The Citizen Soldier

Mark Wilding

AuthorHouse™ UK Ltd.
500 Avebury Boulevard
Central Milton Keynes, MK9 2BE
www.authorhouse.co.uk
Phone: 08001974150

This book is a work of historical fiction, with fictional characters placed in the context of a historical event.

©2010 Mark Wilding. All rights reserved.

No part of this book may be reproduced, stored in a retrieval system, or transmitted by any means without the written permission of the author.

First published by AuthorHouse 8/13/2010

ISBN: 978-1-4520-3531-4 (sc)

This book is printed on acid-free paper.

Authors Note

All characters depicted in this novel are fictional with the exception of the members of the Allied High Command and meteorologist Captain J.M. Stagg.

The main characters within this novel have consciously not been assigned a division within the 101st Airborne. The reason being, I did not wish to detract from the heroic actions that the 'real' Majors and Colonels that took part in the actual invasion of Normandy.

Every effort has been made when researching this novel to keep it as factually correct as possible. Literary license has been used on occasion. Any mistakes that have been made are mine and mine alone.

Many thanks to my agent Darin Jewell and his team at Inspira Group for believing in this novel and their help and advice in enabling this novel to be published. Thanks to my former boss and now friend, Bob Greenwood. The text is now more credible thanks to him pointing out the errors of my ways when reviewing the manuscript as each chapter was completed. Last but by no means least, thank you to my wonderful partner for the last nine years, Sharon Cole. Without her understanding, patience and encouragement this novel would have never been completed.

MW
Waterlooville, England.
May 2010.

To Bianca and Bethany

Was there a man dismay'd?
Not tho' the soldier knew
Someone had blundered;
Theirs not to make a reply,
Theirs is not to reason why,
Theirs but not to do and die:
Into the Valley of Death

- Alfred, Lord Tennyson

PART ONE

Recruited

*call up, conscript, enlist, enrol, induct,
sign on, sign up*

I
10th July 1943
Autryville, North Carolina, USA
03h30 hours

Autryville, with a population of just under 200, is split by route 24 about twenty miles South East of Fort Bragg. As with most small towns, everybody pretty much knew everyone else's business and nothing out of the ordinary ever happened there.

There was no industry to speak of, few jobs and no social scene – just long days of smothering humid heat to endure. . . Long, hot, hazy, humid, seemingly endless summer days.

The monotony was endless.

The door of a jeep opened slowly without the interior light coming on above the windshield. The driver had previously ensured that it had been manually turned off.

Every precaution had been taken.

Nothing was left to chance.

A young man casually slid from the front passenger seat and carefully placed his right foot on the tarmac ensuring that he did not tear the cloth that covered his boot.

He looked down and smiled.

No footprints, baby, we were never here, he thought to himself with a wide-eyed moronic grin. *No way, baby. No one would ever know we were here.*

The smile broadened.

After the left foot had joined the right, he took two careful deliberate steps away from the jeep onto the pavement, his concentration still directed towards the welfare of his makeshift boot protectors. One final check was made that the string that held the covering on his trousers was secure. One final check was made they had not started to tear.

Nothing was to be left to chance.

It never was.

Hence, they had never been caught.

Satisfied that all was in order, he stood to his full height, stuck out his chest and looked up the towards the nights sky with dark vacant eyes.

Twinkle, twinkle little star, baby . . . Twinkle, twinkle . . . Heh there Mr Man in the Moon. How's it going? Whoop . . . Whoop. Turn down the lights, baby. You are shining just a tad too brightly. We were never here, baby.

To the three others, who had also now joined him outside the jeep with the latest fashion accessory covering their boots, the stargazing seemed to go on for an unhealthy length of time. However, none dare venture a comment.

They knew better.

Just let him be – he will be back down to earth soon enough – when he is damn well ready. All deemed it best not to disturb him while the vacant look was present in his eyes. Experience had taught them in the past that any response would be nonsensical, or worse still, violent.

Very violent.

Seconds passed without a word being spoken. Seconds turned into minutes. Nervous glances were exchanged as the stargazing continued. Weight was shifted from one foot to other by three of the four. The anxiety and tension they were already feeling intensified.

Tick . . . Tick . . . Tick . . . Tock . . . Tock . . . Tock . . .

Enough was however enough.

'Heh man, are we going to do this, or what?' One of them eventually built up the courage to whisper. The question was followed by a quiet nervous laugh. A hand was quickly placed over his mouth in fear of any sudden retribution. He glanced nervously towards the non-star gazing members of the group. They cringed and stared at their respective shoe leather. No reassurances were given.

To everyone's relief, none was forthcoming. Three audible sighs of relief were made in unison. The staring at the stars continued. Two nods of reassurance were received to indicate that the bravest of the group should repeat the question.

'Why me?' He thought, but spoke up anyway. 'Did you hear me, man? Are we going to go through with this, or just stand out in the

street and wait to get caught?'

The vacant eyes suddenly narrowed.

The 'Star Gazer's head slowly lowered and then looked towards his inquisitor. 'We sure are, baby . . . WHOOP, WHOOP. We sure are. Could do without this damn moon lighting up the goddamn place though . . . WHOOP. Yes sir, just too damn bright,' he whispered back. His jovial expression was then replaced with an evil grin that could turn a mere mortal to stone.

Resembling a mob of meerkats, all four heads then looked from left to right down the street to ensure there was not any unwanted late night strollers.

God help them if there were.

Satisfied that this was the case, there were three further audible sighs of relief. The consequences did not bear thinking about, not to mention the inconvenience of trying to hide the bodies.

'Mr Star Gazer' nodded to the others that they should start to get on with the matters in hand. His demeanour suddenly changing to indicate that the madness had temporarily left him. His 'all business' head was now on.

WHOOP, WHOOP! Yes sir; all business. Time to do some business. WHOOP.

'Okay. Time to get some beer tokens, guys,' he said as he slowly opened the small rusty gate, looking at it accusingly. *No time for you to be creaking and giving the game away, 'Mr Squeaky',* he thought as he did so.

The gate opened up into a well-kept front yard of a small yet pleasant detached house. After one final check to ensure the street was still quiet, he crept down the path leading to the front door. The remainder of the group followed.

'Mr Star Gazer' then slowly bent down and picked up the small plant pot to the left of the front door. 'There's the baby,' he whispered to himself and then picked up the key that was supposedly hidden safely beneath it.

He looked round to his three companions for looks of approval with a look of 'I told you so' written all over his face. Three nodding heads greeted him with forced smiles.

With his trademark moronic grin now appearing on his face once more, he carefully eased the key into the lock, gently turned it to the right and then pushed the door with his right shoulder. It opened with a minimum of noise.

No squeak to worry about this time . . . WHOOP!

He turned to the remainder of the group and then gestured to them by nodding his head sideways twice in quick succession to follow him into the small hallway. They did so eagerly, urgently, without hesitation – anything to get out of sight – the last of the group gently closed the door behind them giving the street one final cursory glance.

Still nothing . . . nobody to be seen.

The quiet within was deafening. All four hesitated and simultaneously held their breath. Not one of them wanted to be the first to take the first step. No one wanted to be responsible for the making the slightest of noises. A game of 'musical statues' commenced without the accompanying music.

Eventually, 'Mr Star Gazer' fell on his sword and was the first to be eliminated. He motioned towards the others to walk into the kitchen through the first door on the left. He then pointed down to the right hand side of the hallway and shook his head.

Two of the three obediently followed him along the left side. The rear of the group ignored the instruction made only seconds earlier.

Creak.

He slowly picked up his right foot.

Creak . . . Creak.

Three menacing looks were immediately thrown in his direction.

The 'Star Gazer' went one better. He slid his right forefinger across his own throat to indicate what would happen to him if he were stupid enough to stand on the offending floorboard again. A suitably shame-faced expression was returned. He knew that the suggested threat was not an idle one.

Once all had entered the kitchen, the door was quietly closed by the member of the group that had not been so stealthy in the hallway, who then let out a nervous laugh. This immediately had the effect of the others putting their right index finger to their lips in unison, albeit they too were all now trying to suppress their own individual nervous laughter.

They failed.

A chorus of childlike chuckling escaped their lips. Closing of the eyes and biting of fingers followed in an attempt to overcome the overwhelming desire for a good old 'guffaw'. Several seconds passed with four shoulders all moving up and down.

Once a modicum of control had been restored, 'Mr Star Gazer' whispered, 'It's in here,' while opening up a cupboard which was on the immediate left to the sink. He then set about quietly removing a couple of cans of food and placed them on the sinks draining board. After reaching to the back of the cupboard, his hand came across the object he was looking for; an old faded red tin.

'Here we go, fellahs. Let's see how the beer fund is doing, shall we?' He whispered, raising the tin aloft triumphantly as if he had successfully withdrawn Excalibur from the stone.

His face was lit up by the moon shining in through the window giving him the look of 'Dr Demento'.

After examining the contents, he looked at each of the other members of the group with a mischievous grin and whispered, 'Nice to see some things never change.'

The stash was removed and quickly counted. After a brief moment of contemplation, he then reluctantly shared the contents out amongst the group members, ensuring he kept the majority for himself.

Half for them, half for me, baby . . . WHOOP. My job, my stash. WHOOP.

Three faces darkened. Albeit the remainder of the group all realised they were all being stiffed . . . again . . . not one of them felt it prudent to make a complaint. It was not the time or the place for a full on argument or stand up fight. That could wait for later . . . maybe . . . maybe not.

As the lid was replaced on the tin and was about to be returned to its original place in the cupboard, footsteps could be clearly heard coming down the stairs.

It was apparent that not only the hallway floorboards were in need of repair.

The group all looked towards 'Mr Star Gazer' who was now staring intently at the kitchen door.

Three concerned faces all quickly changed to ones of confusion. All looked towards each other and then looked back to their leader with a shrug of the shoulders being exchanged beforehand.

Being discovered was obviously not part of the original plan but the 'Star Gazer' was now definitely smiling. The three confused looks were now replaced with dread.

They all knew what was coming next.

The 'Star Gazer' was true to form. He always was . . . Always. He looked from one to the other of his three companions with a look than made their flesh goose-bump.

One of the group members had the audacity to shake his head with a pleading expression.

It was ignored.

This is going to get interesting, the 'Star Gazer' was already thinking. *WHOOP! Yes. Very interesting indeed. Time to get down and dirty, baby; and boy . . . does this bastard have it coming . . . WHOOP.*

2
31st May 1944
Portsmouth, England

Over the centuries, Portsmouth had taken part in the preparation and departure of many famous military and naval expeditions. King Henry VIII's favourite warship, The Mary Rose, had sunk just outside the entrance to the harbour on 19 July 1545 on its way to engage the French fleet to name but one.

None however throughout history could compare to the scale of the military build up to D-Day in June 1944. The whole of the south coast of England had become one huge armed camp and restrictions on movements around Portsmouth itself were in place around the city. Southsea seafront had become a completely restricted zone in August 1943.

During the period between 11 July 1940 and May 1994, Portsmouth had paid a high price for its strategic importance as the home to the Royal Navy. Just fewer than 1,000 civilians had been killed and over 80,000 properties had either been badly damaged or destroyed without trace.

It was estimated that 1,320 high explosives bombs, 38,000 incendiary devices and 38 land mines were dropped into the city.

The majority of the city's streets now lay in ruin.

It was in these streets that Davey Dwyer was now walking back to his one small room bedsit in High Street – located at the southwest corner of the city – after leaving the Dockyard through Victory Gate into 'The Hard.'

In days gone by, 'The Hard' had always brought a slight smile to his face (although he would admit somewhat immaturely) thinking how ridiculous that was for a street name. *Better than Mr Softy,* he used to think to himself. *Who in their right mind would consider naming a street with such suggestive smutty overtones?*

The smiled had now disappeared.

The walk to and from work had become more and more depressing over the last four years due to the fact that his beloved birthplace had been totally devastated by the German bombing raids during 'The Blitz'.

Many of the buildings on his route home had either completely disappeared without a trace or were now in a pile of rubble, broken glass and masonry.

Madness.
Complete insanity.
Total bollocks.
All of the above.

Within the city there now seemed to be an omnipresent endless howling of sirens – either air raid or fire engines – fire rising angrily to the sky greedily consuming everything in its path and a continual plume of spiralling, grey, choking smoke.

On this particular day however, his spirits were – for the moment at least – reasonably high. He was now working increasingly long hours as an engineer, primarily working on the refit and repair on the Naval fleet. Because of his considerable expertise and willingness to take time to teach anyone that was not as skilled, he had been seconded to the Royal Navy full-time. As a result, he had avoided the call-up into the armed forces.

His work gave him a great deal of satisfaction, as he believed that the well-being of the Royal Navy was partly in his hands. The satisfaction he was now feeling after successfully completing the repair of a generator before his deadline now quickly disappeared.

He was back on the streets of despair and destruction.

Dwyer found himself staring at the pavement while he walked rather than take in the demolition that lay around him.

Such was his anger; he had previously volunteered to join the army . . . twice. He wanted to get some payback. A lot of payback. Much to his disgust, he had been refused on the grounds of his importance to the maintenance of the naval fleet.

'Importance to the fleet my arse,' he mumbled to himself as he trudged the mile long walk home whilst dwelling on the recruitment officers words.

Your work is to too important to the Navy and thus your occupation remains reservist. I am sure there would many who would like to swap places with you.

'They could replace me in the blink an eye,' he added to his own private conversation. He then quickly glanced round his immediate vicinity to make sure that nobody had heard him.

The fact that his 'importance' had intensified over the last few weeks due to the build-up within the Dockyard kept his mind occupied from dwelling on such matters whilst at work. However, the walk to and from home was his only quiet time of the day which allowed him to brood – and brood he did.

More often than not, he tried to convince himself that the recruitment officer was correct. That being, he was one of the fortunate ones that was not about to be placed in harm's way.

It rarely worked.

He could not even fool himself and he often felt that he was in some way not doing his patriotic duty.

Goddamn recruitment officer. Surely, they needed every man they could get their hands on.

Surely?

Most, if not all his friends, had now been drafted and the fact that he had avoided it played heavily on his mind. He felt that he was somehow letting them down not being able to stand toe to toe with them on the battlefield. Truth be known, they would have only been too happy to stand beside him. Behind him in fact, if push came to shove.

As he walked past the pontoon for the Gosport ferry, his mind then wandered – not for the first time – back to the worst night of his life. Apart from the almost seemingly total destruction of his hometown, this was the main reason for his quest for vengeance. A vengeance that was so great, it kept him awake at night tossing and turning in his bed.

He stared at the pavement with hunched shoulders as the uninvited painful memories came flooding back as if a dam had broken and there was not a small boy available to stick his finger in the hole to prevent the relentless, inevitable onslaught of anxiety, sadness and depression that accompanied them.

First, the sensation of his mouth becoming dry started, then the palpitations, closely followed by a smothering sensation and shortness of breath. More often than not, once the physical symptoms had been brought under control, Dwyer found himself becoming overcome with a sense of guilt. A sense of guilt that he felt eating him away inside of him, inevitably, leaving him feeling empty.

Why did it have to happen to them?
Why is it they were taken away and not me?
WHY?
Goddamn war!

The guilt was then replaced by feelings of low self-esteem, hopelessness and helplessness. What made matters worse, was that he considered all of the symptoms and emotions to be some kind of weakness in his character.

Surely I am stronger this. Why can't I just put all this crap behind me and get on with my life . . . .
WHY?

He never talked about his feelings with anyone. He would never consider for a second of sharing his grief, never consider sharing the burden. He tried at all times to shrug them off and put on a brave face. All this achieved was that at times, it made him become irritable and intolerant of others, albeit he was very aware of it and made every effort to keep himself to himself when such feelings descended upon him.

It was better that way . . . for everyone else at least.

Still staring at nothing in particular on the pavement, he absently kicked at a small stone sending it skittering off into the road.

More than one concerned glance was aimed in his direction, as he stood motionless at the side of the street staring off into space. The look on his face, however, prevented anyone asking about his well-being. Instead, they looked away and went about their own business.

The steeliness in his eyes made sure of that.

No one was ever in any doubt what Dwyer was feeling, his face gave him away. You knew when he was happy . . . you certainly knew when he was not. As the memory from over three years ago overwhelmed his every sense, his facial expression could only be described as looking totally and utterly depressed.

3
10th January 1941.
The Still & West
Portsmouth, England

Happy Birthday to you,
Happy Birthday to you,
Happy Birthday dear Davey,
Happy Birthday to you.

Twenty-one day,
Twenty-one today,
You've got the key to the door,
Never been twenty-one before.

For he's a jolly good fellow . . . Blah, blah, blah . . . Applause . . . Applause . . . Applause . . . SPEEEECH!

'Yes . . . Yes . . . Thank you. That's just what I need. A large dose of the clap,' said Dwyer concentrating on every syllable in an earnest effort not to slur his words. 'And who the hell has been mixing my drinks? He added as his raised his glass up to the light and looked at the contents suspiciously.
Looks like someone has pissed in it.
They probably have, knowing this lot.
Nice.
'I must confess I'm feeling slightly pissed . . . Not like me, eh lads?' This last statement was followed by an enormous belch and a foolish boyish grin.
'You have got to be joking me, mate,' shouted Joe Simcox, one of Dwyer's neighbours and workmates. 'You could get pissed just walking past and sniffing a pub, let alone drinking in one.' He ended his jibe with, 'You big queer bear!'
More applause and laugher erupted from the gathering.

Dwyer got up from his barstool and stood to his full height - which was considerable – and looked round the pub until all was quiet to deliver his comeback.

There was a brief delay while he concentrated on, and eventually managed, to stop swaying.

'Well, you can't beat the real thing can you now, Joey? And you would know sweetie pie. Word is that you are rather partial to a hairy arsed matelow once in awhile,' Dwyer replied holding his half-empty glass up again.

Drunken hysterical laughter broke-out throughout the pub and all eyes now returned on Simcox for his repost.

'You wish big boy. Now whose round – '

The merriment and banter abruptly ended with the sound of the air raid sirens invading the party through the pubs open windows like an uninvited sadistic imposter.

The lights were switched off immediately.

'Anyone got a light?' Someone shouted from the rear of the pub, which broke the newly formed tension. Pockets of laughter broke out albeit that it was forced and nervous.

A glass smashed on the floor.

The landlord suggested that whoever it was responsible for breaking it would have to pay.

He was told to, 'Get stuffed.'

'You have got to give it to those Germans,' said Dwyer to himself. 'Their timing is excellent. Ruined a perfectly good night out . . . Again,' he added now feeling suddenly completely sober.

'Aint that the truth?' A voice said from immediately behind him.

The Still & West's – situated on the east side of the edge of the entrance to Portsmouth Harbour – foundations shook along with the timber beams in the ceiling as the first bomb hit in the region of High Street, approximately two hundred yards away. Further glasses were smashed and tables knocked over as everyone to a man and woman dived to the ground for cover. An eerie silence then followed with everyone holding his or her breath.

This time, the landlord kept his own council.

The silence was the worst part. Waiting for the next explosion.

However, once the raids started, the wait was never long. THUMP, THUMP, THUMP . . . Silence . . . Then hysterical screaming and shouting. THUMP . . . Silence.

When believing the worst was over, Dwyer eventually raised himself up to his feet and shouted, 'Is everyone okay? Anyone hurt?'

Silence.

He persisted, 'Joe. Are you there? Answer me, mate.'

'Yes mate,' was the muffled reply. 'Apart from having someone's arse in my face. I'm absolutely fine.'

'I hope it belongs to a woman . . . for your sake,' a voice from the darkness replied.

A few further sniggers of nervous laughter could be heard from around the pub.

'I aint staying here. Too close to the Dockyard,' said Dwyer urgently, ignoring the attempt of frivolous humour. 'They are bound to be going for it again. I am off home. You coming? . . . I'm leaving right now!' He added with the tension evident in his voice.

'What about the shelter at St Peters?' Simcox mumbled nervously. The arse had now been removed from his face. He was now just plain crapping himself.

'No mate . . . I'm going home. Make sure my folks are okay. The shelter is probably full now anyway.'

Simcox reluctantly got to his feet and joined him.

On leaving the pub, they were greeted with a horrendous but nonetheless amazing sight. Night had turned into day as the city burned. Everywhere they looked was surrounded by a ring of fire. A huge orange glow angrily raced up to meet the darkness above from the direction of the centre of the city.

'Looks like the Guildhall as has copped it,' said Simcox looking off into the distance with wide petrified eyes.

'Seems so,' said Dwyer. 'By the looks of things, so have most places.' His own words striking a lightning bolt of fear through his body, which spurred them both into action.

They started to sprint down Broad Street and into High Street, their progress impeded by taking in huge lungfuls of smoke. What was once the George Hotel was half its original size with flames doing their best to reduce it further to mere pile of ash. They both stopped and stared.

'Jesus,' said Simcox. 'Good job your parents didn't get their way with the surprise party.'

'What?'

'Your parents.'

'What about my parents and a surprise party?'

'They were trying to hire the hotel for a surprise party for you but it was already booked. Lucky, eh?'

Oh my God!

Dwyer looked towards the burning wreck and slowly shook his head. 'You serious?'

Simcox nodded and coughed at the same time.

'Not so lucky for the poor bastards that did,' said Dwyer shaking his head again with a forlorn expression.

They continued to make their way toward home in Norfolk Street, coughing and wheezing as they went. Twice they had to pick themselves up from the ground after being flattened by the aftershocks of nearby explosions.

'Mate, this has got to be the worst one yet! The whole fucking city is on fire,' shouted Simcox now struggling to keep up with the pace set by Dwyer.

Dwyer was becoming more and more anxious, which had the effect of steadily increasing his speed due to an overdose of adrenaline. An ever-increasing sense of dread was taking over his thoughts. He felt that something truly terrible had happened. Whether it was a premonition or a sixth sense, he would never know but his haste increased further. So much so, that Simcox was eventually left trailing in his wake.

On reaching the corner of Norfolk Street, Dwyer came to an abrupt halt and stared in disbelief and horror. It appeared that half the people that lived in the street were running around like ants as if their nest had been disturbed. They were shouting and screaming at each other unintelligibly. The houses on his side of the street that had not been destroyed were on fire.

Mrs Jackson that lived opposite him gave him the news. 'I am sorry, Davey . . . I am so sorry . . . Their gone . . . They are all gone,' she shouted through floods of tears. She then ran off down the street waving her arms frantically in the air resembling a newly decapitated chicken.

Dwyer's mouth dropped open. He watched the manic Mrs Jackson run from one side to the street to the other unable to comprehend the news she had just shared with him. Unwilling to comprehend it, now petrified to turn round, face his house and see for himself what she had meant.

They have all gone . . . gone where?
That is not what she meant, and you know it.

Simcox then suddenly appeared out of the smoke in front of him crying uncontrollably. He then sat down in the middle of the road and held his head in his hands.

Snapping himself out of his trance, Dwyer half walked, half stumbled towards his home seemingly oblivious to the chaos surrounding him. On reaching it, he dropped to his knees and lowered his head.

That IS what she meant . . . Oh my God!

What was left of his lifelong home was ablaze. Mother, Father, Sister – gone. Just like that – as if someone had just switched a light switch off. One minute he was saying goodbye to them to go out to celebrate his twenty-first birthday with some friends and work colleagues – the next, he came home to find them buried in a burning wreck. A wreck that had once been the source of many happy memories, memories was all that was now left . . . . Only memories.

For what seemed like an eternity, he stared at the fire on his knees with streams of tears running down his cheeks creating streaks in the dust and grey smoke residue that now covered it.

One day, somebody is going to pay for this . . . BIG TIME.

He was broken out of his hypnotic state when the ear piercing screams invaded his senses.

4
31st May 1944
High Street, Portsmouth, England

As by some strange twist of fate, Dwyer now lived only a couple of hundred of yards from the Still & West which he had left that night over three years ago to discover the fate of his family. As he entered High Street, with his thoughts still on that hateful night, he stopped and removed the newspaper cutting that he had carried in his wallet since.

> ## THREE CHILDREN SAVED FROM BURNING HOUSE
>
> During the air raid on 10th January, three young sisters were heroically saved from certain death.
> After returning home from his 21st birthday celebrations and after discovering that his own parents and younger sister had been killed after their home had taken a direct hit, Davey Dwyer, who resided in Norfolk Street, selflessly broke down the front door of his near neighbours and rescued the three young sisters from a certain death.
> Mr John Stevens, himself a resident of Norfolk Street, stated that the girls were all screaming at their parents from the upstairs bedroom window to help them. He stated that the parents appeared to be 'immobilised with fear.'
> Mr Dwyer was then reported to have broken down the front door with his shoulder, entered the inferno, and returned within seconds with all three girls under his arms.
> Mr Dwyer, an engineer recently seconded to the Royal Navy, has been unavailable for comment.

Davey folded the cutting carefully and replaced it in his wallet. He stood motionless for a moment and stared wistfully down his street. The brief report playing heavily on his mind.

That seems like a long time ago.

When is this crap ever going to end?

His reverie was then disturbed by the sound of an American jeep cruising slowly, almost suspiciously along the street. The occupants of which all appeared to be staring at him whilst he was still stood still on the pavement with hands stuffed in his boiler-suit pockets, wearing his troubled and forlorn expression.

Dwyer returned their stare briefly, which seemed to him to prompt the jeep to speed up – not before the driver had flashed an insincere smile in his direction and mimicked a salute.

The salute was not reciprocated.

Arsehole!

Immediately dismissing the cocky little shit, his thoughts returned to the events that followed the night of his family's death as he walked slowly towards home.

Due to the newspaper article in the *Portsmouth Evening News*, Dwyer had become a minor local celebrity in the city. He had gladly taken on the role of a 'second father' to the three girls for a brief time and whenever he could, despite the food rations, treated them to sweets. The children had since been moved out into the country as part of the evacuation program so he had now lost touch.

You are the lucky ones girls, he thought to himself. *Lucky you do not have to witness the systematic dismantling of this place. You are definitely the lucky ones. I only hope that there is something left for you to come back to one day.*

He shuddered at the thought that there may well not be.

Dwyer was now twenty-four years of age and had lived in Portsmouth his entire life. Despite the fact the city was now literally a 'bomb site', the thought of living some place else had never once entered his head.

He especially liked the area of the city in which he now lived. He had taken delight when as a small boy his grandfather told him stories that had been handed down through generations of how poor unsuspecting souls were Press Ganged into joining the navy in the streets of Spice Island – two hundred yards from his bedsit, which was only a minor part of the city's rich maritime history.

He had in fact only left the city a handful of times throughout his life. When he had, he had not been overly impressed with anything else he had seen elsewhere. He considered the naval city streets – what was now left of them – to be his own, and until recently, had viewed any 'outsider' with suspicion.

What were those Americans doing driving around in that jeep?
I thought they had all been restricted to base.
Didn't like the way the driver smiled at me.
Cocky bastard!

5

To anyone that would listen, Dwyer would inform any 'outsider' that Portsmouth is the United Kingdom's only island city. Anyone coming from the north of the tiny strip of water named Port Creek separating it from the mainland fell into this 'outsider' category as far as Dwyer was concerned, along with the majority of others in the city, which shared his 'Islander' mentality.

On one occasion, he had only just avoided a fistfight after jokingly accusing one poor lad from Petersfield that he was a 'Northern Monkey.' His friends on fearing the worst for the poor lad, were quick to remind Dwyer, albeit jokingly, that that was somewhat harsh as Petersfield is only about ten miles north from Portsmouth as the crow flies.

Dwyer had suggested to him that it was not a good idea to take exception too strongly when he stood up from his bar stool, and on seeing Dwyer's full size, the 'northerner' readily agreed.

Didn't like the way the driver smiled at me.
Cocky bastard!
Why are they cruising round the streets in that jeep? – In my street.
I thought they had all been restricted to base.

Dwyer was what can only be described as a beast of a man. He stood at six foot eight inches in his socks and carried his 18 stone of weight without an ounce of fat. Known as 'Moose' to his friends, of whom he had many, he literally filled any room when he entered it. Men that did not know him tended to try to avoid his gaze when it happened to fall upon them. Women had in the past fought over each other to do the exact opposite.

The fact that the Dockyard was now overflowing with army and navy serviceman from America, Canada and all points north from England, would have ordinarily not sat comfortably with him. The military build up over the last week and had been steadily increasing so he guessed that Eisenhower and Montgomery had stopped messing about up at Southwick House and were actually going to give the green light to the Invasion of Normandy. Rumours were rife within the Dockyard that it was any day now, weather permitting.

When is this crap ever going to end?

Maybe that is why they are here?

Why would they be in my street though? Were they MPs? I thought everyone else had all been restricted to base.

Oh well – who gives a shit?

6

The death of his family had left Dwyer alone in the world as far as family was concerned, as both his parents had been only children. However, just two weeks after his family's tragic deaths, he had met the love of his life, Sally Clark.

In the past, Dwyer had never had any trouble attracting the opposite sex. Until Sally came along, he had only viewed them as objects of fun after a night out with his friends. One of his conquests had spread some gossip around the pubs and clubs that his manhood was equivalent to the size of a babies arm with a clenched fist. He therefore rarely went home alone after a night out, much to his late Mothers disgust.

Sally however was different and had totally stolen his heart. She was tall for a girl at 5 foot 11 inches and had a body to die for. Her lumps were definitely all in the right places. Her piercing blue eyes were accentuated by her long natural blonde hair, but when standing next to Dwyer, as did almost everyone else, she looked tiny.

Dwyer especially liked the fact she made him laugh with her wicked sense of humour. He had actually found a girl that he truly loved spending time with and actually liked talking to, rather than just wanting to play 'hide the sausage' all the time.

For nearly a year, Dwyer had been trying to persuade Sally to move into his room with him but as she was from a strict Catholic background, the thought of mortifying her parents had thus far prevented it.

'You will just have to marry me first,' she would say to him every time the subject came up with a sparkle in her eyes.

Although he worshiped the ground she walked on, he always found himself quickly changing the subject.

Dwyer's mother, who he had also worshiped, always scolded him while he was playing the field and would often say that he would go all the way round the orchard and end up with a crab apple. She also said that one day he would find his true soul mate and settle down.

As usual, his mother had proven to be correct and made him

realise that he now suffered from an emotion that he would never before thought possible.

'The Green Eyed Monster.'

Where Sally was concerned, Dwyer was consumed with jealousy.

Albeit that Dwyer was a man mountain and had never lost a fight in his life, he was not overly aggressive and avoided trouble where possible. If however he was not given that option, or if someone was messing with one of his friends, he would seal their fate. No warning would be given; he would just put them to sleep for a while.

His considerable reputation throughout the city had grown further recently since he had been with Sally. Dwyer hated it when other men even looked at her briefly. If anyone had the audacity to talk to her, it sent him into an inner rage.

On more than one occasion, unsuspecting males of the city's population had been taken aside, forcibly if necessary, and advised that they should concentrate their affections on someone else. To date, nobody had not taken the advice on board and offered reassurances that it would never happen again.

In the main, he did manage to control his temper. He was afraid of his own strength. However, one unfortunate soul went too far and stupidly pinched Sally's arse outside the Still & West down at Spice Island only a week earlier.

Dwyer beat the living crap out of him.

After two short-arm jabs, both with his right hand, he then picked him up from the floor, smacked him again for good measure, and then threw him over the railings into the harbour.

The fact that it soon became obvious that his victim could not swim, he immediately regretted his actions, dived in, fished the bloke out, made sure he was okay and then bought him a beer.

The beer was readily accepted after a sincere apology had been made. He would never have been so forward if he had known she was his girlfriend . . . never. Surely, he knew that. Surely, he knew that he would never deliberately mess with him . . . Surely.

The apology was accepted by a pat on the back and a reassuring smile. The smile was then replaced by a look of shame as quickly as it had if formed due to the look of disgust on Sally's face. She had not been amused or impressed with his 'macho' performance.

He smiled to himself as he finally reached home and looked skywards, leaving his thoughts behind him. 'Hope your okay mum, look after dad and Lucy,' he said aloud to the heavens above.

His smile then broadened as he remembered how Sally had finally forgiven him that night after returning to his bedsit. The springs on his mattress had been given a rigorous and lengthy workout.

She had left to go home with a contented smile.

7

It was Sally that Dwyer now noticed across the street as he was about to put the key in the front door of his apartment building. He had arranged with Sally to come over for the night and cook dinner although Dwyer had no idea what with, his cupboards were bare. He was hoping she was going to bring something tasty with her and that the mattress would undergo a further vigorous workout later on in the evening.

She was talking with four American soldiers whose jeep was parked up on the pavement opposite by the entrance of the Cathedral. His brow furrowed as it appeared to him that she seemed to be a very unwilling recipient of their attentions.

There they are again.

What were those Americans doing driving around in that jeep? In my street.

I thought they all been restricted to base?

Now I do give a shit!

What do they want with Sally?

Dwyer just stared, for which seemed like an eternity, and could now feel the anger build up inside of him. He felt his cheeks physically redden. It was as if all the blood in his body had decided that his face was now the only place to party. The only place to party in the vast vessel that was Dwyer.

'Mr Irrational' thought process now made an appearance.

All the locals in the city know by now not to mess me about where Sally is concerned.

Now the voice of reason quickly joined in the debate with its counter-argument.

How could they know that? They are American, you dick head!

Mr Irrational back again.

I don't care. Right now, it makes no difference to me. They are flirting with my girl . . . And don't call me a dick head.

Voice of reason wins the argument.

Why don't you stop being such a jealous idiot? Go and find out what they are talking about.

Okay. I will!

Good. Anytime time today would be fine.

Now desperately trying to keep his emotions in check along with 'Mr Irrational', he crossed the street as casually as possible.

Remember to stay calm. Sally hates it when you get jealous.

He immediately caught her eye.

A few of his friends in the Dockyard had been complaining recently about how their girlfriends had dumped them and started going out on the town with these cash rich Yanks, most of which were mechanics who were now based in Hilsea. He had scoffed at the idea that this could happen to him in the past and now the fact that these four pricks in uniform were now clearly trying it on with *his* Sally was still making his blood boil, still predominately in his face it seemed.

Just calm yourself down you moron. It is probably perfectly innocent.
I still do not like the way that driver looked at me.
Stay calm.
Cocky bastard!

'Hi, Davey,' Sally said and looked down while starting to fiddle nervously with one of the buttons on her blouse. She knew that Dwyer would not like her talking to strange men, especially foreign troops. 'These gentlemen were just asking where the best place to go to get lodgings for one night is.'

Told you it was perfectly innocent.

'Oh, right,' said Dwyer looking visibly relieved. His blood had now become apparently bored with the party in his face and returned home to all points south.

'There are a couple of places just round the corner on the right. You can't miss them,' he said as he pointed down the street into their direction. 'The chances are they are going to be full though,' he added.

'Yes, this pretty young lady has just told us,' the largest soldier of the four said with a sickly grin.

Dwyer clenched his fists.

Not only is the driver a cocky bastard but so is his friend.
Watch yourself Davey, there is definitely something not right about

this one.
Yeah right. Nothing I can't handle.
Just stay calm.
Maybe.
Stay calm
Shut it!

8

Corporal James Carter of the 101st Airborne and his three pals were making the most of not being confined to barracks at Greenham Common. They had been ordered to drive to Portsmouth to deliver a pouch containing confidential papers, and were instructed to return to base by 10h00 hours the next morning. This was going to be their last chance for a night on the town for God knows how long and they were determined to make the most of it.

Making the most of it in his eyes, definitely meant that the opposite sex was on the agenda.

The fact that his attempt to pull this young girl was being hampered by this giant of a 'limey' did not sit well with him.

Goddam it, this bloke is a shithead.

'Yes she is pretty isn't she?' Dwyer said trying to accept it as a compliment, although he knew this cocky bastard American was trying his luck. 'Thank you,' he added, trying not to grit his teeth.

Stay calm.

The demeanour of the American changed. His eyes appeared to blacken as if a cloud had temporarily blocked out the sun.

'Thank you,' Corporal James Carter repeated. 'Why thank me? I paid her the compliment, fool, not you.' The sickly grin appeared again and the colour now returned to his eyes.

What a fuckwit!

Stay calm.

Dwyer looked to the ground briefly to compose himself. It took every ounce of self-control to stop tearing this idiot a new arsehole right there and then.

'She happens to be my girlfriend,' Dwyer said now returning the Americans stare and forcing a smile. 'And less of the fool okay mate. Not really necessary for insults, is it?' He paused and then added as an afterthought. 'I am trying to help you out here after all.' His tone remained calm.

The cloud blocked out the sun again within the Americans eyes.

Dwyer felt an urge to shiver as if someone had just walked over his grave. He knew his fair share of 'nutters' in the city but there was something very wrong with this guy. Nothing he could properly articulate, but something not right nonetheless.

It is like looking into the eyes of a man with no soul, he thought to himself.

The urge to shiver would not abate.

On not immediately receiving a verbal response, Dwyer turned to Sally and held out his hand to take hers suggesting that they should now walk away.

The American took a pace forward.

'Is that a fact?' Carter said before they had a chance to do so. 'Don't suppose you want to loan her out for of the evening, would you?' He then turned to the other three to seek approval who were all smiling and nodding agreement.

Stay calm.

Fuck you.

Dwyer looked briefly skywards and took a deep breath. He positioned himself between Sally and the four troops and then one by one stared each of them down. They could not make it more obvious that they were deliberately trying to provoke him. He could not help notice how young and fresh faced they looked. He was also annoyed with the fact that they all still had stupid smug grins on their faces and did not look the least bit intimidated by him. Something he was not used to.

Take another deep –

'Is something funny, lads?' Dwyer asked as he looked again from one to another interrupting his voice of reason.

Not one of them avoided eye contact. They were brave. Dwyer was almost impressed.

'No. Nothing is funny,' said Corporal Carter eventually. 'But you need to stop being so selfish. You are preventing this young gal from having the time of her life,' and then looked away from Dwyer's glare towards Sally and winked at her.

Again, this was met with smiling faces and nods of agreement from his companions.

Okay. Fair one. Enough with this stay calm shit.

Really? Are you sure?

Yes. You have my blessing to do your worst. Go to it.

Dwyer took one pace toward Carter and stabbed him in the shoulder . . . hard, with his right index finger.

'Do you know what? My friends and me are sick to death of you Yanks swaggering around our city thinking you can pick up our women anytime you like. Well this time you chose the wrong girl as she's with me, okay?'

Dwyer then looked at each of the four in turn to measure their reaction. To his annoyance, they were staring right back at him and still smiling. All except Carter. He was trying to mask the pain he was now feeling in his right shoulder.

Jesus these blokes are smug!

I said go to it.

He then continued. 'If you have any ounce of brain in that thick skull of yours and know what's good for you, you will piss off out of my street and go back to where you came from.'

Dwyer ended his speech by shoving Carter with the flat of his hand in his right shoulder. He then glanced towards Sally to ensure she was sufficiently far enough away from him to be out of harm's way should the Americans wish to purse the argument further a little more vigorously. He had no doubt whatsoever in his mind that they would.

She was about six feet away staring down at the pavement and biting her bottom lip pensively.

As if they were joined by telepathy, the four Americans immediately spread out and formed a circle round Dwyer. Each standing with their arms straight down by their sides with their fists clenched.

Sally looked up and started to cringe. She knew what was coming next. The thought of calling for help did not even cross her mind. These poor young American lads had just screwed up big time. All the army training in the world was not about to save them from getting a proper good kicking. She was however incredibly proud of her man. His restraint up to now had been admirable.

One last chance. Try to stay calm.

You reckon?

Just one last try.
You said go to it.
They are probably tooled up.
Probably.

'Look lads,' said Dwyer as he looked back to each of them in turn. 'You really don't want do this. You need to go . . . Now,' and gestured with his right thumb towards their jeep.

Private Jack Henderson, who was now immediately in front of Dwyer started to pull back his arm with his fist clenched.

Have it your way.
Time for a tear up.

Within a split second, Henderson was on the ground holding his mouth and spitting out teeth. Dwyer had thrown a straight right with incredible speed for such a big man and Henderson's legs had buckled like a newborn baby giraffe.

I tried. They didn't give me any choice.
You did, well done you.
Thanks.
Stop talking to me and do the fuckers!
Good point.

A further second later, Privates Dan Hickey & Private Tony Garcia had joined him, also both now in need of a good dentist. One left and right had taken care of them.

Dwyer now turned his attention to Corporal Carter who had taken a crowbar from the back of the jeep and was raising it above his head ready to strike. However, his attack lacked stealth. He was screaming like a banshee.

Oh, bollocks!
Told you they would be tooled up.
Now is not the time for 'I told you so.'
Fair one.

Dwyer swivelled to his right and hit him so hard in the chest with his right fist, Carter's sternum and part of his rib cage shattered and severed the arteries to his heart.

Corporal Carter was dead before he hit the ground.

Dwyer stood and admired his handiwork. He had no idea that the last blow he had thrown had caused a fatal injury. He glanced over to his right at Sally whose eyes had suddenly became the size of saucers. He then briefly felt a sickening blow to the back of his neck, which made everything go dark.

What the hell happened then?
Don't know.
It's dark in here.
Anyone got a light?

He went down in a heap for the first time since he was fourteen years old when his father had given him a slap for disrespecting his mother.

9

During the melee, nobody had noticed Constable Gavin Evans who had turned the corner of Pembroke Road entering High Street whilst walking his beat. He had recognised instantly what was about to go down and before he could get his whistle to his mouth to attract attention, Dwyer, who he had known all his life and had been in the same class throughout school, had ended the debate.

Acting purely on instant and adrenaline, Evans sprinted across the street, pulled his truncheon from his belt and made a swing towards Dwyer's head like a clean-up baseball hitter, which fortunately, hit him on the back of the neck. About an inch higher, it would have put Dwyer to sleep forever.

Evans then immediately regretted his actions as soon as he realised who he had felled. He had immediately recognised Sally after he glanced to his right just after he had hit him.

He had always liked Dwyer who had more than once intervened when he was being bullied at school. They had kept in touch after leaving and occasionally went out for a few beers together. Dwyer had even been an usher at his wedding.

Evans looked down to Dwyer deeply concerned and could see that he was clearly out of it. His eyes were rolling in his sockets, spittle was coming out of his mouth and he made absolutely no sign of being able to get back on his feet anytime soon.

Sally then started to scream, *'How could you do it?'* Very loudly.

The three remaining Americans were back on their feet, wiping the blood and broken teeth from their mouths and looking down at Corporal James Carter.

His face had now turned completely white.

Evans bent down and rolled Dwyer onto his side as he had been taught, to avoid him swallowing his tongue. After gently pulling both of his arms round his back and handcuffing him, he turned his attention back to Sally who was jumping from one foot to another, which to Evans, resembled some kind of witch doctor's rain dance. She was now screaming hysterically, and if possible, it was even louder than before.

He got back up to his feet and said, 'Sally. You have to calm down and tell me exactly what happened.' He then grabbed her by both of her shoulders gently which seemed to have the necessary calming effect he desired as she suddenly became still.

'How could you? You bastard,' Sally said with a now incredible amount of calmness in her voice. The transformation from two seconds earlier was remarkable. 'He is supposed to be your friend. You could have killed him hitting him that hard.' She then added, 'I wouldn't want to be in your shoes when he comes round, Gavin, that's for sure.'

Evans was now the one becoming anxious and replied, 'He *is* my friend, Sally, so please tell me exactly what happened. I didn't know it was him. I would never deliberately hurt Moose.'

He then looked back towards Dwyer to see if there was now any sign that he was making any kind of remarkable recovery.

On quickly realising he was still out of it, he looked back into Sally's eyes and said, 'The last thing I want to do is get him in a load of trouble. He has looked out for me my whole life. Who started this? You have to tell me if you want me to get him off!' He emphasised the last point by gently shaking both her shoulders simultaneously.

A voice from behind Evans said, 'Get who off what, Constable Evans?'

Oh, shit! Was that –

10

Detective Inspector David Williams had heard the commotion made by Sally whilst walking home from the station. He also lived in High Street about one hundred yards from Dwyer and was very aware of his existence. On hearing Sally's screams, he ran the distance between them to investigate.

In the minds of all of his colleagues, Williams was an absolute stickler for the rulebook and had absolutely no sense of humour. Evans had once joked that the only time he ever cracks a slight grin is when he coughs in his undies.

Williams was however an outstanding police officer with a brilliant analytical mind, and unfortunately for Evans, the most senior office in his station.

Evans turned on his heels and when realising it was his commanding officer, he knew that Dwyer was in a world of shit. The chance of any cover up and getting Dwyer of the hook was now gone, and at this particular point in time, he had no idea that Dwyer's last punch had killed Corporal Carter.

That was about to change.

Out of the corner of his eye, Evans's saw one of the Americans', Private Tony Garcia, run screaming at Dwyer and kick him squarely in the balls – hard. Fortunately, for Dwyer, he was still unconscious and did not show any sign of feeling it (that would later change when they had swollen up to the size of two small grapefruits).

'He is dead you son of a bitch, you have killed him, you have killed him,' Garcia screamed and then kicked Dwyer in the stomach once more for good measure.

Again, there was no response from Dwyer.

At this point, it all kicked off again.

Sally flew into a rage and tried to scratch and bite Garcia. Evans and Williams became busy trying to prevent Privates Henderson and Hickey from carrying out further retribution on Dwyer. Dwyer remained lying on the pavement oblivious to the pandemonium. Relative peace was only restored when two American MPs, who were both almost the same size as Dwyer, quickly appeared on the scene and wrestled all three Private's to the ground and handcuffed them. Evans eventually managed to calm Sally.

DI Williams then briefly examined the body of Corporal Carter and immediately realised that he was not breathing. After getting up from his kneeling position, with a growing amount of concern, he quickly surveyed the scene around him.

Two enormous American MPs were standing over the three troops who were all shouting obscenities up at them.

The MPs had seen it all before. They were both staring back down at them impassively. Evans was holding the young woman by the arm and Dwyer was still clearly unconscious on the pavement. Behind him across the street, were three female onlookers that were clearly enjoying the afternoon's entertainment.

After a few seconds hasty contemplation, he approached the two MPs and said, 'Gentleman. I am Detective Inspector David Williams and currently Portsmouth's most senior police officer. I do not have many facts at present but it appears there has been an altercation here in the street and a young American soldier has lost his life.'

The two MPs did not offer any comment and both just stood staring at Williams waiting for him to continue.

'I do not want to hear one word from either of you over jurisdiction on this matter. This incident took place on the streets of this good city and my fellow officers and I will be carrying out the investigation.'

Williams then paused again for a reaction from them. Both remained quiet and still continued to stare at him.

So far so good, he thought.

'I do offer my thanks however in assisting my fellow officer and me in restoring order. You may of course be present throughout any questioning of your compatriots later on this evening. I will leave it to you to alert your senior officers of the situation yourselves.'

Before either of the MPs decided, they *were* going to comment; Williams quickly turned his back on them and proceeded to march towards Evans.

On reaching him, he said, 'Constable Evans, please call for additional officers. Arrange for our three American friends and this young woman to be taken to the station where I will interview them later. In addition, arrange for an ambulance for the deceased and interview the three ladies over there across the street to see if they saw any of the events unfold.'

Williams then looked towards Dwyer who was now trying to sit up. He failed and collapsed back down on the pavement banging the back of his head with a sickening *THUD* as he did so. Williams winced at the thought of the damage that may cause.

He then looked back towards Evans again and said, 'It appears the suspect in this crime was trying to make some kind of a recovery, albeit briefly. Arrange for him to be taken directly to the station. His well-being and state of health can be monitored from there for the immediate future. Notify the duty doctor immediately on your arrival and be sure to tell him that he has received at least one blow to the back of the head. I will meet you there in one hour from now.'

'Yes sir. Why one hour from now though, sir?' Evans asked looking incredibly flustered because Williams was seemingly leaving everything to him.

'I have to return home where Mrs Williams will have no doubt prepared my evening meal. It would be very improper of me not to take the trouble in eating it as she does go to an awful lot of trouble with what meagre rations we have,' Williams said.

He paused, waiting for a response from Evans. Evans knew better to than argue or question his orders.

'One other thing, Constable Evans, this will give you a suitable amount of time to come up with an explanation regarding the comment I overheard you make to the young lady on my arrival at the scene.' He then abruptly turned round and walked at a brisk pace down High Street towards home.

Evans looked over towards the two MPs. One of them was shaking his head and said, 'You Goddamn limeys. No doubt he won't turn up back at your station before he has at least three cups of tea as well.'

Without realising, Evans slowly nodded his agreement.

11

Constable Gavin Evans was a now a very worried anxious young man. As he stood at the reception desk of his station waiting on the arrival of DI Williams, he was frantically trying to come up with some kind of excuse (without any success) of how he was going to explain away the comments the DI had heard him make to Sally at the scene.

Truth be known, there was no way in the world now that Corporal Carter had died, he could have covered for Dwyer anyway. Rather than dwell on it any further, he decided to just come clean and tell the DI the truth. That being that Dwyer had been a true friend all his life and he wanted to do anything he could for him.

The fact that Dwyer did not seem to have any idea of his own strength had blown that scenario out of the water.

Evans shuddered at the thought of the strength Dwyer must possess in order to kill a fit young soldier with just one punch to the chest. He knew he could handle himself, *but only one punch.*

His thoughts were interrupted by DI Williams entering the station. He was now dressed in an extremely smart grey suit, black brogues, white shirt and red tie. His appearance reminded Evans of a city banker rather than a copper and he had to fight hard to suppress a grin thinking that was what Williams really wished to be.

Definitely missed your true vocation in life, didn't you?

He had never struck Evans as the sort of person that would wish to interact with the low life's they had to deal with on a daily basis, if not a banker, then definitely some kind of diplomat or politician.

'Good evening, sir,' Evans said. 'I trust Mrs Williams is in good health and you enjoyed your dinner?'

Christ. Did I just say that aloud?

He is definitely going to realise I am taking the piss out of him!

Williams eyed Evans suspiciously looking for the slightest hint of sarcasm in his demeanour. Fortunately, Evans loved a game of poker with his mates when off duty so he had been practising looking expressionless for years, which was not difficult. Although well-meaning and enthusiastic about his duties, he was not exactly the sharpest tool in the toolbox.

Far from satisfied that Evans was not making a joke at his expense, Williams decided not to make an issue of it and said instead, 'Yes thank you, Constable Evans. She is in good form, as is her liver and bacon. A real treat I will have you know in these troubled times.'

Again, he looked for a reaction from Evans. He still stared back at him with a blank expression.

'At least I think it was liver,' he then added. 'Would have been terribly impolite for me to seek confirmation, don't you think?' He then raised his right eyebrow to finally illicit some kind of response from Evans.

Evans still declined to comment. He just nodded and smiled instead. He was somewhat taken aback from the response. The fact that Williams had addressed him with a tiny hint of a smile on his face got Evans to thinking that maybe he did have an element of humour in his personality after all.

Maybe.

'Now then young man,' Williams continued. 'Down to the matter at hand. Before we begin the questioning of the participants of today's incident, at which you will be present throughout, you will accompany me to the interview room and describe the events as they unfolded throughout the afternoon from your perspective.'

Evans nodded.

'After I am satisfied that you have described every event in the fullest of detail, you will explain the comments I heard you made to the young lady upon my arrival at the scene. Is that clear?'

Evans now feeling like a suspect himself, just met Williams stare and said nothing. He had the most horrible sinking feeling that his career and livelihood were at stake. What the hell would he do if he lost his job? One that he truly loved.

'Is that clear?' Williams repeated with a slightly raised voice.

'Yes sir. Crystal clear, sir,' Evans replied trying to disguise the fear in his own.

'Good man, good man,' Williams said with that tiny hint of a smile again. 'But first things first, let's have a cup of tea, shall we?'

Evans immediately thought back to the comment one of the MPs had made earlier and this time his poker face cracked as he turned away from Williams with a wide grin appearing.

12

Evans carried the tea into the interview room on a tray. The windowless room was no more that twelve feet square with a single table in the middle with four chairs that were fit for the scrap yard.

Williams had once suggested that if a suspect should lose complete control when being questioned and started to smash the place up, at least it would not cost much to replace them.

Not a bad point, Evans had thought at the time.

The walls were painted with a truly horrible shade of light green, which was peeling away from all four walls. The permanent smell of stale tobacco did not do much to improve the ambiance. A single light bulb hung from the centre of the ceiling without a lampshade.

Williams was sat at the far end of the table and gestured to Evans to sit opposite. Evans placed the tray in the middle of the table and suggested that Williams help himself to milk. The smallest of drops was deliberately poured into the chipped cup, which was decorated with some kind of flower that Evans did not recognise. Williams seemed to be deep in thought as he slowly stirred his brew, which seemed to Evans to last for hours. He felt a bead of sweat slowly fall down the side of face. It had nothing to do with the temperature of the room.

I have had it.
I know I have.
Mr Rule Book is going to have my guts for garters.

After what seemed like another hour of Evans' life, one that he was never going to get back, Williams simply put down his cup, picked up his pen, arranged the blank pieces of paper on the table into a perfect square and raised both eyebrows. This was Evans' cue to begin his statement.

He cleared his throat and then hesitantly and nervously began.

'Well sir, I started walking my beat at 16h00 hours as normal and at about 16h45 hours I turned left out of Pembroke Street into High Street. I looked across the street towards the cathedral and witnessed four men in uniforms that I recognised as American surrounding one bloke wearing civvies. It turned out to be one of my friends whose name is Moose... I mean Davey Dwyer, although I didn't recognise him at the time. He had his back to me see.'

Good plan.

Get the fact that he is your friend bit in their first.

Evans now paused looking towards the ceiling carefully considering the next part of his verbal report. Williams looked up from his papers with a frown, which prompted Evans to get on with it. Patience was not one of Williams' virtues.

'I had an instinct that it was about to kick-off so I started to reach for my whistle. In the blink of an eye, Dwyer had flattened all four soldiers. One of them had tried to hit him with a crowbar. As I said, I didn't know it was Davey so I ran across the street, drew my truncheon and clouted him round the back of his neck. He went down. I probably overreacted but he is massive and I didn't stop to think.'

Evans now stopped and *did* start to think. He stared down at the floor slowly shaking his head still regretting his hasty actions.

Sally was right, I could have killed him!

He then looked back at Williams and continued. 'The next thing I knew, his girlfriend who is called Sally Clark, who I then immediately recognised, started screaming at me, 'How could I do it?' Or something like that. I obviously then realised it was Davey who I had hit and I felt terrible, him being a really good bloke and a friend and all. I guess I panicked and tried to calm her down by suggesting to her that I could get him off. As I said, he has been a good friend to me over the years.'

Evans took a deep breath and offered no more to the report. Williams throughout had been scribbling notes furiously. He put down in his pen and glanced over what he had written.

Williams finally looked up and said, 'A good friend of yours you say. How long would you say you have you known Mr Dwyer?'

Evans was immediately encouraged that Williams' first response was not one of scorn. He quickly replied, 'I've known him since school, sir. He used to stick up for me and fight my battles for me. We have remained friends ever since. He is the salt of the earth, sir, a real good sort. I cannot believe I just had to lock him up in a cell.

Sure Davey can really handle himself but he aint no troublemaker. He just sort of ends it if it comes his way.'

'So it would seem,' said Williams while slowly nodding his head looking towards his notes on the table.

Evans quickly then tried to defend his friends character further. 'Yes sir, he tries to avoid it mostly though. You saw the size of him, sir, he is as big as a house. That is why his mates call him Moose. He does have the tendency to get very jealous if anyone tries to chat up his girl though. I suspect that was what the fight was about, sir.'

Think. Think you idiot!
What else can I say to get out of this?

Williams started to nod his head again and then looked Evans in the eye. Unbeknown to Evans, Williams was already very aware of his friendship with Dwyer.

'I commend you young man,' Williams said and then paused. Evans expression instantly turned to one of astonishment, his poker face had now disappeared completely.

Williams enjoyed the moment. He paused for an unnaturally long time watching Evans jaw drop lower and lower before continuing.

'Although I can never condone perverting the course of Justice, I admire your loyalty very much and the fact you decided to tell me the truth in this meeting has saved me the trouble of pursuing this issue further. I will say no more about it and strongly suggest that you leave out that particular piece of commentary with Miss Clark from your written report.' Williams ended his statement but staring calmly into Evans' eyes.

Huh? Did I just hear that?

Evans felt his eyes grow wider and his mouth drop open further, it that was possible, and just managed to say, 'Yes sir, and thank you, sir.'

He could have kissed the old geezer.

'As I just said, say no more about it,' Williams repeated with a dismissive wave of the hand. 'Now tell me, what has happened since your return to the station?'

Evans now made a concerted effort to stop catching flies and closed his mouth before answering.

'Yes sir. The three Americans have all been placed in separate cells apart from each other and they are all going on about diplomatic immunity. Not sure that applies to soldiers though?'

Evans waited for an answer but as one was not forthcoming, he continued.

'The duty doctor has given them a once over and apart from a few missing teeth and a few bruises, they all appear to be fine. Miss Clark is in the waiting room next to reception. She has not stopped crying since arriving. Davey went in and out of consciousness whilst the doc was examining him so he gave him a mild sedative, which should put him out until the morning. He has quite a concussion and he is going to be walking with a limp for a while. You saw that kick he got in the crown jewels?' Then immediately regretted the last part of his update.

Oh God, I said that aloud too.

Wind your neck in Gavin!

It was now Williams' turn to suppress a smile. He had never heard of testicles referred to before in that manner. Although he would never admit it, he found Evans' description somewhat amusing.

'What about the three lady onlookers I asked you to interview at the scene? Did they witness any of the events?' Williams asked.

Evans had deliberately not questioned them earlier and his poker face, which had now resumed again, was now being tested to its limits as he said, 'No sir, they didn't see anything.'

Williams eyed Evans suspiciously for the second time of the evening but for reasons only known to him, and he alone, did not pursue the matter further albeit that he was far from convinced that Evans was telling the truth.

Evans now thinking he had managed to pull the wool over the DI's eyes, quickly added, 'There is one other thing that I need to notify you about, sir.'

Williams nodded for Evans for to continue.

'Well sir, it is about the two MPs that helped us out at the scene,' he said and then paused.

'Yes, the two MPs. Spit it out Evans,' said Williams impatiently and then took a sip of sea in attempt to hide the concern he was now feeling. Nothing that they could have to say was going to be good news. Again, for his own personal reasons, he dreaded what Evans was about to say next. It could only complicate matters.

'Yes sir. They went with the deceased, Corporal Carter, to the hospital in the ambulance. They mentioned to me before leaving that the shit was going to hit the fan as apparently he has an uncle over here that is based up at Greenham Common who they were going to contact immediately, a Major in the 101st Airborne, the same Division as the deceased.'

The shit has hit the fan.
For Christ sakes Gavin, get a grip!

Williams' worst fears on the matter were realised. He hid his anxiety by correcting Evans. 'Constable Evans. When in future you are providing me with a verbal report, please ensure you leave out the profanity. It is totally unprofessional and unnecessary,' Williams said, albeit his words were not heartfelt.

Knew I would not get away with that one.
Oh well, you can't win 'em all.

'Sorry sir. Well anyway, one of the MPs said he would no doubt want to speak to you tonight, sir, and they thought maybe it would be a good idea if you didn't leave the station until he had the chance to meet you. Apparently he is not the sort of bloke to take disappointment well.'

'Very well, very well, duly noted. I think we can now start the interview process. We will start with Miss Clark. If you would be so kind to go and get her from the waiting room.'

'Yes sir.'

'One final thing, Constable. Who else is aware within the station of the incident?'

'Nobody sir. Well . . . apart from the Desk Sergeant.'

Williams looked down into the last remains of his tea thoughtfully and then said. 'Good. Please ensure you keep it that way for the time being and tell the Sergeant I wish to speak to him immediately.'

'Yes sir.'

Evans left the interview room puffing his cheeks and blew out a long cleansing breath. *The rest of the blokes are not going to believe this* he thought.

Maybe we have been too harsh on the old fart.
Surely not?

13

Sally was still crying as she entered the interview room as the Desk Sergeant was leaving, looking clearly confused. Why a veil of secrecy was being placed on the latest arrest was beyond him, but he knew better not to question it.

Williams took out a handkerchief from his jacket pocket that his wife had ironed, handed it to her, sat her down at the table and gestured to Evans that he should stand at the door.

Evans stifled a grin.

Ironed handkerchiefs no less.

I wonder if his wife irons his underpants as well.

You didn't say that aloud did you?

No.

Okay. Thank God. Get a grip though will you!

The amount of noise Sally made when blowing her nose into the handkerchief was incredible. Evans would wager any amount of money that Williams would not want it back. This did seem to have a calming effect on her however, and after examining the omissions from her nose, which was plentiful, she promptly folded the handkerchief up and offered it back to Williams.

'No, no my dear. You may keep it,' Williams said quickly with a straight face.

Evans could stifle his grin no longer.

Sally then broke the brief silence between them spoke with a considerable amount of defiance in her voice. 'How's Davey? I am not saying anything to you until I know how he is . . . When can I see him?' She then proceeded to start biting her bottom lip.

Evans for once could predict Williams' response to that one.

Not going to happen I am afraid, Sally.

Our boy is in deepest darkest dingiest poo.

Williams articulated his response in a far more professional manner.

'Mr Dwyer will be taking a little nap until morning I'm afraid, so you will not be able to see him until at least then,' replied Williams.

'He will no doubt be waking up with quite a headache, and once recovered; we will want to start questioning him.' Williams paused and then added with the best look of concern he could muster. 'He is in very serious trouble my dear. You do know that young American soldier died earlier in the fracas earlier today? That somewhat complicates matters.'

Sally gave her bottom lip a further ferocious gnawing and then whimpered. The handkerchief was given a further inspection.

It reminded Evans of the noise young children make when their parents tell them to stop crying or they will be given something to cry about. He also wondered what she could be possibly looking for in the snotty rag she seemed to holding onto for dear life.

Sally went to open her mouth as if to say something but just nodded instead, looking thoughtfully back at the handkerchief.

The handkerchief was then again brutally attacked by her seemingly relentless nasal onslaught.

'Now then,' Williams said with an air of authority in his voice ignoring the imitation of a fog warning. 'I wish to make this as quick and painless as possible so you can return home without further delay. I believe Constable Evans has informed your parents that you are here and so no doubt they will be worried.'

Evans nodded confirmation towards Williams.

'In your own words, please describe to me what exactly took place on High Street and approximately 16h45 hours this afternoon.' He then picked up his pen and waited for Sally to start.

After one final violent assault on the linen, Sally took a deep breath and began.

The only details she added that Evans and Williams had not witnessed between them, was the fact she was meeting Davey at his home where she was supposed to make dinner. She was about to cross the street and go into the flat after lighting a candle in the cathedral for her aunt who had recently been killed in a bombing raid, when four men in uniform pulled up in a jeep, got out, and asked where they could find lodgings for the night. She did not realise they were American until she had heard their accents.

After pointing the way up the street, the tallest bloke, the one that was killed, started to insist that she joined them and asked her if she had any friends as pretty as she was. Sally said she told them that she couldn't because she had a boyfriend and he would be home at any minute.

At that point, she saw Davey walking across the street. She advised Williams and Evans that Davey had also told them where the guesthouses were. Davey then told them that she was his girlfriend when they said that she was pretty.

Sally then paused and looked backwards and forwards from Evans to Williams almost as if to seek confirmation that she was.

Evans believing that to be the case nodded his agreement. Williams remained impassive.

Sally then continued. She was in fact actually trying to gage their reaction to her description of the events. Evans nodding his head provided her with some degree of encouragement that she was doing just fine.

They then said he was being selfish and that he should let them show her a good time. That got Davey mad and he told them to piss off home and then shoved him in the shoulder. Again, she informed them that that was towards the tall one that had died. All four of them surrounded Davey as if to start attacking him. Davey said they did not want to do it and needed to go. Then the fight broke out.

Evans looked towards Williams to see if was going to chastise Sally for swearing and wondered if he had written, 'go away home' in his notes instead.

Williams making no comment on her profanity asked for some further clarification instead. 'Are you sure that the Americans acted in aggressive manner and circled your boyfriend, Miss Clark?'

Oh, I see. One rule for one and one for another, Evans thought and smiled inwardly to himself.

'I am absolutely positive, officer,' said Sally nodding furiously. 'I remember feeling sorry for them because I know what Davey's like when he loses it. They didn't stand a chance, even if there were four of them. They all surrounded him with their fists clenched.'

Sally looked towards to Evans with wide eyes looking for support.

He looked away instead.

Shut up Sally!

Do not tell him he loses it and kicks the shit out of people.
He doesn't as a rule!

'Very well, Miss Clark,' said Williams shuffling the paper he had just been writing his notes on, 'I will not detain you any longer. Constable Evans will show you to the front desk where you will be asked to produce a written statement. Once completed and signed, you are free to go for the time being. I will of course be in contact in the near future.'

As Sally stood up to leave she said, 'What's going to happen to Davey? It wasn't his fault . . . They didn't give him any choice you know. They were deliberately looking for trouble.' Her voluntary statement was ended with a small whimper.

Evans took Sally by the arm as he did not expect any further comment from Williams and was then amazed when he replied, 'I am not sure yet, Miss Clark. It could be argued that there is an element of self-defence and provocation involved here, but the fact that a death is involved means that Mr Dwyer is likely to face at least a manslaughter charge. Good evening to you,' he said without any hint of emotion.

Oh, nice!
That will put the poor girls mind at rest!
Jesus Christ!

Evans glared at Williams, which went unnoticed by him.

Before Evans and Sally had a chance to leave the room, Williams looked up and added, 'Constable Evans. The questioning of the three Americans can wait until I have had a chance to speak with Major Carter whose arrival I am sure is imminent. In any case, the MPs have not arrived yet and I gave them the opportunity to be present earlier. Please bring the Major to my office as soon as he arrives. I am not to be disturbed in the meantime.'

'Yes sir, anything else, sir?' Evans said unable to hide the sarcasm in his tone.

Williams ignored the obvious jibe. Instead, he made the pretence of reading the notes he had written.

I take back what I thought about you joining the diplomatic service, Evans thought as he led Sally out. *And we were definitely not wrong about you either. Old fart!*

'I will take that as a no then,' he said instead.

14

Major Edward Carter of the 101st Airborne sat in the front passenger of a jeep (finally driving through the Portsmouth City streets) which seemed, at least to him, to be devoid of any suspension. The Private, his designated driver, did not seem to notice.

Fortunately, throughout the horrendous sixty mile drive from his base at Greenham Common the Private had maintained silence.

Carter did not feel like talking.

His ass felt like that it had kicked repeatedly by a mule. This was not improving his mood, which had steadily gone from bad to worse since arriving in England. He hated the food, the climate, and most of all, he missed North Carolina. Last but not least, he now had to clear up the latest mess that his God forsaken nephew and his three accomplices had created.

For as long as he could remember the boy had been trouble. It now turned out that he was continuing the trend even after his death. The thought of now having to clear up after him – again - sickened him to the stomach.

And to think, it was me that had sent him on the Goddamn simple errand in the first place. Anything to get the low-life piece of crap off base for a day or so.

He believed he had been doing the rest of the men a favour. Maybe he had. It now turned out that he would never be returning.

Now that he had been killed, he briefly wondered if anyone would miss him back at base . . . apart from his three degenerate friends.

Extremely unlikely was the hasty conclusion he came too.

They would more likely throw a party on hearing the news. Somewhat perversely, he looked forward to the condolences that would be offered. Brushing them off would be misconstrued as him putting on a brave face. Nothing could be further from the truth.

Since being contacted by the MPs from the hospital, he had surprised himself that he felt absolutely nothing. Not one moment of remorse had he felt for a single second. Truth be known, he found himself feeling somewhat relieved. The world would now be a better place.

Good riddance to bad rubbish, he thought.

It was almost inevitable that his nephew's fate would end this way. His only regret was that it was typical that it had happened before he had had a chance to see combat. At least then if had died in battle his life would have served some purpose and not been a total waste. That being he would have at least depleted the enemies ammunition supply by a single bullet. Maybe even got in the way of a more worthy soul that did not deserve to die young.

That at least would be something.

He surprised himself further as he was now actually looking forward to making an appearance at the police station to come face to face with Garcia, Henderson and Hickey. A slight smile formed on his face thinking about how they would react to seeing him standing outside their cell.

'Probably shit their pants,' he said aloud to himself with a slight smile forming on his face.

'Excuse me, sir?' The driver said with a surprised look towards his officer sat next to him.

'Nothing Private,' Carter said with a more stoic expression.

'I think this is the place, sir. Sorry it took so long. Not the best road I have driven along, sir,' said the driver.

'Very good, Private, not your fault, you can stand down for about a half-an-hour. I should not be any longer than that,' replied Carter.

They both got out of the jeep and stretched in unison.

The urge to give his backside a good rubbing was overwhelming but as his subordinate was looking right at him waiting for further instructions, he resisted.

Instead, Carter took a shilling from his pocket and flipped it towards the Private. 'I noticed a pub over the road. Perhaps you can get them to provide you a bowl of soup or even something stronger while you wait, only one mind. You are to drive me to Southwick House later this evening.'

'Thank you very much, sir.' The private saluted and immediately crossed the street. He did not need a second invitation even if the beer over here looked like dirty dish water and was nearly always warm.

Beer was beer.

Carter straightened his tie, stuck his shoulders back and walked towards the entrance of the police station. His pace quickened as he was more than curious of meeting his nephew's slayer. If what he had been informed over the phone of the 'incident' earlier in the day was only partly true, he must be something to behold.

On walking through the door, he was pleased to see that the MPs that had accompanied his nephew's body to hospital, and who had made contact with him, had already arrived.

They immediately jumped to their feet and saluted.

Carter saluted in return and then approached the reception desk where Evans was waiting.

'Good evening. My name is Major Edward Carter and I am here to see Detective Inspector Williams. He is expecting me I believe?'

'Yes sir,' replied Evans. He did not know whether to salute or not. He thought better of it. 'I am to escort you to his office, if you would like to follow me. The Inspector said to take you to him without delay as soon as you arrived.'

Carter nodded, smiled, and then gestured towards the MPs that they should follow.

They immediately fell into line.

15

Evans knocked twice and opened the door to Williams' small office, which as usual, was incredibly tidy. The wall behind the wooden desk had shelves stretching the whole width of the room and from top to bottom. They were covered by Police procedural and law books. Evans suspected that Williams had the contents of all of them committed to memory. Four filing cabinets lined the wall in front of the desk, which was to the right of the door. Two wooden chairs were placed opposite Williams' desk. A small window was on the opposite side to the entrance.

Evans entered first and then ushered the three Americans into the room. Williams seemed oblivious for the briefest of moments that he now had company.

As was his norm, he only had the report that he was reading on his desk along with a small lamp and pencil sharpener. The remainder of his paperwork was placed neatly in an in-tray on top of the cabinet nearest the door.

Suddenly becoming alert, Williams stood bolt upright and extended his hand towards Major Carter over his perfectly organised desk. He noticed that Carter eyes looked incredibly sharp, without a hint of sadness.

'Very pleased to make your acquaintance, Major. I only wish it was under more pleasant circumstances,' Williams said as Carter shook his hand, which had a vice like grip. He consciously tried not to show any of the discomfort he was now feeling once his hand was eventually released.

'Thank you, Detective,' said Carter. 'I wonder if you would allow me five minutes alone with the two MPs here before we have our meeting. Is there a room we can use?'

You can speak to them as long as you want. You will not be taking over the investigation though. No matter what story you think up amongst the three of you, Williams thought.

'Of course there is,' Williams said instead. 'Constable Evans, will you take the gentleman to the interview room please.'

Evans nodded and the foursome left the office without further comment.

Much to Williams' surprise, Major Carter was true to his word. He returned alone to Williams' office in no more than *four* minutes. Williams realised that this man was all business after all.

Major Carter sat down in one of the chairs opposite him and said immediately, 'Inspector, let me make this easy for you. You are obviously aware by your kind words earlier that the deceased is my nephew. Please be assured that I have not come here tonight to start up some witch hunt, in fact, quite the opposite.'

Carter then paused and looked for a reaction from Williams, who had to this point, remained impassive.

Wouldn't want this guy in our Friday night poker school back home, Carter thought. *The guy is unreadable.*

'As fate would have it,' Carter continued, 'I have to attend Southwick House later this evening to meet with my superior officer, so I was due to make the trip to the south coast anyway.'

Williams felt both his eyebrows rise at the same time now due to the indifference in which the Major had delivered his last statement.

So much for unreadable, Carter thought. He was actually beginning to enjoy himself.

After noting the 'tell,' Carter continued, 'I see my attitude to today's events surprises you, and may well it should. Let me explain why.'

He paused briefly staring into Williams' eyes. His stare was returned. Carter noted the curious frown.

'The truth of the matter is that Corporal Carter is not my *real* nephew, although nobody within Army is aware of that fact. My brother and his wife were unfortunately unable to have children so they adopted James when he was a baby. His natural mother abandoned him in a dumpster in Jacksonville, Florida.'

Again, Carter paused and tried to read the body language of Williams in front of him. As his eyebrows had now returned to their normal position and remained there, he continued.

'Throughout his childhood James was nothing but trouble, and to cut a long story short, my brother gave up on him. I agreed to pull a few strings for him to join the Airborne a year ago and this is his first posting. We thought the Army discipline might do him good. It must have done to a certain extent as somebody saw fit to bump him up to Corporal but frankly, Detective, James was a walking time bomb waiting to go off. It was only a matter of time before something like this happened. Today seems to be the day. He appears to have finally met his match.'

Williams remained quiet hoping that Carter would continue. For once in his life, he had no idea where this was going. To his irritation, there was a knock on the door and the Desk Sergeant entered.

'Excuse me, sir, sorry to interrupt, the medical report for the Carter case has just arrived from the hospital. I thought you would wish to see it immediately,' he said, whilst giving a sideways glance to the Major who was sat staring at him.

'Thank you Sergeant,' Williams said. 'Please close the door on your way out.'

The Sergeant left.

'I would be very interested in the contents of that folder,' said Carter.

Again, William's both eyebrows jumped to attention simultaneously. *Why the sudden interest in your nephew now?* Quickly sped through his mind.

'Of course, if you will just give me one moment.' Williams read the short written report more deliberately than he would have done normally, and then eventually looked up at Carter.

'It states that Corporal Carter was killed by his sternum and three of his ribs splintering after receiving a severe blow to the chest. This then severed his right coronary artery and punctured the right atrium of his heart. He would have died instantly.' Williams then studied Carter's face for any sign of remorse.

'This guy Dwyer must be some piece of work. The MPs certainly didn't exaggerate,' Carter said as casually as if he was discussing the weather.

'Excuse me, Major, how so?' Williams said unable to hide his surprise at the Majors comment.

'It transpires that they both witnessed the incident from afar. Before they had time to react, it was all over. They both told me separately they have never seen anything like it in their lives, and they have seen their fair share. Sort of goes with job I guess. He took out four guys in the blink of an eye and hit one so hard in the chest that he killed him . . . Very impressive.'

This time Williams' eyebrows reached the top of his forehead. 'Major Carter, may I remind you that a crime was committed today which resulted in the death of your nephew, even if he wasn't a blood relative. I hardly believe the word 'impressive' is hardly appropriate,' he protested.

Carter smiled.

'Piece of shit nephew from poor blood stock, Inspector,' Carter said remaining casual. 'Forgive me. Have you interviewed the three other Privates yet?' He then looked straight into Williams' eyes with a bland expression on his face.

Williams was now becoming unnerved by the Majors disinterest in his nephew's demise and looked away from his gaze towards the report on his desk. He said, 'No, Major Carter, not yet. I did inform the MPs earlier that they could attend, but they arrived only minutes before you did.'

'That will not be necessary,' said Carter too quickly. He then paused and added, 'Detective, can I ask you to keep them in custody overnight. I will of course speak to them before I leave. I would then very much like to attend their interviews in person tomorrow morning. I could be back here no later than 08h30 hours. In addition, if I may, I would also like to attend the first interview with Mr Dwyer himself. Would this be acceptable to you?'

Before Williams could think of any reason why not, he hesitantly replied, 'Of course.'

He then regretted it immediately as it would be a highly irregular practice for a member of the deceased's family to be present when questioning the suspect, even if he was a Major in the U.S. Army.

'Excellent,' said Carter quickly before Williams could change his mind. 'If you could then arrange for me to be taken to the cell block I will advise my men they are to remain here overnight and then take up no more of your time.'

Williams frowned.

Agenda; went through his mind.

16

Major Carter followed Williams to the reception area where they met Evans. Williams immediately instructed him to take Carter to visit the American soldiers detained below. He then positioned himself behind the reception desk and waited on their return. To say the meeting had gone quite the opposite too how he had expected would be an understatement. He fully expected the American Officer to be full of bluster and demanding retribution.

Agenda?

Carter's calmness throughout was curious to say the least. It was obvious that there was no love lost between him and his adopted nephew, but Williams sensed that there was far more to this lying beneath the surface of his apparent apathy of his nephew's sudden and violent demise. No matter what family issues they had in the past, the complete lack of compassion displayed by Major Carter was, to Williams' own mind, disquieting. Before he could dwell on his troubled thoughts much further, Evans and the Major returned.

'That is that all squared away then. Thank you for your time, Detective,' said Carter. 'Until tomorrow then.' Carter did not wait for a response or offer a handshake. He just quickly turned on his heels and exited the station.

Carter's driver was waiting in the driver seat of the jeep. 'How was your soup?' Carter asked as he slid into the front passenger seat.

The private retuned the shilling to Carter that he had given him earlier and said, 'Seems I was not very welcome in there, sir. The word seems to be round about some guy they have locked up in there and there must have been at least thirty elderly gentleman looking not best pleased. They were one tough looking bunch, sir, even if they were old. They didn't seem to appreciate seeing my uniform for some reason. I thought it best not to hang around and ask why.'

'Very wise, Private,' said Carter. 'Thirty you say. He must be popular. Now, if you would be so kind, Southwick House is our next port of call and not a word to anyone about this unscheduled stop.'

'No sir.'

Back in the station, Williams and Evans were still in reception, both watching the jeep drive away through the window. 'Did you by any chance overhear the exchange of words between the Major and the other three soldiers, Constable Evans?' Williams asked as the taillights disappeared from view.

'Yes sir. That bloke does not muck about, does he? As soon as the three of them saw him standing outside their cells, they all just stared at him with their mouths open. It seemed strange to me that they didn't salute him though. Not one of them did. They all looked proper worried, sir. He just told them they would be interviewed here tomorrow, at which he would be present, and that they were staying in the cell overnight. That was it. He then just turned round and walked back up the stairs.'

'I see,' said Williams with his brow now furrowed.

He did not appear to Evans to be going to offer any other comment.

'May I say something, sir?'

'Certainly, what is on your mind?'

'Well it seems to me, sir; you would think that the Major would want to get his men released as soon as possible. He didn't seem at all that interested in their well-being. I just wondered what you made of that, sir. Seems a bit strange to me.'

'I couldn't agree more, Constable. It would appear that Major Carter seems to have some kind of personal *agenda*, which at present is not clear to me. I have no doubt that all will become clearer when he returns tomorrow. I shall be making it my business to find out.'

Evans nodded his agreement.

'Have you checked on Mr Dwyer's condition?' Williams added.

'Yes sir, he's snoring his head off.'

'Very well, get yourself off home, Constable. I will see you at 08h00 hours tomorrow.'

17

Although he would have no recollection of it later, Dwyer had briefly gained consciousness. He had been placed in the last cell of on the left by Evans within the cellblock, three cells away from nearest of his earlier combatants.

In his now drug induced haze, he became vaguely aware of an angry, urgent conversation.

'Make sure we all stick to the same story –

– he attacked James first.

– just defending ourselves.'

The voices trailed away somewhere off into the distance.

With his eyes remaining closed, his expression was a mixture of pain and confusion. He tossed and turned, groaned, briefly opened his eyes, and then groaned again.

Is that those Americans again?

It is.

His eyes now shot open and searched urgently around his unfamiliar surroundings. His look of confusion returned but with more intensity.

Why are they in my flat?

Don't know. Maybe you should get up and find out.

What are they doing in my flat?

Get up and find out.

I thought they had been confined to barracks

Silence.

I said, I thought they had been confined to barracks.

This is not my bed!

Silence.

I said this is not my bed. Who the hell's bed is this?

Silence.

God by balls ache.

His head rapidly whipped from side to side on the thin pillow provided causing a sharp, stabbing, violent pain behind his eyes. A loud audible groan escaped his lips.

The voices returned.

- son of a bitch that killed him.
- make sure he will get his.
- if we get out.

Tell them to shut up . . . I can't sleep.
Listen to what they are saying.
They didn't give me any choice.
No . . . they didn't.
What choice did I have?
None.
This bed is crap.
Get up then.
Can't.
Why not.
Too tired . . .

His inner conversation then came to abrupt end. His skin prickled and the hairs stood up on the back of his neck. He now had an overwhelming sense of dread as he felt he had been joined by a sinister, hateful, loathsome presence in the room. He felt as if every muscle in his body tensed in unison, fully expecting something atrocious to happen to him.

'Who's there?' He whispered closing his eyes, too frightened to open them, which actually sounded like 'ooos thaaa.'

There was no response.

'Ooos thaaa.'

The voices returned.

- What did that son of a bitch just say?
- make sure he will get his.

Just shut up.

With every muscle still taught, he slowly brought his knees up to his waist, held them tight with both hands and closed his eyes tightly. The resultant pain behind his eyes and temples was a welcome one. It took the focus away from the fear.

Slowly but surely, he started to relax.

Just as the darkness was about to completely consume him again; he thought he heard a woman scream.

'DAAVVEEYYY! Nooooo!'
Sally? Is that you?
The welcome oblivion was then gratefully was restored.

18
31ˢᵗ May 1944
HMS Dryad, Southwick, England
22h00 hours

On approaching, the manor house located just North of Portsmouth in the Hampshire countryside; a slight smile appeared on Carter's list. He relished the history and the importance of the place.

'This house was built in 1800, Private, and was then requisitioned in 1941 following the heavy bombing of the Dockyard. It then became the new home of HMS Dryad,' Carter said with enthusiasm.

The Private remained quiet and only just managed to stifle a yawn. He had heard the speech before . . . every time he had driven Carter there previous.

Carter continued. 'In 1943, with the planning of D-Day already underway, the house was chosen to be the location of the Supreme Headquarters Allied Expeditionary Force.'

'Yes sir,' the Private said. 'You have mentioned it before.'

Carter did not take the hint that he maybe boring him. 'Within only the last few months, the Allied Commanders such as Admiral Ramsay, General Eisenhower and General Montgomery have made it their headquarters.'

The Private happily pulled up outside the entrance. 'This okay here for you, sir?'

'Yes Private, see you in the morning.'

After entering, and then being led to wait outside the Library, Carter sat in an upholstered chair listening to the gale force wind and rain lash against the walls and windows. He felt like the British elements were conspiring to lift the house from its foundations. He briefly thought how Dorothy must have felt in the Wizard of Oz when the tornado picked up her house in Kansas.

Within the library was the largest gathering of high-ranking military leaders Carter had seen in one place in his entire career. He guessed the decision on the date regarding the Invasion was on the agenda, and that his immediate superior Colonel Franklin Harrison had been requested to attend a final planning meeting.

Pieces of information had filtered down to Carter over the last few days that Air Vice Marshall, Trafford Leigh-Mallory had been in fierce debate with Eisenhower over the deployment of the airborne divisions. He believed that dropping them into the Cotentin Peninsula would cause 70 percent loss of gliders and over 50 percent troop casualties. In addition, recent intelligence had revealed that the Germans 91st division had been placed where they scheduled to drop the 82nd Airborne.

Ignoring the storm for a moment, his mood darkened at the thought of the imminent battle. It was to be the first time he was going to experience combat and lead his men into harm's way. The responsibility was weighing heavily on his shoulders.

He did not consider many of the men under his command to be anything more than boys. The fact that many would not be returning back home to their families sickened him to the stomach.

The Library door opened and Harrison came out alone disturbing Carter from his troublesome thoughts. On seeing him waiting, he turned to close the door behind him and then gestured to Carter to follow him. He stood up and followed Harrison into the spacious dining room whose walls were lined with oak panels with framed pictures of famous historical military leaders. Harrison closed the door behind them.

Carter stopped and studied the portrait of Lord Admiral Nelson. 'Remarkable character,' he said whist still gazing one of Britain's most famous naval officers. 'Do you know he requested his subordinate officer Captain Hardy aboard HMS Victory to kiss him moments before he died? That would be the last thing I would consider with the crowd we have.'

'I certainly wouldn't want you to kiss me, that's for sure,' Harrison replied.

He then smiled and extended his hand to Carter and added, 'Thanks for coming down, Ed. Sorry to drag you all the way down here but you can't take too many chances with the phones at the moment. Never know whose listening these days. Can I get you a drink?' He picked up a glass next to a decanter of Brandy and waved it at Carter.' 'Large one or small one?'

'Depends what you are about to tell me, Frank,' said Carter while forcing a smile.

'Large one it is then, take a seat.' Harrison then poured out two extremely large measures and sat opposite Carter at the table. He briefly studied the contents in his glass gently swirling it around and then looked towards Carter.

'Right, business first, and then maybe we can go and get a bite to eat in that charming little village down the road. I hear the meat pies they serve up in the pub are almost edible. They must have their own cows considering the current rations that are being imposed,' Harrison said raising an eyebrow with a smile.

'Sounds good,' said Carter. 'But we will have to get a move on. It's getting late.'

'Not a problem. They appear to stay open all hours. Cannot seem do enough for us. I must say these Brits can be very accommodating at times.'

Carter just smiled and thought how different things were only a few miles south. His driver had been genuinely worried about his own safety while waiting for him in the pub.

'Okay. This is the way it is, at least at the moment,' Harrison said. 'It looks like we are going in on the 5th June weather permitting, which means we will leave Greenham on the night of the 4th. That is four days from now, although the weather here seems to be impossible to predict. I trust the order back at Greenham has been given to confine all the men to barracks?'

'Yes sir. It has been a place for a week now. With the exception for those required to perform the occasional special duty.' He shifted in his seat uncomfortably at the thought of the screw up his nephew had made of the latest such 'duty' he had ordered.

'Right, let me fill you in on a few details. Eisenhower has overruled Leigh-Mallory and advised that the capture of St-Mere-Eglise and the causeways are imperative to protect the flank of the 4th division. If not accomplished, the landing at Utah beach would have to be cancelled. I must say I agree with him, as it is too late in the day to start amending the whole Overlord operation. That of course means we will indeed be dropped in the Cotentin Peninsula west of Utah

Beach.'

'Very good, sir,' said Carter. 'Excellent news, I am sick of waiting, as are the men. The sooner we get in there and get this over with the sooner we can get home.' He hoped that his false bravado was convincing.

Harrison took a sip of his brandy and nodded his agreement.

They then spent the next hour intently studying maps of the intended drop zones and the mission objectives along with known enemy positions. One thing that they were grateful for from the Brits, apart from their meat pies, was their intelligence gathering which in most cases could be relied upon.

Once satisfied all was committed to memory Harrison said, 'Okay then. Let's go get that meat pie shall we?'

Carter briefly hesitated, and then went for it.

'There is one more thing you need to know before we go, sir' Carter said in his normal all business tone.

He then spent the next five minutes informing Harrison of the events that had took place in Portsmouth earlier in the day, what he had told DI Williams about his nephew and the conversation he had with the MPs. He also added further information when briefing Harrison that he had deliberately neglected to inform DI Williams earlier. He then asked permission to execute a plan that he had hastily formulated after speaking with MPs at the police station in Portsmouth.

Permission was granted.

19

On the journey back to the Police station the next morning, Carter couldn't help think that this small Island seemed to have been at war since time began. Evidence of previous wars and conflicts were everywhere in this part of the south coast of England. His driver had taken the scenic route. Instead of continuing along Southwick Hill Road into Cosham, he had turned left onto Portsdown Hill Road. He had advised Carter that the slight detour would afford panoramic views of the city.

Carter was keen to see it.

'Pull in here, Private,' Carter requested eagerly.

Carter got out of the jeep and truly admired what an excellent vantage point this was.

Immediately due south of him was Portchester Castle which was built as early as the 3rd Century which had then acted as a staging-post during the hundred years war for expeditions to France and repelling cross-channel raids. The Dockyard sprawled away to his right, which was filled every imaginable type of warship. Dotted about in the Solent were Forts that were built in Napoleonic times and the Isle of Wight was off in the distance.

Unfortunately, the rest of city, due to its destruction by the German bombing raids, rather spoiled the landscape. For a brief moment, he forgot about home and thought that might be nice to spend some more time here once this madness was over. To to able to spend some time viewing these historical buildings rather than just reading about them would be nice.

More than nice.

He hoped there would still be some left to see when this madness was all over.

Reluctantly, Carter pulled himself away from the view and returned to the jeep. He was still going to be early. He smiled to himself on how he was about to play DI Williams.

A worthy mind game opponent indeed. I would bet the farm on that, he thought to himself. He gazed through the windshield absently as the jeep descended the hill towards the destruction below.

20

DI Williams was surprised to see Evans at the reception desk as it was only 07h30 hours. 'Early start, Constable Evans, everything okay?' He said.

'Yes sir. I wanted to get in early to see how Davey was in case he woke up. I have been here since 05h00. Miss Clark was waiting for me when I got home last night. She is worried sick. I promised I would try to be there when he came round and then let her know.'

Poor girl is going out of her mind thanks to your comment to her about manslaughter last night!

'And has he?'

'No sir. He stirred a couple of times but he is still out. The Americans are all awake though. They have been given tea and toast and have all been remarkably quiet.'

'Tea sounds like an excellent idea. If you would be so kind, Evans, I will be in my office.'

What am I? The charlady all of a sudden?

'Sir, Major Carter is already here. He is in the interview room. He wanted coffee but we aint got none.'

'Already here?' Williams repeated anxiously and then quickly regained his composure. 'It seems he is not the only one that didn't get much sleep last night. You look terrible, Constable Evans. Please use the facilities in the WC and make sure you shave. Then join Major Carter and me in the interview room.'

Nope. We have not been too harsh on you. You are definitely an arsehole!

Careful you do not say THAT aloud.

Oh, shut up. You can piss off as well. He is an arsehole.

Williams was not happy. He hated attending meetings without extensive preparation. Nevertheless, he went straight to meet the eager beaver Major and entered the interview room.

'Good morning, Major Carter, I trust your meeting went well last night?' He said as he entered the depressing green, stale tobacco smelling room.

Carter rose from his chair before replying, 'Yes thank you, Detective. I realise I am early and I am happy to wait if you have other duties to perform before 08h30.'

'No that's quite alright, Major,' Williams lied. 'No time like the present. Constable Evans will be with us shortly and then we can begin. Unfortunately, Mr Dwyer's sedative does not seem to have worn off and he is still sleeping. If you will excuse me one minute, I need to fetch some writing material from my office.'

'No problem, Detective, I have no time constraints.'

The way Carter fidgeted and looked towards the floor when he delivered his final remark made Williams think that the opposite was more the truth. 'I think not,' he said to himself as he walked the corridor towards his office.

On returning to the interview room, Evans had now arrived and looked worse than he did earlier. He had obviously cut himself shaving and several pieces of blood stained tissue were now stuck to his face.

Williams declined to comment.

'Constable Evans,' Williams said. 'I think we will start with Private Garcia. Please go and bring him up from the cell block.'

'Yes sir,' Evans said and then looked towards the Major. He was sat bolt upright in his chair staring at the wall. He wondered why Williams was allowing him to be present.

Williams then turned to Carter and soon as Evans had left and said, 'I trust you are here only as an observer, Major Carter. You will be leaving all the questioning to me?' This was said as more of an instruction rather than an enquiry.

Carter nodded his agreement. He picked up his chair and moved to the corner of the room.

Evans returned with Private Garcia whose lips had swollen up to twice their normal size. Garcia took a seat opposite Williams and seemed to fix his gaze about a foot above Williams' eye-line.

'Excuse me, sir,' said Evans. 'Constable Blake has just told me that Mr Dwyer has just woken up. May I tend to him?'

A slight smile appeared on Major Carter's mouth.

'Tend to him? I'll tend to him alright,' said Garcia and carried on staring at the wall.

'Private. If you know what's good for you, you will keep mouth shut until asked a question by the Detective here,' said Carter in a calm, matter of fact manner.

Garcia did not look in his direction, he acted as if the Major had not spoken and just continued to stare above Williams' head.

'Thank you, Major,' said Williams after looking at Garcia for any noticeable reaction following the Majors rebuke. As one was not apparent, he turned towards Evans and said, 'Yes you may, Constable, but see to it that Constable Blake joins us immediately.'

Evans nodded and left the room.

Williams turned to Garcia and started his questioning.

'For the record, you are Private Anthony Garcia of the 101st Airborne currently based at Greenham Common?'

'Tony.'

'I beg your pardon.'

'It's just Tony Garcia. Not Anthony.'

'What was the purpose of your visit to Portsmouth yesterday . . . Tony?'

'We delivered a secure pouch to the Dockyard.'

Williams turned to Carter for confirmation who simply nodded.

Maybe having the Major here could be quite useful after all, Williams thought and then returned his attention back to the clearly truculent Garcia.

'Why were you in High Street? It would appear you were lost.'

'To look for lodgings for the night, we didn't have to return to barracks until this morning.'

Again, Williams looked towards Carter who again nodded confirmation.

Yes, this is definitely saving some time.

'Very well, please describe to me the events that took place at approximately 16h45 hours in High Street yesterday.'

Garcia now shifted his gaze towards Williams' eye-line.

'We were asking a young lady if she knew where any lodgings were in the area. This guy then marches across the street, starts getting in James' face about stealing his woman, and then shoved him in the shoulder. We all thought that he was going to hit one of us so we spread out and tried to avoid him.'

Garcia then looked towards the ceiling as if to collect his thoughts before continuing. He did not look back into Williams eyes this time.

'The next thing I knew I was on the lying on the floor and spitting out teeth. I didn't even see it coming, and this guy is huge. After I picked myself up, I checked on James whose face had gone real white. I checked his pulse and listened for his heartbeat. I knew pretty much straight away that he was dead. I lost my temper and ran at the guy who was now on the floor himself, I don't know how that happened, and kicked him.'

'I see. Was any one of you insisting that the young woman join you for a drink? Were you complimenting her on her looks at all? Asking her if she had any friends that may wish to join you?'

'No.'

'Are you positive about that?'

'Yes. I am absolutely positive. I just said so, didn't I?'

Williams ignored the aggression being displayed.

'The young lady told us that's exactly what you were saying.'

'She's lying.' Garcia said quickly. He then lowered his gaze to meet Williams' eyes again.

'Why would she lie about something like that?' Williams said returning his stare. 'Why would she go to such lengths to make up such a story?'

'I don't know. Ask her. But it should be obvious to you that she is trying to protect her boyfriend.'

Constable Blake then entered the room and remained by the door looking towards Garcia.

Williams continued his questioning. 'Did any one of you suggest that the young lady would be better off with you for the night? That her boyfriend was being selfish not letting her join you.'

'No.'

'I see.' Williams said still meeting's Garcia gaze. He then said, 'You said that you thought this *guy* was going to hit one of you.'

'Yes.'

'Why didn't you all just walk away? Why did you circle him?'

'We didn't circle him. We just spread out and tried to avoid him. As I said.' Garcia now pretended to look bored, yawned, and stretched his arms at the same time.

Williams just passively stared at his juvenile antics and waited for him to finish. He then stated, 'I have two witnesses that have told me independently that's exactly what you did and it appeared to both of them to be an act of aggression.'

'They're mistaken.'

'Including one of my officers?'

'Yes.'

'So you are saying that a trained police officer does not recognise an act of aggression when he sees one?'

Blake glared at Garcia waiting for his response. His expression then darkened further when Garcia said matter of factly, 'Yes, that is exactly what I am saying.'

Williams passively stared into Garcia's face and played the old, 'I am not going to say anything else' trick until you volunteer further information without prompting.

To Garcia's credit, he sat staring above Williams' head once again and offered nothing further.

Eventually Williams realised that his ploy was not working and said, 'Very well, that will be all for the time being. Constable Blake, will you please escort Private Garcia back to his cell and bring up Private Hickey.'

Garcia stood up without offering any other comment and waited for Blake to open the door. He then sauntered through it with his shoulders back and chest stuck out, smiling.

Blake refrained from the urge of shoving him through the door.

The smile on Garcia's face as he left the interview room had been noticed by Carter. He was now struggling to maintain his calm demeanour. Calm was absolutely the last emotion he was feeling. He had an overwhelming desire to race across the room and kick Garcia through the doorway.

When they had both left the room, Williams turned to address Carter as he felt he owed him an explanation. 'It was Constable Evans that incapacitated Mr Dwyer with his truncheon. He has been guilt ridden ever since as they have been friends since childhood and apparently Dwyer has fought more than one battle on his behalf. He didn't realise it was Dwyer until after he had hit him, just thought you should know.'

Carter just nodded and refrained from comment. He was already aware of the fact as the MP's had witnessed it and informed him in their brief meeting the night before.

Over the course of the next twenty minutes both Hickey and Henderson answers to the same questions were almost verbatim to what Garcia had answered earlier. Apart from kicking Dwyer while he was unconscious on the floor. Garcia had in fact deliberately forgotten to mention in his statement that he had in fact kicked him twice.

Williams had noticed that not one of the three Americans had made any eye contact with Major Carter throughout all three interviews. It was almost as if he was not there with them in the room.

Carter waited until only he and Williams shared the room, and then said, 'I trust you have gathered that they are all lying through their teeth, forming a circle round a combatant is something they learn in training. They had every attention of attacking Mr Dwyer.'

'Indeed,' said Williams. 'Thank you, I had come to the same conclusion.'

'Truth be known, Detective, those three are the dregs of humanity, along with Corporal James Carter. The fact that Mr Dwyer is no doubt going to go away for manslaughter is a travesty of justice. A medal may be more appropriate.'

Agenda?

'Williams could not contain his curiosity any further. 'Major. Maybe it is time for you to tell me what your true *agenda* is. I realised you were formulating one last evening but cannot quite figure it out what it may be. I do not like unsolved puzzles, Major.'

Carter sat back in his chair and smiled. *A worthy opponent indeed* he thought.

'You are very astute, Detective. Let me fill in the blanks for you.'

21

Evans had sent word to Sally that Dwyer had surfaced. He suggested in the message that she did not come to the police station at this point. She would not get to see him for a least a couple of hours. In addition, he was now starting to feel the effects of hardly any sleep the night before and the last thing he wanted to do was deal with her likely hysterics.

As he walked towards the end of the cellblock, he was dreading what Dwyer's reaction was going to be once he came clean about the fact that it had been him that had hit him from behind. Sally's comment from yesterday about *'not wanting to be in his shoes'* was starting to play heavily on his mind.

On reaching Dwyer's cell, he unlocked the door he saw that Dwyer was sat up on the bed holding his heads in his hands.

'Hello Moose. How's it going?' Evans said.

Dwyer looked up and was visibly relieved to see one of his friends stood at the doorway. He said, 'Mate, what the hell is going on?'

'Don't you remember?' Evans asked although he was not entirely surprised he could not.

Dwyer's face was a picture of confusion. His shook his head and stared at the floor. After a good thirty seconds, he looked up at Evans and said, 'I had a scrap with some Yanks, didn't I? How'd I end up in here?'

'It was me, Moose. It's my fault you are in here.'

Dwyer just stared at Evans in disbelief and then eventually said, 'What the hell are you talking about it's your fault?'

'I didn't know it was you, mate. I'm sorry.' Evans felt like he was going to cry.

Get a grip of yourself, Gavin.

'You *didn't* know it was me?' Dwyer repeated and continued to stare at him with a now more than confused look on his face. It had turned into disbelief. He then added, '*How* could you not know it was me? We have only known each other most of our *lives!*'

Evans stared at the floor, counted to ten silently in his head and then explained what he had seen, how and why hit him with his truncheon, why Dwyer's balls probably ached and what had since happened with the Americans.

If there were a picture of the word 'shock' in the dictionary then it would have had a photograph of Dwyer's current facial expression in it. It appeared to crumple in on itself and his mouth hung open so wide you could have fit a bowling ball in it.

The events of previous afternoon now came flooding back.

I told you to stay calm.

They had it coming. Boy did they have it COMING.

Your fists have got you in the shit now though, haven't they?

They didn't give me a choice. It was self-defence!

Yeah right. Your word against three.

Sally was there. She would have told them what happened.

Silence.

After Dwyer eventually gained control of his jaw and after he had vanquished his unwanted voice of reason from the forefront of his mind, he asked, 'Where's Sally?'

It immediately returned.

Where is Sally? You are up to your eyeballs in shit and you ask where Sally is?

Evans immediately responded before it could question him further.

'She's at home, mate. Probably be here in a couple of hours. She was here last night. The DI questioned her about what happened and then let her go.'

Dwyer reflected on this for a while and then said in almost childlike voice, 'I can't believe it. I just cannot believe it. How could I have *killed* one of them?' He then looked up at Evans for an answer.

You have always been scared of your own strength.

I have . . . that's true.

Now you know why.

Evans shuffled from one foot to another now looking towards the floor again and said, 'Seems that you splintered the breastbone and ribs of the last one you hit. It ripped up his heart and he died instantly.'

Evans looked up to see Dwyer's reaction. He had resumed his

open-mouthed pose and looked like to him that he had suddenly aged about ten years.

After returning his gaze to floor, Evans mustered up the courage to say, 'And it gets worse, Moose.'

Dwyer looked up at Evans in horror and said, 'How can it get any *worse?*'

'There is this Major from the regiment of the soldier that died. Turns out, he is his uncle. He's been sniffing around since last night, he seems like a right hard bastard as well. He is with Williams now.'

Dwyer then went suddenly into serious panic mode. He stood up from the bed and pointed at Evans menacingly. 'You have to do something to get me off, Gav. There is no way I am going to no prison, no fucking way. I couldn't. I couldn't. I just couldn't hack it. I get claustrophobia. You have got to get me off. It would be my worst fucking nightmare.'

You should have that of that before you hit them.
Will you just shut up!

Dwyer then looked at the four white walls of his windowless ten foot square cell suspiciously as if they were about to close in on him.

His face then turned a pale shade of green. If had been in the interview room he would have blended in like a chameleon. Whether it was the fact that he had stood up or that he was now hyperventilating and sending the blood round his body at an increased rate, he doubled up in pain clutching his groin. He collapsed on the bed.

He then let out a blood-curdling cry of anguish and shouted, '*Oh my God! My bollocks are killing me. Jesus H Christ.*'

If this whole situation were not so screwed up, Evans would have laughed hysterically. Instead, he turned round to see Constable Blake enter the cell.

'The DI wants to see you upstairs, Gav. What you done to him?' Blake said and nodded towards Dwyer writhing around on the bed holding his groin with both hands.

'I aint done nothing have I. Seems he just realised that one of those Yanks tried to kick his balls into touch yesterday. Did the DI say want he wanted?'

'Nope, just that I was to come and get you.'

'Okay mate. Look after him, will you?' Evans asked as he quickly left the cell to go back upstairs.

22

When Evans entered the interview room, both Williams and Carter were sat at the same side of the table, which Evans immediately thought to be strange.

Very strange.

He sat down in one of the chairs opposite and looked from one to the other waiting expectantly for one of them to say something.

Williams eventually broke the uneasy silence and said, 'How is Mr Dwyer?' Is he ready to come and speak to me yet?'

'Not sure that he is yet, sir. It obviously came as a massive shock to him when I told him that one of the American soldiers had died. At first he didn't remember anything.'

'What was his exact reaction when you told him about the fatality?'

'He sort of went into panic. Said that there was no way he could go to prison. He said it would be his worst f – his worst nightmare, something about suffering from claustrophobia, sir. Then he collapsed on the bed.' Evans deliberately left out the *'you have got to get me off'* part.

Twice in two days was not going to happen.

'Why did he collapse on the bed?'

'Seems to be the after effect of the kick he got yesterday, while he was on the floor.'

'He didn't try in any way to deny striking the soldiers then?'

'No sir, he eventually remembered he had a fight with them and at first thought that was the only reason in was in here.'

Williams turned to look at Carter. After a couple of seconds of what seemed like a staring contest Major Carter just nodded his head.

Oi, Oi. What have these two been up too? Evans thought.

Williams turned to Evans and said, 'Let's just *pretend* for a minute, shall we, that there may be an alternative to prison. How do you think Mr Dwyer would feel about that?'

This left Evans bewildered. Especially considering the lecture, he had received from Williams the day before about perverting the course of Justice. Just how Williams thought he was going to manage that was anyone's guess. He would bet handsomely that getting people 'off' was not a chapter in one of his many procedural books in his office.

'An alternative, sir? I expect he would bite your hand off,' Evans eventually said unable to hide the look of astonishment on his face.

Evans then turned to Carter and stared into his eyes. The Major did not flinch and just stared right back at him.

'Forgive me for speaking out of turn, sir, but what is exactly going on here?' Evans said whilst still staring at Carter. 'Have you got to the bottom of the *agenda* you referred to last night?'

Carter then broke his silence, 'How well do you know Mr Dwyer, Constable Evans?'

Evans eyed him suspiciously.

'Known him all my life, I am lucky to have him as friend. He would do anything for anybody. You do not want to mess with him though. He is the hardest bloke I have ever met. He is – '

'Thank you, Constable,' said Williams cutting Evans short. 'See to it that Mr Dwyer is given a hot drink and offered some food. Then bring him here to meet us in half-an-hour.'

Evans looked to Williams if he was about to try to finish his sentence.

'That will be all, Constable Evans,' he said quickly and then added, 'Not a word of this is to be mentioned to Mr Dwyer. Do you understand? Not a word,' with the sternest of looks he could muster.

Evans nodded and reluctantly stood up. He gave one last glance towards Carter and left the room.

Something here stinks to high heaven, Evans thought as left the room.

Of course, I will not tell Moose anything about our little chat. Yeah right!

23

When Evans returned to Dwyer's cell, Blake was still stood inside the door. Dwyer was curled up in the foetus position with both hands still holding his groin. He noticed a pile of vomit on the floor of the cell. Blake was just staring at it, reluctant to be the one to clear it up.

'Best you get a bucket of water,' Evans said to Blake. 'I need to talk to him alone.'

Blake seemed happy to leave. It was starting to smell badly and he quickly walked outside.

'You okay, mate?' This seemed in hindsight to Evans to be a stupid question.

Dwyer shifted his position on the bed, looked up at Evans and said, 'It feels like an elephant came in here while I was asleep and jumped up and down on my nadgers.'

Again, this would normally have made Evans laugh but he was now all seriousness.

'Look mate. I have got to tell you something, but you can't let onto the DI that I told you.'

'Why? What's going on?' Dwyer said now suddenly getting his hopes up that Evans had pulled a few strings for him after all.

Yeah right. What strings can a lowly Constable pull?

I aint going to tell you again.

Just pointing out the bleedin obvious.

Will you just F –

'I aint got a clue what is going on. That's the thing. I just had a meet with the DI and this Major, and they asked me what you would think about an alternative to prison.'

Dwyer sat up quickly on the bed and immediately regretted it. After the pain that had shot up through his stomach had subsided, and he stopped clinching his teeth, he said excitedly, 'What did you say? You must have said I would go for it?'

'I said that you would bite his hand off, but I do not trust this Major, something aint right here, Moose.' Evans said. He then waited for a response from Dwyer who was now staring down at vomit on the floor with a rueful expression.

'The DI told me to get you some food and hot drink,' Evans said eventually when realising Dwyer was in too much inner turmoil to say anything further. 'Do you want anything?'

'No thanks, mate,' Dwyer said shaking his head looking up towards Evans. 'I would probably just throw it back up at the moment.' He then looked back towards the pile already he had made earlier on the cell's floor. 'When do I get to see the DI?'

'In another twenty-five minutes time, and remember, I never just told you that. Just play dumb, which shouldn't be too difficult for you,' Evans said with a forced smile.

Now he is even calling you dumb.

Dwyer smiled back, ignoring his increasingly annoying inner voice of reason, which he wouldn't have thought likely considering the mess he was in and said, 'You only said that because you know I can't do anything about it at the moment in my condition.'

'You got that right, mate. Not in any position to run after me, are you?'

No! I'm not.

God my balls ache!

24

Dwyer was led to the station interview room at no more than a slow shuffle deliberately ignoring the glares of Garcia, Henderson and Hickey as he passed their cells. He gave the appearance of having ankle-cuffs on.

He was in fact restraint free.

The shortness of his breath he was now experiencing, he put down to the fact he had never been so scared in his life and he was suffering from some kind of anxiety attack. The lump in his throat seemed to be expanding and he had a pain across his chest that was getting steadily worse with every step he took.

Murder.

You have committed a Goddamn murder!

He briefly wondered if this was what a heart attack felt like. As he entered the room, the two figures that were sat at the table seemed to blend into each other, as he could not gain his focus. He was vaguely aware of being told to sit down.

Stay calm.

That is easy for you to say.

Take a long deep breath. You will be fine.

Murder.

You have committed a Goddamn murder!

Major Carter was studying Dwyer intently. This was the first time he laid eyes on him. For the briefest of moments, he had some sympathy with his deceased adopted nephew and the three Privates who were still in the cellblock below. The thought in getting involved in a fistfight with this bloke was not in any way appealing. He could clearly see that he was in a great deal of pain, the fact that he visibly winced when sitting down gave it away. Now that he appeared to be trying hard to disguise it, was to Carter, a sign of strong character. He immediately started to take a liking to him.

His thoughts were disturbed when Williams said, 'Good morning, Mr Dwyer. My name is Detective Inspector Williams. To my left is Major Carter of the 101st Airborne of the US Army and Constable

Evans, who I know you know; is also present standing behind you.'

Dwyer nodded.

'Can you please confirm for the record that you are Davey Dwyer currently residing in High Street, Portsmouth?'

Dwyer nodded again.

'You will have to speak up, Mr Dwyer,' said Williams.

Dwyer felt beads of perspiration break out on his forehead and a further tightening in his throat. The fact he could not catch his breath made him feel like he wanted to belch.

Stay calm.

He made a concerted effort to compose himself and said, 'That's correct, officer,' in a barely audible breathless whisper.

'You are currently employed within the Dockyard as an engineer, is that correct?'

'That's correct, since I left school eight years ago. I have been seconded to the Royal Navy for about three-and-a-half years now though.'

'Very well, please note that you have not been formally charged with anything yet. I will be asking you a series of questions now, which you might at first think strange. You will have to humour me however. I will be trying to establish your character. I advise you, Mr Dwyer, to answer honestly at all times. Is that clear?'

What? Where the hell is this going?

I don't know, but –

I know, stay calm.

No. Answer honestly! Are you deaf as well as dumb?

'Yes officer.' Dwyer said now trying to focus on maintaining eye contact with Williams.

Have you ever been in trouble before?' William asked returning Dwyer's now steely gaze.

'I have never been in trouble with the police before, no.' Dwyer shook his head to confirm his answer.

'Have you been in any fights in public places before?'

'Yes. When you are as big me as I am, there is always someone who wants to try his luck. I try to avoid them where possible, especially now. My girlfriend doesn't like it.'

'That would be Miss Sally Clark?'

'Yes officer.' This time adding extra confirmation by nodding his head.

'So you would say that you are the type of person that does not deliberately look for trouble then?'

'No officer. I never have. Gav will back me up on that one,' Dwyer said turning to look at Evans who was already nodding agreement.

'Have you ever lost a fight, Mr Dwyer?' Williams asked once Dwyer had returned his attention towards him. He suspected by the size of the man that was now in front of him, he already knew the likely response.

What kind of question is that?

Just answer it. Just say it how it is.

'Not that I can remember,' Dwyer said and now looked towards Carter who was staring at him intently. He then looked back to Williams and said, 'As I said, I try to avoid them where possible.'

'Apart from the fact that your girlfriend doesn't approve, why would that be?'

'Look what happened yesterday,' Dwyer said and shrugged his shoulders. 'I tend to hurt people badly when I hit them.'

Good answer.

Williams and Carter exchanged glances. Williams noticed that Carter's eyes had a glint in them and they appeared to him to be smiling.

The Major's demeanour was also noticed by Dwyer.

I am not sure I like him.

No. What does he have to smile about?

On turning back to look at Dwyer he said, 'That Mr Dwyer would be an understatement, would you not agree?'

Dwyer refrained from comment. He instead looked back towards the Major who definitely appeared to Dwyer to be enjoying himself.

'Tell me now about the events that took place on 10 January 1941,' Williams continued.

Dwyer looked visibly shocked. 'Why do you want to know about *that?*'

'As I said, Mr Dwyer, I am trying to establish your character. Please continue.'

Dwyer shifted awkwardly in his chair and began. 'I was out with my friends celebrating my 21st birthday at the Still & West in Spice Island. The air raid sirens went off and I ran home. Just before I got there, my house in Norfolk Street had been flattened and was on fire. My mum, dad and my younger sister were all killed.' Dwyer then became silent as he thought this was a sufficient account of the events.

'What happened next?' Williams persisted with a degree of sympathy now apparent in his tone.

'I heard the three girls that lived next door but one screaming. They were only little. The oldest was seven I think. They were shouting from the window and crying. Fire was coming out of every window accept the one they were screaming from.' Dwyer then paused remembering how the petrified howling had made his very soul cringe. He then seemingly reluctantly continued. 'So without really thinking, I broke the front door in, ran up the stairs, scooped them all up under my arms and ran out.'

'So you undoubtedly saved their lives?' Williams said leaning forward and almost smiling.

'I suppose so, yes,' Dwyer replied and slightly lent back in his chair.

'I believe you became quite the local hero?'

Williams already knew the answer to this after remembering reading the report in the *Portsmouth Evening News*. He also remembered that Dwyer had modestly refrained from comment at the time. A follow up report had been written two days later after the original with an interview with Dwyer's *'Gaffer'* within the dockyard. He could not praise highly enough his subordinates character and his work ethic which Williams was also aware of. His reason for his line of questioning now was to make Major Carter also aware of his character.

'Not really, it was written about in the paper and that, but anyone would have done the same thing. No one could just stand there and watch them die.'

'Is that so, Mr Dwyer? What were the children's parents doing why this was going on?'

'They were stood outside.'

'So their father did nothing, and you took it upon yourself to act?'

'I guess so,' said Dwyer who was starting to become completely confused by this line of questioning. He looked back at Carter who still seemed to being having fun, as a slight smile was clearly visible on his face.

'I see. Where are the children now?' Williams asked.

'A family out in the country took them in. A farm just outside Hambledon I think. I used to see them once a week before they left. Used to make sure I gave them sweets whenever that was possible. They were beautiful kids, really polite too.'

Williams leaned back in his chair and now appeared to be in deep thought. The palms of his hands were laid flat on the table surface, which he was staring at with a vacant look on his face. He then abruptly stood up straight and said, 'Mr Dwyer, I am now going to leave you in the hands of Major Carter here. There is something he wishes to speak to you about.' As an afterthought he added, 'Good luck, Mr Dwyer.'

Eh?

Williams gestured to Evans to follow him and they left the room, with Williams deliberately closing the door behind him without looking back.

Evans left scratching his head.

25

Dwyer could now feel the perspiration on his forehead again. Evans had told him that the soldier he had killed was this bloke's nephew and God only knew what he had him store for him.

He thought it wise to say something first.

'Major Carter. I am sorry about your nephew. He didn't really give me any choice. He came at me with a crowbar. I just hit him. There is no way I intended to kill him . . . obviously.'

Carter stared long and hard into Dwyer's eyes, who held his gaze, and then said, 'I don't consider that low life piece of shit my nephew, Mr Dwyer, in fact unbeknown to you, you have partially solved a problem of mine . . . I am actually in your debt,' Carter said without a hint of any kind of emotion in his voice.

Dwyer nearly fell of his chair such was his surprise.

Didn't see that one coming did you Davey boy?
No. What the hell does he want with me then?
Let us just wait and see, shall we?

'That particular story is for another time,' Carter continued. 'I have had to make Detective Williams aware of the full details and he has assured me of his secrecy in the matter. What I am about to say to you now is a onetime offer and you have to make your decision immediately I am afraid. I have to return to base, ASAP.'

Dwyer was not sure he wanted to hear what was coming next. He again fidgeted in his chair waiting for what he was sure going to be something unpleasant. All previous concerns over his aching body parts had now, for the time being, seemed to disappear.

Carter continued. 'I have arranged with Detective Williams, now that you seem to have passed his moral fibre test, to forget about this little episode. I have made it possible that the US Army will not pursue the matter further and I have my superior officer's permission to do so. You can be rest assured; no one will miss Corporal Carter.'

Dwyer was now totally bewildered and considered his next response carefully. He ended up just simply saying, 'What about his three mates?'

What about his three mates?
They are going to want to cut your Goddamn heart out!

'Ah yes. You can leave them to me. My proposal is that you accompany me back to Greenham Common this afternoon where you will be enlisted in the 101st Airborne. You will remain extremely close to me when we go into France, which no doubt you know is imminent due to the fact you work in the Dockyard on naval vessels. I am sure the place must have rumours flying around it everywhere.'

Carter paused to let the enormity of what he had just said sink in with Dwyer before continuing and did not expect to receive an answer to his question anyway.

Dwyer was wide-eyed and open-mouthed, not for the first time of the day.

What did he just say?
He wants you to enlist in the American Army.
What? I mean, why?'
Silence.
Why?
Silence.

'Your alternative is to remain here and face the consequences of your actions yesterday and no doubt go to prison,' Carter said, and after he considered a suitable amount of time had elapsed he added, 'That is the only way Detective Williams agreed to shall we say. . . make this incident disappear. He will not simply release you back on the streets.'

'It sounds to me that you need a bodyguard,' was Dwyer's immediate response.

Hey. Quick thinking Davey. Nice one!

'That is an excellent deduction, Mr Dwyer. Well done.' Cater did not volunteer as to the reasons why.

Ask him why?
Will do, thanks.

'Why would a Major in the US Army need a bodyguard? Haven't you got enough men under your command to do that for you?'

'As I said to you earlier, that is a story for another time. Your decision please, Mr Dwyer.'

Dwyer's head started to spin.

This was all happening *too fast*. Yesterday afternoon he had been walking home from work expecting to have a nice dinner with Sally. Now, he was being asked to set sail in some ship in the next few days, and be shot at by Germans . . . real live ones. The thought of leaving her was horrendous. What would she think? Would she wait for him? Realisation then took hold, which made his shoulders visibly slump, as the chances were that he would almost certainly *not ever* see her again anyway.

Oh, crap.

After these thoughts had raced through his mind, he looked at Carter and started to smile. Smiling then turned to laugher and he said, 'This has got to be some kind of joke, right?'

It must be, and it aint even a funny one.

Carter's expression did not change when he replied, 'I can assure you Mr Dwyer that this is not a laughing matter. I do not make jokes. Not about issues such as this.'

Bugger.

The smile was wiped from Dwyer's face when he suspected that this Major might actually have been serious. He stood up and limped slowly around the room with his hands behind his head staring up at the ceiling.

After eventually sitting down again he said, 'You are being serious, aren't you?'

Carter just stared him in the eye and nodded.

'I could probably plead self-defence and get off this charge. Why the hell would I want to join the American army?' Dwyer said. 'I would be about as popular as a fart in a confined space when your boys back at base find out what I did to one of their own!'

Carter just shook his head and then said casually, 'No way you can get off. You killed a man. Even if it was self-defence, you will still get a manslaughter charge. Williams said so himself. In respect of the men back at base, you will just have to trust me. You will be fine.'

Yeah right!

Dwyer then stood up, returned to his previous pose limping round the room slowly, and then bowed his head. He then sat back down and looked Carter in the eye and said, 'There is no way I could handle prison. I guess you have your man. I have previously volunteered anyway, just never envisaged that it would be with the Americans though.'

Carter allowed himself a smile.

'Never been on a ship before though. Well, not while it was sailing anyway. I hope I don't puke all over you,' Dwyer said without a hint of humour in his voice with a forced grin.

Carter remained smiling, his being genuine. 'You won't have to worry about that, Mr Dwyer. The clue is in the name. The 101st Airborne are going in by parachute! Please do not repeat our conversation to anyone before we leave.' He then abruptly got up from his chair and left the room, closing the door behind him.

Dwyer definitely now knew he *was* going to be sick again.

Davey Dwyer was going to take part in D-Day. *Well,* he thought to himself with a certain amount of gallows humour, *you have the right initials for it.*

26

After leaving the interview room Carter slowly walked down the dimly lit corridor towards Williams' office. His thoughts had now turned to the three soldiers that were still being held in custody in the cellblock in the floor below.

He was about to take part in one of greatest amphibious operations ever conducted. He had been advised that it had been estimated that 160,000 troops would cross the channel on the first day of the assault, made up of forces from Canada, the United Kingdom and the Unites States. If all went according to plan, 3 million would have landed by the end of August. They would then be joined by further forces from The Free French, Poland, Belgium, Czechoslovakia, Greece, Holland and Norway.

The fact that he was now once again spending his time thinking about these three sorry cases of humanity in the cells below was becoming more and more of an irritant. His men deserved better from one of their offices to be continually distracted at a time such as this, who in the main he nothing but admiration for. Now that Colonel Harrison had advised him that they were now going in now only *three* days, his thoughts should have been consumed with planning and the men he would be leading into battle. Every Division always had one bad apple, until yesterday's events, his had had four, rotten to the core.

Carter knocked on the door of William's office still preoccupied and entered without waiting for permission to enter. The young Constable Evans was standing opposite Williams who was seated behind his desk. It appeared to Carter that they been in the middle of a heated exchange. He ignored the fact that the younger of the two men was now glaring at him.

'Excuse me gentleman,' said Carter. 'You seem to be in the middle of something. Would you like me to come back when you have finished?' He hoped that this was not the case as he was now anxious to get back to base . . . Immediately.

'Not at all, Major, please take a seat. Constable Evans was just leaving,' Williams said lying for the second time of the morning.

That's news to me, Evans thought.

Evans turned and glared at Carter even more severely.

Carter managed to stifle a grin.

The young Policeman obviously wanted to have a pop at him. Carter believed it to be endearing. He admired the loyalty he was showing towards his friend.

As Evans left the office, he deliberately slightly dropped his shoulder and tried to make out to accidently make the smallest of contact with him.

It had the opposite effect that he desired.

Carter subtly side stepped him, which made Evans lose his balance and fall through the door and hit the wall on the opposite side of the corridor. He turned his head back towards Williams' office, glared at Carter again and then stomped off down the corridor towards the interview room where he believed Dwyer still was.

He wasn't.

Williams made a mental note to deal with Constable Evans later but decided not to make an apology on his behalf to Carter on the matter. He had a degree of sympathy with Evans because his friend's fate had been kept from him, however, attempting to shoulder barge an officer of the US Army was not acceptable behaviour for an officer of the law, no matter what the circumstances.

'So Major Carter, how did Mr Dwyer react to your proposal?'

'He went for it,' Carter replied, with no intention of adding anything further.

'I see.' Williams tried hard to hide his surprise. He never thought for a second that Dwyer would have agreed to the Major's plan. The fact that he grossly miscalculated Dwyer's reaction to it had the effect of three deep lines furrowing across his brow.

He regretted now that he had gone along with it. All he wanted to do was give him the option. He suddenly found himself thinking, *what have I done?*

After all, what chance did a Dockyard engineer have in military combat without any sort of training? No matter how tough he was.

He also regretted the fact that he had tried to portray Dwyer in a good light during the earlier questioning.

What was I thinking to go along with this madness?
Williams broke the uneasy silence that had become apparent and to try to hide his new feelings on the matter.

'Then we must start making arrangements for his release. Do you have any thoughts on the three other soldiers currently in custody?' Williams said, not doubting for a second that Carter had not already fully thought that particular issue through.

'I do, Detective,' Carter said quickly. 'If you will release them into my custody, I will ensure they are put up on a public disorder charge when they return to barracks. The two MPs you met yesterday have retrieved their vehicle from High Street and are waiting outside to drive them to Greenham Common. I suggest we leave it one hour after I leave with Mr Dwyer so I can wait on their arrival. Somewhat conveniently, they will have been AWOL for at least three hours to add to the trouble they are already in. They were due back at barracks today by 10h00 hours.'

'Indeed,' said Williams. 'Do you attend to leave immediately?'

No stone left unturned, Williams thought. *How long did it take you to come up with that? Not long, I suspect.*

Agenda. Always an agenda.

'I do,' said Carter who then stood, as did Williams. Carter then added, 'May I take this opportunity to thank you for your cooperation during these proceedings, Detective. You have afforded me a great service.'

'Think nothing of it, Major. We all have skeletons in our cupboard you know,' Williams said as he extended his hand for no doubt another crushing handshake.

Carter's curiosity got the better of him. How this straight-laced man in front of him could have any kind of dark secret was intriguing, 'Really, Detective?' Carter said raising an eyebrow. His immediate thought was of Williams dressing up in women's clothing and then fought desperately hard to quell the raucous laughter that was trying to escape him.

Williams looked towards the ceiling and appeared to be deciding whether to continue. He then looked Carter in the eye and began. It had nothing to do whatsoever with cross-dressing.

'My parents were sweethearts since school. My mother became

pregnant out of wedlock when she was only fifteen. My father being the same age. It was kept quiet are as far as possible as it was quite the scandal, as I am sure you can imagine?'

Williams looked towards Carter to gauge his reaction to what he still considered to be, shocking news. Carter just stared back at him impassively, now regretting his earlier thoughts.

Williams continued. 'She gave birth do a daughter, which was immediately given away for adoption. Both sets of parents believing this to be the most appropriate course of action. My parents then married four years later. I was only made aware that I had a sister when my mother informed me on her deathbed four years ago. She died of cancer.'

Williams then paused to take time to compose himself and clear his throat.

'My sister was later killed on 10 January 1941. Her name was Margaret Dwyer.'

Williams paused again briefly to gage Carter's reaction and then added. 'As you have no doubt deducted, Major, Davey Dwyer is in fact my nephew. It seems we have much in common.'

Carter was amazed. 'Obviously Dwyer is not aware of this,' he said.

'No Major, and I will now be relying on you secrecy as you are mine.'

'If I may intrude, Detective, why have you not informed him of your family connection in the past?'

Williams seemed embarrassed by the question. He thought long and hard before offering an answer.

'As I said, I was only made aware that I had a sister a few years ago. I fully intended to make myself known to her one day but it transpires I left it too late. With regards to Davey, I have never been able to find the right words.' Williams now looked Carter straight in the eye, with the British stiff upper lip now returning. 'As I requested, I would appreciate it you did not mention the matter to him . . . ever.'

'You have my word,' replied Carter. He then pushed back his shoulders, gave an exaggerated salute, about turned and walked out of Williams' office.

Williams sat down behind his desk, rested his elbows on the surface and then slowly lowered his head into his hands.
What have I just done? He thought.
What was I thinking?
Why have I placed my only blood relative in harms way?

27

Dwyer had been in the bathroom while Carter went to inform Williams. He had stood at one of the sinks splashing cold water over his face and staring at his refection in the cracked mirror. It now appeared to him that he aged about ten years overnight. He at least he would not have to worry about getting a haircut. He wore his jet-black hair at crew cut length. Sally had always joked he looked like he should have been in the Army, wearing his hair that short. How prophetic her jests had turned out to be.

Many a true word spoken in jest, eh Davey?
Yep. Many a true word indeed.
Not very funny this time though.
No.

He now started to wonder if Sally had turned up at the station, and surprisingly, he found himself hoping that she had not. He could not imagine what her reaction would be. He would have to leave it to Evans to tell her if she did not make it in time. He would write to her as soon as he got to Greenham Common, wherever that was.

Soon after they had met, Dwyer had told Sally that he had volunteered to join the Army and she had thought him mad. She thanked God that she did not have a brother that would have been drafted.

'Thank your lucky stars that you have a reservist occupation,' she had said. 'I like you just where you are. With me.'

Not anymore!
No. Not anymore!
Maybe never ag –

He quickly stopped the thought formulating in his mind. His voice of reason was turning out to be a real pain in the arse again.

As he walked out of the bathroom, Carter walked past in the corridor with Williams following. Carter turned towards him and said, 'Ready then, Mr Dwyer? It's time we were leaving.'

Already?

Dwyer just nodded without comment. He fell in to line and

followed them into the reception area where Evans was standing behind the desk. Evans gestured by moving his head upwards with a creased brow towards Dwyer as if to ask him what was going on.

Dwyer looked away and stared at the floor.

Wow this happening so fast.
Too fast!
Stop the roundabout.
I want to get off... right now!

'Good luck, Major. Good luck, Mr Dwyer,' said Williams trying to remain as impassive as possible.

He then turned to Evans and requested that he join him immediately, in his office.

Evans' face was a picture.

He looked from Dwyer, to Carter, to Williams, and then repeated the process again. He looked like someone had just told a joke that he did not understand and that everyone else was laughing at raucously.

What the fuck is going on? He was actually thinking.

Carter and Dwyer then left the station into the drizzle outside.

Carter instructed Dwyer to get in the back of the jeep where his driver was waiting. He then walked over to the MPs who sat inside the Jeep that had been driven to Portsmouth a day earlier by the four 101st Airborne troops. He advised them that the Private's would be released in an hour. Without further delay, he then returned to his own transport and instructed the driver to return to base.

A lump started to expand in Dwyer's throat again.

So fast.

28

Williams sat behind the desk in his office with an expectant Evans in front of him, clearly waiting to be filled in on the details that he had been kept in the dark. Williams took his time before putting him out of his misery, pretending to read a report on a different case instead.

Williams wanted to choose his words carefully.

He finally closed the brown manila folder, placed it in the middle of his desk, and looked up at Evans.

'Well?' Evans said doing the double teapot with both of his hands resting on his hips.

'I am afraid, Constable Evans I cannot share the full facts of what has taken place this morning with you. I have given my word to Major Carter that the majority of what he has informed me of this morning will remain within my confidence. He in turn has returned the favour to me with regards to something I have shared with him.'

Evans expression returned to the same one earlier when Carter and Dwyer left the station.

'What I can tell you is this that Mr Dwyer will be travelling to Greenham Common with Major Carter where he will enlist in the 101st Airborne. There he will remain for the foreseeable future as a kind of personal assistant to the Major, and inevitably go into France with him. Between the Major and me, we have agreed that this sorry mess is best forgotten. The three other American soldiers will be released in one hour and driven back to Greenham where they will be charged by Major Carter.'

Evans looked like all the wind had just been knocked out of him. He sat down in the seat opposite Williams and said, 'Joined the *American Army*? What the *hell* is going on, Detective?' Evans yelled.

Williams bristled. 'I can understand how you must feel about this, Constable. However, do not take the tone with me. In addition, your behaviour towards Major Carter earlier when you tried to shoulder barge him was inexcusable. I am on this occasion prepared to overlook this, considering the circumstances. The only thing I can tell you further is that this was the only way Mr Dwyer was going to avoid prosecution, and almost inevitably prison. That will be all.'

That will be all?

That will be fucking all?

'What do I tell Sally Clark when she arrives?' Evans said unable to hide his exasperation.

'Please bring her into me immediately when she does, without saying a word about this matter.' Williams then pretended to return to the report on his desk.

Evans was shaking his head all the way back to reception.

How the hell could the DI allow such madness? He also wondered what secret he had shared with the Major. If he had a thousand guesses, he probably would not get it right. His thoughts were disturbed when he noticed Sally standing at the reception desk. She looked towards him, almost accusingly.

Oh, shit!

'Hi Sally, do you want to follow me?' Evans said feeling incredibly uncomfortable.

'How is Davey? Can I see him? Sally said looking anxiously at Evans now sensing something was horribly wrong.

'You need to speak to the DI first,' Evans said trying to avoid her gaze.

He then led her to the DI's office without speaking, knocked on the door and entered. 'Miss Clark, sir,' he said and left immediately.

Good luck in trying to explain this one away, you arsehole. The whole damn city is going to know within five minutes of her leaving the station. Shit. What a mess!

Williams looked up from the report, of which he had still not read a word. 'Take a seat, Miss Clark. Can I get you some tea? Some water perhaps?'

'No thanks. I don't want anything. I just want to see Davey.'

The look on her face convinced Williams that the next two minutes were not going to be his easiest.

'I am afraid that will not be possible for the foreseeable future, Miss Clark.'

'What do you mean that will not be possible?' Sally said now close to tears again.

Williams then spent the next two minutes explaining, as fully as he could, how Major Carter and he had allowed Dwyer to avoid prosecution. He finished his explanation by saying, 'I am fully aware that many of Mr Dwyer's friends and acquaintances will by now know the events of yesterday. Please tell them, Miss Clark, that it was his choice to go with Major Carter. If anyone should take it upon themselves to start to ask too many questions, I will of course have to face the consequences of my own actions.'

After taking a handkerchief from his suit pocket and wiping his brow, he then added, 'I will come up with something to tell his employer. I will share with you what I decide to tell them first before doing so.'

Sally just sat and stared at Williams as if she had seen a ghost. Her face had turned completely white and she appeared to Williams that she had stopped breathing.

He stood up and looked down at her with genuine concern. 'Are you alright, my dear? I realise this must have come as a terrible shock to you, but you have gone terribly pale.'

Sally opened her mouth to reply but could not form any words of her own.

She stood up, and then promptly fainted.

PART TWO

Training

education, guidance, instruction, preparation, schooling, teaching.

1

Dwyer was now experiencing the same problem that Carter had the night before. The lack of suspension in the jeep was causing him a considerable amount of discomfort. However, there was one major difference.

> Do your balls hang low?
> Do they wobble to and fro?
> Can you tie them in a knot?
> Can you tie them in a bow?
> Can you throw them o'er your shoulder?
> Like a continental soldier?
> Do your balls hang low?

Yes to all of the fucking above, thought Dwyer miserably.

He sat staring out the back of the Jeep at the City streets where he had grown up, now holding his groin with both hands once again. Not once did he see anyone that he recognised which left him with a feeling of despair. He had a sudden feeling that whole city had decided to turn its back on him.

Enough with the self-pity.

Not for the first time, and certainly not for the last, he ignored his voice of reason.

They had driven down the London Road and left Portsea Island via Hilsea. The Jeep literally crawled up Portsdown Hill and then went off through into the countryside passing through Hambledon. Dwyer searched in vain for the three girls he saved from the burning house over three years earlier and wondered how they were now fairing.

Kids grow up so fast.
Probably would not recognise them now anyway.
I wonder if they remember me?
Of course they do! Surely?

The last time Dwyer had left the city was on a trip to watch

Portsmouth F.C. play in the FA Cup Final at Wembley in 1939 against Wolverhampton Wanderers. His father had managed to get two tickets (he never did find out how) and they had travelled up to London along with thousands of others on the train. Pompey won the match 4 -1 with two goals from Cliff Parker and one a piece from Bert Barlow and John Anderson. Dwyer had managed to get so drunk celebrating their victory, the day after he stayed in bed for the entire day. Due to the start of the war, that was the last time the final had been played any many Portsmouth fans claimed that they had held the cup for the longest period, including Dwyer.

This trip, however, was very different, not to mention more uncomfortable. An endless stream of every kind of military vehicle imaginable was travelling in the opposite direction towards the coast.

Something is happening. We must be going in . . . and soon.
So fast.
Yeah, and now you are going with them.

In an effort to dismiss such thoughts from his mind, he began to concentrate on the rolling green Hampshire countryside and started to wonder what Northern France would be like. He guessed that it would be very much the same although geography had never been one of his strongest points. He tried to imagine what it would be like to fight an armed battle in such a place.

What do I know?

The closest he had come to firing a gun was when he played with his sister when they were very young in the street outside with a water pistol.

He closed his eyes and almost instantly fell into a fitful sleep dreaming of Sally.

Sally was standing at the end of the corridor outside Williams' office at the police station. She was shouting something, which he could not hear, and she was crying. The walls of the corridor were closing in on them both and he felt like somebody was pulling him backwards away from her as if he was floating in mid-air. There was not one thing he could do to stop it.
Who is pulling me back? . . . Who? Is that you Gav? . . . Who –
The clouds blocked out the sun.
Who is there?
Two dark eyes appeared with the clouds blocking the sun . . . What goes

around comes around a voice said.

Manic laugher followed.

DAAVVEEYYY! Sally was screaming again only now he COULD hear her.

DAAVVEEYYY! Nooooo!

He woke up with a start when at the same time the jeep came to an abrupt halt. He quickly rubbed the sleep from his eyes with a strange feeling of déjà vu regarding the dream.

What the hell was that all about?

Probably best not to dwell on it.

It appeared to him that they had reached their destination. A fence with barbed wire at its top, stretched off into the distance in both directions, which was being patrolled by armed guards.

Carter quickly jumped out of the jeep and briefly spoke with the two sentries' that were on guard duty on the gate. There was lots of nodding and saluting and, 'Yes Sirs.'

On entering the base, they turned right driving round the perimeter of the fence.

Carter broke the silence.

'Welcome to Greenham Common,' he said as they passed the accommodation blocks. 'This will be your new home for the next few days.'

Only a few days?

Dwyer looked out the window and frowned. The view was not much to right home about.

The Private grimaced; he knew what was coming next.

'Greenham Common was reassigned to the USAAF on 1 October 1943. From out of this base, we have conducted a number of training exercises, which lead to a final exercise, codename Operation Eagle. It was held over the Berkshire Downs and its aim was to test the D-Day operation as closely as possible. All of the 101st Airborne that are about to take part in the invasion have now been fully trained on glider towing and paratroop drops by day and night.'

Again, the Private driving the jeep stifled a yawn.

Dwyer was not listening.

He was too busy looking at the hangars that they were driving past. The second of which, they parked just inside the entrance.

2

Dwyer felt like you could have cut the tension with a knife as he followed Carter and the Private that had driven them both from Portsmouth. He nervously looked from left to right trying to take in his surroundings. He noticed that four mechanics that were working on a plane, of which he did not know the name, had stopped working and were staring at him suspiciously. At first, Dwyer wondered what their problem could be. He then realised that he was probably the only bloke on base not wearing a uniform. They were no doubt wondering who this civilian was wearing an oil-covered boiler suit and a round neck sweatshirt that had both definitely seen better days.

Rather than look away immediately, he smiled and nodded in their direction. Due to the fact, not one of them reciprocated, Dwyer thought it best to look at the floor instead and concentrated on watching the feet of the Private.

On reaching a small office at far end of the hangar, that had an overpowering smell of paraffin, Carter summonsed the Private in and told him to shut the door.

Dwyer was left outside standing alone.

Carter sat down behind his cluttered desk and then lit his first cigarette of the day. He inhaled deeply into his lungs and then blew out a satisfying long plume of blue-grey smoke. Now instantly feeling a little light headed, he loosened his tie and put his feet up on the desk. After taking another huge lung full of smoke, he addressed the Private.

'Your orders yesterday were to drive me to Southwick House,' said Carter matter of factly.

'Yes sir.'

'If anyone should ask, which I doubt, that is what you carried out, and that alone.'

The Private did not respond.

'As I ordered yesterday, you will say nothing of our two detours to the police station in Portsmouth to anyone. Do I make myself clear? Carter said and looked straight into the Privates eyes.

'Yes sir,'

'You will especially not mention anything about the fact that that we picked up the gentleman now standing outside from the police station.'

'No sir. Not a word.' The private said standing bolt upright with his arms down by his side.

'Very good, there is one other thing, Private. Please ensure you take that damn jeep to the motor pool and get the suspension fixed. I feel like I have been the recipient of the efforts of the winner of a butt kicking contest, dismissed.'

'Yes sir.' The private smiled, saluted, about turned, and left the office. He deliberately avoided looking at Dwyer as he walked back to the jeep.

Carter now returned his attention to his cigarette. He studied the lit end and watched the ash form as the tobacco slowly burned away. He became deep in thought on how he was going to manage Dwyer's appearance on base. The fact he had just ordered his driver to stay quiet on the subject was a waste of time. Not that he suspected the Private would talk and it was already squared away with Colonel Harrison who was due to return to base in the evening. The men in general were going to be more of a problem, especially when Henderson, Hickey and Garcia returned. He could contain that particular issue in the short term, but at some point, they were bound to meet.

Imagine the surprise he thought, when they ran into the slayer of their buddy in an American Uniform with a screaming eagle insignia on his sleeve. In addition, it would get round the base that his alleged nephew was killed in a street fight whilst on special duty in Portsmouth. He smiled to himself that most of the men would probably want to shake Dwyer by the hand.

Carter finally decided that he had too many other important issues to think about in the next few days. Rather than taking the time to think up an elaborate plan, he decided that they should all reunite immediately once the MPs had brought them back to base. He somewhat perversely looked forward to it. After all, he thought, the chances were that it would not matter anyway if Air Vice Marshall Trafford Leigh-Mallory turned out to be correct.

Chances are we will all be shot to shit within minutes of landing.

Carter had been in such deep thought that the cigarette had now burned down to the butt and started to burn his fingers. He quickly stubbed it out in the ashtray and brushed the ash that had dropped onto his jacket to the floor. He then stood up and opened the office door, and ignoring Dwyer for the moment, called across the hangar to a Private that was walking past with a clipboard.

'Private. Please will you go to the stores and tell Corporal Manning that I wish to see him at once please, on the double.'

The Private immediately went into a jog towards the exit of the hangar.

'Must be nice having these men running about for you,' said Dwyer with a sarcastic look on his face.

Carter did not respond to the jibe. He just turned to Dwyer and said, 'Inside and sit down.'

Dwyer thought better of it to say anything further and did as requested. He had not yet grasped the concept that such requests would be known as orders within the next hour.

Carter followed Dwyer into the office that now smelled of a mixture of stale cigarette smoke and paraffin and sat behind his desk. Carter then lit another cigarette just to add to the splendour of the room's aroma.

'Bit dangerous don't you think? Smoking in here. Smells like a petrol station,' said Dwyer nodding towards the cigarette and began to wave the smoke away with his right hand.

Again, Carter ignored the jibe and said, 'Would you care for one yourself?'

'No thanks. Don't smoke,' said Dwyer.

'I am prepared to bet my house back home that you will be within a few days, Mr Dwyer, considering what we have in store for us.'

Dwyer just smiled. He doubted it, but in the past, he seemed to lose most bets he made and what would he want with a house in the States anyway?

'Okay, Mr Dwyer. Here is the thing. You are shortly going to be reacquainted with the three men you had, shall we say, a disagreement with yesterday. As you can no doubt imagine they are going to be somewhat surprised to see your presence here on base.' Carter said with his usual calm demeanour.

Did he just say somewhat surprised?

He did.

Dwyer now burst out laughing. The Major seemed to him to be the master of understatement. Much to Dwyer's surprise, Carter joined in with the laughter, which had the effect of making Dwyer stop.

Why does he think it is funny?

Once Carter had composed himself, he checked the end of his cigarette to ensure that he was not going to burn his fingers again and took a deep drag. He then proceeded to blow four perfectly formed smoke rings by forming his mouth into a circle and moving his jaw up and down. He appeared to Dwyer to resemble a fish that was fighting for his life after being yanked out of the water.

Carter then continued. 'Once I have spoken to the three of them, word will spread round the base like wild fire about what happened to their Corporal yesterday. I will of course order them to remain silent on the matter, but I will be wasting my breath.'

Dwyer nodded agreement while Carter took another long drag on his cigarette.

'Following orders is not their strong point,' Carter continued. 'I suggest once you have been kitted out and filled out the necessary paperwork, you should remain in your accommodation hut at least for the rest of the day and keep your head down. We can then revaluate the reaction towards you tomorrow evening, if you are still alive that is.' Carter ended his statement with a genuine smile.

Is he joking?

No. I don't think he is.

Smashing.

Dwyer went into deep thought, which had the effect of creasing his brow. After some consideration he said, 'What interests me is how you got DI Williams to agree to let me get off without any charge as long as I came with you? My mate Gav, Constable Evans who you met at the station, has always told me that he imagined him reading the rulebook before he went to sleep every night. Seems strange to me that he would allow any charges to be dropped. He didn't seem to put any resistance at all to your ridiculous plan.'

Carter's attention returned to his cigarette and he then once again blew four smoke rings after taking what seemed to Dwyer as an excessively long drag.

Whatever he says next is going to be bullshit. He is obviously taking this much time to respond to make up some elaborate lie, Dwyer thought to himself.

He remained staring at Carter impassively while waiting for the considered response.

'As I advised you back at the station in Portsmouth that is a story for another time. Maybe if we get through this great adventure we are about to embark on, I will let you know then.'

Oh. Wasn't expecting that!

No. Do not be too quick to judge.

Dwyer put two-and-two together and realised that whatever Carter had told Williams about the three Privates, had somehow managed him to agree to his release.

Yeah, but what did he tell him?

Carter checked his cigarette again and added, 'Detective Williams is a decent man. I hope that one day you will get the chance to talk with him on a social level. I am sure he would enjoy that.'

Eh?

This totally mystified Dwyer. What the hell the DI would want to meet him on a social level for, he had no idea. As far as he was concerned, they did not exactly have a lot in common.

3

Carter and Dwyer's conversation was disturbed when there was a knock on the door. Corporal Manning had arrived from the stores.

'Ah Corporal,' said Carter. 'Please will you be so good to fully equip Mr Dwyer here with a uniform, weapons and washing utensils, without delay.'

Manning looked quizzically at Dwyer and said, 'Yes sir, can you please stand up, Mr Dwyer.'

Dwyer stood up straight to his full height and stuck out his chest. Manning's eyes grew wide as he looked Dwyer up and down. He then looked back towards Carter.

'Wow,' he said. 'I'm going to struggle to find a uniform big enough, sir.'

Maybe I won't have to enlist then.

Manning looked Dwyer up and down again.

'What shoe size are you, Mr Dwyer?'

'Fourteen,' replied Dwyer.

Manning quickly calculated the equivalent into American sizes and then whistled. 'Okay, how tall are you?'

'Six foot eight, I think.'

'How much do you weigh?'

'About eighteen stone, I haven't weighed myself recently.'

Manning made another calculation, that being just over 250 lbs.

'Okay sir. I will see what I can do,' Manning said looking back towards Carter.

'Thank you, Corporal. Can you also please find Mr Dwyer a place to sleep in the accommodation buildings and place his gear on his bed. Then ring me and tell me where.'

With any luck, I will get to share with See No Evil, Speak No Evil and Hear No Evil.

Yeah, that would be cosy.

'Yes sir,' Manning said and left the office. The rumours were about to start. *Why the hell was the Major referring to this enormous limey as Mr all the time? In addition, why he was being asked to kit him out?* Manning was thinking as he returned to the stores.

As Manning left the office, Carter noticed Henderson, Hickey and Garcia walking towards the office with the two MPs. '*Shit*', he thought.

They were quick. Obviously, the jeep they have driven up in was better than the piece of crap I had.

'Please stand against the wall behind my desk, Mr Dwyer,' Carter said as they approached.

4

Carter stood next to Dwyer with his hands behind his back. He too was a big man, and although he stood at just over six feet himself, he seemed to be dwarfed by Dwyer.

The two MPs entered the small office, which obscured the three Privates view of Dwyer. 'Privates Garcia, Henderson & Hickey are here sir, as requested,' one of them said.

'Thank you, Sergeant. You have my permission to requisition the jeep you drove here in and return to Portsmouth.' He then added, 'Please remember, not a word to anyone about these events.'

'What events, sir?' The Sergeant said while smiling.

Both MPs then saluted at the same time, about turned, and left the office.

The MP Sergeant then addressed the three who were waiting outside. 'The major will see you know,' and then marched off without another word with his companion towards their newly acquired jeep.

This had been noted by the other dozen troops that were performing various duties around the hangar and they all stopped and stared. MPs were almost universally hated by the average soldier, as they patrolled areas where soldiers spent their spare time. Not only did they break up fights, but enforced dress code with such enthusiasm that many considered it harassment.

Several singled-fingered gestures were made to them behind their backs as they left.

Garcia, Henderson and Hickey slowly filtered into the office and rather than saluting and standing to attention, all took it in turns for their jaws to drop open so wide, they nearly touched their chests. Garcia was the first to compose himself sufficiently, to say, 'What the fuck is he doing here?' His eyes did not leave Dwyer, although he was asking the question of Carter.

Dwyer smiled and winked at him.

Carter, an expert of keeping his emotions in check, was fighting hard inwardly not to show his disdain. He casually said, 'Don't you mean, what the fuck is he doing here, *sir?* . . . In addition, as Mr Dwyer is about to be my adjutant within the hour, he will be joining the Division as a Corporal, which outranks all of you. So, show your superior some *respect!'*

Good one!

Yeah, that should please them no end.

Dwyer fought hard not to laugh aloud again. Carter was growing on him. He never seemed to be rattled by anything. Dwyer found it a likeable quality. He also seemed to Dwyer to talk like a Brit, except for the accent of course.

Once again, all three jaws dropped wide open. They reminded Dwyer of the clown's mouths you shoot at with water pistols at the fun fair, which then bursts a balloon when full.

That is not a bad idea.

'What? Garcia eventually said. He now did look at Carter. 'Why the fuck would you want some limey bastard who killed your nephew to be your adjutant? You can't be serious?'

Who is pulling me back? . . . Who is it? Is that you Gav?. . . Who –
The clouds blocked out the sun.
Who's there?
Two dark eyes appeared with the clouds blocking the sun . . . What goes around comes around a voice said followed by manic Laugher.

Dwyer tensed every muscle in his upper body to avoid shivering.

Jesus Christ.
I can remember the dream I had in the jeep!
Was it his voice in the dream?
No. Similar though. Very similar.

'You can't be serious . . . *sir,'* Carter said and then sat down at his desk. This left the image of Dwyer standing over his officer as his protector, which Garcia immediately noticed.

Carter then lit yet another cigarette and deliberately blew the smoke towards the direction of Garcia's scowling face.

No attempt was made to wave it away. His scowl intensified.

'By returning to base at 13h00 hours, means that you have been AWOL for the last three hours, not to mention the public disorder charges that has not yet been addressed,' Carter said.

All three faces now scowled in unison.

'What kind of bullshit is that?' Garcia said with a sneer forming. 'The reason we are late is that you insisted we were kept in overnight in the police station, and as for public disorder. How do you figure, Major?'

The question was spat with venom. On not receiving a response from Carter, he continued. 'This bastard kicks the shit out of all of us, kills James, and we are the ones going to be charged?' Garcia then paused and looked towards Dwyer. He added, 'Good luck in getting those charges to stick. I like our chances. Bring on the judge and jury.' He then folded his arms with a look of defiance on his face.

Albeit that Dwyer was still fighting the urge to shiver, he forced a smile and winked at Garcia again.

The sign of affection was not returned.

For the first time, Garcia actually had impressed Carter on how he had articulated his defence – excluding the expletives of course – he could not really argue with any of it. He held his impassive stare at Garcia, and once he returned his gaze away from Dwyer back towards him, he blew smoke towards him again.

Carter then said, 'Not another word out of you, Private. I am prepared to overlook these offences on this occasion. We are going to need all the men we have over the coming weeks, even you three.'

He was now on the receiving end of three sneers. Dwyer's smile broadened. However, this time, he refrained from winking at all three.

'No doubt on leaving this office you will be telling anyone who will listen to you about yesterday's events, and no doubt, not the truthful version. You are ordered to tell the men that Corporal Carter's death was an unfortunate accident. One he brought on himself. I will leave it to the three of you to use your imagination, if you have one between you that is. Are we clear?'

The three of them all looked at Carter with complete and utter contempt.

Carter then jumped from his chair with incredible speed and shouted, *'Are we clear?'* Even Dwyer slightly shuddered behind him at the level of the volume of his address.

All three Privates flinched and in unison shouted back, 'Yes sir.'

With a dismissive wave of his hand and returning to his normal level of speech, he said, 'Get out of my sight.'

They did not need a second invitation.

Carter sat back down and Dwyer moved round from the back of his desk and faced him. On doing so, he realised that Carter was clearly distressed. His cheeks were puffed and reddened and an angry rash had appeared on his neck.

'What is it with you and those blokes?' Dwyer said as looked down at the Major who just seemed to be staring through him. Without receiving a response immediately he added, 'Don't tell me, a story for another time.'

Carter now appeared to have his thoughts back in the room. He looked at Dwyer and said, 'Watch your back with those three.'

No shit, Sherlock!

Dwyer nodded and said, 'Nothing I can't handle.'

Carter did not doubt it for a second.

5

Garcia, Henderson and Hickey walked out of the hanger back to their accommodation block. They had not spoken a word to each other until out of earshot of the troops that were in the hangar. All of which seemed to have smiles on their faces as they had all clearly heard the dressing down they received in Carter's office. They would have to have been deaf not to.

Hickey broke the silence between them. 'What are we going to say about James then? People are going to ask where he is.'

'Goddamn assholes,' Garcia muttered.

'I only said – '

'I know what you said,' Garcia said angrily. 'I wasn't talking to you, was I?' I was talking about those bastards back in the hangar. All laughing behind our backs. I can't believe I let James talk me into joining this chicken shit outfit, and what do you know? Now he is dead and left us to it.'

'Thanks to that bastard, Dwyer,' Hickey said. 'But as I said, people are going to ask where he is. What are we going to tell them?'

'You reckon?' Garcia said. 'Most of these bastards won't give a shit. He wasn't exactly Mr Popular, was he?' He glared back towards the hangar, kicking at an imaginary football on the ground and muttered something unintelligible under his breath.

'That may be, but we will still need to get our story straight,' said Henderson. He looked towards Hickey who nodded his agreement.

Garcia looked from one to the other and said, 'Let me get this right, you are going to do what that son of a bitch Major tells us to do, all of a sudden?'

Neither either confirmed or denied. Instead, they both started to stare at their shoes.

Garcia continued. 'If anyone asks me where he is, I am going to tell the truth.' The imaginary football was then given another good kicking.

'You disobey his order and you are in a whole load of shit, Tony. You know he is onto us. He has been since the beginning,' said

Henderson. 'I don't like this shit. Not one little bit.'

'Me neither,' said Hickey vigorously nodding his agreement. 'That bastard has got something planned for us, and why the fuck has he got that goddamn gorilla in there with him? How the fuck did he manage that? Don't make any sense to me at all. No sir, not one bit.'

'I know he has. I just can't figure out what just yet,' Garcia said. 'That's why we gotta do something about him and his new boyfriend. The Major and that limey bastard are going to get it when we get to France. There will be all sorts of stray bullets flying about. From the looks of things that aint going to be very long now.'

Henderson and Hickey both started to smile.

6

The phone rang in Carter's office, which he immediately picked up. He heard a voice say, 'Hello sir. Corporal Manning here, Mr Dwyer's kit has been sorted. It's on his bed in the last bunk on the left in block B.'

'Is that in the same block as Garcia, Henderson and Hickey?'

'No sir.'

'Many thanks, Corporal,' Carter said and replaced the receiver in its cradle. 'It seems you are all set kit wise. I will take you over to the administration block first and get the paperwork sorted.'

'What did he say about your three friends? Am I in the same block, or what? They must have a spare bed in there now.'

Carter shook his head.

'Shame,' Dwyer said sarcastically.

Carter shook his head again and then sighed. 'I would like nothing more for you to beat the shit out of those three, believe me. However, you will shortly be a part of the US Army, and the US Army has rules. One of those rules prohibits you from making an arse of yourself and picking fights with your fellow soldiers.'

'Shame,' Dwyer said again.

'I am serious, Mr Dwyer,' Carter said now glaring. 'You will avoid them at all costs while you are at Greenham Common. If they get in your face, you will just ignore them, and that's an order.'

Yeah right.

'What about when we leave Greenham Common?'

With any luck, they will not live through the jump, Carter thought,

'Hopefully, they will have to more worry about, like making sure they don't take a German bullet,' he said instead.

'Okay, then what if they come after me while I am asleep while we are still here?'

'No way. Not going to happen.'

'How are you so sure?'

'Too many witnesses. If you are put up on charge of battery while signed-up, you get court marshalled. Court Marshalled means being kicked out the army, and then prison. They are not the sort that would handle prison well. As it turns out, they appear to be not the only one's, doesn't it?'

Fair one.

'Why do you say that? Why do you think they could not handle prison?' Dwyer said, dwelling on his own fear of confined spaces.

'Because they are snitches. Snitches usually have a hard time in the shower block, if you will excuse the pun, and then end up with their throats cut. There are almost never any witnesses.'

Paints nice a picture.

He does.

Dwyer remained silent.

'Are we done?' Carter said.

'Won't they think it a bit strange that I'm English?' Dwyer said, and then added, 'When I sign up, that is.'

'No doubt, but I very much doubt they will ask any questions with me there. One further thing before we go. You are no doubt aware the word will get round the base about yesterday. Those three won't be able to help themselves.'

'I know', said Dwyer nodding. 'If its okay with you, I'm just gonna play it straight. If anyone asks that is. I will just say it was self defence.'

Carter considered this briefly and then slowly nodded his agreement.

'That's settled then. Many of the men will probably want to be your new best friend. Let's go, shall we?'

Really?

Dwyer led the way out of his office and once again attracted the attention of the mechanics the hangar. Once again, Dwyer decided to keep his head down. Carter joined him at his side and had to quicken his stride as they walked towards the daylight at the exit. He felt he had to make twice as many steps to that of Dwyer who simply ate up the ground, even when not appearing to be in any rush.

A mechanic, whose face was absolutely covered in oil and grease, bent over towards his workmate and said, 'Who is that guy?'

'Dunno, but he sure is one big mother, aint he?'

'He sure is. Glad he appears to be on our side.'

'He sounded like he was British . . . Did you hear his accent?'

'He did. Maybe he is one of those secret guys you hear whispers about. You know; the ones that masquerade as French Resistance fighters, what are they called again? The ones that fought in Africa.'

'SAS?'

'That's it . . . The SAS.'

'Maybe, he sure looks the sort.'

7

Carter and Dwyer left the administration block in less than half an hour after arriving. The signing up process had taken less time than Dwyer imagined.

Despite several curious looks from the Staff Sergeant, he had been given three badges and a sewing kit to stitch onto his uniform, which we was now looking at with interest. One was the division insignia of an eagle's head and the other two were both two olive stripes. He looked around at two other troops walking past to make sure him he put the eagle on the correct sleeve.

It was the left.

'Wear that badge with pride,' said Carter as he noted Dwyer looking at the 101st Airborne insignia.

Dwyer nodded thoughtfully and said, 'So tell me, how come I get to be a Corporal and not a Private?'

'I would not get too carried away, Corporal, adjutants are normally at least a Staff Sergeant. Considering your extensive military experience, that would be pushing it a bit, don't you think? However, they usually hold down desk jobs at headquarters like the guy you just met and do not usually go into battle. . . You however, certainly will be.'

Dwyer noticed that he was now being addressed as Corporal and not Mr Dwyer. He rather liked the sound of it, which he found surprising.

'Block B is the second building on the left,' Carter then added as he pointed towards it. 'You will find your bunk at the far end also on the left. I will catch up with you tomorrow at 20h00hours, just to make sure you are okay. I will be in my office in the hangar. Meet me there.' Carter then turned as if to leave.

'Can I just ask one quick question,' said Dwyer urgently. He had a strange feeling that felt like his father was about to leave him at an orphanage.

Carter nodded.

'Why did you want to recruit me? The *real* reason that is.'

Carter looked at Dwyer long and hard before answering and then said, 'It was after I spoke to the two MPs last night. They have never seen anyone take out four guys like you did. They were in awe of you actually.'

'MPs? Some MPs saw the fight?'

'They did.'

'I still don't understand why you would want to recruit me just because of winning one fight?' Dwyer then looked around him and shrugged his shoulders. 'I mean, with all this, with all these men, what difference is one man going to make? My bet is those three dick heads are a real issue for you. Am I right?'

'That is several questions,' Carter said smiling. 'And it is still a story for another time. You will find out soon enough.' He then turned and walked back towards the hangar.

Dwyer watched Carter until he disappeared inside. He then felt the most alone he had ever felt in his life, even more so than we his family had died. At least then, he had his mates to rally around him and soon after, he had met Sally. He turned towards the direction that Carter had pointed out earlier and went to find his bed.

On your own now Davey.
You are a master of stating the obvious as well.
Remember what the Major told you.
What?
Watch your back!
Yeah right, and his by the sounds of it.

8

Dwyer opened the door of accommodation block B and cautiously went inside. It led into a small lobby with a further door in front. On the left wall was a large corkboard with all kinds of notices and rotas pinned to it. He made a mental note to read them later. All he wanted to do now was have a long shower.

He had been wearing the same clothes for well over twenty-four hours and guessed he stank. He sniffed one of his armpits to check and immediately cringed.

Oh, bollocks. That is embarrassing.

He was right.

He opened a further door and again cautiously walked through. Before him was a long straight room with bunk beds on each side of the room. They formed an artificial corridor down the middle of the room. He looked from one side to the other and was relieved that nobody appeared to be around.

'Hello,' he said. 'Anyone here?'

Silence.

Dwyer walked slowly down the room until he got to the last bunk on the left. All the kit that Manning had been told to provide was neatly spread out on the bottom of the two.

There was a lot.

He picked up a towel and the toiletries and then looked around for where the bathroom might be. A further door was in the middle of the wall that was directly next to his bunk. It had a sign above it that read, 'Latrine'.

What is a latrine, for god's sake, why don't they just call it the bathroom like everyone else?

After entering, he took of his clothes and hung them on a peg. He then rolled his head round his shoulders, stretched, and then checked his groin for bruising.

Remarkably, he found none.

Balls of steel, he thought as the dull ache had now thankfully almost completely gone. He took out a bar of soap from the wash bag and then walked to the middle shower and stood back from the jet of water that spurted out enthusiastically. He then tested the temperature of the water with his hand, and to his surprise, the water turned hot within seconds. He stood underneath it turning his face towards the welcome hot spray and let the water wash over his body.

While Dwyer was in the middle of his *overly* long shower, the accommodation block had started to fill up with its temporary tenants. Sure enough, Garcia had spilled the beans to the first group of troops that he came across. He had seen Dwyer enter Block B earlier and given the news to its residents. The level of curiosity about their new houseguest was understandably at fever pitch.

On noticing that Dwyer was not in the sleeping quarters, Privates Ramirez and Hobbs slowly entered the Latrine and looked into the shower block. They went unnoticed by Dwyer who was too busy swearing and trying to rinse the soap out of his now stinging eyes.

Ramirez and Hobbs returned to the sleeping quarters. They were greeted by twenty expectant faces. Ramirez put them out of their suspense. 'That guy is an absolute monster. He's built like a brick shit house and hung like a well hung horse.'

Quiet laughter broke out.

Hobbs nodded agreement. 'Ramirez is right. He is one big son of a gun. He looks like he has lived in the gym all his life. I didn't look at his dick though. Not like this queer,' and then slapped Ramirez on the back.

'Just as well,' Ramirez said. 'You would have had an inferiority complex for the rest of your life if you had.'

Loud laughter now broke out all round the room and then stooped as soon as it started. Dwyer had walked through the latrine door carrying his clothes and only wearing a towel wrapped round his waist.

Oh, crap!

On seeing the group in front of him, whom to a man were all staring at him, Dwyer stopped dead in his tracks.

Fuck me he thought, *the cat can't be out of the bag already.*

He looked around at the sea of faces that confronted him. Not one of them was smiling. However, he quickly took consolation that they did not appear to be scowling either.

'Alright lads, how's it going? I'm Davey Dwyer,' was all he could bring himself to say, which he regretted immediately.

Is that the best I could come up with?

Suddenly, he started to feel extremely vulnerable, as only a towel was preventing him from being completely naked.

The silence that now met his greeting seemed to last too long to Dwyer, he was absolutely convinced that we was about to get jumped and started eyeing each man in front of him to see if any of them looked like a handful.

One of them has to be first.

What went through his mind at a million miles an hour was that if he hit the first one hard enough, maybe the arse would fall out all of the others.

Ramirez was the first to speak up. 'Is it true?'

Here we go.

Dwyer knew the game was up, but said anyway, 'Is what true?'

'The word is, you killed James Corporal Carter and Major Carter saw fit to bring you into the 101st. He paused and then added, 'And last but not least, you are a Brit.'

'I only hit him once. He was coming at me with a crowbar, and yes, I am a Brit,' said Dwyer defensively.

'Bullshit you only hit him once. How'd you kill him if you only hit him once?' Ramirez said.

'Apparently I splintered his breastbone and it messed up his heart.'

This startling revelation was greeted with a long period of silence and many open mouths.

'Is that a fact? Well, I hope you never get mad at me man. Welcome to the screaming eagles,' said Ramirez eventually, starting to smile and offered Dwyer his hand to shake.

With that, the whole group burst out into laugher and lots of hand clapping. It seemed to Dwyer that everyone wanted to shake his hand and pat him on the back at the same time. Such was the vigour of one of the handshakes that his towel slipped down from his waist. Twenty new inferiority complexes were born.

That was unexpected.

Really?

Dwyer was truly overwhelmed. Major Carter had said that there might be many; that would want to be his new best friend. He had thought this to be an attempt to make him feel at ease. It seemed that the Major had been spot on. That arsehole Corporal Carter had definitely not been flavour of the month.

Neither are his three bum chums.

Once the furore had died down, Dwyer sat on the end of his bead and examined his kit. He first noticed that the rifle was broken down into several parts. There was a pistol, a knife, a bayonet, a gas mask, first aid kit that contained syringes and bandages and a rucksack, which already had his surname on it, in black capital letters.

As far as clothes went, there were five of most things including pairs of socks, white T-Shirts, underpants and fatigues. There was a set of combat camouflages, a helmet, pair of boots and a carton of cigarettes. He tried on the helmet and was relieved to find that it seemed comfortable enough. In addition, there were the three badges and sewing kit that he received earlier. He then noticed the dog tags with his name, rank and serial number indented on the metal. There was a note attached that said 'Please notify admin of blood type.' He did not have a clue.

Dwyer dressed in set of fatigues that surprisingly fit him perfectly and then picked up the pieces of his gun.

This could be fun, he thought without the first idea of how to put it together. He put it down again only a minute later, giving it up as a waste of time, and after packing most of the kit into the rucksack, looked round the room.

It was totally filled now with about forty blokes in it. Some were playing cards, some were lying on their beds reading, nearly all were smoking and one bloke was playing a guitar.

Really well Dwyer thought, *even if it is that Country and Western crap.*

Why people felt compelled to sing about their '*daddy being a milkman*' and '*going to jail for shooting their wife's lover,*' bemused him.

Nonetheless, he sure could bang out a tune.

9

Sergeant Luke Nelson, who was almost equal to Dwyer in height at least, approached him.

'Okay if I take a seat?' He said while gesturing towards the end of Dwyer's bed.

Dwyer put down the camouflaged jacket, which he was making the best job possible of sewing on the badges onto, and moved up and made a space for him.

'Be my guest,' he said.

Uh oh. Here comes the third degree.

Just say it how it was.

Nelson hadn't been in the block while Dwyer was making his new acquaintances earlier and wanted to hear it straight from the horse's mouth about a British civilian, after killing one of their own, had then being asked to join the division. By the deceased's uncle no less.

'You are quite the new celebrity around here from what I am hearing,' said Nelson looking at Dwyer with his curiosity apparent. 'I'm Luke Nelson by the way, your Sergeant.'

Dwyer just nodded. He did not know where this was going yet.

'It's quite a story. Wanna tell me what really happened?' Nelson asked.

Not really.

'Okay, but I'm not sure I quite believe it myself yet. Everything is happening *so fast*.'

Dwyer told him everything, including the conversation he had with Major Carter at the police station and the reunion with Garcia, Henderson and Hickey at the hangar on his arrival at the base.

Nelson's expression had been impassive throughout Dwyer's commentary. He had been listening intently, occasionally shaking his head, occasionally nodding it.

When realising that Dwyer was not going to add anything further and said, 'Major's don't normally have Corporal adjutants, especially the likes of Carter.' Nelson then paused for thought and added, 'He must see something special in you though. You are honoured. He is the best damn officer in the division. Everybody respects him.'

'Not from what I have seen. Garcia and his two buddies sure don't seem to like him much,' said Dwyer. 'And the feeling seems to be mutual.'

'Those three mongrels,' said Nelson nodding. 'There were four until yesterday.'

'Pretty obvious those blokes don't seem to be liked by anybody. Do you want to tell me why?' Dwyer said looking towards Nelson raising both his eyebrows.

'No problem,' said Nelson. 'I trust the Major told you to watch your back?'

Dwyer nodded.

'Well, I will tell you what I know and that aint that much. They all joined the 101st at the same time. Seems they have all been tight as brothers since school days. Where Carter went, the other three followed. I expect Garcia will take the lead now. Ever since they joined, they have not been exactly keen to fit in with the rest of the guys. Many think they are responsible for some thefts that have been going on lately, but nobody can prove it. Also, a young private was found badly beaten up outside one of the hangars two days ago.'

Nelson then looked towards the floor and shook his head before continuing.

'Everyone suspects it was them as he had been seen arguing with Hickey earlier in the day, but again, nobody saw it. Even the young lad who was hurt didn't see them. They apparently jumped him from behind.'

Dwyer interrupted. 'That's brave of them.'

Nelson shook his head and continued. 'Obviously word gets round quick within the base and it was Major Carter who sent them to Portsmouth yesterday, no doubt for morale purposes so no one could try and seek revenge.'

Nelson then paused again and waited for a response from Dwyer. When not receiving one he carried on.

'Nobody trusts them, and that is the last thing you want when you are about to go into battle. They are the sort of guys who run off will the medical supplies and ammo and leave everyone else in the shit. The fact you took their leader out yesterday makes you No. 1 top boy around here as far as the most of the men are concerned. It's like having a cancer removed from the division.'

'Glad to of been of assistance,' said Dwyer trying to look nonchalant.

Now who is the cocky bastard?

'One last thing,' said Nelson. 'For some reason the Major has had his eye on them the whole time since they joined. Everyone has noticed it but nobody knows why. No one thinks it was the fact that Carter was his nephew. He sure didn't seem to cut him any slack, quite the opposite in fact.'

Dwyer nodded in agreement. Something had been going on between them and he found himself looking forward to *'the story for another time'*, to satisfy his curiosity.

With that, the men started filtering out of the room. 'Chow time,' Nelson said.

Dwyer was pleased. He suddenly became aware that he was starving.

10

Dwyer was now sat back on his bed, fiddling with various pieces of his rifle. He felt better now. He was clean, his balls had stopped aching, and he had a full stomach. The food had not been great but there was more of it than he expected and at least it was brown and hot.

He had kept himself to himself in the dinner hall, but had noticed many of the troops casting curious glances his way that were seeing this mysterious Brit for the first time. He just kept his head down and tucked in. He deliberately made a point of not looking towards Garcia, Henderson and Hickey who were glaring at him the entire meal.

Hope they get indigestion, he thought to himself.

He imagined how a new *celebrity* criminal must feel on their first day inside at mealtime. Everyone staring at him, whispering, inventing conspiracy stories, exaggerating his exploits – *plotting his downfall?*

He looked up from the puzzle of assembling the pieces towards the commotion that had broken out further down the block. A Private had let off a fart, which was a loud as a ship giving off a collision warning in the channel, and apparently, its aroma was as pungent equivalent to that of a bag of rotting sprouts. This had resulted in the outbreak of a pillow fight in which the offending Private was coming a poor second. He was outnumbered to five to one.

This brought a smile to Dwyer's face and he then noticed that one of the blokes was looking over in his direction. He then smiled and walked over towards him.

'Having trouble?' He said as he gestured towards the rifle still in pieces.

'I aint got a clue mate,' said Dwyer with a foolish grin on his face. 'The longer I look at it, the more complicated it seems to become.'

The Private gave a huge grin back, which revealed that four of his top front teeth were missing. He picked up the pieces; and what seemed to Dwyer to be in the blink of an eye, assembled it and then stripped it down just as quickly.

'There you go. Now it's your turn.'

What just happened?

Pretty impressive, huh?

Dwyer looked up at and said while laughing, 'You are having a laugh, mate. Any chance you can do that again, about ten times slower?'

The Private smiled his toothless grin again and went through the process explaining each step as he went. He then handed the pieces back to Dwyer and said, 'It takes a bit of practice. Let me know if you want any help.' The Private then went to walk away.

Dwyer stopped him and said, 'Wait a minute mate, what's your name?'

'Danny Brooks. I am from Wilmington, North Carolina,' he said smiling.

'I'm Davey Dwyer. Portsmouth, England. Good to meet you,' said Dwyer having no idea afterwards why he added the *Portsmouth, England* part.

'I know,' said Brooks. 'You got a nickname, Davey?'

'Yeah, my mates call me Moose.'

Brooks burst out laughing and then said, 'Why am I not surprised?' He then turned away and went to join in on a card game three bunks further down the room. 'Deal me in,' he said as he sat down with his buddies and slapped the man on his right on the back.

II
10th July 1943
Autryville, North Carolina, USA
03h40 hours

The whole group held their breath. 'Mr Star Gazer' frantically gestured for everyone to get down on the floor. He was wasting his time. The remainder of the group all stood like statues with shocked looks on their faces.

Goddamn. These are three stupid sons-of-bitches . . . WHOOP, WHOOP . . . Yessiree, real stupid sons of bitches.

Clearly now showing his frustration, he rapidly moved his right hand up and down to insist that they follow his lead by crouching down onto the floor. On realising that they were too scared to move a muscle, he stood back up shaking his head in disbelief and joined them all standing.

The footsteps stopped. 'Is anyone there?' A voice called out. 'If there is, you better come out. I have a gun.' A huge amount of anxiety could be detected in the voice.

All looked towards 'Mr Star Gazer'. He shook his head slowly to try to give assurance that the male owner of the house was bluffing. *Maybe he was, maybe he wasn't . . . Very interesting. Yes indeed . . . WHOOP, WHOOP . . . WHOOP.*

'This is your last chance,' the voice said again with now even more anxiety apparent. 'Come out with your hands up in the air. I mean it.'

No one made a move to follow the instruction within the kitchen.

The owner, now realising that the trespassers he thought he had heard were clearly not going to come out, gently pushed down on the handle and pushed the kitchen door with the palm of his hand to look inside.

That was the last action of his life.

The member of the group nearest the door immediately raised

the baseball bat that he was carrying and sent it crashing down on his head. Blood exploded everywhere in all directions in the same manner juice would fly from a grapefruit if hit with a hammer.

The owner of the house slumped to the floor. A pool of blood rapidly formed round his head in the hallway.

'Mr Star Gazer', now wearing his moronic grin again, walked out into the hallway and stepped over the body carefully avoiding the ever-increasing pool of blood. He bent down to see if he was alive. He first listened to his chest and then checked his pulse. He then violently slapped both sides of his face.

On satisfying himself that he was dead, he looked towards the member of the group that had carried out the assault and whispered, 'Oh well, this son of a bitch definitely had it coming.'

Yes indeed . . . Whoopdie fucking doo. . . WHOOP. Definitely had it coming.

The other members of the group all looked towards each other and started to snigger like a group of nursery school children.

'*What the hell have you done?*' Shouted a hysterical female voice from the top of the stairs.

The sniggering stopped abruptly as all four faces turned towards her. *The meerkats had all detected the now apparent danger at the same time.*

All members of the group then looked back and forwards at each other and then back up towards the middle-aged woman and then back at each other for what seemed like an eternity. They all then sprang into action in unison.

'Mr Star Gazer' took the lead. He bounded up the stairs two at a time towards her. The remainder of the group all followed suit.

The sniggering had returned.

The woman's eyes grew wide and she quickly backed away from the top of the stairs and collided with the landing wall behind her. This had the effect of her bouncing back into the arms of the 'Mr Star Gazer' who had now made it to the top of the stairs.

'Well hello there, bitch. Have you missed me?' He said with his mouth only inches from her face.

She moved her head to the side. One out of fear, two, because of the overpowering odour of his breath.

You need to just be real quiet now,' Mr Star Gazer said placing his right hand over her mouth and grabbing the back of her neck with his left. 'Quiet as a mouse. *Squeak. Squeak.* Quiet as a little mousey . . . WHOOP.'

The woman's eyes grew wide as saucers and a muffled groan escaped her.

'Mr Star Gazer' looked towards the rest of the group and then said, 'Time for a bit of R&R boys . . . WHOOP . . . WHOOP . . . Yessiree.'

He then grabbed her by the throat and threw her backwards into her bedroom. Once the whole group had followed her in, the door was slowly closed behind them.

12

The words of Sergeant Nelson had played heavily on Dwyer's mind whilst he was eating his dinner earlier, regarding his likely popularity. He had decided that he was going to make every effort to fit in as best as possible. After all, he would no doubt be relying on these blokes at some point soon to be watching his back and probably even saving his life.

He realised that the many of these young kids had not seen combat before, but at least they had been given extensive training and knew how to fire a weapon.

Which is more than you have.
I am aware of that thanks.
Just saying.

Dwyer could not help but notice the camaraderie between these young men. Although they were always making jokes at each other's expense and did not seem to able to agree on anything, especially baseball, they clearly would fight tooth and nail for each other when push came to shove.

It reminded him of the friendship he had with his own group of friends. You take one of them on and you took them all on.

He then suddenly felt homesick.

He had only left Portsmouth that morning but it already seemed like a lifetime ago and about a thousand miles away.

His attitude towards the Americans had now however completely changed.

Before the build up of troops over the last few days in Portsmouth, there had not been that many Americans based there. Most of them on the south coast of England were encamped east of Portsmouth along the coast in Chichester, and west along the coast just outside Southampton. Those that were now within Portsmouth were in the main, confined to barracks either on ship or within the Dockyard.

Dwyer's attitude towards the American serviceman had been earlier prejudiced by his friends, who some of which, had lost their girlfriends to them. As far as he was now concerned, they were all okay by him. He was having a very hard time trying to understand how they could welcome such an unusual newcomer, especially under the circumstances.

Fair play to them, he thought.

After he had finished sewing the patches onto his camouflage jacket, of which he had made a surprisingly good job, he lay back on his bunk and started wondering about what Sally was doing. He could not imagine what she was now thinking. His thoughts turned to the content of a letter he would write to her, but within seconds, he had fallen asleep.

DAAVVEEYYY! Nooooo!

His dream earlier in the jeep when travelling up to Greenham Common started where it left off.

He turned back towards Sally. She was slowly floating backwards down the corridor towards Williams' office door, which was opening and closing in a violent, threatening, malevolent manner. Her arms outstretched, pleading, begging him to reach out to her.

'What goes around comes around' the voice said again behind him.

He turned as if in slow motion. Not wanting to, but unable to stop himself, to see who had said it.

Corporal James Carter was now standing ten feet away from him with blood running out of his both of his eyes and was raising a pistol slowly to fire at him.

He turned back toward Sally, again in slow motion. She had reached interior of the office. The door then abruptly shut closed as if to take her away from him forever . . . He heard the sound of the pistol firing . . . And then . . .

Oblivion.

Two hours later, Dwyer became aware of being shaken from his slumber. He woke to find Private Brooks kneeling down beside his bed. Such was the deepness of his sleep; Dwyer momentarily forgot where he was. The look of confusion on his face must have been mistaken as aggression. Brooks quickly stood up to back off and hit his head on the top bunk. This brought Dwyer back into the present, and the sight of Brooks now vigorously rubbing the back of his head, made him start to laugh.

He had an only a vague recollection that he had a horrendous dream. Something about –

Best not to dwell on it.

You might wish you hadn't.

Dwyer sat up and swung his legs off the bed remembering to duck down to avoid hitting his own head and said, 'What's up, mate? What time is it?'

'It's 21h00 hours. Sergeant Nelson told me to wake you up. Apparently Major Carter wants to see you in his office.'

'21h00 hours,' repeated Dwyer. 'It feels like I have been asleep for hours.' His head felt like he had drunk to much the night before. 'What does he want? He said he didn't want to see me until tomorrow night.'

'I don't know, but you better not keep him waiting.'

13

Major Carter had been joined by Colonel Harrison who had now returned from Southwick House. They had once again been going over the plans for the imminent invasion and both men could hardly contain their excitement that it was now only a few days away. The more they discussed the plans the more enthusiastic they were becoming. The waiting to execute them was becoming unbearable.

It had nothing to do with wanting to go into battle. It was just that waiting for it to happen, seemed worse.

Much worse.

Both men had been discussing at length that whilst training in England, the 101st three formal exercises had simulated capturing causeway bridges behind Utah Beach. In the latter of these exercises, they practised actually jumping out of planes as opposed to just the backs of trucks, which they had used earlier. This was their full dress rehearsal for its role in the actual invasion. Both Harrison and Carter believed that all had gone well.

Next on their agenda came their objectives. Again at length, they had been going over the detail of seizing the positions west of Utah Beach and to eliminate the German's secondary beach defences, thus allowing the 4th Infantry Division to continue inland once ashore. In addition, they were to capture the causeway bridges between St.Martin-de-Varreville and Poupeville, destroy two railroad bridges northwest of Carentan and establish two bridgeheads on the Doule River at le Port.

Carter and Harrison were in the process of folding up maps and finishing for the evening when Dwyer appeared at the door of the office.

Carter waved at him to enter.

'This is Colonel Harrison my immediate superior officer. Colonel Harrison, this is our latest recruit, Corporal Davey Dwyer,' said Carter.

Harrison stood up and then immediately thought better of it and sat straight back down again. He was only five feet eight inches tall and the presence of this giant now in the confined space of the office, at first, made him feel in some way inadequate.

Dwyer bit his tongue to avoid laughing, as Harrison's actions reminded him of a toy jack-in-the-box. Carter noted his reaction, who briefly looked away himself to eradicate the grin that he felt appearing on his face.

'I see you didn't exaggerate, Major,' said Harrison.

Dwyer looked towards Carter and assumed he was referring to his size. Carter refrained from comment.

Harrison then stood again, gave Dwyer a last glance and said, 'I will see you at 05h00, Major. Good night,' and quickly left.

Carter waited until Harrison's footsteps grew distant in the now deserted hangar before he said, 'His curiosity got the better of him. He wanted to meet you.'

Dwyer just nodded and waited for Carter to continue.

Carter then sat down behind his desk and lit a cigarette, which prompted Dwyer to look at the ashtray. It was overflowing which explained the visible line of smoke that appeared to be hovering about a foot from the ceiling. He fought back the urge to cough.

'What has the men's reaction been towards you?' Carter finally said breaking the silence.

'It's been unbelievable. They seem to think I have done them a favour. Just like you said.'

Carter took a deep drag on his cigarette and then seemed to take an age to Dwyer to blow an endless plume of smoke to the ceiling. He found himself disappointed that there were not any smoke rings this time.

'I hoped as much,' said Carter. 'Made any friends yet? He asked.

'Not really, although Danny showed me how to assemble my rifle.'

'Do you mean Private Brooks?' Carter asked now looking enthusiastic.

'Yes, that's him. Seems like a good bloke.'

'Excellent,' said Carter. 'Private Brooks is an excellent soldier with a good character. He is also without doubt the best shot in the entire Division. I will instruct him tomorrow to not leave your side over the next three days and get him to show you the ropes. In addition, he will be told to instruct you on military etiquette. Please tell him to come and see me when you return to your sleeping quarters.'

'Military etiquette,' Dwyer repeated with a quizzical look on his face.

'Yes, Corporal Dwyer, military etiquette. Knowing how to stand to attention, when to salute and say sir to superior offices when appropriate. You are after all in the U S Army now. I suggest you go and get some sleep. You are going to need it.'

'I was asleep before you made me come in here,' said Dwyer.

'That will be all, Corporal. Good night.'

Dwyer just nodded and left Carter's office. On his way walking back to the accommodation block, Dwyer wondered if he should have saluted and said 'goodnight sir' when he left.

This is going to take some getting used to.
Without a doubt.

On his return to the accommodation block, Dwyer saw that Brooks was still playing cards. The majority of other troops were now tucked up in bed.

As he walked towards Brooks, he noticed that one of the men was snoring like what he imagined an angry bear to sound. With that, the troop in the bunk below kicked his bunk, which had the necessary effect of him rolling on his side and stopping; not without a couple of loud snorts of protest first.

I wonder if I snore.
Believe me. That is the last of your worries!

'You okay, Danny?' Dwyer said as he reached the card game. 'The Major wants to see you. It seems you are going to be stuck with me for the next few days.'

'Yes Corporal.' Brooks said and immediately got up and jogged to the exit.

Yes Corporal. I like the sound of that. Three bags full corporal. Maybe I should try it out on Garcia and his flock – see how they like those onions.
Watch your back.
Would be funny though.
Watch your –
I know. Shut up will you.

14

It *was* now a case of déjà vu for Dwyer. He woke again to find Brooks shaking his shoulder, only this time Brooks did not bang his head when Dwyer opened his eyes. He was vaguely aware of Brooks saying something to him.

'Time to rise and shine,' Brooks had been saying. *This guy is one deep sleeper,* he thought as he had been shaking him for a full ten seconds.

Dwyer slowly came round and said, 'What time is it?'

'05h00,' was the reply.

Are there two five o'clocks in the same day?

'05h00,' Dwyer repeated with a pained expression and disbelief in his voice. He closed his eyes and desperately hoped that Brooks would piss off and leave him alone. He had noted the night before that the Colonel and Major had arranged to meet then, but did not think for one minute that that ridiculous time to get up in the morning would also apply to him.

'Come on big guy. Up and at em,' Brooks persisted. 'Get yourself into the latrine and then get dressed. From what the Major tells me, we have a long day in front of us.'

Long day – no kidding – not surprising if you get up 05h00, is it?

'You sound like my mother used to when she was trying to get me up for school,' said Dwyer who was now reluctantly crawling out of his nice warm bed rubbing his eyes.

Brooks started to laugh and then said, 'That's right. You just think of me of has your new ma and pa. From what I heard last night whilst talking to the Major, it looks like I will even have to teach you how to wipe your nose.'

Dwyer now stood to his full height and loomed over Brooks. He tilted his head back so Brooks could see straight up his nose and said, 'How does it look?'

'Wow, that's disgusting, man,' said Brooks albeit that he was smiling at the same time. 'C'mon, have a shit, shower and shave and we can get some breakfast.'

The thought of more food spurned Dwyer into action and he trudged off towards the latrine. After entering, he then immediately returned to his bunk and got out his towel and toiletries that he had forgotten to take from the cupboard beside it. He just did not function well in the mornings.

He felt something resembling human though after he had showered. On leaving the accommodation block, he became even more alert due to the coolness of temperature outside, although it did look like it was going to be a beautiful day for a change. There was not a cloud in the pale blue sky. The sun was beginning to do its best to start to warm up the base.

The image was ruined when the three stooges all walked past him. Garcia flipped him the finger.

Dwyer waved back, smiling.

15

After breakfast, which consisted of toast, powdered eggs that and a cup of brown strong smelling liquid that Dwyer guessed to be some kind of coffee - so thick you could stand your spoon up in it - he walked with Brooks towards the hangar where Carter's office was situated.

He was actually starting to 'buzz', which he put down to the brown liquid he had just forced down his gullet.

Carter and Harrison were walking towards them. Brooks immediately saluted as he walked past. Dwyer of course did not and made a mental note. Lesson number one in respect of etiquette had been learned.

C'mon, keep up.

Once inside the hangar, Brooks led Dwyer over to a truck and told him to climb up onto the back. After giving Brooks a quizzical sideways glance, and looking around the hangar to see if anyone else may be watching, Dwyer reluctantly did as instructed, muttering as he did so.

'Okay. First lesson of the day, how to land properly from a parachute jump,' said Brooks. 'Just jump off and I will see what you do.'

'Just jump off?'

'Yes. There more to it than you think.'

Just jump off?
That's what he said.
How hard can that be?

The same group of mechanics that were working on the plane the day before, now all stopped work and observed.

Dwyer just simply jumped off without further hesitation and landed flatfooted with his legs straight. This had effect of sending up a jolt up through his body that started at his feet and then ended by rattling his jaw, which made him bite his tongue.

It also brought back the painful memories of the groin problem from the day before which he had until then, forgotten about. He did not know whether to grab his jaw or his balls first. Instead, he just ended up doubling over. Such was the pain; no sound came out of his mouth that was now wide open.

His voice of reason could have dined out on that one for a month.

Oops!

This sent Brooks and the group of mechanics into a state of hysterical laughter. Tears were literally rolling down Brooks' face and it was not until a full two minutes later that he regained any kind of composure. Dwyer, however, was failing to see the funny side of it. He did eventually start to smile at the thought of causing so much hilarity.

'If you do that when it's for real, you will break your back,' said Brooks eventually, trying to look serious. 'We will be going in with a shit load of kit and by the looks of you, will make you weigh well over 400 lbs.'

The two mechanics that had been discussing Dwyer's likely British regiment the day before looked at each other. 'Maybe he is not in the SAS,' one of them said.

The other agreed nodding his head furiously unable to control his belly-laughter.

Brooks then climbed up on the back of the truck himself and demonstrated the proper procedure.

He picked himself up off the floor and said, 'Did you see what I did there? I made sure my knees bent on landing, rolled down onto my side and then brought my legs over with my feet together. Now you try it again.'

So soon. You can do one, mate!

Too fast.

'You are going to have to give me a minute, mate,' said Dwyer looking towards his audience over by the plane. 'My balls feel like they have jumped up into my throat at the moment.'

Hysterical laughter broke out again. The mechanics did not have the slightest intention of returning to work. Dwyer's next attempt was not to be missed. Unfortunately, for them, Major Carter then appeared at the entrance to the hangar so they quickly pretended to busy themselves repairing the landing gear of the plane. They did however ensure they watched out of the corner of their eyes.

'How is our new recruit coming along, Private Brooks?' Carter said.

Don't tell him.

Dwyer glanced over at Brooks and dreaded his response.

'He's doing very well, sir,' he lied.

Dwyer gave the game away by visibly looking relieved, which was noticed by Carter.

Idiot. You just ruined a perfectly good lie.

'Really, well let's see a demonstration then, shall we?' Carter said.

Dwyer cringed.

He definitely needed more time to recover from his first attempt. He reluctantly climbed up onto the back of the truck and tried to look as nonchalant as possible.

He was making a piss poor job of it.

He quickly went over in his mind what Brooks had shown him and then jumped. He nailed it, much to Brooks' and the mechanics surprise, who could not help themselves from completely downing tools again, regardless of the presence of the Major, to watch.

'Excellent. Carry on,' said Carter who then walked towards his office with his hands behind his back.

Dwyer picked himself off the ground with a stupid grin on his face. 'What's next? He said.

'Not so fast. You probably just got lucky then. Get back up and do it again,' said Brooks.

Bollocks!

Much to Dwyer's dismay, he actually climbed up on the truck and jumped off a further twenty times before Brooks said that he was satisfied.

'How's your fitness?' Brooks asked.

Not bad normally, but my balls are suggesting otherwise.

'Okay,' said Dwyer with suspicion. He was reluctant to know where this was headed.

'Let's see, shall we? Follow me,' said Brooks.

Brooks then led Dwyer outside the Hangar. 'Try and keep up,' Brooks said and then started to run towards the perimeter fence.

'First one to the camp entrance and back following the fence,' he shouted back over his shoulder.

Never one to avoid a challenge, Dwyer set off in pursuit. With what appeared to be only a dozen large strides, Dwyer caught Brooks up and past him. He reached the camp gates first where he was eyed suspiciously by the guard duty who thought briefly that one of the troops was trying to make a run for 'freedom'. He then turned round and ran back towards to Brooks who desperately trying to keep up. Dwyer reached the hangar a full hundred yards in front of him and turned round to watch Brooks belatedly arrive.

It was now Brooks' turn to bend over double. While gasping for breath he looked up at Dwyer and said, 'Well, we won't be doing that again in a hurry.'

Thank God for that.

Yeah, and if my balls could talk, they would agree.

Dwyer smiled. He was absolutely exhausted but refused to show it.

'Okay, let's go back to the accommodation block,' said Brooks. 'You can practise assembling and stripping your rifle now.'

Yes, lets.

16

On returning to the block, they were confronted by Garcia and his two sidekicks Hickey and Henderson who were walking towards them.

Brooks nervously looked towards Dwyer to see what his reaction would be. To his amusement, Dwyer just carried on walking with what seemed to be without a care in the world.

Brooks heard Dwyer say, 'Alright lads, how's it going?'

Dwyer strode past without waiting for a response but did turn around to measure their reaction once sufficient distance was between them.

Brooks quickened his pace to keep up.

Their reaction was that they all stopped and stared after him. All three of their faces simultaneously adopted a scowl.

Dwyer blew them a kiss.

'That's right, arsehole,' said Garcia. 'You just keep walking, real cocky mother, aint you? You will get yours soon enough,' sufficiently quietly so that Dwyer could not hear him.

Brooks caught up with Dwyer and said, 'Those guys looked really pissed, Corp.'

'Can't imagine why,' said Dwyer with a slight grin. 'Let's go and see about this rifle, shall we?'

Definately watch your back.

Did you see the look on their faces?

Yes – pure hatred.

It took Dwyer over two hours before he truly got the hang of the assembly and stripping of the M – 1. At one point, he felt the urge to throw it out the window such was the level of his frustration.

All of a sudden, it all fell into place, and after a few swift movements, he had mastered it. He looked up at Brooks with a goofy grin, looking for approval.

Brooks managed a toothless one, and said, 'There you go. Aint so difficult, is it?'

'Not anymore,' Dwyer replied and then proceeded to go through process three further times.

He then looked towards Brooks and said, 'Thanks for being so patient, Danny. I really appreciate it.' He was not so sure he could have had so much while watching his initial pathetic attempts. Patience was not one of his virtues.

'No problem at all, Moose. You picked it up a lot quicker than others I have seen.'

'Really?'

'Really,' Brooks confirmed.

They exchanged smiles. Dwyer liked the fact that Brooks had just called him by his nickname and he believed they were going to become firm friends.

God knows I could use one right about now.

Dwyer then returned to his rifle and continually repeated the process of assembling and stripping it until he could do it with his eyes closed.

Brooks went to the hangar to find Major Carter.

Unbeknown to Dwyer, Carter had requested regular updates throughout the day. The Major was sat behind the desk studying a map with his customary cigarette in hand. Brooks knocked on the door and Carter waved him in without looking up.

'Private Brooks reporting, sir. On Corporal Dwyer's progress.'

Carter just nodded for him to continue now showing a good deal more interest in his visitor.

'He's doing really well, sir. I have left him in the accommodation block practising assembling his rifle. It took him a while at first but he has the hang of it now. One thing, sir, he is a very good runner, completely kicked by butt,' Brooks said with a smile.

'That is excellent news, Private,' Carter said.

Carter then quickly filled out a slip. 'Take this to the stores and draw some live ammunition. Take him to the far end of the base. He can now learn how to fire his weapon as he has learnt to put together. If he is half as good as you by the end of the day, you will have performed your duties well.'

'Yes sir, and thank you, sir.' Brooks took the slip of paper from Carter, saluted and then marched out of the office.

He then sprinted back to the accommodation block after leaving the stores. The fact that he could now spend the rest of the day doing what he definitely believed to be his best talent had quickened his step.

He literally burst through threw the accommodation blocks doors and shouted down the room at Dwyer, 'Moose, get your gun and come outside, will you?'

There were a number of other troops carrying out various activities now within the block and most smiled at the thought that Brooks had called Dwyer Moose. Brooks had not shared the fact that it was his nickname with anyone the night before.

They all agreed that it suited him.

Dwyer quickly put on his boots and jogged towards the exit with his rifle slung over his shoulder. 'What we doing? What's the rush?' He asked Brooks when he reached him.

'My absolute favourite thing my friend, we are going shooting.'

Dwyer's face lit up. He was starting to enjoy his new life in the Army.

17

On reaching the end of the base, which was by in large the end of a large field, Brooks placed a number of large rocks on a weather beaten rusty metal table that had seen better days. He then walked back fifty paces and lay down on the ground in a firing position.

Dwyer did the same.

Brooks then briefly targeted the rock on the extreme right and fired.

The rock flew off the table.

'And that's how you do that,' said Brooks and looked over at Dwyer lying next to him. 'Your turn, just place the rifle into your shoulder, aim and gently squeeze the trigger.'

Dwyer did as instructed. Nothing happened.

Eh?

'You forgot to take the safety off,' said Brooks and showed him how.

Idiot!

Dwyer took aim once again and fired. The rock in the middle of the table that he had been aiming at flew of the table. He then proceeded to subtly shift his position and hit all of the remaining rocks without missing.

Nothing to it.

'Look at what we have here,' said Brooks. 'It seems that you are a natural,' and then slapped Dwyer on the back, toothlessly grinning from ear to ear.

I wonder what happened to his teeth?

Brooks walked back to the table and placed a further five rocks on the table. He then walked back, this time counting a hundred paces.

'Try it from here, hotshot,' he said.

Dwyer lay on the floor and took aim. He did not miss one.

Brooks whistled through the gaps in his teeth. 'Outstanding,' he said in genuine surprise.

Davey smiled a goofy grin up at him from his firing position lying on the ground.

'Nothing to it,' he said aloud.

'So it would seem,' Brooks said and then walked towards the table to replace the targets.

Once more, all were removed without missing.

It was not until they went back one hundred and fifty paces that he missed occasionally. Dwyer continued practising until his shoulder became sore.

On the way back to the accommodation block Brooks made a detour to Major Carter to tell him the good news.

18

The next morning, Dwyer once again had to be woken by Brooks. He had gone to bed early the night before as his activities and made him more tired than he could ever remember being before.

While he was showering, he reminded himself to write a letter to Sally and take it to the admin block for them to post. He had no other way of contacting her as nobody he knew had a telephone; and even if they did, he did not think he would be allowed to make personal calls from a phone at the base.

The day's activities were almost an exact replica of the day before with the exception of the run round the perimeter fence.

Brooks had learnt his lesson.

On returning to the accommodation block that evening, he borrowed some paper, an envelope and a pen from a young Private named Baker, who since Dwyer had arrived, had either been reading the bible, praying, or writing to someone. Baker had handed over them over to him without saying a word or looking up.

'Thanks,' Dwyer said on receiving the writing material. 'I don't suppose you have a pencil I can borrow as well, do you?'

Baker handed him a pencil, again without saying a word.

'Not very talkative, are you?' Dwyer said smiling down at him. 'Is that a good book?' He added, nodding towards the bible.

'I talk to the Lord,' Baker said. 'Considering what we have in store for us soon, I suggest you do the same.' He then picked up the bible and started to turn the well-thumbed pages, dismissing Dwyer as if he were not standing only a few feet away.

'I will bear it in mind,' Dwyer said awkwardly. 'Thanks again for the paper.'

Baker ignored him.

Dwyer then returned to his bunk and immediately started to write:

My Dearest Sally,
    No doubt, you know where I am by now. It must seem pretty unbelievable to you. It does to me. Everything has happened so fast.

I just want to say how sorry I am about the other day. I should have just walked away. I hope though, that you realise that I tried to and they didn't give me a lot of choice.

I don't know what Gavin or Williams would have told you at the Police Station, but by going with Major Carter was my only chance of avoiding prison – this seemed to me to be a better option.

I hope so.

The fact that I do not know when I am going to see you again absolutely breaks my heart. It already feels that we have been apart for ages.

Please don't worry. It is actually okay here and there is one bloke that I have met, called Danny Brooks, who is a decent lad. At least I have made one friend already. The rest of the men are really good blokes as well. Those I have met are at least.

I do not know when I will be able to write again so please know that I absolutely love you to death and I am missing you so much it makes me want to cry.

Take care of yourself sweetheart.

I love you

Davey

p.s. Say Hi to your mum and dad for me.

Dwyer kissed the letter before sealing it in the envelope, wrote Sally's address on it and walked out of the block. He was turning the corner to the administration block where he ran into Garcia and his two stooges.

They were all smoking.

On seeing Dwyer, they stood shoulder to shoulder and blocked his path.

Morons.

'Good evening, lads,' said Dwyer instead. 'Can I get by please?' He said, with a wide grin on his face.

They did not move. They appeared to Dwyer to try to give their toughest stares, which had the opposite effect they desired.

Dwyer started to laugh in their faces.

As they still appeared not to have any attention of moving, Dwyer said, 'Get the fuck out of my way or I will move you.'

He had stopped laughing.

Garcia stood aside and said, 'After you, chief,' without any expression on his face.

Dwyer walked through the gap Garcia had created with his fists clinched. He deliberately kept Garcia in his peripheral vision.

Nothing happened.

A sense of disappointment overcame him. He was just in the mood for a bit of a tear up after dwelling on the fact that he was now separated from Sally. He would have gladly accommodated all three of them if they had been up for it.

They are definitely have something in mind for me at a later date, he thought.

Watch your back.

Really?

As he was about to open the door to the administration block, Dwyer heard Garcia call him an 'asshole'. He stopped, turned round and walked towards him.

'Say something?' He said when he stopped and was only a few feet away.

Garcia took a step back before saying, 'Not a word, chief. You must be hearing things.'

'Thought so,' Dwyer said casually. 'I didn't think you had the balls to repeat it, you coward piece of shit.'

Garcia glared at him, his eyes wild with fury. Hickey and Henderson's eyes were wide with fear.

Dwyer began to smile again. He then shook his head, chuckled and then turned round to deliver his letter.

He did not look back.

While delivering his letter, Dwyer asked for confirmation three times before he was satisfied that the Staff Sergeant was going to make sure it was posted. He would have asked a fourth time but the Sergeant had turned his back on him after saying, '*YES . . . Enough already!*'

When he returned outside – fully expecting another confrontation, and still totally up for the exercise – they had gone.

He went back to his block and went straight to bed. He was exhausted again. The writing of the letter to Sally had also left him emotionally drained.

Such was his tiredness, no dreams were to be had that night.

19

Dwyer woke up next morning due to the sound of a door slamming, to find he was almost alone in his accommodation block. His new alarm clock had let him be this morning.

Where the hell is everybody?

In a state of confusion, he quickly washed, dressed and then jogged to the food hall.

The room was absolutely buzzing.

He looked round the room and tried to find Brooks. He was nowhere to be seen. However, he did receive the customary glares form his latest three admirers.

Again, he smiled back at them.

His second look round the room was more successful, Brooks was now stood up and waving him over. He waved back, but decided to get some food first.

When eventually joining Brooks, he asked what all the fuss about. Brooks could hardly contain himself and spoke so rapidly, that Dwyer had to get him to repeat his news twice. The word was; they were going tonight.

Too fast.

Brooks ended the news by saying, 'The waiting is finally over.'

What do you mean; the waiting is finally over?

I only just arrived!

Once it had fully registered what he had been told, Dwyer felt like his stomach did a summersault . . . several times. Sweat immediately formed on his brow and his shoulders started to ache.

Since arriving at Greenham Common, everything had seemed to be no more than a great adventure. The severity of his situation now meant that he felt like someone was pressing down on his shoulders. He was also suffering from the same shortness of breath he had previously when meeting with Williams back in the police station in Portsmouth. He sat down next to Brooks and pushed his tray away from him.

He no longer felt like eating. Instead, he took five huge breaths and let out an enormous belch.

He ignored the several looks of disapproval from his table companions. He now felt marginally better. The lack of etiquette alleviated the tightness in his chest.

'You okay?' Brooks said noticing that the colour had drained from Dwyer's face.

No.

Dwyer nodded his head, blinking rapidly.

Oh, great! Now I can't see shit!

'Not eating that?' Brooks said.

Does it look like I am?

Dwyer shook his head. Brooks immediately tucked in.

It's for real now Davey boy.

It is.

No more playing at cowboys and Indians in the field, firing at rocks.

No.

You get to go in a plane tonight for the first time – and then jump out of it.

Thanks for the reminder.

Then you will probably be shot at.

Enough already. Shut the hell up.

Dwyer's voice of reason got the better of him. He placed both his elbows on the table, held his head in his hands and then groaned.

What was I thinking?

What have I got myself into?

I am not ready for this.

Aint that the truth.

His stomach agreed. It growled, did a further summersault, and then growled again. Dwyer knew it was not because he was hungry. He suddenly concentrated on his bowels, ensuring that everything was clenched . . . tight.

When he was confident that he could fart with confidence, he did so . . . loudly.

'Jesus Christ,' a voice said from further down the table. 'Were you brought up in a pig sty?'

Dwyer ignored the question.

'So this is it then?' He said, to nobody in particular.

Brooks assumed he was talking to him and said, 'Looks that way.'

It was 05h30 hours.

20
4th June 1944
HMS Dryad, Southwick, England

The weather for the two days previous had been excellent with clear blue skies and hardly any wind. It had however started to deteriorate. It had become cloudy and the wind had come up.

Eisenhower had set a conference for 04h00 hours to get a final update on the weather. Many ships had already departed their various ports and were now sailing in the channel and forming up convoys. He was advised that the weather was to get worse throughout the 5th June and asked his subordinates for their view. With a difference of opinion, Eisenhower made the decision to postpone for at least one day.

This was at 06h00 hours.

21

During the 4th June, the troops in the 101st Airborne had started to pack their equipment and carry out numerous weapons checks.

Dwyer felt completely empty in side and walked around as if in some kind of trance. He checked his rucksack repeatedly to ensure he had not forgotten anything.

He was finding it incredibly difficult to concentrate. So much so, he had not noticed the commotion that had broken out in the block all around him.

Brooks approached him and noticed that he was still as white as a ghost. He stood still and watched him taking his equipment and weapons in and out of his rucksack.

Dwyer was oblivious of his presence.

'Is everything okay, Moose?' He said, with a concerned look on his face.

So fast – too fast!

'What? What did you say, mate?'

'I said, is everything okay? You look like shit, man.'

Dwyer saw Brooks' mouth move but could not make out what he was saying. He noticed that he had a very quiet ringing in his ears. In addition, he had to keep blinking his eyes to regain any normal kind of focus.

His vision was still screwed up.

'What did you say, mate?' Dwyer said again.

'I said is everything okay?' Brooks said. Only this time, he shouted.

After one final high-pitched ring in his ears, everything at all once returned to focus for Dwyer, including his hearing. He took a deep breath and said, 'I am having a nightmare mate. I keep thinking I am going to forget something,' and then looked down at the rucksack suspiciously as if it was conspiring against him.

Brooks grinned his toothless grin, and said, 'Well it doesn't matter now, does it?'

Eh?

'What do you mean, it doesn't matter now?' Dwyer said quickly, wondering how Brooks could possibly find anything to smile about.

To his annoyance, the smile broadened.

'Didn't you hear? It has been postponed because of the bad weather. The word is, we are going tomorrow night instead,' Brooks said and then nodded his head vigorously to confirm that it was true.

Didn't your hear? It has been postponed. We are going tomorrow night, because of the weather.

Obviously not. For fucks sake!

Dwyer sat down on his bunk, what seemed to Brooks to be in slow motion, and put his head in hands. He let out a large groan and then lay down fully outstretched. His feet were hanging over the end of his bunk, which struck Brooks as comical. He managed to hide his amusement as he could see Dwyer was struggling emotionally – big time.

You have been banging on about it being 'too fast'.

Now it is slower.

What is your problem?

Brooks was about to leave him be when Dwyer said, 'I aint ready for this, mate. Two days training is bullshit. What have I let that Major get me involved in? Right now, the prison option seems better to me.'

Brooks' brow furrowed. He did not understand Dwyer's reference to prison. He was about to ask him what he meant by it, when he heard a voice behind him say, 'Will you accompany me back to my office, Corporal Dwyer?'

Brooks turned round to see Major Carter standing there. He looked back at Dwyer who was slowly getting to his feet.

He still looked like shit.

22

On arriving in his office, Carter turned to Dwyer and said, 'Ready start to smoking yet, Corporal?'

Dwyer forced a smile, shook his head, and said, 'Not yet.'

'Perhaps you would prefer something a little stronger then?' Carter walked behind his desk and opened a draw in his desk. He produced a bottle without a label on it and two glasses. He poured them both a generous measure and handed a glass to Dwyer.

'Thanks very much,' said Dwyer. He inspected the contents of the glass and then added, 'Cheers.' He downed it one gulp.

'I see Private Brooks has not had much success with regards to your etiquette training,' Carter said with a hint of a smile.

Dwyer was trying not to splutter everywhere, as the liquid that assumed was whisky, burned all the way down to his stomach. It made him feel immediately light headed. He shook his head and eventually said, 'Must have slipped his mind.'

Carter leant towards Dwyer and refilled his glass with and even more generous measure.

'Thanks very much,' he said again. What is this? It's good stuff.'

'Brandy.' Carter said without elaborating further. He studied Dwyer's face carefully who was now only taking a few small sips at a time.

'As you will now by know, the likelihood that we go tomorrow night is very high.' Carter then paused and waited for a reaction. On not receiving one, he continued.

'We will be boarding the same plane and our mission will be to take out the German defences close to the beach. Your role will be to remain close to me and to protect me all times. I will jump first and then you will follow. Considering your size, you will probably go past me on the way down. I will then follow you. Then I will find you on the ground. Is that clear?'

Dwyer took a larger sip this time and then said. 'I am really looking forward to that I can tell you. Never been in a plane before and thought of jumping out of it in the dark into God knows what aint my idea of great night out.'

Carter could not agree more. Now that the waiting was *finally over*, Carter found himself smoking more and more. He reached for his pack on his desk, took one out, lit it, inhaled and then blew his customary smoke rings.

Dwyer watched their progress to the ceiling before they slowly lost their form and then dissipated completely.

'You will be fine, Corporal.' Carter said eventually. 'Private Brooks has informed me that you are an excellent shot, and your jump training went well eventually. Any man that states he is not scared or nervous about going tomorrow is only fooling himself. It is a perfectly natural emotion.'

'Including you?' Dwyer said.

Carter nodded. 'Including me.'

Dwyer finished his drink and put the glass on the desk hoping that Carter would fill it up again.

He did not. He simply said, 'I will see you tomorrow. Make sure you try to get plenty of sleep tonight.'

Dwyer got to his feet and said, 'Thanks for the drink,' and left.

Oops!

I forgot to salute again!

23

As Dwyer arrived back at the accommodation block, Brooks joined him immediately. The grin of his face had now disappeared. He seemed to Dwyer to be highly agitated.

He started to tell him about his hometown of Wilmington in the States, and proudly showed him a picture of his sweetheart waiting for him back home. She reminded Dwyer of Sally a little, as she too was blonde-haired and blue eyed. As far as Dwyer was concerned, there was no comparison in their beauty.

Sally makes her look like a right uggerbug.

He kept his thoughts to himself.

Dwyer wondered why Brooks had now decided to share his private life with him. No such conversation had taken place before. He guessed that this was his way of dealing with his own insecurity and anxiety and allowed him to continue without interruption. Even when Brooks repeated for a fourth time how they planned to marry as soon as he returned, Dwyer smiled and nodded and urged him to continue. If that was his way of dealing with his anxiety, he was happy to help. He just wished that he knew what his was.

It was then Dwyer realised that he did not have a picture of Sally with him and suddenly found himself with an overwhelming desire to cry. The feeling consumed his every thought. When Brooks started in on his fifth rendition of his marriage plans, he excused himself and retuned to his bunk and began to brood.

It was not that Brooks' ramblings had started to bore him; he just started to feel guilty. Guilty about the fact that he had not asked Sally to marry him. Most of his friends were married. Some already had children. They all seemed happy enough. They still found time for their friends. Friday nights were sacred. Nothing could get in the way of blowing a proportion of their weekly wage on the local brew. Nothing could get in the way of the weekly male bonding session. The difference was; they went home to a welcoming warm bed.

He went home alone.

Now that he was with Sally, the days of picking up a more than willing slapper five minutes before last orders was over. He did not even miss the days of waking up on a Saturday morning and find himself wishing to chew his arm off rather than waking up some of the monsters he had picked up in the past. He did not miss have to come up with excuses of why he could not spend the rest of the day with them. He did not miss counting the seconds before they finally dressed and left him to suffer from his hangover in peace.

Why had he been so pigheaded about remaining single? Why? A question that was now playing heavily on his mind.

Rather than torture himself further, he swung his legs over the side of his bunk and looked around the block. Rather than the normal games of cards, guitar playing and loud banter, Dwyer noticed that there was now an eerie silence. Most were either lying or sitting on their bunks staring off into space. Some appeared to be reading letters from loved ones, one of the youngest of the group appeared to be wiping tears from his cheeks.

Dwyer was in two minds to go over and try to comfort him. Talk to him about anything just to get his mind off his own inner demons. He immediately thought better of it. He wanted to be left alone. No doubt, the young lad did as well. He left him be.

His thoughts then returned to home and Sally. Rather than dwell on them, he stood and walked towards the forever praying Private Baker.

'Heh, Baker. Is it okay if I borrow some more of your paper?'

Baker did not acknowledge him. He was on his knees by the side of his bed, and true to form, he was praying for forgiveness for this that and the other.

Rather than interrupt his attempt at salvation, he reached over the top of Baker's head and just took a single piece of paper and an envelope, which was loose on the middle of his bed.

'Okay if I take this?' Dwyer said.

Again, Baker ignored him.

He returned to his bunk and sat down to write a further letter to Sally.

His mind went blank.

What the hell am I supposed to put in this letter?
Just tell her what you are feeling.

Maybe, but I am not sure what that is right now.
Silence.
What the hell am I supposed to put in this letter?
Silence.

He gave up trying to force the words and looked round the room once more. He noticed that one of the blokes kissing his own letter and then placed it in the front top left pocket of his camouflage jacket.

Must be a 'if I do not make it back letter'.
Must be.

He began to write:

My Dearest Sally,
If you are now reading this letter, it will mean that I will not be coming home. I am so sorry sweetheart.
I am not going to tell you to not to be sad as I know this to be a stupid thing to say. I just want you to know that you were the love of my life and my true soul mate.
I can only be thankful of the time we spent together. I was a very lucky man.
I will always be with you.
Your Davey
x

He then placed the letter inside the envelope, addressed it, then picked up his jacket and placed it his pocket.

He had never felt so miserable and alone in his life.

24
5th June 1944
HMS Dryad, Southwick, England
03h30 hours

Eisenhower was driven to Southwick House from his trailer through the mud, the wind and the rain. It was still not too late to postpone again and delay to the 19th June, which would mean ordering the ships back to harbour. This order could be given by him and him alone.

The previous evening as the gale force winds once again rattled the mansions doors and windows, Eisenhower had once again asked for the opinions from the Allied High Command seated around the long table in the library.

Leigh-Mallory wanted to delay to the 19th. Both Ramsey and Tedder were reluctant, Smith believed it to be a gamble. Montgomery said, 'I would say go.' At 21h45 hours, the Supreme Commander made a preliminary decision and stated, 'I am quite positive that the order must be given.' The final decision would be made after attempting to try to get a few hours troubled sleep. There would be still time to change his mind.

Everything now hinged upon the weather briefing. Eisenhower called for meteorologist Captain J.M. Stagg. With a confident grin, Stagg advised that the storm would break by dawn. After pacing the room, where the minutes seemed to turn into hours, the Commander turned to his staff and said quietly but firmly, 'Okay. Let's go.'

In under a minute the room had emptied as the commanders rushed from their chairs to get to their command posts. The Invasion of Europe had begun.

PART THREE

Invasion

attack, assault, foray, incursion, offensive, raid.

1

When the order had reached Greenham Common, Dwyer found himself feeling surprisingly relieved. He now just wanted to get it over and done with. An air of calm had now seemed to come over him as opposed to the anxiety that had gripped him the day before.

In the afternoon, he started getting ready for battle. He organised his M-1 rifle, 160 rounds of ammunition, an assortment of five grenades, a knife, a bayonet and a pistol. In addition, a Mark IV antitank mine was added to the already considerable weight along with a *'clicker'* that was used to be as recognition devise. One *click-click* was to be answered with two *click-clicks*. He also had three days of field rations, first aid kits, a gas mask and three cartons of cigarettes. He only took the cigarettes to give to the Major.

After the process of checking and re-checking that all was present and correct, he then gathered around with the rest of the men in his regiment and received a last pep talk. This was then followed by their platoon leaders giving out some final instructions.

The 101st however were honoured. Eisenhower, who had spent the morning in Portsmouth watching the ships leaving, had made the journey to Greenham common and had arrived at the base about 19h00 hours. He was circulating amongst the troops trying to boost morale. Dwyer heard him say to one soldier, 'I've done all I can; now it is up to you.'

Dwyer made a conscious decision to try to avoid being questioned by him. He believed that Eisenhower would think it strange that a Brit was dressed in combats and ready to go to war with them, at least within the same Division. The game would be up as soon as he opened his mouth and he heard his accent.

He could not take his eyes of him.

The very presence of the great man commanded respect and it appeared to Dwyer at least that if his visit was in fact to improve morale, it was definitely working.

As he wondered round the group of troops, he came across Brooks and Carter. They both nodded a welcome. Dwyer bent down slightly to whisper in their ears simultaneously and said, 'The great man isn't very big, is he?' Smiles broke out all around.

Unbeknown to them, Garcia, Henderson and Hickey were observing them from behind.

All were wearing their customary scowls.

'Quite the little threesome, aren't they? They will be holding hands and taking windy walks together next,' said Garcia.

'Not for long though, eh Tony?' said Hickey.

'No.' Garcia replied. 'You got that straight,' he added while slowly nodding his head. 'Not for long.'

2

At 22h00 hours, the order was given to 'chute up.' Dwyer failed miserably whilst trying to buckle his parachute up and Brooks had to help him.

So fast.

Too fast.

'You sure you have put it on right?' Dwyer said when Brooks had finished.

'I think so,' replied Brooks.

Dwyer looked at him with a horrified look on his face, which remained until Brooks winked at him. They both then burst out into laughter. It was a welcome relief to both of them. It broke the tension that they were both now inevitably feeling.

I cannot believe I fell for that.

Dick head!

Again, they were being observed. Again, they were having aspersions being cast on them.

'You will not be laughing for much longer, you Goddamn limey bastard,' Garcia said through gritted teeth. 'You may as well make the most of it while you can.' He then began to smile thinking of what he had in store for him.

Dwyer and Brooks then marched towards their designated Dakota C-47, which had three white bands painted around the fuselage and both wings. They fell into line behind Major Carter who looked to Dwyer that he did this sort of thing every day. He could not believe how calm and relaxed he looked and wondered what he was really feeling inside. As Dwyer boarded the plane, he noticed Garcia, Henderson and Hickey up in front.

Happy Days!

Why did those three morons have to be on my plane?

Watch your back.

Don't you mean, watch my front?

To what seemed immediately to Dwyer, his plane started its engines along with every other.

The noise was deafening.

It then lurched forward and started to taxi towards the runway. Dwyer closed his eyes, the anxiety had returned and his chest felt like that he had swallowed a rhino sideways. True to form, he took in three large gulps of air and then let out a loud belch accidentally in Carter's right ear.

You can shove your etiquette, he thought.

Carter acted is if nothing had happened. Unbeknown to Dwyer, he was crapping himself, but nonetheless, his expression remained stoic.

The plane then turned left and slowly and came to a brief stop. The engines then started to scream and just when it seemed they must surely explode, the pilot released the breaks and the Dakota started lurching down the runway.

Dwyer closed his eyes and whispered, 'Fuck,' repeatedly. Nobody heard him over the noise of the engines. Half of the men were joining him in the chorus.

This was followed by a series of jolts and shudders until it finally left the ground and gradually crawled up into the night's sky. Dwyer had suddenly found religion. He closed his eyes and instead of whispering obscenities, he began his own special way of talking to the heavens above.

Jesus Christ! Oh my God!
You have never been a God botherer before.
Now's a good time to start as any.
What makes you think he is going to answer your prays?
Never too late to start.
Yeah? Well, he is probably busy right now answering everybody else's on this plane.
Including Garcia, Hickey and Henderson?
No, but Baker is probably monopolising his time – get to the back of the queue.

Eisenhower had been standing at the side of the runway calling out, 'Good luck,' and waving. When returning to his car after the last plane had taken to the skies, he said quietly to his driver, 'Well – it's on.'

3

Dwyer eventually found the courage from deep within and opened his eyes. He glanced around the plane at his fellow passengers. No one appeared to be talking. Everyone seemed lost in their own thoughts. One of the troops appeared to have fallen asleep which considering the noise, Dwyer thought to be unbelievable.

Private Baker was holding some rosary beads and was praying.

Told you.

Carter then interrupted his thoughts by saying, 'Remember, I will jump first and you are to follow me immediately. Do not attempt to find cover when you reach the ground until I have found you. If I am not with you by five minutes, carry on without me.'

Do not attempt to find cover! Are you having a laugh?

Dwyer nodded . . . reluctantly.

With that, Carter then looked forward and appeared to Dwyer to be staring at Garcia.

Brooks had taken the picture of his girlfriend out from his jacket pocket. He was staring at it and appeared to be gently stroking the face of the image that was smiling up at him.

Dwyer now concentrated on the pain in his chest. He consciously slowed down his breathing and tried to take his mind off his current situation by thinking of home.

The fact that he had been seconded to the Royal Navy was a big enough adventure as far as he was concerned. The army recruitment officer had made sure of that. The thought of sailing into the channel for the first time and repairing any ship that was in distress appealed to him. At least he would be able to sit his own grandchildren on his knee one day and tell them of his participation in the war. He smiled to himself on thinking how different his stories would be now.

So fast.

His thoughts now turned to Sally. There was no doubt in his mind that he wanted her to be the mother of his children. He was now furious with himself that he had not proposed to her before now. He could not imagine with being anyone else and he was sure she felt the same way. She had after all dropped enough hints. If he ever got out of the mess he now found himself in and eventually made it home, it would be the first thing he did.

Why didn't you tell her that in your letter then you idiot?

He closed his eyes again and tried to keep his anxiety in check by trying to remember specific moments with her.

The first image that immediately sprung to mind was the night he had met her on the beach at Southsea. He had been walking along it with a friend with a couple of bottles of beer. Both of them were occasionally throwing stones into the Solent.

After hearing girlish laughter behind him, he turned to see the two girls that had been following them, about ten yards behind.

He was immediately drawn to Sally and her blue eyes that seemed to be sparkling at him. He then noticed her long blonde hair that was being blown about in all directions by the wind and her frantic efforts to keep it under control. On realising that he was staring at her with his mouth open, he consciously made the effort to give her his best smile.

It was Sally that spoke first. 'By the looks of the size of you, you could probably throw those stones over to the Isle of Wight,' she said with a cheeky grin on her face.

He smiled to himself at the memory while still keeping his eyes closed.

The second thought was when she had finally agreed to go back to his flat with him one night. Just as Dwyer was reliving the moment when he first took off her bra . . .

His brow started to furrow as unwanted horrifying image suddenly appeared.

DAAVVEEYYY! Nooooo! The door of Williams' office slammed shut behind her.

What goes around comes around a voice behind him said.

Dwyer's eyes snapped open. He was looking straight at Garcia who was grinning at him.

4

> 'When you look into the abyss,
> the abyss also looks into you.
> - Friedrich Nietzsche

Carter was off on one again.

'There is over 430 Dakota's carrying the 101st Airborne into Normandy.'

'That many?' Dwyer said trying to look interested. He was actually more concerned with the look on Garcia's face.

Carter nodded enthusiastically. 'Yes. Right about now, our planes are probably spread across about 300 miles and flying in V formation without radio contact.'

Dwyer forced a smile.

Garcia mistook it for it being aimed his direction. He immediately began to scowl. Dwyer's smile broadened.

This bloke is so easy to wind up. It is not even a challenge.
Maybe.
I know. Watch your back.

'Our altitude while crossing the channel will be about 500 feet to try and escape radar detection. Only when we fly over the Channel Islands will we climb to about 1,500 feet to avoid the German antiaircraft batteries, and then return to about 600 feet when we reached the French coast,' Carter added.

Is his little story trying to make me feel better?

The smile was removed.

On noticing the concerned look on Dwyer's face, Carter got the hint. The remainder of the flight was spent in silence.

At almost exactly at the point where the sea meets land, the sky lit up with explosions, tracers and searchlights.

Oh, crap.

Dwyer's Dakota started to twist and turn violently which threw the men around like rag dolls and sent cargo scattering around all over the floor.

They had been standing since flying over the Channel Islands in readiness. There was then an enormous jolt and the Dakota's engine noise started to whine, splutter and then whine again. The light above the door turned from red to green, which was their signal to jump. While the troops were trying to scramble to their feet, the Dakota banked sharply to the left with the engines now screaming which sent the men flying around the cabin again whilst they were trying to hook up. Two troops fell out of the open door screaming into the night.

Dwyer felt himself being hauled to his feet. He looked round to see Carter screaming into his face shouting, *'Follow me.'*

They both hooked up.

Carter then appeared to dwell at the door. 'We are going too quickly,' he shouted over his shoulder towards Dwyer. He looked down, staring into the abyss below and then without further delay, threw himself from the plane. Without hesitation, Dwyer did the same. They were closely followed by Brooks.

It all happened so quickly –

so fast

that Dwyer did not had a chance to feel the fear that he fully expected to grip him when it was his time to jump. He had imagined that they would form an orderly line and then wait to take your turn.

He looked up above him and saw with great relief that his parachute had opened and he was gently descending to earth, although it did appear to him to be too quickly.

SO FUCKING FAST!

He then noticed a handful of troops following him down who appeared to be on a different heading to him. He started to wonder where the others were, when he noticed the plane he had been in only a few seconds earlier bank sharply left and screamed downwards back out to sea. To his horror, it did not pull up and crashed into the channel in the distance.

He could not see the Major.

Dwyer looked away down to the ground trying to pretend that he had not just witnessed the horror of the plane crashing. He then noticed that it was rapidly coming up towards to meet him.

He appeared to be coming down into the middle of a field and noticed a number of shapes in the darkness almost immediately beneath him. While he was desperately trying to remember what Brooks had told him in the hangar on how to land, he hit the ground.

Instinct took over and he performed the landing perfectly. After rolling onto his side, he sprang to his feet, pulled in his chute and unbuckled it. He then knelt down on one knee and resembled an athlete about to start a sprint race.

Everything was deathly quiet.

To his dismay, it appeared that nobody else had landed anywhere near him. Certainly not in the same field.

Thank God that is over and done with!

No shit . . . talking of which –

The smell gave away what the objects were that he had noticed when descending to the ground.

'Cows,' he said to himself and then immediately hoped there was not a bull in the field with him. He quickly checked them all quickly for any pointy horns that he hoped would not be sticking out of their heads.

None did.

They had all stopped chewing on the grass. Each and every one of them seemed to be now staring in his direction.

His concerns regarding the gender of the occupants he shared the field with were soon forgotten. He realised that while performing his landing, he had rolled through a cowpat. He was now covered from head to toe, in foul smelling crap.

'That's just absolutely great,' he said to himself and then tried to make himself as small as possible – which wasn't easy considering his size – and started to wait for Carter.

5

Dwyer was still alone in the middle of the field ten minutes later – it seemed to him to be ten times longer – except for the cows who had now lost interest in him and had all returned to getting back to the business of chewing the grass, and to Dwyer's adolescent amusement, occasionally farting incredibly loudly.

'Be careful you don't eat your own shit,' he whispered at them. It was everywhere and the smell of his camouflages was now making him feel sick. He was not used to the country air and at this particular point in time; he thought he never would be.

No, sir. Give me the smell of diesel fumes and oil any day of the week.

Yeah, and twice on Sunday's.

I hate cows!

It felt like he had been waiting for Carter for hours.

Where is he?

Just as he decided that he had better start looking for any of the other troops, he heard a *click-click*. The sound was coming from the corner of the field where the only gate was located. The cows also gave away where from where the sound originated from as they in unison lifted their heads, still chewing, and looked towards it.

One click-click is responded by two click-clicks.

Yep, definitely.

You sure?

Oh, bollocks! . . . I think so . . .

Go for it.

Dwyer eventually took out his own *clicker* form his jacket pocket and returned two *click-clicks*. On not hearing any kind of response, he stood up and slowly crept towards the gate in a stooped position. When he was about twenty feet from it he whispered, 'Who's there?'

'It's me.'

'Who is it?' Dwyer said unable to hide his irritation in a now louder whisper.

'Keep your voice down.' Brooks appeared from behind the hedge and gave him the thumbs-up. They walked towards each other and hugged.

Dwyer could have kissed him. He was so relieved that he was now not on his own. The fact that it was Brooks made it all the better.

'Oh my God,' said Brooks pulling away from Dwyer quickly. 'You stink like shit, man.'

'You are not wrong. That is exactly what it is. I landed in it!'

Both men then literally bit into their fingers to stop themselves from bursting out laughing.

Once both had stopped seeing the funny side of Dwyer's predicament, with Brooks making every effort to keep a suitable amount of distance between them, Dwyer asked, 'Have you seen the Major?'

Brooks shook his head. 'The last time I saw him was when he jumped out of the plane. You are the first one I have come across.'

'Others got out. I saw them when I looked up to see if my chute had opened. I saw at least four but one of them must have been you. Did you see what happened to the plane?'

Brooks just nodded and looked at the ground. It was clear to Dwyer that he did not want to talk about it. He had no doubt just lost some close friends. The subject was not brought up again.

On looking back up again at Dwyer, he said, 'Okay, let's get rid of our chutes, then go and try to find the Major. You never know, we might find some others along the way. No offence, Moose, but I think our chances of taking on the German army on our own are pretty slim.'

'Don't seem to be anyone around here, mate. We are in the middle of nowhere,' Dwyer said.

WATCH YOUR BACK!!

'That's for sure,' said Brooks nodding in agreement. 'Keep your eyes open though. One thing I do know is that we are nowhere near where we are supposed to be and I do not have a clue where.'

Dwyer's earlier felt euphoria when he met Brooks left him as quickly as it had arrived. They were supposed to be with a whole regiment; not standing in a field up to their ankles in cow shit playing hunt the Major.

They both set about digging shallow holes with their bare hands and then covered over their chutes with the mud. They both added a few leaves and twigs for good measure.

'That will do,' said Brooks. 'If anyone should happen to find them, we will be long gone. C'mon, let's get out of here.'

They then crept along the edge of the field staying close to the hedgerow. Dwyer continually kept looking over his shoulder into the surrounding dark countryside. He could not shake off the eerie sensation that they were being watched.

After just over one hundred yards, they reached the end of the field. Dwyer could see over the top of the hedgerow that now blocked their progress and could see that a narrow lane was on the other side below. A six-foot high bank led up to the field in which they were standing. On the other side of the lane was a small brick wall.

Click- Click

Both Dwyer and Brooks froze and stared at each other with open mouths. Eventually, Brooks responded with two *Clicks* of his own.

They walked about 10 yards along hedgerow where they then found a gap just about big enough to get through. Immediately, they both scrambled through sending a number of the local bird population chirping their protests up into the night's sky. They both looked to their right and saw a figure slumped against the wall in the lane. Both slipped as they scrambled down the bank.

'Not very stealthy, are you? I could hear you coming from fifty yards away,' said Major Carter in a pained voice. 'Why don't you just fire off a couple of shots and announce our presence, once and for all?'

'Is everything okay, sir? Are you hurt?' Brooks asked as he rushed towards him.

'I hit this wall when I landed. I think I may have broken my ankle. I cannot put any weight on it. Not without wanting to scream at least.'

Even though Brooks did not have any medical training, he bent down to examine the Major's ankle. He very carefully undid the laces on his left boot and slowly removed it from his foot. He then gently squeezed the ankle, which was already swollen to double its normal size.

Dwyer stood in the middle of the lane rapidly looking one way and then the other. His eyes were playing tricks on him. Every bush and tree now appeared to transforming into a German soldier, just waiting to put a bullet in his head.

The Major's face contorted into agony and it took every ounce of his self-control not to let a blood-curdling scream.

'Sorry Major,' said Brooks as he jumped away from him, fearing the Major might lash out in some kind of retribution. He then added, 'You said you can't put any weight on it. Have you tried to get up?'

Dwyer snapped out of his paranoia.

Blimey Brooksie, not even I would have asked such a dumb question, he thought. He then immediately resumed his search of the hedgerows.

'Of course I have tried to get up. How the fuck else would I know that I cannot put any weight on it, Private?' Carter whispered angrily through gritted teeth.

'Yes sir, of course sir, sorry sir,' said Brooks looking suitably shame faced.

The Major's expletive now had Dwyer's complete attention. It was obvious for all to see that he had lost his normal calm demeanour. He stopped looking one way and then the other up and down the lane and studied Carter. 'Well you can't stay sat in the middle of this lane. We need to get you hidden,' he said.

Brooks nodded his agreement.

He casually bent down and picked up Carter up with the ease an adult picks up a small child.

'C'mon Brooksie, jump over the wall and then take him off me when you get to the other side,' Dwyer said.

Brooks hesitated. Not for one minute did he believe that he could handle the weight of the Major as easily as Dwyer. He looked towards the wall, then at the Major who was grimacing, back at the wall and then at Dwyer.

The look on Dwyer's face made up his mind. He had *'just get on with it'* written all over it.

As he suspected, he did not manage as well as Dwyer when the weight of the Major was transferred to him. He promptly dropped him, landing broken ankle first. The Major punched the grown trying to stifle a further scream.

Brooks looked mortified while Dwyer turned away to hide his amusement, more at the mortified look on Brooks' face, rather than the Major's anguish.

Dwyer almost seemed to step over the wall, which was three feet high, and sat in front of the Major waiting for him to make some kind of recovery. The Major eventually stopped clenching his teeth and then made a conscious effort to slow down his breathing and compose himself.

'Sorry Major,' Brooks offered.

His apology was ignored.

'Okay,' Carter said eventually. 'I have absolutely no idea where we are. One of you is going to have to go down the lane and try and find some kind of landmark or road sign.'

You can do one mate.

The thought of walking along a country lane in the middle of the night with God knows what round every corner did not exactly appeal to Dwyer. He looked towards Brooks who busying himself – or pretending to at least – looking through his rucksack.

You aint kidding anyone, Brooksie.

'Well,' Carter said impatiently.

Brooks continued to make himself busy, making sure he avoided eye contact with Dwyer at all costs.

Oh, Bollocks!

'Okay – which way?' Dwyer reluctantly asked after giving Brooks a withering look, which he again pretended not to notice. He had looked up grinning from ear to ear after Dwyer had *volunteered*.

'North.'

Dwyer looked all around with an incredulous look on his face and then scratched his head. 'Which way is north?'

'Oh for Christ sake – that way,' Carter said sternly and pointed to his left.

How am I supposed to know which way fucking north is? Dwyer thought to himself, as he climbed over the wall.

You have a compass. Dick head.

Fair one.

6

Dwyer had only walked about fifty yards, when turning a slight bend in the lane, he noticed three German soldiers standing outside the door of a barn. They were all looking skyward and appeared to be in deep conversation. Dwyer made like a statue as he watched the nodding and shaking of heads. He could not hear what they were discussing, which was immaterial; he did not know a word of German.

Oh, shit! They must have heard our plane.
Really? You think!
Yeah, and if they heard it, how many others did?
Silence.
Oh, shit.

Once convinced that they had not noticed him, he took a dozen tiny backward steps round the corner until they were out of sight. He then turned and quickened his step back towards the Major and Brooks.

Jesus Christ. This is for real!
Yes. Those were real live Germans back there.
They were. What is that lying in the road?
He froze.
The image in front of him did not compute.
Is that Brooks?
Silence.

He took two silent steps forward, blinked, and then realisation struck him. Brooks was lying flat on his back in the middle of the lane. A further American soldier was kneeling down next to him and appeared to be searching through his rucksack.

How did the Major get back over the wall?
Silence.
Wait a minute –

Dwyer crept forward. When within fifty feet of the pair, Dwyer realised it was Hickey that was kneeling beside Brooks who then finally noticed him returning. He looked up at him with wide terrified eyes.

'What do you think you are doing?' Dwyer said far too loudly considering their current predicament.

Keep you Goddamn voice down will you!

Hickey did not respond . . . verbally. He simply sprang to his feet and ran towards the gap in the hedgerow.

Dwyer did likewise, and just as Hickey was about to start climbing the bank, Dwyer flattened him with a shoulder barge. Hickey jumped back up instantly and then lunged at Dwyer with his knife. Dwyer side stepped to his left, caught Hickey's arm with his right hand, and twisted it round his back putting his left hand over his mouth.

The knife fell to the ground.

He then pushed him towards to Brooks who was still laying flat on his back motionless on the road.

Dwyer did not know whether the darkness was playing tricks on his eyes but it appeared to him that Brooks had an enormous grin on his face. He also appeared to be drooling out of his mouth.

Something is very wrong with this picture.

His mouth appeared to be much lower than it should have been and at least five times larger. After staring at Brooks for a full five seconds, reality then came crashing down around him and he suddenly realised that Brooks had had his throat cut. He was not drooling. It was his blood flowing freely from the wound.

What the f -

A bomb went off inside Dwyer's head. Without saying a word to Hickey, he moved his left hand from over his mouth, grabbed hold of the top of his head, pulled it back with one swift movement slightly to the left and snapped Hickey's neck.

Crack.

He then forcibly threw Hickey's dead body to the floor and kicked it. He then knelt beside Brooks and immediately realised that he was kneeling in his blood. Two lifeless shocked eyes stared back up at him.

'Oh my God, Danny,' he said and then repeated it a further two times with his head bowed. Trying to control his emotion, he tilted his head back and stared up into the night's sky seemingly looking for some divine intervention.

Maybe you should have watched his back as well.
What the hell is going on? Americans killing each other?
For what reason?
Why Goddamn it?

His voice of reason was now silent again. It had no idea.

Eventually he looked back down towards Brooks. He took out the photograph of his girlfriend and the letter from Brooks' top left jacket pocket and put it in his own. He then jumped up with the hairs standing up on the back of his neck and quickly searched the surrounding area.

This scumbag would not act on his own. He aint got the balls. Where are Garcia and Henderson?
They are probably looking at you right now.
I know. Where are they?

There was no sign of them. After one final look up and down the lane, he bent down and picked up Brooks' body. His arms hung limply to the ground. Dwyer walked towards the wall and very deliberately, lowered him over the side before gently dropping him down the last six inches.

Although he knew Brooks was already dead, he still felt the need to be extra careful with his body. He then repeated the process with Hickey, but this time, he threw him over. Whilst doing so, he nearly tripped over something in the road.

Bollocks!

He looked down accusingly. He was ready to pick a fight with anyone or anything. It was the Major's boot. Brooks had obviously gone to retrieve it when he was jumped from behind by Hickey.

Dwyer looked for from left to right once again checking that all was quiet in the lane. He also made one final check that Garcia and Henderson were not anywhere to be seen. Satisfied that this was the case, he gathered up the Major's boot, Brooks' rucksack, the knife Hickey had dropped and then jumped over the wall.

Major Cater was still sat slumped against the wall staring at the lifeless body of Brooks with a map in his hand.

'Is there any chance of you now telling me what the hell is going on with those three bastards? That prick Hickey has just killed

Danny,' Dwyer said doing the double teapot with both hands on his hips. 'He cut his throat for God's sake.'

Carter said nothing. He just continued to stare at Brooks' body for a few seconds with a distant expression on his face and then started to study the map by torchlight.

7

Garcia and Henderson had indeed witnessed the demise of Brooks. They had also observed Dwyer take out Hickey. After following Dwyer and Brooks walking through the field after landing, they had climbed up a tree that overhung the lane. On seeing the ease at which Dwyer has disposed of Hickey, Garcia had to prevent Henderson from raising his rifle and shooting him. They too had no idea where they had landed. However, Garcia was no fool. The last thing he wanted was for a rifle shot to be heard. Before he would consider taking on the enemy, Dwyer and the Major were to be taken care of first.

As Dwyer suspected, Garcia instructed Hickey to care of Brooks, in the lane, when he had climbed over the wall opposite. He had appeared to be searching for something on his hand and knees. He had also instructed him to take care of the Major on the other side of the wall afterwards. They would all then deal with Dwyer when he returned.

Hickey had exited the field through the same gap as Dwyer and Brooks had earlier.

He then pretended to be relieved to meet Brooks.

'Thank God I am not on my own. Never thought I would be so happy to see your sorry face, Brooksie,' he had said.

On hearing Hickey move through the hedgerow and slip down the six-foot bank, Brooks had turned towards him and raised his rifle. On seeing who had made the same amount of noise that he and Dwyer had earlier, and then listening to his greeting, Brooks relaxed, located the Major's boot and told Hickey to follow him. On turning his back, Hickey grabbed him from behind and stabbed him in the neck. Then with five savage slashes from left to right, he cut his throat so deep it had severed his windpipe. Brooks made several unsuccessful attempts to gasp for breath as his life slowly escaped from him.

Why then Hickey had started to go through Brooks' rucksack rather than take care of the Major was a mystery to Garcia, one that would never be solved thanks to that bastard, Dwyer.

That was two of his lifelong buddies that he had killed and the self-control it took him to stop Henderson from blowing him away right there and then was considerable.

'We are just going to have to wait,' he whispered. 'We are going to have to find a way to jump him from behind. Failing that we will just shoot him in the back and take our chances with the noise it makes.'

Garcia, if nothing else, was realistic. There was no way if Dwyer saw them coming they would have a chance of taking him out in hand to hand combat, especially as now there was only two of them. They both waited in the tree to see what Dwyer and the Major's next move would be.

8

Dwyer had now crouched down behind the wall and was staring at the Major angrily waiting for some kind of response. The one he finally got once the Major had finished studying the map was not what he expected.

'How long would you say we were in the plane after it sharply banked left?' Carter said looking up at Dwyer.

What?

What about Danny?

'How the hell do I know, I was grovelling around on the floor getting hit on the head by the stuff flying around until you got me to my feet,' Dwyer said making a poor job hiding the irritation from his voice.

Carter stared off into space.

After looking over his shoulder and realising that the Major was looking at nothing in particular, he decided enough was enough. He could not stand the silence between them any longer.

'Did you hear what I said earlier? Brooks had his throat cut by Hickey,' and then pointed towards the body of Brooks to help emphasise his point.

Carter made the faintest nod of his head to indicate that he had heard him.

Unbelievable.

As he had still not received what he considered a suitable response, he looked up and stared off into the night's sky.

He was starting to feel panicked.

The Major had clearly lost it since breaking his ankle and not only did have to worry about the German Army, but it appeared that the he also had to worry where Garcia and Henderson were. They would no doubt try to repeat Hickey's actions on him.

Carter then finally said, 'Did you see anything of note when you walked down the lane earlier?'

Dwyer shoulders slumped. He had started to respect the Major but his total indifference to Brooks' fate was really starting to annoy and frighten him. He looked to his left and stared at nothing in particular and said, 'About fifty yards down is a slight bend. Just beyond that, there is a barn on the right. Three Germans were outside looking for our plane they no doubt heard. When I saw them, I came back. That is when I noticed Hickey kneeling over Brooks. He was going through his rucksack.' He then returned his gaze to the Major to see if the fact that Brooks was dead had now registered with him.

'That son of a bitch. I see you have taken care of Hickey though,' said Carter looking down to his right.

Dwyer was suddenly encouraged. It appeared that the Major was returning to the present moment. He waited for Carter to continue.

'No doubt Garcia and Henderson are around somewhere. Hickey would not have acted without their instruction. Keep your eyes open,' Carter said.

Watch your back.

Dwyer nodded and then quickly looked round again just to ensure that had not materialised magically out of the darkness.

'A barn sounds like a good idea to me. If you can help me up and support my left side, we can see what we can do about taking over its occupation.'

Eh?

'But first, take the ammunition from Brooks and Hickey's rucksacks. You can ditch the mines. It will make your rucksack to heavy to carry,' Carter said. 'Oh, and do not forget the cigarettes and food rations as well.'

Dwyer was still dwelling on the matter of fact statement Carter had made about taking over the barn.

'I saw three Germans come out of that barn I mentioned. I have no idea how many more there may be inside,' said Dwyer.

'That's what we are going to find out,' said Carter.

Oh, crap!

Dwyer did as instructed and packed his rucksack with the Major's aforementioned necessities after taking out the mine. He then picked up Carter and helped him over the wall. He then stared down at Brooks and said, 'What about Danny?'

'You are going to have leave him I am afraid.' Carter said and looked away down the lane towards the bend.

'We just can't leave him here. We need to bury him or something,' Dwyer said with a disbelieving expression on his face.

'We are now in the middle of a war, Corporal, not to mention lost. I am afraid that there is not time for such niceties,' Carter said now staring at Dwyer. 'Besides, we appear to be clean out of shovels, in case you hadn't noticed.'

'We could use our hands,' Dwyer said petulantly. 'We used our hands to bury our parachutes.'

'I am not arguing with you, Corporal. Now, are you going to assist me walking down this lane, or am I going to have crawl along on my hands and knees?'

I will throw you down there if you talk to me like that again.

Instead of sharing his thought process, Dwyer looked down at Brooks one last time and then reluctantly climbed over the wall. He then walked round to the left side of the Major who then reached up to put arm on his shoulder and started to hop up the road beside Dwyer. Due to the progress being so slow and the amount of noise that they were making, Dwyer just scooped the Major up and carried him in his arms.

9

When within ten yards from the barn, Carter indicated to put him down in a small drainage ditch that had started to run between the lane and the brick wall. There was just sufficient space for him to kneel down and sit in a firing position. He gestured to Dwyer to bend down so he could whisper in his ear.

'Try and see if there is any way you can see inside. Then come back and tell me what you see,' said Carter.

Dwyer stood to his full height and glanced towards the barn. Without hesitation, he slowly crept passed the ten yards of hedgerow that briefly replaced the wall and then a small driveway that led to a double door entrance to the barn. He then passed the side door that the Germans had exited from that opened straight onto the lane. He looked further down the lane, which turned to the right about fifty yards further down. He did not notice any other buildings.

The barn was part brick and part wood. The brick gave way to the wood after about three feet as if it had been deemed too costly to carry on with the more sturdy building material. There was a three-inch split in one of the word panels, which Dwyer looked through. He could see the entirety of the interior. It was almost completely empty apart from a motorbike with a sidecar attached to his left, and a square wooden table with four chairs positioned at each side. To Dwyer's relief, the three Germans he had seen earlier were the only occupants. A kerosene lamp was casting a shadow around the interior, which was hanging from a beam over the table. The soldiers were all smoking without seemingly talking. He took one more look around to make sure they were the only three. Once he had confirmed to himself that that was the case, he returned to Carter.

'It's pretty empty apart from the three Germans and a motorbike. They are all sitting round a table smoking.'

'There are definitely only three?' Carter said.

Dwyer nodded. 'Definitely. I double-checked.'

'How far is the table from the door?'

'From the door that leads onto the lane, about four paces.'

Carter just raised his right eyebrow.

'Leave it to me. Be back in a second,' said Dwyer.

I cannot believe I am doing this.

No worries. Just get on with it. It is no different from a Friday night out on the town.

Yeah, but these blokes have guns!

He returned to the side door of the barn and gently knocked on it. He then moved to the left of the door and stood with his back against the side of the barn. He heard a brief conversation and voice shout something out that he did not understand.

He waited.

Just as Dwyer was about to knock on the door again, it opened. He quickly moved to the frame of the door, which he filled, and said, 'Hello mate, how's it going?'

The German's mouth dropped open as he looked up to what appeared to him to be a foul smelling giant that had materialised in front of him from out of the darkness.

Dwyer grabbed the unsuspecting German soldier by the throat and lifted him towards the table. In only three large strides, he slammed him down on its surface. He then let go of his capture, grabbed the two others who had remain seated with stunned looks on their faces, and smashed their heads together.

Both fell to the floor.

Dwyer now returned his attention to the German soldier on the table that was starting to try to get up. Dwyer hit him with a straight right, which knocked him out cold, breaking his jaw in the process. He slipped off the table and sent one of the chairs flying to the side of the barn. Satisfied that all were unconscious, he once again returned to Carter.

That was easier than I thought.

'Job done,' Dwyer said as he bent over to pick up Carter from the ditch.

Instead of carrying Carter, he helped him hobble to the barn. On reaching the door, Carter cautiously looked inside to see the three soldiers laid out on the floor. The kerosene lamp was swaying that hung above the table. He hopped to one of the chairs and sat down.

Dwyer began to drag all three of his victims to one side of the barn and then looked towards the motorbike.

What a result.

It had its keys in it. He then turned and shut the door.

'That might come in handy,' Dwyer said and pointed towards the bike enthusiastically.

Carter looked over and nodded whilst spreading his map out on the table. He then began to study it intently. Dwyer looked over his shoulder to see for himself what was so interesting.

'We were supposed to come over the Cotentin Peninsula from the West,' said Carter whilst drawing an imaginary line with his finger across the surface of the map. His finger then abruptly stopped and pointed. 'Due to the evasive action taken by the pilot and the direction we flew in, my guess is that we are around thirty miles or so too far east of our intended drop site. That however is a complete and utter guess.'

He sat back, contemplated this for a moment, and then looked up at Dwyer with his trademark blank expression. 'I hope to God I am wrong.'

'Why's that?' Dwyer said urgently.

'Well, if my guess is correct, that puts up somewhere between Colleville-Sur-Mer and Vierville-Sur-Mer.'

'So,' said Dwyer as Carter had paused. He felt his heart now thumping in his chest almost not wanting to hear the answer.

There was then an unwanted interruption as the German laying nearest to Dwyer now started to stir. He was groaning trying to get up resting on his forearm and elbow.

Dwyer casually turned and kicked him in the head sending him straight back to his previous unconscious state.

'So,' Dwyer repeated as if nothing had just happened.

'That places us right in the middle of the beaches that the Americans will be landing on tomorrow morning, codename Omaha.'

Dwyer could not understand why the Major was so pessimistic. The fact they were to be joined by thousands of troops had to be a good thing . . . *Didn't it?*

It was not difficult for Carter to realise that Dwyer had not grasped the situation they now found themselves in, confusion was written all over his face.

'This means, Corporal, that in about three to four hours, this area we now probably find ourselves in is going to have the shit bombed out of it by the allied air forces, not to mention the bombardment from the navy before the troops land.'

Carter let this sink in with Dwyer before continuing. To his credit, Dwyer's expression remained impassive.

In addition,' Carter continued, 'The fact we have only come across three of the enemy so far, is to say the least, very fortunate. This area must be crawling with them. I can only hope if Garcia and Henderson are out there somewhere, along with any others, they avoid capture.'

The big picture fell into place for Dwyer and he nodded, 'If they find them they will start looking for more.' He paused and then added. 'Will let's just hope we find them first.'

Dwyer then put both hands flat on the table and leaned towards the Major and said, 'One question I do have though. What were you doing while Hickey killed Brooks?'

Carter slightly leant back in the chair feeling extremely intimidated and said, 'Just before Brooks went to retrieve my boot, he gave me a very small shot of morphine for the pain from his first aid kit. I am afraid I was out of it for a while, as you may well have noticed.'

Fair enough, I suppose.

Dwyer nodded. That would explain his indifferent attitude towards Brooks' murder earlier.

Carter then added, 'And by the way, Corporal, you absolutely stink. I am not sure what is worse, the pain in my ankle or your odour. I am beginning to think I need another shot.'

Dwyer smiled as he looked down at his camouflages that were stained in now *dry* cow shit and blood.

Carter folded up his map and returned it to the inside pocket of his jacket. He then took off his helmet. The next twenty seconds were spent gently massaging his temples with his index and forefingers in a slow rhythmical circular motion. He then looked towards the motorbike briefly and then down at the unconscious Germans. On looking around the barn further, he noticed their helmets that had been placed on a shelf at the back of the barn.

'We can't stay here. There is every chance that our friends here will be joined by any number of others at any time. Have you ever ridden a motorcycle before?' Carter said.

Dwyer shook his head and said, 'Nope, but there is a first time for everything. How hard can it be?' He turned to look at it suspiciously not feeling the confidence he had tried to portray.

Carter did well to hide his disappointment.

'Go and get those helmets will you,' Carter asked and nodded towards their location at the back of the barn.

Dwyer did as requested and took off his own. He tried one of them on for size, which fitted him okay. He then handed the other two to Carter.

'We need to find out our exact location. I suggest that we use the motorcycle. You cannot continue to carry me everywhere, even if you do appear to make it look effortless. We are just going to have to take the risk of the amount of noise it will make. I don't see that we have any other option.'

Dwyer was not convinced. Again, he threw a suspicious glance towards the bike.

'The darkness for the time being should hide our uniforms and we can wear their helmets. We should be okay if anyone only gets a glimpse of us passing by.'

Dwyer finally nodded his agreement and then took a jacket off one of the Germans and handed it to Carter. There was no way any one of them was going to fit him.

10

The side door that lead to the lane flew open and Henderson and Garcia walked through with their M-1 rifles both pointing at Dwyer.

'That's a damn good plan, Major,' said Henderson who for once was taking the lead. 'I think we might just have to do the same thing ourselves.'

Carter was still sat at the table whilst Dwyer was stood on the opposite side to him.

Henderson had advanced just one-step too far into the barn.

Now!

In the blink of an eye, Dwyer had parried Henderson's rifle away with his left forearm and pulled the kerosene lamp from its hook on the ceiling.

He smashed it into Henderson's face.

The remaining fuel soaked Henderson's jacket and then still lit wick ignited it. He let out an ear-piercing scream and his arms started to windmill, thrashing around his body furiously. His hands appeared to be trying to grab hold of thin air. He then backed towards Garcia who promptly pushed him away back towards Dwyer by raising his foot and shoving. Garcia then ran out of the door into the darkness.

Ignoring the flames, Dwyer picked up his rifle, which was leaning against the table, and cracked it into Henderson's chest. He went crashing to the floor. Dwyer then stamped on his chest and stabbed the bayonet attached to his rifle into the front of his neck and twisted it. Henderson's screams turned into a loud gurgling sound resembling the last of the water draining away from a bath, and then eventually, silence. Dwyer then removed a jacket from another of the unconscious Germans and put out the flames.

'Jesus Christ,' he said as he now looked towards Carter. 'They probably could have heard him screaming back in England!'

Dwyer then went to the open door and looked left and right down the lane looking for Garcia. He was nowhere to be seen.

After spending a full minute looking up and down ensuring that Henderson's screams had not attracted any unwanted visitors, he closed the door and looked towards Carter.

'Heart of a lion that one. Running off and leaving his friend, to die like that,' he said while nodding towards the door that Garcia had just fled out of.

Carter had remained motionless throughout the excitement. He had not actually witnessed Dwyer in action to this point and was amazed how coolly he dispatched of Henderson with such ease.

He had only heard the earlier attack on the three Germans whilst sat in the ditch. In addition, he was incredibly impressed of the speed of thought shown to silence Henderson and then prevent the spread of flames. The last thing they needed was for the whole barn to go up and send out a beacon to all within a mile of their position of their unexpected arrival.

He became *even* more impressed when Dwyer took the rucksack of Henderson's now smouldering back and took out the ammunition, first aid kit, food rations and cigarettes.

'Oh my God, what a smell,' Dwyer said waving the air from under his nose. The smell of burning flesh had filled the barn. 'Lucky the fire didn't get to the ammo, would have been fun if those grenades would have gone off,' he added as he now looked towards Carter for confirmation. He was now pinching his nose with his thumb and index finger.

You are a fine one to talk.

Eh?

You still smell as if you have shit yourself.

'That was extremely quick thinking, Corporal, a truly outstanding performance,' was all Carter allowed himself to say. He was actually thinking that bringing Dwyer along was the best decision he had ever made. Seventy-five percent of his problem had now gone away and he could not wish to be in better hands, especially as he was now incapacitated.

As if Dwyer was reading his mind, he said, 'Three down, one to go, eh Major? Are you ready to let me in on your little secret that you shared with Williams yet?'

'A story for another time,' said Carter smiling.

Dwyer started to laugh and then said, 'You know what. You are an American version of Williams, the way you speak and act. You sure you are not his long lost brother or something?'

Carter smiled again and said, 'I will take that as a compliment.'
If only you knew, he thought.

11

Dwyer turned the motorbike and sidecar round towards to face the entrance with the double doors. Not without first crashing it into his shin, which made him hop about like a demented frog whilst trying not to let out a cry of anguish.
You clumsy bastard.
I am aware of that thanks!
Carter had remained seated desperately trying hard not to laugh at his expense which he eventually failed by letting out sound that was more like a loud sneeze. Dwyer had looked round at the Major trying to control himself from belly-laughter and then let a small childlike giggle himself with his hand over his mouth.

'Okay here goes nothing,' said Dwyer as he climbed onto the motorcycle and turned the key in the ignition. He then stamped down on the kick-start. The engine did not exactly roar into life. It sounded more like a cat gently purring . . . Quietly.

Dwyer looked over his shoulder towards Carter and said, 'Chances are nobody will hear us on this thing.'

He then gently pulled back the throttle and slowly drove out of the barn, turned left and slowly drove round in a circle in the driveway. He then drove into the lane and parked outside the entrance to the side door of the barn.

Carter was looking at his compass. He looked up at Dwyer who had now joined him, and said, 'The way you have the bike facing is roughly north. I suggest we go as far as is safely possible and see how far from the coast we are.' He then slipped over the German jacket that Dwyer had given him earlier to cover his own.

Dwyer helped the Major into the sidecar and gave him the three extra rifles to hold that they had gained from Brooks, Hickey & Henderson, along with their own two helmets.

Dwyer then walked back into the barn to retrieve his own rifle and now over laden rucksack. 'What about them?' He said, and nodded towards the pile of unconscious German bodies.

Carter contemplated this for a moment, and then said, 'It depends how hard you hit them. If they wake up anytime soon they are going to send out the alarm.' He paused for further thought and said earnestly, 'We must make every effort not to compromise the surprise of the beach landings.'

Every effort?
That is what he just said.

Dwyer got the message. He picked up his rifle and systematically performed the same process he had done on Henderson earlier.

As he put his foot on the first Germans chest he said, 'That's for my sister,' and then thrust the bayonet into the still unconscious German neck and twisted. 'That's for my mother,' he said to the second and, 'That's for my father,' as he finished off the third.

Was that really necessary?
Yes.
You sure about that?
Not now!

By the time he was finished, his right boot and camouflage trouser leg were drenched with blood. He dragged all the bodies into one corner and then piled them on top of each other. He then placed a large piece of tarpaulin over them that he found folded up in the corner of the barn. *That will have to do,* he thought, and left.

Did that feel good?

His voice of reason persisted.

It did. I said someone was going to pay for the death of my family.
That's right, you did – BIG TIME!

As Dwyer sat on the bike he said, 'You know what it is funny?' Carter shook his head.

'I was about to go prison for accidently killing someone a few days ago, now it appears to be my job.'

Carter put on his newly acquired German helmet, and said matter of factly, 'War is hell. Let's go.'

12

Even rotten apples do not fall far from the tree. On running from the barn, Garcia had turned right and almost immediately noticed a gap in the bottom of the hedgerow big enough to crawl through, which was fortunate. The gaps were few and far between.

His mood improved when he realised it offered excellent cover. The grass at the base of the hedge was longer than anywhere else in the field. He lay flat on his stomach and peered back through it with his rifle at the ready.

He had seen Dwyer come to the door and look up and down the lane, and at one point, he was convinced that he had been spotted by him. Dwyer's gaze seemed to linger in his direction just a fraction too long.

He now realised that he had been lying there fretting unnecessarily. Dwyer and Carter had just passed him slowly on the motorbike wearing German helmets and had not even given a cursory glance in his direction.

The Major was even wearing one of their jackets!

He was in a total state of anxiety and the fact that he was so indecisive, prevented him from taking a shot at them as they passed.

He curled up in a ball in the grass and started to whimper, hugging his rifle close to his chest. So many emotions were now running through his mind at the same time he came close to putting his rifle in his mouth and pulling the trigger. His emotions changed from rage, self-pity, fear and then back to rage again. He started to rock gently back and forth. Then loneliness hit him.

He was God knows where in northern France thanks to their plane getting hit, and when he and his only two remaining buddies in the world did manage to get out, and had all landed miraculously together, that bastard Dwyer had now killed them both. If there was, one thing he was going to do was shoot the bastard.

What happened to him after that, he did not care.

Garcia slowly got to his feet and trudged through the field next to the hedgerow in the direction Dwyer and Carter had driven previous.

You never know your luck, he thought. *Maybe they will drive straight into a division of German troops.*

He quickly dismissed the idea. He wanted the satisfaction of standing over Dwyer's dead body himself. Then he would take care of the Major. He thought of lots of interesting ways of how he could do it slowly, and very, very painfully.

He started to smile. His insanity had come to the surface again.

It had been awhile.

13

Dwyer found the riding of the motorcycle remarkably easy. He was temporarily lost in his thoughts of what he had accomplished in the last few days. He had fired a gun for the first time, flown in a plane, jumped out of a plane with a parachute, landed his jump perfectly, killed three of the enemy, and now he was driving a motorcycle. He had even killed two troops that were supposed to be on the same team. Three if you counted Corporal James Carter back in Portsmouth.

His feeling proud of himself (apart from James Carter, although that he now thought that seemed fair enough considering the company he kept) abruptly came to a halt when he failed to notice a huge pothole in the lane. He rode straight over it, which had the effect of him biting his tongue in the same place previous when he attempted his first practice parachute landing in the hangar at Greenham Common.

Bollocks!

He glanced at the Major who was wincing with pain that the jolt had no doubt caused to his ankle.

Keep your eyes on the road Davey, he thought, and then started to smile.

On leaving the barn, the lane turned right at almost ninety degrees and then slowly climbed up at a hill gradually before turning left again. The lane was incredibly dark and was like driving through a tunnel due to the hedgerows on both sides and the overhanging trees. The hedgerows appeared to be huge to Dwyer, which sat on top of least six-foot banks with an occasional gap for the local farmers to enter.

The progress they were making was painfully slow and he fully expected the bike to conk out at any second.

His appearance to any one that could have seen him was comical. His helmet was bobbing up and down due to the unevenness of the lane and the lack of suspension. His right leg was also sticking out at right angles due to the fact his size made it look like a child's toy beneath him. His left knee next to the sidecar was level with his chest.

As they now started to start slightly descend a hill, Carter abruptly threw his arm in front of Dwyer and motioned to him to stop and cut the engine. He then pointed to a road sign at a junction ahead that read Saint-Laurent-sur-Mer, pointing to the right. What was to the left was anyone's guess. The sign did not indicate that there was anywhere.

Carter took out his map from his inside pocket and quickly checked his map.

He looked towards the sky and sighed heavily. 'This is the one time in my life that I wished I was wrong,' he whispered. 'We are about two miles south west of Colleville. We have to ditch this bike and take cover. Turn around and go back to the barn.'

'Why?' Dwyer said. 'We have not seen anyone yet. What's the problem?' He asked looking towards Carter.

'The problem is that St Laurent will be filled with Germans. Not all of them will be sleeping in their beds. Just turn the fucking bike round, will you?'

Oh, right. I see what you mean.

For the first time Dwyer could clearly detect panic in Carter's voice. He now followed the order without further debate.

Immediately after turning the bike round, they both noticed a gap in the hedgerows entering a field that was at such an angle that they had missed when travelling in the opposite direction. In the middle of the entrance to the field were two German soldiers standing by a machine-gun nest that was pointed directly at them.

Oh, crap.

The Germans had noticed them earlier and thought nothing of it. The fact that they had now just taken a U-turn, were stationery in front of them, and one of them had appeared to be looking at a map with a small torch, now had the better of their curiosity. They started to walk towards the two men that were on a motorcycle who were about twenty yards away.

'Give me a pack of your cigarettes,' Dwyer whispered as he as casually as possible dismounted the bike.

Carter reached into his pocket and did so.

Dwyer winked and slowly turned round to the two soldiers that were now only ten feet away. He took out a cigarette, put it his mouth, and gestured to the soldier in front of him to his left for a light by simulating striking a match.

Both of the Germans had quizzical looks on their faces. They both noticed that the huge stranger in front of them odour was overpowering and there was something not right about his uniform. Although dawn was fast approaching and some birds had already started to sing in the trees, it was still sufficiently dark enough for them not to instantly recognise it as one of their own.

The soldier to his right spoke first and appeared to be asking him a question. Dwyer looked towards him, smiled and then narrowed the gap between them. When within striking distance, he flattened him with straight a right. In the same movement, he smashed his left elbow straight into nose of the soldier to his left. Both went down as if they had had their legs chopped away with an axe.

Without looking towards Carter for any instruction this time, Dwyer took the knife from his belt and thrust it to both of the front of their necks. This was followed by a brief gurgling sound this time and Dwyer noticed that an air bubble formed and then popped at one of the entry wounds. An arc of blood also erupted from each victim, which provided an additional coating on his jacket sleeve.

On finishing the second one off he said, 'That's for bombing the shit out of my city.'

Dwyer then hauled each one up in turn, carrying them in a fireman's lift into the field where they had been guarding the entrance. He looked round for a suitable place to hide their bodies.

To his right was a ditch that was partially covered with weeds and long grass, which was about two feet in depth. After walking twenty yards up the border of the hedgerow, Dwyer placed them down in it and then moved back ten paces to see if he could notice them.

He could not.

He then took one glance around the field to ensure it was empty, which it was, and then returned to Carter.

In Dwyer's absence, Carter had sat in the sidecar and shuddered. The calmness that Dwyer demonstrated in ending the life of the two unsuspecting soldiers was something to behold. This was his first time in combat and he doubted he could carry out such a brutal execution without batting an eyelid.

Only a week earlier Dwyer was living his life as an engineer in the streets of Portsmouth, and apart from the occasional scrap with some foolhardy locals that wanted to take him on, had never had any remote armed combat experience or even training. His sudden transformation into a ruthless killer was starting to alarm him slightly.

He was not the only one that was becoming alarmed. Dwyer's voice of reason now spoke up again.

Are you actually beginning to enjoy this?
No.
You seem like you are.
It is them or us.
You could have just left them unconscious.
The Major said that we could not compromise the beach landing. They might have come round and sounded the alarm.
Oh, that's right. Blame the Major, why don't you?
Look. This is hard enough without you making it worse.
Okay. It was just an observation.
Well, just keep them to yourself in future.
Silence.
I said, just keep them to yourself.
Silence.

Dwyer suddenly stopped before leaving the field and stared down at his boots briefly. His voice of reason had a point.

What the hell is happening to me?

He then violently kicked a stone into the hedgerow, now disgusted with his actions. A startled bird squawked its disapproval at being disturbed and flew off into the night. He took a deep breath and then continued back to Carter and the motorbike.

Carter looked back towards the entrance to the field and noticed Dwyer returning. On reaching the bike and straddling the seat Dwyer said, 'What did that bloke ask me?'

Carter looked forward and shook his head.

'Boring conversation anyway,' Dwyer said with bravado that he did not feel. He then proceeded to drive down the lane back towards the barn.

Your bravado is not fooling anyone Davey – You are changing. So fast.

Carter did not offer any comment. He continued to stare in front of him searching the hedgerows for any other unseen guarded entrances that they may have missed earlier. He was thinking to himself somewhat disconcertedly that Dwyer was now beginning to enjoy himself.

14

The short journey back to the barn was considerably quicker. Apart from the initial incline after the despatching of the German soldiers, it was downhill all the way. On arriving, Dwyer swung the bike into the small driveway and parked outside the double doors.

The side door leading to the barn straight from the lane was slightly open. He was sure he had closed the door before leaving and he suddenly became extremely alert.

Alarm bells were suddenly ringing.

He also now noticed a gate at the rear of the barn for the first time that led to a field behind.

Dwyer gestured to Carter to be quiet by placing his index finger over his mouth and slowly approached the double wooden doors and placed his ear to them. He could hear a voice quietly pleading and repeating, 'I had nothing to do with it.'

Realising that the voice was speaking in English, without hesitation, he opened one of the doors and entered.

He stopped dead in his tracks.

Two German soldiers were standing over a body curled up on the floor with their guns pointed at it. He quickly estimated that they were about ten feet in front of him.

Dwyer's new found animal instinct took hold and he advanced on the nearest one to him. He punched him on the top of his shoulder, which sent the German flying into his compatriot. They both fell to the floor.

Dwyer sprang towards them and stamped on the face of the first he reached. The sound resembled a bunch of twigs being snapped simultaneously. He then dropped to his knee, taking his knife from his belt in one swift movement, and then carried out his now trademark finishing move on the second. There was a brief gasping of breath and then silence. Wide terrified eyes stared up at him.

Dwyer now stood and looked towards the soldier that was curled in a ball on the floor. He bent down towards him and pulled his shoulder back so that he could see his face. Staring up at him were the also terrified eyes of Tony Garcia.

Dwyer smiled. 'Hello mate, fancy seeing you here.'

He grabbed him by the scruff of his neck, pulled to him his feet, slapped his face with the palm of his hand and then shook him like a rag doll. He then pushed him towards the open door of the barn.

Outside, Carter was trying in vain to get out of the sidecar. The pain in his ankle prevented it. He relaxed and sat back down in the seat when he saw Dwyer exiting the barn. He was more than surprised when he realised that it was Garcia, he was manhandling out of the barn.

Garcia had been captured within a minute of walking along the hedgerow. Two Germans, who were walking to their pillbox on the coastline on the opposite side of the field, had noticed him and gone over to investigate. Such was Garcia's concentration on his thoughts about inflicting pain on the Major that he was not aware of them until they were five yards away. Once they challenged him, the game was up.

They had then dragged him back to the barn, discovered the horrendous smell and the pile of dead bodies under the tarpaulin, and then started in broken English to interrogate him.

'Look what we have here . . . The third little piggy,' said Dwyer. 'What do you want me do with him?'

Carter studied Garcia who was visibly shaking. He was then drawn to the damp patch that had appeared in the groin area of has camouflage trousers.

'Well, well, well. It seems that this cocky low-life scumbag is so petrified, he has pissed his own pants.'

Garcia began to whimper due to a mixture of the embarrassment and the fear he was feeling.

Carter continued. 'There is no way we are taking him with us. He will stab us in the back the first chance he gets.'

Garcia instantly feared the worse believing that Dwyer would deal with him the same way he had dealt with Hickey earlier. He let out a blood-curdling scream of, '*NO,*' and broke free of Dwyer's grasp. He headed straight towards the immobile Major with his hands outstretched in attempt to grab his throat.

Dwyer took one huge pace forward and grabbed the back of his collar. Without breaking a sweat, he pulled him back towards him. He then spun him round, grabbed him by the scruff of the neck with his left hand and hit on the jaw with his right, twice. Garcia crumpled to the ground in a heap.

Without a further word, Dwyer dragged Garcia's body into the barn, picked him up and threw him next to the pile of bodies he had created earlier.

A moan escaped from the German who he had stamped on earlier. Dwyer casually turned towards him, placed his left foot on his chest and ended his life with the bayonet of his rifle. He then placed his body on top of the increasing pile and replaced the tarpaulin. He then returned his attention back to Garcia to make sure he was still out.

He was.

After a brief pause for thought, he kicked him in the balls before leaving . . . really hard.

Now we are even.
Did that feel good?
You bet your arse it did.
Did you have to kill the German though?
Don't start that again.
Why didn't you finish off Garcia?
He is supposed to be on our side.
How naive are you? He is on his own side . . . Really? Go and finish him off.
No. He is supposed to be on our side. Germans is one thing. Americans would be . . . Would be murder!
Don't say I didn't warn you.

On leaving the barn, Dwyer noticed that Carter was now looking down at his map and appeared to be smiling.

'Well that appears to have taken to care of the three little pigs. Some Germans can pick him up later on. He won't be able to talk to them again anytime soon.'

On not receiving any kind of response, Dwyer continued, 'Ready to spill the beans yet on the reason why I am here? My guess is that my work here is done,' said Dwyer.

Carter continued to study the map and said without looking up, 'Maybe later.'

15

'We are here,' Carter said pointing to a dotted line that represented the lane on the map, which was just South of Saint-Laurent-sur-Mer.

'Northeast from here is a number of fields and then eventually a wooded area. At present, we are only about one mile from the coast as the crow flies. The wood is just a fraction further northeast. If we head towards it, the more chance we have of being killed by our own side due to the imminent aerial and naval bombardment. If we stay in the fields, there is a strong possibility that will be discovered due to the fact they appear to have most of the gaps in the hedgerows armed with a machine-gun.'

Fantastic!

Carter then studied the map further and nodded once he made his final decision.

'I suggest that we head for the wooded area on the bluff near Coleville and take our chances with the bombing, causing as much trouble as we can when the beach landings begin. There is also bound to be some form of shelter to take cover. More than this barn would provide. That's for sure.'

'Okay,' said Dwyer. 'You're the boss.'

Are you out of your mind? You are deliberately going towards the area that is going to be bombed.

He knows what he is doing.

Good luck with that!

'The closer we get to the coast we will no doubt come across more and more of the enemy, not to mention bunker systems, pillboxes and gun battery positions,' Carter said.

Any more bad news?

'You should know that the chance of making it to the bluff unnoticed is probably impossible.'

That would be a yes then.

'If, or when, we do engage with the enemy, we cannot fire our rifles or pistols giving away our presence here, not at least until the bombing commences. However, to this point, that does not seem to be a problem for you.'

Even he has noticed you are enjoying yourself, or appear to be.

Appearances are sometimes deceptive.

Dwyer did not comment. He just helped Carter get out from the sidecar.

They spent the next two minutes deciding the best way to carry the equipment and Carter. They ended up packing as much equipment as possible in one rucksack, which Carter would wear on his back. The remainder would be carried by Dwyer whilst carrying the rucksack in his hand. He would carry Carter on his back.

The three additional rifles they had gained from the previous deceased were left in the barn against the wall. They now had 960 rounds and 30 grenades between them.

After Dwyer has pushed the bike back into the barn, Carter climbed onto Dwyer's back and they set off towards the gate at the back of the barn.

It was 03h00 hours.

16

On entering the field, Carter immediately became anxious. Having to be carried by Dwyer was one thing. In addition, the hedgerows that surrounded the fields gave the impression of being trapped inside a large open prison.

Apart from the field in which they were now in there was absolutely no visibility of anything else that may be awaiting them, not to mention the fact that it was still fully dark due to the cloud cover. Not even the moonlight could now help them.

'What's wrong?' Dwyer said over his right shoulder.

'Nothing's wrong. Why?' Carter replied defensively.

'Bullshit. You are fidgeting about as if your arsehole is infested with a thousand fleas. Keep still for fucks sake, or I will probably drop you on your bad ankle.'

Carter blanched at the rebuke. 'Will if you must know,' he hissed. 'I was just thinking how crap your intelligence has been on the terrain we now found ourselves in.'

'What?'

'British Intelligence.'

'What the hell are you on about, British Intelligence? Are you calling me stupid or something?' Dwyer said, with every intention of now letting Carter walk.

'Not you,' Carter said with exasperation clear in his tone. 'The British Intelligence operation. Ordinarily, it is second to none. But it sure seems to have fucked up this time.'

Dwyer was far from appeased. 'Why? What's the problem?'

'Well, it seems to me that they have spectacularly failed in respect of the hedgerows that surround the fields here.'

Dwyer looked around him. It was still none the wiser and had no clue what Carter was referring too.

'What about the Goddamn hedges?'

'Look at them,' Carter said hastily. 'They are nightmare.'

'Eh?'

Carter struggled to maintain his patience. He sighed and said,

'You said you were 6 feet 8 inches, right?'

Dwyer nodded.

'Well in case you haven't noticed, most of them don't start until they are about level with your head due to the mounds of earth they are sitting on. They also appear to be almost impossible to climb through and do not seem to have any gaps in them.'

'So?'

'So, the photographs that I have seen of the area did not pick any of this up. I just hope to God that they are not all like this.'

'Why?'

'Because they will provide the German Army with excellent defending positions. That's why. Look directly to your left.'

Dwyer looked directly to his left.

'Do you see those slits in the hedge?'

Dwyer nodded.

'That is not natural. They have been cut out deliberately. They will either place a machine-gun nest at the entrance to the field or dig down into the banks as they have there, in order to fire through.'

The penny dropped. Dwyer got the picture.

Oh, crap.

Carter felt Dwyer tense beneath him. He did not cut him any slack. 'So, keep your wits about you. The fact that that slit is there may well mean that we have some company at any time.'

Dwyer did not have to keep his wits about him for long.

After they had walked just under half the length of the field, Dwyer came to an abrupt halt. He slowly bent his knees and lowered the Major to the ground. Twenty yards in front of them was a lone German soldier that was resting against a machine-gun nest. He appeared to Dwyer to be asleep. He looked over his shoulder towards Carter and shrugged them both for confirmation on what action they should take.

Carter carried out a full three-sixty observation of the field and looked at his watch.

It was now 03h05 hours.

From what he remembered from the overall invasion plans, the aerial bombardment of the area would commence around 05h15 hours. This gave them over two hours to travel the mile or so left to the wood and find suitable cover.

There was time to back track and try the other side of the field.

Just as Carter was about to advise Dwyer that this should be their course of action, the German stood up from his position, yawned, stretched and slowly turned round and looked towards them. Carter's hurriedly made plan had instantly gone out the window.

The German began to walk towards them. After ten paces, he stopped and said, *'Es ist an der Zeit, wo waren Sie?'*

Dwyer and Carter remained motionless.

After not receiving a response, he took two further paces forward, and said, *'Karl, Reiner, ist dass Sie?'*

Both Dwyer and Carter now realised the size of this curious German in front of them. He was every bit as tall as Dwyer and looked to weigh in the region of about 300 lbs. There did not appear to be a noticeable gap from where his shoulders ended and his head began, such was the size of his neck.

Dwyer stood up. The only response he could think to come up with was to put his finger to his lips and gave an audible *'Shhhh'* as he walked towards him.

Instead of becoming overly concerned about being discovered and possible capture, Carter looked on with morbid curiosity. How Dwyer would deal with this giant of a man that was now that challenging them was anyone's guess. Carter strongly believed that he had more than met his match.

'Wer sind Sie, wo ist Carl und Reiner?' said the German who was now becoming increasingly alarmed.

'Sorry mate, don't speak German,' Dwyer said as walked towards him.

The Germans eyes grew wide as he whispered, *'Englander?'*

Dwyer took advantage of the visible shock now being displayed and grabbed the German by both his shoulders pulling him towards him. He placed a well-aimed head-butt onto the bridge of the Germans nose and simultaneously brought his right knee up into his groin.

To his credit, the German did not go down. The only noticeable difference to his appearance was that his nose was spread halfway across his face and the look of shock on his face was now doubled.

Dwyer then took the rifle slung over his shoulder and crashed it into the side of his head. His worthy opponent started to bend over towards him. Dwyer repeated the process, this time aiming the blows towards the back of his head. He finally went down. Six further sickening blows to the skull were performed to ensure he would never wake up.

Job done.

Jesus. Look at the mess you have made of his head!

I know. Would not have thought it possible to make him look even uglier.

How can you make jokes at such a time?

Whatever it takes to get through this crap.

Dwyer then rolled him over, took off his jacket and then sat him upright against the machine-gun nest, making sure that it was similar to the position he was in when he and Carter had first discovered him. He then put the jacket on over his own, which was almost a perfect fit and returned to Carter. As he did so, he outstretched his arm and started to goose step.

'Do I wear it well?' Dwyer said to Carter as he reached his side.

Without a hint of expression on his face Carter said, 'If I was a betting man, I would have just lost my money. I definitely thought that would have gone fifteen rounds.'

'Yeah well,' said Dwyer. 'You don't lose many fights if you get the first punch in, and as far as I know, you can't go into boxing ring with a rifle. In addition, I am fairly sure you can't head-butt people and knee them in the balls either.' He then looked down at his newly acquired clothing, and added, 'At least we both have a jacket now,' matter of factly.

Carter's calm demeanour now crumpled.

It now took his every ounce of self-control to stop laughing aloud. His silhouette looked comical in the darkness, as his shoulders were moving up and down so rapidly that it looked like he was trying to shake his head off his neck. A broad smile also appeared on Dwyer's face, although he was not sure what the joke was.

Wasn't that funny!

'How long do you think we have before somebody notices?' Dwyer said nodding towards the newly deceased which had the effect of eventually sobering Carter up from his state of mild hysterics.

'Well, it is pretty obvious that the word has not reached here yet that out troops have landed on the Cotentin peninsula. They would be swarming around the place like bees if it had. The short answer is that it is anyone's guess. Maybe we will get lucky.'

'What time does the cavalry arrive?' Dwyer asked.

'The bombing should start just after 05h00 hours. The troops should then start to land at around 06h30.'

'That gives us about two hours then to find cover,' said Dwyer as he looked at his watch.

'Agreed, I had worked that out earlier but who knows what time somebody notices the fleet sailing towards the coast. My guess is that it will be anytime soon. We have to get to that wood and try to find cover as quickly as possible. The fact we both have jackets now will help us. On the negative side, the fact we are walking around looking to have a piggyback fight with anyone that's brave enough, will not. I suggest we take this exit to the field and use the lane. If we turn right we will be headed in the right direction.'

Good plan. Told you he knows what he is doing.

Silence.

I said I told you he knows what —

I'm not listening.

Without further discussion, Carter climbed onto Dwyer's back and they set off out of the field. On immediately turning right, they almost collided with a further German soldier walking down the lane. He casually looked up and said, *'Entschuldigen sie bitte herrn,'* and continued along the lane away from them.

Dwyer and Carter stared after him and ensured that he did not notice anything untoward about the German that slumped over the machine-gun nest at the entrance to the field. Fortunately, for him, he was far too preoccupied with his cigarette, which saved him his life. Dwyer was ready to give his most recent victim someone to sit with, albeit without any conversation to be had.

The dirt lane was about teen feet wide and had the same tunnel effect that the one they had ridden down when using the motorcycle. This one however was devoid of trees. After about one hundred yards, Carter noticed a small slit in the hedgerow and immediately after, a voice said, '*Warum sind Sie mit ihm? Was ist das Problem?*'

Oh, shit. What is he saying?
How do I know?
I wish paid more attention at school.
You didn't learn German at school, you idiot!
Good point and well made.

Carter just laughed and waved. He then simulated a jockey spurring his horse into action by squeezing his legs on Dwyer's thighs and moved them back and forth . . . ignoring the pain this caused to his ankle.

Dwyer immediately quickened his stride in fear of being whipped. They both held their breath as they walked the next fifty yards. Thankfully, their unseen inquisitor was obviously not that concerned, as he seemed not to be attempting to follow them or challenge them again.

Just as they were both to expel a large breath of air, they heard, '*Warum sind Sie mit ihm? Ist er zu faul zu laufen?*' Again, Carter waved and Dwyer's pace hastened.

17

Dwyer and Carter had now reached the junction at end of the lane. A narrower path, lead from left and right. Immediately in front of them were a number of trees and a further hedgerow. Ten yards down to the left was a rusty gate, which was partially open. Carter tapped Dwyer on the shoulder and pointed him towards it.

Dwyer hesitated. He fully expected a further machine-gun nest to be present. He liked his chances better if he was on his own.

After relieving himself of the weight of the major, Dwyer crept towards the gate. On reaching the end of the hedgerow, he slowly peered round the corner.

He was filled with euphoria.

Not only was there nobody waiting to open fire on him but the wood, which seemed fairly dense to Dwyer in the darkness, was only thirty yards in front of him. He quickly returned to the Major.

'It looks like we had made it, the wood starts just behind the gate. Let's go.' He then knelt down so Carter could straddle his back.

'Good news, but watch where you step,' said Carter as he climbed aboard. 'Did you see any cows?'

'No I didn't, and I have seen enough of cows for one day thanks. Not to mention their Goddamn shit.'

'No cows probably means mines, so be careful,' Carter said.

Did he say mines?

He did.

For fucks sake!

Dwyer's earlier euphoria now turned rapidly to despair. He stared at the ground suspiciously, for what seemed like an eternity, afraid to put one foot in front of the other.

'C'mon then. What are you waiting for?' Carter said.

'How the hell I am supposed to see them, especially in this light,' Dwyer said with almost a whiny childlike tone to his voice.

'You won't be able too. Just watch where you tread. If there is any sign of the ground being disturbed, avoid it.'

I thought walks in the countryside were supposed to be FUCKING

FUN!

'Anything else you wanna tell me while you are at it?' Dwyer said.

'No. That will do for now; lets get on with it, shall we? You can take some consolation that if we do tread on one, you should not feel a thing.'

No. Only my arsehole being blown through my brains.

'Thanks.' Dwyer said simply and trudged off towards the gate.

On entering the open ground, Dwyer looked towards the wood in front of him as if it were the resting place of the Holy Grail. Never would he have thought he would be so excited about the prospect of visiting one.

He turned his gaze to the ground in front of him, and with intense concentration lines etched on his face, took his first tentative step towards it.

No explosion.

One down, about thirty to go, he thought.

So slow was their progress that it reminded Dwyer of a game he used to play in the playground at school. One child would stand with their back to everyone else and intermittently turn around to try to spot anyone moving. If they could, then that person was out. The winner of the game would be the one who got closer enough to touch them on the back. The delight he felt on finally reaching the edge of the wood was far greater than he ever remembered when he had ever been declared the winner of the childhood game.

What was the name of that game?

It is not important right now.

I know, but what was it?

Silence.

He had not in fact had to deviate from a straight path once, as nothing look overly suspicious as far as the ground was concerned. It led him to believe that this particular area was clear.

The Major however was not so optimistic. He urged Dwyer to remain vigilant even when they entered the wood.

After walking twenty yards under the cover of branches and leaves, Dwyer placed the Major next to a tree in order that he could lean against it. Due to the tension and carrying the extreme weight for just over a mile, his legs and back were in need of a good rest. He realised for the first time that his forehead was aching also.

That German had been one big ugly bastard.

His thoughts were then disturbed by Carter providing him some further unwelcome news.

18

Dwyer looked towards Carter who had remained silent since being seated at the base of the tree. He could just about make out, that the Major seemed to be grimacing and looking ruefully towards his ankle.

'Giving you grief?' Dwyer said.

Carter ignored the question and said instead, 'Okay, I suppose you better hear the bad news.'

What now?

'Our original objective was thirty miles to the west of here so I am not entirely clued up on this area, but I will tell you what I know.'

'I am not sure I want to hear it,' Dwyer said.

Again, Carter ignored him.

'Codename Omaha Beach is a five miles long stretch between Sainte-Honorine-des-Pertes to Vierville-sur-Mer. Its strategic importance to the Normandy landings is to secure a beachhead from Port-en-Bessin and the Vire River and thus ensuring that a continuous line of troops around the Bay of the Seine.'

'Sorry Major. Those places mean nothing to me,' Dwyer said scratching his chin.

'It doesn't matter, just listen. Once secured, the troops of the 29th Infantry Division, the 1st Infantry Division are to link up with the British landings at Gold Beach to the east and the troops landing at Utah Beach to the west.

The Beach we are above is split up into eight sectors as part of Operation Overlord named Charlie, Dog Green, Dog White, Dog Red, Easy Green, Easy Red, Fox Green and Fox Red.'

Enough was enough. 'Very interesting that is, but it means absolutely fuck all to me. It also aint going to help me get you out of here.'

'Perhaps this will,' Carter said casually. 'The sectors I just mentioned are probably defended by Belgian Gates and a continuous line of logs driven into the sand facing seawards. Both will be mined.

Then there will be a line of 'hedgehogs' which are anti-tank obstacles made of angled iron approximately 150 yards from the shoreline. The area between the sand bank and the bluffs will also be mined, as will the bluff slopes.'

'Really? What are Belgian Gates and hedgehogs?'

'They are both anti-tank obstacles. Belgian Gates are steel fences about three-metres wide and two metres high, which can be mounted on rollers. The hedgehogs are static and made out of angled iron.'

'How do you know all this?'

'Intelligence reports.'

'British intelligence reports?'

'Yes.'

Not so crap now, are we?

'How many men are around?' Dwyer said instead.

'Excellent question.'

After a brief silence, Dwyer said, 'Well, how many are there?'

'I have no idea.'

'None?'

'All I can tell you is that defences along the beach will probably have a number of strong points or 'resistance nests' which will be interconnected by a series of trenches and tunnels. They will probably have light artillery pieces deployed within them, the heaviest of which were will be in gun casements with the lighter pieces in pillboxes. In addition, there will probably be a number of anti-tank guns.'

'Jesus,' Dwyer said wide-eyed. 'Sounds like our boys are sailing into a Goddamn nightmare.'

Carter shook his head.

'No. What do you mean no?'

'Remember the aerial bombardment I told you about?'

Dwyer nodded.

'By the time they have finished, and the Navy has shelled the shit out of the rest, there should not be much left to worry about.'

Dwyer decided to change the subject.

'I haven't seen you smoking since we got here. Why don't you have one? It might make you feel better,' Dwyer said now looking at Carter's ankle. He then thought back to the German they had almost stumbled upon, when leaving the first field. 'You may as well, everyone else seems to,' he added.

Carter contemplated the idea briefly and then shook his head. 'We cannot do anything to attract anyone to us, and believe me, although we can't see anyone at the moment, they are all around us.'

Dwyer looked round into the darkness suspiciously, and then said, 'Just blow the smoke down your jacket, there is nobody about.'

'Okay. If you insist,' Carter said. He lit his first cigarette for over six hours and inhaled so deeply that it lit up like a torch.

Dwyer looked around again nervously just to ensure they were still alone.

Send up a search flare, why don't you?

'You should be a medic Davey. That has certainly hit the spot,' Carter said and then took another deep drag forgetting to blow the smoke down his jacket when he exhaled.

And Indian smoke signals while you're at it!

Dwyer waited for him to finish the whole cigarette before saying, 'Shouldn't we look for somewhere with a bit more protection than this. Not sure this tree is going to stop a bomb.'

'Take five minutes rest. You must be tired after carrying my sorry arse around for the last half-hour.'

Dwyer ruefully nodded his agreement. He leant fully back against the tree and stared upwards towards the branches and leaves. It suddenly dawned on him that he knew nothing about the Major apart from the fact he was an officer in the U.S. Army.

'What did you do before you joined up?' He asked.

Carter lit up another cigarette and this time cupped the lit end in his hands. 'I was a high school history teacher as well as being in the National Guard, similar to the British Territorial Army. I joined up fully when the 101st was activated in 1942.'

'Are you married?'

'No. I never seemed to meet the right girl. To be honest I have always been more interested in history books.'

Really? Not surprised you are single.

'How old are you?' Dwyer said instead.

'I will be forty-four tomorrow.'

'Well if I don't get the chance later, happy birthday for tomorrow. It seems a crappy way to celebrate it though.'

'That it is. How about you, any plans of getting married in the future?'

'It's the first thing I am going to do if I ever get home. I am an idiot not to have asked her already. My Sally is just the best person I have ever met, and she is beautiful too.'

Carter moved his leg and winced in pain. 'I think I am going to have to have another small shot of morphine.' He then opened the lighter of the two rucksacks and searched for one of the first aid kits.

'I will no doubt be slightly out of it for about ten minutes. While I am, you should have a look round for somewhere for us to hide up and take cover from the bombing. Leave your rucksack with me.'

Oh great. A walk in the woods in the middle of the night on my own. This just gets better and better.

Yeah. And there be monsters.

Who asked you to pipe up?

Well there are. Watch your back.

Dwyer stood up and checked that his ammo pouch on his belt was full. He then took off the safety of his rifle for the first time since landing and said, 'Don't run off. I will be back in a minute.'

Oh my God! Aren't you just the comedian?

Fair one. I can't believe I said that.

After taking about ten steps, he remembered Carters advice about being careful of mines, even when in the woods. Due to the fact that he was under a blanket of leaves, he could hardly see the ground anyway. He tried to dismiss the thought of being blown into a hundred tiny pieces from his mind, and carried on and just hoped for the best, without continually looking down.

A gap then appeared in the trees above and he could see that it was now starting to get slightly lighter.

Dawn was approaching.

He checked his watch. It was 03h50 hours.

19

Dwyer now fully realised how close to coast they were due to the fact he could hear the sound of the waves lapping onto the beach. It was so loud in the stillness of the night that he wondered how he had not noticed it before. He then noticed a path just beyond the where the tree line ended. He cautiously walked towards it, and just as he left the cover of the trees, German soldiers started to run towards him in all directions out of nowhere.

Jesus Christ.

He looked down and immediately noticed a trench, which seemed for the moment at least, to be unoccupied. While he was making up his mind to jump down into it, or turn round and go back the way he had come, one group passed by within two feet from him.

He did neither.

His body parts all ganged up on him, ignored the mixed messages being sent from his scrambled brain, which resulted in him being rooted to the spot.

All he was now capable of was thinking of was, '*Fuck me,*' repeatedly.

They appeared to him to be running in slow motion. He held his breath.

'*Die innvasion begonnen hat, die invasion hat begonnen. Nehmen Sie Ihre Position,*' a shoulder towards the rear of the group shouted. They ran past, mostly ignoring him.

Thank fuck for that!

His brain started to get back into gear. He only recognised the words '*innvasion*' and '*position*' and looked towards the channel.

Is that – ?

It is.

He squinted for a few seconds and then began to smile. He could just make a line of black shapes on the horizon. He checked up and down the path, made sure nobody was taking too much notice of him and then slowly walked back into the trees. He then sprinted back to the Major.

Be careful of the mines.

Fuck the bloody mines; we need to find some bloody cover.

When he eventually found him, due to not following the same route back, the Major was slumped against the tree and appeared to be asleep. Dwyer knelt down beside him and gently shook him.

Carter just groaned and tried to push Dwyer's hand away.

Dwyer desperately now tried to think how long it had been when he had left him earlier with Brooks. He did a quick calculation in his mind and thought it could not have been longer than ten minutes.

Depending when he injected himself, he believed that it must have been away from him longer this time. Especially as he had managed to get lost whilst returning from the bluff.

His attention was distracted by hearing further voices towards the coast. Urgent, panicked stricken voices.

Crapping yourselves now, aren't you?

The only downside was that so was he.

He looked at his watch.

It was now 04h05 hours.

'It must have been at least fifteen minutes,' he said aloud to himself. 'We still however had plenty of time if he was correct about the timing of the bombing raid,' he added.

Instead of trying to revive the Major again, he sat down next to him and tried not to think what lay ahead of them. He picked up the packet of cigarettes that lay on the Majors lap.

If ever there was a time to start smoking this was it, he thought. Instead, he opened the Major's top left pocket and placed them inside.

With that, the Major stirred. He looked quizzically at Dwyer and said, 'How long have I been out?' With a slight slur.

God knows.

'At least fifteen minutes I'd say.'

'Did you find anywhere suitable for us to hold up?'

'I'm afraid not. I reached a path that is quite close to what appears to some kind of cliff above the beach and then Germans started running about everywhere. One shouted something to me about getting into position as the Invasion had begun.'

'How would they know that already?'

'Probably because someone saw the ships coming, I looked out towards the sea quickly and saw dark shapes on the horizon. I then ran back here.' He then added an afterthought, 'It's starting to get lighter as well.'

'What time is it now?'

Dwyer looked as his watch again. 'It's 04h10 hours.'

'Okay. Then we have just over an hour. How far are we from the coastline?'

'I would say about three hundred yards.'

'Three hundred yards is not very far from where they will be aiming the bombs. There will definitely be a number of stray ones and they will start bombing inland soon after the initial phase to prevent reinforcements coming up.'

Wonderful.

Dwyer swallowed hard, intently staring at Carter waiting for his next instruction about their immediate course of action.

Carter then looked Dwyer in the eye with a slight grin and said, 'How lucky do you feel?'

Lucky? Are you taking the piss?

'What do you mean?' He said instead.

'Well, we can take our chances here or look for something better. Our German friends will now be busy looking out towards the Channel rather than looking behind them.'

You are asking for my opinion. How the hell should I know?

Dwyer looked nervously upwards just to make sure that it was not all going to kick-off early. On only seeing the branches and trees above him he said, 'My vote is to try somewhere else. You are right. They are all going to be shitting themselves watching the ships coming in right about now.'

'That's settled then,' said Carter nodding his head in agreement.

Dwyer helped Carter to his one good foot. 'I will carry you are as far as just before the tree line, and then go slightly down the cliff on my own and look for some kind of shelter.'

'The correct term is bluff, and be careful. Anywhere off the beaten track will probably be mined.'

'Bluff then,' Dwyer said. 'And will you shut up about the Goddamn mines.'

'Shut up, *sir*,' Carter said.

'And you can stick your *etiquette* up your arse as well.'

Both were smiling when Carter once again climbed onto Dwyer's back. They had walked half way to the path beyond the tree line when they noticed a German soldier squatting down in front of them about twenty feet away.

Oh, crap.

Exactly right.

You are making jokes, at a time like this?

The German turned towards them and said, '*Was sind Sie beide denn hier?*' It was obvious from his tone that he was not best pleased to see them and being disturbed whilst in the middle of his very early morning constitutional.

Hope he doesn't crap on a mine.

No. What a shower of shit that would literally be.

Dwyer casually walked up towards him, and when within five feet away, he put down the Major who let out a simulated moan when he placed him on the ground.

The German turned his attention solely to Carter and said '*Was ist los mit ihm?*'

Dwyer pulled the knife from his belt, grabbed him by the top of his head, pulled it back and slit his throat in one brutal movement. He then immediately put his hand over his mouth.

After the life quickly ebbed away from Dwyer's latest victim, he let go of him so he fell backwards into his own excrement. Dwyer then dragged him between a tree and a bush and placed a fallen branch over his body.

'I told you they would be shitting themselves,' Dwyer said as he returned to Carter. 'What a way to go. One minute you are parking your breakfast in the woods, the next you are lying in it dead.'

Carter looked away with an incredulous look on his face.

'I can't help but notice that taking other people's lives does not seem to have any effect on you,' Carter whispered while being pulled to his one good foot.

I told you. You are enjoying it too much.

Shut up and listen.

'Don't let my joking around fool you,' said Dwyer looking sincerely mournful. 'It's just my way of dealing with it.' He then looked back towards the dead German. 'For all I know, he may have had four kids who are never going to see their dad again.'

Carter nodded slowly.

'I wish I hadn't just said that,' said Dwyer looking miserably towards the ground. 'I am now going to have to spend the rest of my life getting that thought out of my head.'

Carter saddled up and they made their way towards the path. He now regretted his comment regarding Dwyer's actions. He looked visibly upset that he thought he had become so ruthless.

20

Dwyer left the cover of the tree line at the same place that he had earlier. All now seemed to be quiet in comparison. However, it was not all good. The trench that been empty was now fully occupied. He could clearly see soldiers looking over the top of it five yards in front of him all. They were all looking seaward, most of them through binoculars.

At least they are all oblivious to us.
For now.

Dismissing the last pessimistic thought from his mind, he took one further glance towards the horizon. Pessimism turned to optimism in an instant.

He could not believe his eyes.

As he scanned from left to right, the dark shapes that he had seen earlier were now more in focus to him.

Much more in focus.

Although he still could not clearly make out the features of the individual ships, he could tell there were hundreds of them. *Thousands maybe.* He had been on an emotional roller coaster since boarding his plane at Greenham Common. He now felt like screaming for joy.

Probably best not to at the minute.
Watch your front.

Dwyer had no idea how many troops the ships carried towards the coast but he guessed it must have been tens of thousands. He believed there was no way this sorry lot he was stood behind were going to have a chance fending them off.

From what he had seen there was nothing like that number of Germans in this area. They had hardly come across any on their way to the woods. Little did they know they were just about to be dumped on from above in under an hour. He was suddenly filled with an overwhelming sense of well-being. His only concern was to survive the aerial bombardment himself.

With this now suddenly consuming his every thought, he turned his attention back to the trench in front of him. He looked to the right and noticed that that the trench stopped and their appeared to be a gap about ten yards further away. He went back to the trees and came out again opposite. A further trench started on the right. Both ends of the trenches appeared from his line of sight that they had bushes going down the bluff that would provide some cover if he walked through the middle.

He took a deep breath and moved closer.

His mood improved further when he realised he was correct. He stuck his shoulders back and walked through the gap as casually as possible, stopping in between the bushes on each side that were for the moment preventing from being seen from either trench.

There was a sudden drop of about four feet immediately now in front of him. He lay flat on his stomach, looked over the edge and then realised that he was on an overhang. There appeared to be sufficient room below it for both he and Carter to shelter under.

This will have to do, he thought.

He slowly stood up, dusted himself down, and then as casually as possible walked back to the tree line.

21
10th July 1943
Autryville, North Carolina, USA
03h45 hours

The woman scrambled to her feet and looked at each member of the group in turn with defiance. Her eyes became wild with fury. The immobilising fear she had felt earlier, now completely dissipated.

Her first instinct was to start screaming for help but she immediately thought better of it. Her fear and rage were held in check. A smile started to smile form at the corner of her mouth. Her emotion then turned towards to contempt towards her captors.

'What have you got to smile about, you bitch?' 'Mr Star Gazer' said grinning inanely himself.

She ignored the insult and quickly stole a glance towards the closet door to her left and then looked back towards her abuser. She thought of the hunting rifle that was on the top shelf and now prayed that it was loaded. Something she had always poured scorn on her husband about in the past. Her husband that was now lying in a pool of blood downstairs in the hallway.

Please God. Let it be loaded. He didn't do much that I asked him to. So please, don't let him have started now. Just let it be loaded . . . **PLEASE!**

The thought then quickly entered her head why he had not taken it with him when he went downstairs to investigate the noise that had woke her up earlier. A sense of uncontrollable guilt now descended upon her.

Why am I such a light sleeper?

The slight forced smile on her face now broadened and she forced herself to laugh which sounded similar to a witches cackle. She threw her head back and cackled as hard as she could.

All members of the group looked at each other in confusion.

This was her cue. With the agility of a woman half her age, she sprang across the bedroom floor towards the closet door.

22

Carter could tell Dwyer was bringing good news when he saw him approach by the nature of his body language. He was now sat up against another tree with his left foot resting on his rucksack. The slightly raised angle seemed to alleviate the pain and the morphine was definitely doing its job.

Whilst Dwyer had been off carrying out reconnaissance, Carter was in remarkably good spirits, considering the circumstances.

He had escaped from the doomed Dakota and survived the drop – dismissing the fact that he had broken his ankle and landed miles from his intended target. The four bastards that had plagued his life in the last year had been systematically taken out by Dwyer (albeit that Garcia was still alive), and thus far, they had escaped capture and discovery. Last but not least, he estimated that the beachhead would be secured within the next three hours and he would be on his way back to England by the end of the day.

He allowed himself a celebratory cigarette cupping the lit end in his hands. He did not even seem to care when he inadvertently burnt the palm of his left hand.

His thoughts turned to Dwyer and marvelled at the man's calmness and ferocity in the face of adversity. Although recruiting him had been an act of complete selfishness on his part, he consoled himself that he would not be able to perform his duties properly whilst continuing looking over his shoulder. Not that it mattered now. At least Dwyer had avoided prison as he had given him the option of coming with him. No matter how outrageous a plan that may have been at the time.

He knew that if he lived through the rest of the day, he would be indebted to Davey Dwyer for the rest of his life and started to think how he could arrange for him to join him when he returned to England, later in the day.

He did not think that him being his adjutant would be sufficient, but it was a good enough place to start any subsequent argument that he may have to have.

His thoughts were interrupted by Dwyer's return.

Dwyer sat down next to Carter and whispered into his ear. 'There are two trenches about fifty yards from here that have a break in the middle. There is a bush either side that leads to an overhang. It look's ideal.'

He then went onto describe the scene he had witnessed out on the channel.

It was now Carters turn to whisper. He turned his head towards Dwyer and said, 'Excellent news, I suggest we go as close as possible to the trenches at 05h15 hours, whilst still under the cover of the trees, and then wait for the first bomb to be dropped. As soon as it hits the ground, we go for it.'

Carter then looked at his watch. 'It is now 04h55 hours.'

23

> 'War is a series of catastrophes that results in a victory.'
> - Georges Clemenceau

The twenty-minute wait seemed like an eternity. They had both sat in silence the whole time and apart from hearing the odd instruction shouted in German, all was quiet except for the waves below. It seemed surreal to them both that one of the biggest invasions in military history was about to take place.

At 05h15 hours, Dwyer stood up and slung his rifle over his shoulder. He then helped Carter on with the heavy rucksack containing the majority of their ammunition, then handed him the other whilst he was still sat down. He then pulled him up into a standing position.

Carter momentarily lost his balance and put some weight on his left foot. Instead of grimacing, he just hopped around a bit and then gingerly put some weight on it again to test it out. He immediately withdrew his foot from the floor. He shook his head towards Dwyer to indicate that there was no improvement who then immediately turned round so he could once again climb onto his back.

Considering the combined weight of the two men, plus the ammunition and equipment they carried, Dwyer walked the fifty yards to the break in the trenches in almost total silence. He stopped five yards within the tree line, standing behind a tree with the thickest trunk in the immediate vicinity.

Out of nowhere, all of his worst nightmares arrived at once. He had an overwhelming desire to sneeze. He stood with his eyes closed waggling his nose from side to side as quickly as possible whilst moving his head up and down desperately trying to prevent it.

Carter, who had his head resting on Dwyer's left shoulder, glanced sideways and immediately recognised his predicament. He reached round with his left hand and grabbed Dwyer's nose. As if on cue, the first explosion hit, followed with what seemed to be at least a million others. The noise was deafening and the ground shook as if they were experiencing an earthquake.

Pumped with adrenaline, and with fear being a great motivator, Dwyer literally sprinted from the tree line, through the gap in the trenches and jumped down the four feet drop from the overhang. On landing, he immediately leaned backwards. Carter fell off Dwyer's back and screamed when his left ankle hit the ground.

The noise he made was an irrelevance. They had no cause for concern about giving away their presence. Dwyer did not even hear him from a foot away. They then crawled as far back as possible under the ledge and curled up into two small balls. Never has a six foot eight inch man weighing just over 250 lbs looked so small.

There then appeared to be a lull.

Is that it?

Can't be.

Dwyer started to lift his head when a further round of explosions hit nearby slightly inland of their position. Dirt and stones fell from the overhang above onto Dwyer's upturned face and he immediately cowered back down to the floor.

Maybe not.

While clenching everything that could be clenched, he wondered how long the bombardment would last and what chances they had of living through it.

24

Dwyer and Carter were still huddled together under the overhang. Each time a bomb landed, they both jumped out of their skin. It was not as if they did not know the next one was coming, it was just the fact the earth shook beneath them and they could not get used to the shock.

Dwyer had experienced bombing raids before back home in Portsmouth. Whist walking a young lady home one night in late 1940 along the seafront at Southsea, they had both taken off their shoes and swam out into the Solent on hearing the sirens and the subsequent first explosion. Dwyer had suggested that the bombs would be aimed inland as opposed to the water.

His was proven to be correct as not one of the bombs landed anywhere near them.

Nothing he had experienced before had compared to this. Not even the night his family was killed and more than half the city was destroyed could compare to this.

It was the sheer quantity and the concentrated target area that made this experience one that he would not wish on his own worst enemy. His teeth began to ache due to the ferocity in which he was clinching his jaw and he felt pain across the side of his forehead due to closing his eyes so tightly.

Everything remained clenched except for one part of his body. A bomb which seemed to land on top of them, scared him so badly, he farted. For the briefest of moments, he nearly laughed thinking back to cows earlier when he landed.

You are not the only ones that fart like a foghorn.
No, but you probably need a bucket and sponge to clean yourself now.
Dwyer then began inwardly cursing Carter.
What kind of dumb idea was this?
I told you earlier, but would you listen?
To deliberately walk into this position was utter and complete madness.
I just said I told you earlier.
Oh fuck off you know it all smug bastard.

He could now not believe that he agreed to it. He was about to try to make his thoughts heard, when there was a definite lull in the explosions. They both slightly raised their heads and looked at each other.

Carter braved sitting up and opened one of the rucksacks. He took out two sets of binoculars and gave one to Dwyer. They both went into a kneeling position and looked out to sea.

The view from their hiding place was incredible. There were ships as far as the eye could see, along with hundreds of landing craft. To Dwyer's dismay, there was no sign of them coming ashore and offloading troops and he noticed that there seemed to be far more positioned to his left along the coast. Very few in comparison, were directly in front of their position.

He was about to say as much to Carter when they then both had to dive for cover when a further series of explosions landed directly behind them. They were both covered once again with soil and stones falling from the overhang above. Dwyer had realised all along that any bomb being even close to being a direct him, would mean that would be all she wrote. He believed it was only a matter of time. There was no way the strip of earth, which was about two feet in depth, would protect them. However, he consoled himself that for the time being, they were still alive and kicking.

More by luck than judgment.
It's better to be lucky than good.
Good point.
My God. Coming from you that is high praise indeed.
Silence.

Dwyer then returned to his kneeling position, now choosing to ignore the explosions behind him believing that curling up in a ball would not be the least bit good in saving him should a bomb land straight on top of their position.

It's amazing what you can get used to.

He looked through the binoculars too see if any of the landing crafts were getting any nearer to the shoreline.

He then took them away from his eyes immediately and checked the lenses at the front. Something appeared to be obscuring the view, which he guessed to be some dirt that had fallen from above.

As nothing appeared to be untoward, he looked up. A German soldier was now standing no more than three feet in front of him. They had a quick competition to see who could have the most surprised expression on their face, which the German marginally won.

What went quickly through Dwyer's mind was that he had no idea why he would have left his trench and could only think that he knew of this spot and was now trying to take cover there.

A shot rang out.

Dwyer felt the bullet whiz past his left ear. The Germans mouth formed a perfect O, and then tumbled backwards down the bluff. There was then a further explosion, which seemed insignificant, compared to the last ten minutes, but this time, body parts flew everywhere. The German had landed on a mine in his descent down the bluff and disintegrated into several different parts. One of his hands still attached to his forearm landed at Dwyer's knees.

What the f -

At first, the image in front of him totally confused him. Once realisation struck, he quickly picked it up as if it were a grenade about to explode and threw it down the bluff to reunite it with the rest of the bits and pieces that remained. He had also noticed that the Germans watch was still attached to the wrist. He turned his head downwards to the right and violently vomited.

When he had finally stopped dry reaching, he wiped his mouth clean on the sleeve of his jacket and immediately regretted it. The vomit had now joined the remnants of the cow shit and blood from earlier and he could now taste both in his mouth. He vigorously started to spit onto the floor.

It didn't work. He vomited once more for good measure.

Never did Dwyer think that the taste of his own vomit would be preferable to something else.

After what seemed like a lifetime of spitting and throwing up, he turned to Carter who was slumped against the back of the overhang with his rifle still pointing towards the Channel. Dwyer noticed for the first time that the back of the overhang was actually concrete and guessed that it must be the outside wall of a tunnel connecting the two trenches.

A further bomb fell close to their position and rattled the teeth in Dwyer's mouth. It also set his ears off ringing again. He shook his head to relieve himself of the sensation and then shook Carter's right shoulder. He definitely seemed to be away with the fairies again.

It's not the morphine this time.
What's the matter with him?
I don't know. Ask him.

Carter arrived back in the land of the living with a sudden jolt and grabbed at Dwyer's wrist. Dwyer roughly pulled his hand back and then took hold of both Carter's shoulders.

'Snap out of it Major,' Dwyer said, which was the first time he had addressed him in such a manner. He quickly went through his mind that he did not know his first name.

This did the trick. Carter's eyes seem to focus on him properly without the glazed stare that had been present seconds earlier.

'I'm sorry,' Carter shouted and then repeated it.

'Sorry about what?' Dwyer shouted in reply.

There then seemed to be another lull in the explosions around them and the Major said more quietly, 'I lost it again there for a minute. That is the first time I have killed anyone before . . . Doesn't feel very good, does it?'

Dwyer looked away briefly and shook his head in agreement. He then turned back to Carter and said, 'What's your first name?'

'What?' Carter said with a confused look on his face due to being asked such a random question considering the circumstances.

'What is your first name?' Dwyer repeated. 'I am not going to die here without knowing the first name of the man I have been carrying around all night.'

Carter's face broke into a broad smile and said, 'It's Edward. Everyone calls me Ed.'

'Eddie it is then,' said Dwyer.

They both know broke out into silly big grins which left their faces as soon as they arrived as further 500-pound bomb landed inland, no more than 100 feet away from their position.

Carter now raised himself to his knees and started to look out to the Channel with his binoculars. As he moved his head from left to right he said, 'You know, there is something very wrong here. All the bombs seem to be landing inland. There is certainly no damage to the trenches directly above us, as no doubt we would be buried underneath them if there had.'

He then put down the binoculars and looked at Dwyer.

'I have also noticed that there are very few landing crafts headed our way. There are considerably more off to our west.'

Dwyer nodded agreement and said, 'I noticed that earlier.' He then looked for himself and checked their progress. They still did not appear to be any closer and most of them appeared to be circling.

He turned to Carter and shouted as another huge explosion went off inland, 'Why aren't the Germans shooting at the ships? They appear to be just sitting here doing nothing.'

Good question Davey.

Thank you.

Another wave of B-17's had just dropped their contents from above and the ground shook again, all around them. Dwyer who was still kneeling actually felt the top of the overhang drop slightly and touch his German helmet.

Both men flew themselves to the ground and Dwyer ended up lying on top of Carter.

When the shock wave had died down, both men started to try to sit up.

The ground rocked again.

They were thrown violently back down to the same position. They lay in the somewhat suggestive pose together for a full twenty seconds before braving sitting up again.

When Carter managed to return to a sitting position, he felt the side of his mouth and then spat out one of his back teeth into his hand. He stared at it with a certain degree of fascination. He then looked towards Dwyer.

'To answer your question from earlier, I have no idea why the Germans are not shooting at our ships, but I can tell you one thing.'

He paused.

'Well?'

'I am starting to get a really bad feeling about this.'

A minute later, their question was answered. The German batteries opened fire on the fleet.

It was 05h35 hours.

25

Dwyer's eyes grew wide behind the binoculars that he was still using to watch the progress of the troops landing.

He had been looking left and right confirming to himself that the number of landing craft were fewer in number directly opposite their position on the beach. In addition, he was trying to see how effective the German guns that were now firing shells from their positions, both sides of him. He then threw himself to the floor and pulled Carter down with him.

At 05h37 at Omaha Beach, the Navy joined the Allied Bombers in bombarding the Normandy coastline.

The noise was incredible, which had sent Dwyer diving to the ground with Carter.

The subsequent huge explosion sent flames in every direction on the coastline, a number of small fires broke out in the grass and bushes on the bluff and several mines exploded.

Once again, the ground shook.

If someone would have told Dwyer that their perilous predicament would get worse once the aerial bombing started, and the fact that they were hiding within feet of the enemies frontline position, he would have thought them totally and utterly insane.

His face now looked liked that he rubbed it in a bowl of flour due to the amount of dust now plastered all over it.

After eventually taking the chance to raise his head, he then violently shook it to get the dust and earth out of his ears. He then rubbed his eyes and looked down at Carter who was looking up at him. It appeared to Dwyer that he was laughing at him. He then realised that he could not hear anything and to make matters worse, his vision was blurred. A shell then exploded about twenty yards to the right, which knocked him off balance.

After regaining some kind of composure, he looked back at Carter.

He is definitely laughing at me.

He put his fingers in his ears and moved his jaw slowly up and down, which had the desired effect of partially restoring his hearing. He then commenced blinking rapidly, which returned the focus to his vision.

'What the hell can you possibly find to laugh about?' He shouted at Carter.

'You should look at yourself in the mirror. You look like a panda,' Carter shouted back.

Dwyer rubbed his hands all over his face to remove the excess dust and then to his amazement, Carter sat upright, leaned against the concrete wall at the back of the overhang and calmly lit a cigarette with a satisfied goofy grin.

Why the hell is he so calm all of a sudden?

He gave the impression of someone casually sitting on a park bench watching the ducks on the lake rather in the middle of utter and complete chaos. His demeanour did change however, when a further bomb landed inland behind them off to the right, which for a brief second, threatened to collapse the overhang again.

Turning his attention away from Carter, Dwyer raised himself into a kneeling position and surveyed the scene that was unfolding in front of him. The visibility of the fleet was now slightly obscured due to the amount of smoke drifting across the Channel. The smoke was also preventing him from clearly seeing the progress of the landing craft. Giving it up as a waste of time, he moved back in under the ledge and opened one of the rucksacks.

A carton of cigarettes was removed. He hastily took out a pack, tapped a cigarette into his hand, took the cigarette off Carter that he was still smoking and lit his own. After taking a long drag, he closed his eyes and inhaled.

Oh, bollocks.

He immediately started to splutter, which was then followed by an enormous hacking series of coughs. Unperturbed, he took another large lungful of smoke and then blew it out without the previous ill effect. He then placed his right hand on the ground in an effort to kneel up again, right in the middle of the pile of vomit he had prepared earlier.

Fuckety fuck.

The incredulous look on his face as he quickly wiped it onto his jacket sent Carter into raptures of silent laughter again. He then proceeded to lie down on his side with his body visibly shaking. He had been studying Dwyer with a quizzical look as he had now decided that this was time to start smoking.

Once he had his hysterics under control, he partially rested his weight on his left elbow and looked back towards Dwyer slightly over his shoulder.

'At least my home is safe,' said Carter as he nodded towards the cigarette in Dwyer's hand.

'I didn't take the bet,' replied Dwyer looking slightly indignant.

Dwyer was briefly annoyed with the *'I told you so'*, look on Carter's face but then looked out towards the Channel now smiling. He then took another long drag of the cigarette with a thoughtful look on his face.

'Well, I have seen the calming effect that they have on you so I thought why not. Chances are we are not going to last much longer anyway,' Dwyer said.

'I think we are over the worst of it,' said Carter as they heard the whine of a shell approach and then explode away to their left, which seemed extremely close to Dwyer.

'You reckon?' He said after they had once gain dived for cover. It seemed to him that the whole fleet seemed to open up on the same position as the last shell just hit. They spent a full five minutes laying flat on their faces as at least one hundred rounds slammed into the side of the bluff.

Carter eventually shuffled along the ground so he could speak into Dwyer's ear rather than shouting. 'The shells from the ships are far more accurate than the bombs dropped earlier. They will be aiming at the concrete gun placements and pillboxes. There does not appear to be any really close to us so we should we be okay.'

Dwyer gave Carter a disbelieving look.

Carter continued. 'The planes that are dropping the bombs above must be B-17's because we can't see them. They fly at high altitude. If they were Marauders, we would have been able to see them flying at low level. The problem is most of the bombs seem to be landing inland, probably due to the cloud cover.'

Would have seen them?

I am not entirely sure I would have been looking skywards and shouting don't aim at us 'we're friendly's!'

I was too busy trying to protect my head by trying to bury it up my own arsehole!

'How much longer do you think the bombing will last?' Dwyer said instead.

Carter looked at his watch. 'It is 05h55 hours now. The bombing will probably stop ten minutes before the first wave of troops hit the beaches. The Navy will continue to fire away at the German inland gun positions over their heads as they land, so maybe about half-an-hour.'

Dwyer took the last drag of his cigarette and put it out on the ground next to him. He then immediately lit another one as the ground shook around him. The thought of waiting for a stray bomb falling right on top of them in the next twenty-five minutes was worse than waiting for the hangman.

At least with the latter you knew your fate.

26

Dwyer now sat up with his back resting against the concrete wall, brought his knees up to his chest and rested his chin on them. He closed his eyes and started to count the seconds off in his head as he had done when he was a child and could not get to sleep.

One . . . One thousand.

Two . . . Two thousand.

Three . . . Three thousand.

How long are you going to keep this up for?

As long as it takes for the world and his wife to stop trying to blow me up into tiny pieces.

Should have stayed at home. At least they don't drop bombs on you every other second in prison. Maybe once in awhile. But not every other second. These are big mothers too.

Maybe.

Maybe? What do you mean, maybe?

Well at least I avoided prison and don't have to worry about dropping the soap in the shower here.

That's true. You would have been out in a maximum of five years though. You would have never got more than a manslaughter charge. After all, they didn't give you a choice, and considering your size, I'm sure you could avoid the bum tickling in the shower block. Just take the top 'Chutney Ferret' out by giving him a good kicking, and no one else would have bothered you again.

At least I got to kill some German's.

That won't bring back your family though, and besides, it wasn't the poor bastards that you ruthlessly stabbed and beat to death that flew the planes that dropped the bombs that killed them. Everyone is just following orders.

Everyone is just following orders?

Of course. Even you. Why else would you be here in the middle of hell on earth? If you feel that strongly about it, why don't you just march your way up to Berlin and stick a bayonet in Hitler's throat. He is ultimately to blame.

Maybe I will.

Well, good luck with that.

Every time I close my eyes, I see the lifeless eyes of the men I killed staring up at me. This is going to haunt me for the rest of my life.

As the Major said, 'War is Hell.'

Master of the understatement, the Major.

Maybe, but remember. You didn't have a choice. Given half a chance, anyone of the Germans you killed would have done the same to you. You didn't start this war. You just want it to end... Like almost everyone else. Almost everyone.

Thanks. But that's not much consolation. I can see their eyes looking up at me NOW!

You have to shut it out. Do whatever it takes to get through this. Remember, it's nothing personal.

Right. It's nothing personal.

That's right.

Just do what it ever takes to survive?

That's right.

Do whatever it takes to get back home to Sally?

Yes. She's worth fighting for.

You're right. I have to have a focus. A will to continue. Something has to drive me on. Sally is my focus. Sally is my motivation.

That's good. Focus on Sally.

I wish I had a picture of her though.

27

Only one minute and thirty seconds of Dwyer fighting with his inner turmoil had passed, when he felt Carter nudge him in the arm.

'Are you okay? You were muttering something to yourself.'

That's one of the first signs of madness Davey. Talking to yourself. You have to keep our little conversations private. Okay?

Okay.

'I'm fine. I was just thinking of Sally.'

'That's good. You have to have a focus on something unrelated to the war to keep you going.'

Is this bloke a mind reader or something?

Dwyer disguised his astonishment by nodding and looking away to his right. He felt goose bumps appear on his arms and a prickling sensation break out on his scalp.

That was spooky. How loud was I muttering?

He rubbed his arms and then took off his helmet and scratched his head.

Carter's voice brought him back to his terrifying reality.

'When the troops land, see if you can do something about the trenches above. There are no doubt machine-gun positions in them.' He handed him a fragmentation grenade. 'Just pull out the pin, wait for a few seconds, throw it in there and get down.'

He wants me to do what?

Dwyer's eyes grew large. He studied the weapon of death intently and rolled around it around in hands slowly examining every detail. His attention finally settled on the circular pin. He had not paid them any attention when he had been packing his rucksack whilst in an almost hallucinogenic haze back at Greenham Common. He had been in too much haste when transferring Brooks', Hickey's and Henderson's, into his own rucksack.

More death.

At least you won't have to look into their eyes this time.

No, they will probably be blown from their sockets.

'Just pull the pin, wait a few seconds, throw it in there and get down,' Carter repeated looking at Dwyer with real concern for the first time.

He was beginning to realise that Dwyer was staring to show signs of severe signs of stress.

He did not blame him.

The effect of shooting the German soldier earlier had had more than an unsettling effect on him. With any luck, he would be headed back across the channel towards Portsmouth in a hospital ship in a couple of hours with Dwyer at his side. This hideous ordeal would be then behind them.

Dwyer nodded and gave the grenade back to him. He then lit a further two cigarettes and handed one to Carter. He then proceeded to study the lit end of his own and watched how the tobacco and cigarette paper slowly burned down leaving a cylinder of gray ash in its trail behind its relentless quest towards his fingers.

'Ashes to ashes, dust to dust,' he muttered to himself and then stubbed the cigarette out without taking one drag when he felt the warmth reach his skin. He then lit a further one and took a deep, long soothing drag, which made his head spin.

His previously tensed shoulders relaxed.

'Feel better?' Carter said who had been observing him the whole time.

'Just fine and dandy,' said Dwyer now smiling realising that Carter was staring at him with a look of concern. 'Don't worry Eddie; I'm just having a bad five minutes.'

The worst was yet to come.

28

The Allied bombing and shelling continued. Both Dwyer and Carter were now almost oblivious to thunderous noise surrounding them.

It's amazing what you get used to.
Aint that the truth.

Dwyer's stomach rumbled, trying to compete with the noise made by the latest 500-pounder exploding inland.

'I am absolutely starving. I could eat a horse,' said Dwyer

'Careful what you wish for,' said Carter with a slight smile. 'If you stay in France long enough you may get to do that very thing.'

'What?'

'Apparently they eat them over here. Or so I have been told.'

He must be pulling my plonker.

'You're joking, right?'

Carter shook his head with a now broadening smile appearing at the corner of his mouth.

Dwyer suddenly burst out into uncontrollable laughter.

Carter welcomed the break in the tension and watched Dwyer have his moment of hilarity. 'What's so funny?' He said when Dwyer had stopped wiping the tears from his eyes.

'I just had a vision of Walter Nightingall returning to the stable and seeing the stable lads each tucking into a leg of Straight Deal like some enormous chicken.' The laughter resumed. He held the sides of his stomach and then eventually said, 'Just imagine the look on his face when he realises the stud rights have gone down the shitter.'

Again, Carter let him calm down before asking, 'Who is Walter Nightingall?'

'He was the trainer of Straight Deal who won The Derby in 1943.'

'Presumably that's some kind of big horse race over in England?'

Dwyer looked towards Carter. 'You don't follow horse racing?'

Carter shook his head.

'Me neither normally, but yes. It's the richest horse race in

England. If memory serves, it's the last time I won a bet with the bookies. I only bet on it because of the name.'

That's something a girl would say.

Shut it.

'Straight Deal,' Carter repeated. 'I like that.' He was then overcame with a sense of guilt, as he had been far from straight with Dwyer up to now regarding why he got him in the mess in the first place.

He looked away to his left to ensure that his facial expression was not exposing his inner thoughts.

In a further attempt to hide his embarrassment, he opened one of the rucksacks and took out two tan-coloured rectangular boxes which had 'US ARMY FIELD RATION K' printed on them. He then took out one smaller box from each with **BREAKFAST** printed on and handed one to Dwyer.

Dwyer looked at the box suspiciously, which had the letter B printed on both ends. With a great deal of curiosity, he opened it. It contained a can of ham and eggs, some biscuits, a cereal bar, a fruit bar, some gum, soluble coffee, sugar and water purification tablets, a can opener or key, a spoon, four cigarettes and even a small supply of toilet roll.

That will come in handy. No doubt, I will shit myself at some point if this gets any worse.

He put the four cigarettes into his pocket and then went straight for the tin of ham and eggs. He then carefully peeled back the lid with the key provided, picked up the spoon and ate hungrily. He looked towards Carter whose first choice was the cereal bar. He appeared to have at least half of it is in mouth and was chewing away furiously. They both gave each other foolish boyish grins and tucked into the remainder of their feast.

Once finished, Carter gestured towards Dwyer for his empty can and then cleaned out the inside (which Dwyer had done a pretty good job of with his spoon). He then produced a hit flask from the inside of his jacket pocket, poured half its contents of Brandy into it and handed it to Dwyer. He then repeated the process for himself.

'I think the word you Brits use is Cheers,' Carter shouted as he raised his tin.

'Down the hatch,' shouted Dwyer back and they touched tins.

Both men slowly raised the tins to their lips and took small sips. Neither felt that this should be rushed. Every last drop was to be savoured.

Dwyer looked towards Carter and said in his best imitation posh voice, 'Thank you Major, terribly decent of you old boy,' and then burst out laughing.

Carter raised both his eyebrows. The joke was lost on him.

'I feel like I am on the beach at Southsea seafront having a picnic. All we need are blazers and straw boaters and we would be complete,' said Dwyer.

With that, a shell slammed into the bluff about twenty feet below their position. It sent earth flying around in all directions. Some of which, landed in Dwyer's drink.

He looked down forlornly. He then shrugged his shoulders, fished out a couple of the offending larger pieces, flicked them away and carried on drinking.

After finishing it off, he turned to Carter and said, 'That's better. At least I can't taste cow shit, blood and puke in my mouth now. How many have we got of those ration boxes?'

'We have thirteen left between us. Three breakfasts, five dinners and five suppers.'

'What's the difference between them?'

'Hardly anything, the dinner has a cheese product and a candy bar, but they are pretty much the same.'

'Throw me over another breakfast then,' said Dwyer.

Carter did so, and took one for himself.

Just as they were finishing, they looked at each other with wide eyes. The aerial bombing appeared to have stopped and the shelling from the fleet had reduced dramatically.

They both raised themselves onto their knees and looked towards the shoreline through their binoculars.

PART FOUR

Chaos

anarchy, bedlam, commotion, confusion, disorder, madness, pandemonium.

I

Dwyer and Carter both held their breath. The deafening noise of the last hour seemed to stop completely. An eerie silence descended. Dwyer shuddered as if someone had walked over his grave.

'Something's wrong. There only seems to be half a company landing here. Something's horribly wrong,' Carter said.

The landing craft approached the beach. The doors opened. The Germans had been ordered to start firing when the enemy reached the waterline. Now, they opened up.

Both Dwyer and Carter ducked initially as the Germans above them in the trench systems began firing.

The results of which were catastrophic.

They both looked on horror as the troops in the first craft were obliterated. The majority were killed before they even attempted to leave the craft. Those that did were either shot in the water, which was up to their shoulders, or soon after when they made onto the beach.

Some appeared to be taking cover behind the hedgehogs. As soon as they made a run for it across the two hundred metres of beach to the sea wall, they were mercilessly cut down by machine-gun fire.

Dwyer was left totally immobilised with fear, and although every sense in his body was screaming at him to look away, he could not tear the binoculars away from his eyes. As he scanned the beach, he could see men literally blown into pieces from mortar rounds, which seemed to him to create red mist as their bodies disintegrated.

One soldier who had braved to leave the cover of the hedgehog was cut in half by machine-gun crossfire. His companion next to him was running in slow motion with both of his arms blown off before eventually collapsing. Another lost both his legs, collapsed to the ground and appeared to be still slowing moving forwards by clawing at the sand with his hands. Two others were decapitated in rapid succession.

This is sick.

Master of the understatement.

Dwyer returned to his attention to a further landing craft that was in process of lowering its ramp. As it was halfway down, a mortar round hit and the whole craft exploded. Body parts were thrown in every direction into the sky. Two crafts immediately behind it that were carrying tanks appeared to be sinking. A further craft to the left had also just been hit by a mortar round and troops were falling over the edge on fire into the water.

This is not happening in front of my own eyes.
I'm afraid it is.
It can't be. What a waste of human life.
Puts the six Germans you took care of into perspective, doesn't it?
They don't have a chance. Why do they keep coming forward?
Just following orders.
Maybe. But this IS personal now.
Why is it personal?
Because witnessing this is going to fuck me up for the rest of my life, that's why.
Focus on Sally.

He scanned the beach closer to the bluff and noticed that some men had almost made it to the sea wall and were now crawling. The more fortunate ones that were still running appeared to be doing so in slow motion due to the weight of their equipment and that their packs were waterlogged.

Dwyer tore his gaze away from the carnage unfolding and looked straight out to sea. He could not see any further craft that would be landing anytime soon, although some did appear to be angling towards their position slowly from the west.

He lowered his binoculars and looked at Carter who was looking westwards further down the beach.

Dwyer followed suit.

About eight hundred metres away, a further group of landing craft had landed almost simultaneously and those troops there were not fairing any better. Due to the distance, everything appeared in miniature.

Dwyer could see men leaving the waterline and instantly falling to the sand or disappearing completely when mortar rounds hit, which created a vertical shower of sand, blood and body parts. He continually checked the progress of those that had dived down onto the sand as soon as they had reached the beach to see if they were moving.

The majority were not.

2

Now consumed by an uncontrollable rage eating him up inside, Dwyer started to shake.

He was witnessing total carnage.

He lowered his head, and for the first time since he was ten years old, unashamedly, started to cry. He then moved to the back of the overhang, wiped the tears from his eyes, took a cigarette from his pocket and lit it.

I can't watch anymore.
No. What can you do to help?
Nothing.
Are you sure?

After taking a huge lungful of smoke, he wiped his eyes once more with the cleaner sleeve of his jacket and returned to his knees.

Instead of looking out onto the horror on the beach, he looked down the bluff below him. Just below their position, he could make out a path weaving in and out of the bushes. He patted Carters arm and pointed towards it.

Carter looked down and nodded, 'That must lead to the beach.'

'I am going to go down there and check it out,' said Dwyer. 'I can't sit here and watch this any further.'

As he bent down to pick up his rifle, a shell exploded into the bank below, which sent him flying to the back of the overhang crashing against the concrete wall. After he picked himself up, he noticed that Carter was laying flat on his back with his legs from the knee down folded underneath him. Blood was trickling from a cut above his left eye and a bruise had immediately appeared. He had been struck by a large stone from the blast from the explosion.

Dwyer gently shook Carter to see if he was conscious and received no response. He then rolled him onto his side and gently straightened his legs. He then shook him again a little more vigorously. Carter opened his eyes briefly; they rolled in their sockets and then closed again.

'Major, can you hear me?'

Nothing.

'Major.'

Nothing.

'Oh that is just great,' Dwyer shouted to himself.

'Wake up,' Dwyer shouted even louder. 'You got me into this fucking mess.'

After not receiving the slightest response, he gave up and returned his attention to the path below. He then took one more look though his binoculars at the beach and noticed further landing craft approaching the waterline. There appeared to be a few more than the first wave, but not many.

I think it's best if you look away.

Dwyer felt completely helpless. He wanted to shout out and tell them to go back, but again, he could not seem to take his eyes of the inevitable slaughter that was about to take place.

This is your last chance. Look away, NOW!

The ramps of the landing craft opened.

Immediately the Germans in the positions above him and below opened fire.

The noise was deafening.

The result was much the same as before, but still Dwyer looked on with morbid, terrified curiosity. He felt like the gates of hell had opened before him and he was being given a sneak preview of what may lie in store.

He looked to his left and saw that two tanks had made it to the shoreline and were firing at a position west of him.

He allowed himself the briefest moment of optimism.

Two lines of troops were following them in taking cover from the murderous firepower raining down on them. His newfound optimism soon evaporated when the more advanced of the two tanks was hit by a mortar shell and exploded with flames shooting out in all directions. The men who had been following close behind turned into human torches. One of them who had not been killed outright by the initial blast appeared to be trying to run back towards the sea in attempt to extinguish the flames that engulfed him. He did not make it as he was then cut in half by machine-gun fire.

Mother of God.

Dwyer now scanned back to his right. Three further landing craft were trying in vain to offload their troops. Those that made it to the shoreline, all now appeared to crawling along the sand as opposed to trying to run in crouched firing positions. Those that appeared to making the most progress temporarily went out view as they were obscured by a shingle bank. He guessed it was forming some form of cover. Periodically, men would appear from behind it and try to run to the base of the sea wall.

He looked on in awe at the bravery these men were displaying. Despite the fact that the sea was now filled with floating lifeless bodies and the beach itself resembled an open burial site littered with body parts, these men still kept pushing forward.

Poor bastards have nowhere else to go!

Dwyer could see that one soldier was taking cover by pushing a dead body in front of him through the water and then continued to do so when he made it to the beach. His progress was halted as he joined the deceased when a mortar round landed right on top of him and sent his body parts in all directions around the beach.

A few of the troops appeared to be running from one prone body to the next and checking on their progress. They would then get up and run to the next. Dwyer guessed these to be medics and once again could not imagine the courage required to go about your duty under the most horrific conditions. He watched in awe as they scurried to one fallen soldier after another, without any seemingly thought for their own safety.

They have a focus.
I bet they are not thinking of their girlfriends back home right now.
Maybe they are, and that is what is keeping them going.
Maybe.

Turning back to the west, he noticed that there were considerably more men running the gauntlet to be what seemed to be the safety of the sea wall. He could not understand why in comparison such relatively few landing craft had approached directly in front of his position and that there appeared to be huge gaps in the line of troops assaulting the beach.

Dwyer checked his watch and saw to his astonishment that it was now 07h45. Over an hour had passed since the first troops had landed which seemed to him be literally minutes ago. He quickly looked out to sea and could not clearly make out if a further wave of crafts were approaching due to the smoke.

He returned his attention back to Carter.

Lucky for you, he thought, he was unconscious and was in a welcome oblivion.

3

Dwyer was then hit by a sweep of depression as if a large wave had crashed on the shingle of the beach and then slowly retreated to the ocean. He briefly questioned his own mortality. He started to think how insignificant he was, in the big scheme of things. The men that were dying on that beach, had families, friends, memories. All of which had now been brutally and mercilessly snatched away from them.

Is this how it is all going to end? A hundred different body parts strewn over a northern French beach.

He shook his head to try to dislodge the misery within.

Focus. Focus on Sally.

Focus on getting back to Sally.

He took the canteen from his belt and unscrewed the lid. He then gently poured a small amount of water onto Carter's face, who immediately stirred. Dwyer then splashed some water over his own face, which despite the small amount, felt incredibly good and soothing.

He lifted Carter to the wall at the back of the overhang by holding him under his armpits and then lit a cigarette and gave it to him. He then lit one for himself.

'How long have I been out?' Carter slurred as if he had been on the source all day.

'I am not sure. I just checked my watch and it has been over an hour since they started to land.'

Dwyer checked his watch again and. A further five minutes had passed in the blink of an eye. 'It's 07h50.'

So fast.

'How are we getting on?'

Dwyer looked to the ground and shook his head.

'It's an absolute bloody slaughter. Another small wave came in while you were out but they did not do much better than the first. There seems to be ten times the amount of troops landing off to our left. I don't understand it.'

Carter raised his hand to the throbbing above his left eye and then inspected his fingers to see if there was any blood. What there were was now dried, with a mixture sand and soil thrown in for good measure.

'It appears that this has been one total fuck up,' said Carter wearily, having now regained his normal speech. 'The fact that our boys got torn to ribbons indicates that the air force and the navy didn't exactly hit their targets. We were supposed to have at least partially secured the beachheads by now. It also appears that they are not landing where they are supposed to.'

I figured that one out for myself.

Dwyer did not comment. He just stared at the Major with a growing sense of dread, as the confirmation of his own thoughts was the last thing he wanted to hear.

Carter then quickly grabbed his rifle, aimed and fired over Dwyer's shoulder, which sent Dwyer tumbling backwards. He turned to his right to see a German soldier start to tumble down the bluff and then once again set off the obligatory mine. Dwyer took some consolation that at least this time flying limbs did not land anywhere near them.

The second of Carter's victims did not have the same effect on him as the first as he casually turned to Dwyer and said, 'Did you check where that path leads to while I was out?'

Dwyer ignored the Majors question. 'Jesus Christ. Where the fuck did he come from?' He said.

'From the path leading up from the beach. Did you check it out?'

Dwyer looked down the path suspiciously to see if any other Germans were descending and eventually said, 'No. I didn't want to leave you on your own.'

Carter allowed himself a smile. He was touched. 'Do you feel like having a look now?' He said.

Eh?

'Not now. . . Not really.' Again, he looked towards the path as if some kind of imaginable beast from bottom of the sea was going to start climbing the bluff towards him.

It is better than doing nothing.

Yeah, but there be monsters down there.

Carter was looking at him expectantly when he returned his wide-eyed gaze towards him.

Sometimes a look can speak more than a thousand words and he was left in doubt the Carter was waiting for him to change his mine.

It is better than doing nothing.

Dwyer took a deep breath and took another untrusting look towards the path twisting downwards below. After a moments consideration, he returned his gaze back towards Carter and nodded.

'Good man,' Carter said. 'Just make sure that when you come back up, you raise your helmet in the air.'

'Why?' Dwyer said.

'I certainly don't want to shoot you, do I my friend?'

Dwyer reached for his rifle.

Assuming I do make it back, he thought.

4
10th July 1943
Autryville, North Carolina, USA
03h50 hours

Just as the woman reached the closet door, she felt a hand grab a handful of hair and yank her backwards. Her scream was stifled by a further hand violently grabbing her mouth.

She was twisted round to look into the eyes of 'Mr Star Gazer' whose face in the half-light looked to her be to be insanely demonic. He slapped her on her right cheek with the back of his right hand.

'Now why would you be trying to run off into the closet?' He said, and then gestured to the member of the group on his immediate right to go in and check it out.

'Let's have a little look what we can find, shall we? Remember, quiet as mouse now . . . WHOOP.'

> Hickory Dickory Dock,
> The Mouse ran up the clock,
> The mouse ran down,
> Hickory Dickory Dock.
> WHOOP. . .

The insane quiet chanting of the nursing rhyme was disturbed by the group member returning from the closet with a shotgun. He handed it to 'Mr Star Gazer', shifting from one foot to another in anticipation.

'Well lookey, lookey here. I wonder if it is loaded, let's see shall we?'

He brought the end of the rifle up to her face.

'Open your mouth, bitch.'

The woman closed her eyes and shook her head.

He once again grabbed a handful of hair and violently pulled. 'I said open your mouth, you fucking bitch.'

She slowly did as instructed with tears slowly running down her cheeks.

The end of the rifle was slowly slid between her lips.

Sniggering filled the room.

'Mr Star Gazers' face blackened . . . and then pulled the trigger.

CLICK.

'Hmm . . . It must be your lucky day . . . not loaded.'

The woman now became completely paralysed by fear. She did not even feel the urine that was now running down both her legs onto the carpeted floor.

'Look at this,' said 'Mr Star Gazer looking down. 'This dirty bitch has just pissed herself.'

He then took a deliberate step back so that he would not be standing in it.

'Maybe we should do what we did to the dog when he did that. Shall I rub your nose in it, bitch?' He hissed.

The woman just stared back into his face with terrified eyes . . . unable to muster up the process of thought to form any kind of coherent response.

'Good idea,' said one of the others. 'Teach her a lesson not to do it again.'

'Mr Star Gazer' then thrust the woman's head down towards the floor, which made her legs buckle. He then commenced to move her head from side to side on the carpet whilst still holding her by the hair.

5

Garcia had regained consciousness thirty seconds before the first explosion courtesy of the allied bombers had exploded.

His first emotion was euphoria that he was still alive, he had fully expected that Dwyer was going to finish him off once he had manhandled him in the barn earlier. He then realised that he had a splitting headache and his jaw and balls hurt like hell.

I guess you think we are even now, do you? You big lump of limey shit, he thought as held his groin doubling over on the floor grimacing.

As he was lying there feeling sorry for himself and trying to get his eyes accustomed to the dark, he heard and felt the tremor of the first thump of the 500-pound bomb that hit the ground.

He gingerly got to his feet, took off his rucksack and opened it. After desperately fumbling around through the contents, he found a small torch and turned it on. The small beam of light did not make much difference to the almost complete darkness of the barn as it was designed for reading maps, but it was better than nothing.

Garcia turned to the wall that he had been previously slumped against. He slowly then moved the small beam of light from left to right along a shelf. To his delight, he found a kerosene lamp, which he then gently shook next to his ear to see he could hear if any fuel remained inside.

It had. He smiled.

Three bombs then hit in the field behind the barn where Dwyer and Carter had set off from earlier. They shook its very foundations, which knocked Garcia off his feet. He struggled to ensure that he did not drop the lamp.

The smile disappeared.

After picking himself up, he quickly placed the lamp on the table and lit it. The interior of the barn was now clearly visible in a slight orange glow.

Garcia slowly looked all around him, taking in his surroundings. He noticed a pile covered by tarpaulin in the back corner and walked towards it. He lifted up one corner and after a second of confusion, he sprang away from it and let out a startled yelp realising that he was looking down into the face of a dead body whose lifeless eyes was staring back up at him.

'Goddamn it! That's enough to give anyone a heart attack,' he said aloud to himself.

On regaining his composure, it then came back to him what the two Germans that had been interrogating him about earlier. They had been asking in broken English about the pile of the bodies that they had discovered lying in the corner. He thought better of it to take a further closer inspection and shuddered at the thought that he been lying next to them while he had been unconscious.

Realisation then struck him that one of the bodies must be Henderson's thanks to Dwyer's earlier handiwork. He silently questioned Dwyer's parenthood.

He then turned towards the motorbike and sidecar that he had seen Dwyer and Carter drive off on down the lane, and which fortunately for him, they had returned not long after.

As his thoughts about getting on it and trying to make some kind of escape from the area entered his head, a further bomb exploded. This time, it was in the field opposite and the aftershock sent him crashing to the floor once again. The kerosene lamp fell over onto its side and slowly rolled towards the edge of the table.

Garcia jumped to his feet and caught it just as it was about to fall on the floor. As the dust from the barn roof gently descended upon him, he placed the lamp on the floor beside the motorcycle trying to decide what he was going to do. Thoughts of gaining retribution on Dwyer and Carter had now slipped his mind. He was more concerned about his own immediate well-being.

He still had no idea where he was.

He sat down leaning against the rider's seat of the motorcycle and took out a map from his inside jacket pocket. After briefly studying it, he shook his head. No matter how long he stared at it, he would never be any the wiser.

As he returned it to his pocket, he noticed three M-1 rifles leaning against the side of the barn. He picked each one up in turn and flicked the safeties off. As he was about to the place the last of three back against the wall, the side door to the barn burst open and three terrified German troops tumbled through.

Such was their haste, not one of them noticed Garcia who immediately raised his own rifle towards them. The last of the three through the door frantically closed it as if this would provide them their salvation. All three appeared to Garcia to be exhausted and were gasping for breath. The nearest to Garcia was bent forwards with his hands on his knees.

He slowly looked up and saw the rifle pointed straight at him. Garcia did not hesitate. He pulled the trigger. The bullet entered the German right in the middle of his forehead and exited out the back of his head taking half the skull with it and a considerable amount of blood. It splattered against the wooden panelling behind him.

The remaining two Germans reacted very differently.

The one to Garcia's left froze.

Garcia turned the rifle on him and shot him in the chest. This sent the German crashing backwards to the wall of the barn just to the left of the side entrance door.

The other instantly withdrew an enormous knife from his belt and charged. He covered the last three feet between them by performing a perfectly executed rugby tackle and collided with Garcia just above the waist.

They both went sprawling to the floor with the German landing on top.

Both men grunted when hitting the floor.

Garcia was the quicker to react. He managed to free both of his arms and raised his hands to the Germans face who was desperately trying to free his hand that was holding the knife that was trapped under their combined body weights.

He didn't make it.

Garcia pressed both of his thumbs into the Germans eyes, raised his head and started to bite down as hard as he possibly could on his nose, smiling and squealing as he did so.

The German let out a piercing scream and rolled away to his left. Garcia immediately sprang to his feet, grabbed the rifle at the same time, swivelled and shot the German in the stomach.

He bent double and raised his right hand up towards Garcia whilst pleading, 'Bitte nicht schieBen.'

Garcia bent his knees and crouched down pointing his rifle towards the now panic-stricken Germans face.

'*Bitte nicht schieBen,*' he repeated, '*Ich habe kinder.*'

Garcia stared down into his face and started to smile.

Now believing that his life was going to be spared, the German smiled back and said in English, 'My name is Anders, please do not shoot.'

'Hello Anders,' Garcia said and ignored his request. He pulled the trigger and shot his prisoner in the face.

A mixture of teeth, blood and bone exploded from his head. Smoked slowly drifted up from the entry wound.

Garcia now calmly slowly turned his head from side to side examining what was left of the young Germans features. He then started to giggle like a child and rocked back and forwards on his heels.

'Wow.' He said to himself. 'Look at you now, Anders. I have appeared to have ruined your rugged good looks.' The demented childlike cackle then returned.

A further series of explosions sent dust falling from the ceiling. Garcia snapped out of his trance like state and returned to some semblance of normality. He stood up and walked to his two earlier victims.

After dragging them towards the back of the barn to the previously formed pile of bodies, he positioned them with their backs against the wall and sat them upright.

He then turned and looked towards the motorcycle and immediately dismissed the idea of his previous thoughts of making a break for freedom.

'Probably not a good idea,' he said aloud. 'Not with all that Goddamn bombing going on. No sir, I think I best stay put for the time being. And besides, there are bound to be a load more Krauts waiting for me out there.'

He then nodded his head in agreement with the speech he had just made.

'Yes sir. I am going to stay put,' he added.

With the decision made, he walked to the side door and opened it. He carefully stuck his head out and looked first right, then left.

He hurriedly retreated inside and closed the door when he saw two further Germans running towards him round the bend of the lane.

'I knew it,' he said aloud.

Garcia looked round the barn looking for a non-existent hiding place. He dragged the table to the right side of the barn, thought better of it than to turn off the kerosene lamp, and then dragged the body of the German, Anders, to the right of the other two to ensure there was a gap in between them. He then sat down in it and aimed his rifle towards the door.

'C'mon inside,' he whispered. 'It's really nice and cosy in here.'

He thought at first that the soldiers had run past without stopping until he heard the excited voices shouting at each other immediately outside the side door. The door burst open and the Germans entered and closed it behind them. On turning round to inspect the barns interior, Garcia shot at them.

The one on his left died instantly as the bullet went straight through his heart. The second staggered backwards as he had been hit in the left shoulder. Garcia sprang to his feet and fired off three more shots at his head. The third of which did the job.

Once again, he dragged the bodies to the wall at the end of the barn and sat them upright against the wall. After positioning himself back in the gap between the bodies he had made earlier, he lit a cigarette and stared at the door once more.

No one else came through it.

Whilst still not taking his eyes off it, he said aloud, 'What do you think of the party so far boys? Anyone having fun yet?'

As if expecting a response he turned his head left both ways to look at the dead Germans sat beside him.

'No, me neither. This place is like a morgue.' He then started his insane laughter again and started to think about where Dwyer and Carter were.

6

Dwyer took one look back at Carter before leaving the area from under the overhang. He went to say something but could not think of anything worthwhile.

He remained silent.

Carter had emptied his ammo pouch and placed three fragmentation grenades in it, which he gave to Dwyer to carry. On passing it to him had simply said, 'Good Luck.'

Luck? I am going to need a bit more than luck.
Master of the understatement.

Dwyer stepped from underneath their hiding place for the last hour and twenty minutes and first looked up towards the trenches above. To his right, he could clearly see two machine-gun positions with men spread about between peering over the top of the trench looking towards the Channel. They were not firing at present due to the lack of landing crafts heading towards their area of the beach.

His first thought was to open fire on them but as quickly as the thought came into his head, he dismissed it. He realised that at most, he could only take out a couple of them before attracting their full attention, which would then have given him a life expectancy of about one second. Instead, he crouched down as low as possible on the path and started to move down towards the beach.

Almost immediately, the path turned to the left. It was flanked by thick bushes on either side. He stopped at the bend at slowly looked round the corner. On seeing that the path was clear, he took two small paces down it and then stopped.

Jesus Christ!

The sight in front of him made him put his hand over his mouth and then took every piece of willpower imaginable to stop from throwing up again. He had enjoyed his two breakfasts earlier and did not wish to part company from them so soon.

The body of one the Germans that Carter had earlier shot was lying in front of him, at least what was left of it. All that remained was his torso and the bottom half of the head. Dwyer could only make out the mouth and about half of the nose. All the limbs were missing. What made the sight worse was that a large rat was gnawing away at the bottom of the torso.

Hello again breakfasts!

It was almost as if his stomach took on a mind of its own. It erupted like a volcano angrily spewing its contents upwards until one final bit of pressure exploded its load out of the crater at the top – or in this case – three craters.

Vomit flew from Dwyer's mouth and nostrils in all directions, making his eyes water in the process. Such was the force of the heave that it was over almost as soon as it had started. Dwyer simultaneously wiped his eyes and spat the last remaining remnants of his earlier feast onto the path below.

He looked back towards the rat accusingly and raised his rifle as if to shoot it.

It was oblivious to his angry presence. Instead, it buried its head deeper into the carcass and carried on with its meal.

This is one fucked up day at the beach – Go for a swim – Buy an ice cream – Fly a kite – Throw up, twice! – Witness a total human massacre – Watch a blown up German be eaten by a rat. Nice . . . Bring the family!

It could be worse.

What the fuck are you on about, it could be worse? Sometimes I wonder about you!

It could be you instead lying down there – FOCUS!

Dwyer took one pace towards the remnants of the body. The rat stopped eating and looked round towards him. He then dismissed him and nuzzled even deeper into bloody mess of innards and entrails.

Dwyer walked past and thought *'brave little bugger'* and let it carry on with its feast.

After another four paces, the path came to a further bend, which this time almost doubled back on itself. The gradient now started to increase. On checking that the path was clear, he turned sideways and took several small steps moving his leg left first downwards and then joined it with his right to avoid descending the bluff too rapidly. Such was his concentration that he was oblivious to the gunfire, explosions and screaming that was taking place all along the stretch of beach. He also could not get the thought of the damn rat out of his head.

First cows, now rats. What is going to be fucking next?

On finally making the steep descent, the path took one final gradual turn to the left and then levelled out after about ten yards. At the end of the path was an entrance to what appeared to him to be a concrete tunnel going from left to right as he looked at it. Apart from going back, there was no place else to go. He could clearly hear machine-gun fire from within, off to his left.

He froze. His feet refusing to obey the instructions from his brain to keep moving forward one in front of the other.

Well done feet. I don't know what the fuck that dumb brain of mine is thinking.

You can't just stand her with your thumb up your arse doing nothing.

Well I can't go in there. They will know I'm not German.

Why? What are you going to do? Introduce yourself and ask them what their favourite football team is.

No. But they'll know as soon as I go in I'm not one of them.

YOU HAVE A GERMAN HELMET AND JACKET ON!

7

Holding his breath, he finally made the decision to move forwards. He crept towards the entrance although due to the noise that had just started erupting again from the inside, he could have been banging a bass drum and nobody would have heard him.

Dwyer stood up straight, and with his rifle pointing out in front of him, he casually walked through the entrance and turned left. He considered this casual course of action to be best in order not to arouse suspicion.

The concrete tunnel was in fact a bunker about fifty feet in length and about six feet in width. At the far end in the direction Dwyer was looking, it turned to the left. Ten feet in front of him the roof opened up and he could see the bushes of the bluff behind him. On the right, there were slits in the concrete that the Germans were firing through onto the beach. Behind him, the bunker turned to the right about ten feet away.

Immediately in front of him, a soldier was enthusiastically firing a machine-gun. The gunner had not noticed him enter and the last thing he imagined the German would have been expecting at this particular moment in time; was an enemy soldier entering the bunker system from behind dressed in a German uniform.

Okay, this is not personal... Focus.

Oh, but it is.

Dwyer raised his rifle and shot the German in the side of the head. After seeing him collapse to the floor, he looked down the length of the bunker to see five others all still looking forward, concentrating on firing at anything that moved on the beach. He quickly strode to the first firing position and glanced through the slit. He could see that he was still about thirty feet above it and a further wave of landing crafts were about to lower their ramps at the waterline.

He fumbled with Carters ammo pouch, his hands shaking, and took out two of the grenades and immediately pulled the pins. He threw the first one gently along the floor and the second a lot harder, both underarm. He then turned and ran out of the exit back to the path on the bluff and threw himself to the ground with his arms over his head.

On hearing the *'THUMP' 'THUMP'* of the grenades exploding, he quickly got to his feet and returned to the bunker. All the machine-gun fire had now stopped and with the exception of one the Germans who was sitting on the floor holding his stomach, all the gunners now appeared to be dead. Dwyer slowly walked towards the sole survivor through the smoke and cloud of concrete dust that remained.

He ignored the plea of the soldier who he assumed was asking him to help him and walked towards the end of the bunker where it turned left. With that, a shell hit the outer wall and exploded which sent him flying into the wall on his left. Fortunately, the concrete structure withstood the force and the shell did not penetrate. Apart from now having the ringing back in his ears, Dwyer was unharmed.

He got back to his feet and shouted through one of the slits, 'For fucks sake. I'm on your side.' Not that anyone could have heard him, but it made him feel better anyway.

He continued down the bunker to its end and looked left round the corner. It turned right after only four feet. He walked the short distance and peered round the corner. The roof had now returned and light was filtering through an occasional firing slit on the right hand side facing the beach. It was empty and was about twenty feet long before it made a further turn to the right.

Dwyer turned round and went back towards the Germans he had just taken care of with the grenades. On turning the corner, he saw five soldiers jogging towards him. One other had stopped and was bending over the survivor from the grenades. Dwyer instantly dropped to his knee and started to fire.

The limited amount of practice that he had managed to get in back at Greenham Common was now put into good use. The first three Germans he aimed at were all clean kills, two of them being shot in the head and one in the chest. One of the remainder had been shot in the right arm and the other in the right shoulder. They were now both on the floor holding their wounds. The soldier who had been attending to the grenade victim now stood with his arms up.

'Nie strzelaj. Nie strzelaj. Polski.'

'Don't shoot. Don't shoot.' he repeated in English.

Dwyer shot him anyway.

He then stood up from his firing position and systematically took care of the injured as both were now crawling towards their rifles on the floor. One shot each to the head got the job done.

On reaching the exit of the bunker to go back up to the bluff, he hesitated. He was convinced he had heard an American accent shouting instructions coming from behind the bushes to his right. As the noise of gunfire and explosions once again filled his ears, he quickly dismissed it as wishful thinking.

Dwyer then continued on to the end of the bunker that now veered off to the right. It was the same as the previous, also being empty. He guessed that they were just interconnecting tunnels to other firing positions as where else would the previous Germans had come from, unless they had come down the path in the bluff. With that, his thoughts returned to Carter and he turned round to leave.

You did well back there.

I was starting to wonder where you have been.

You were busy, I didn't want to disturb. Remember it is nothing personal. Just stayed focussed.

Yes. Focus on Sally.

8

Walking back up the bluff was considerably harder work than waking down it. Whether it was something to do with the fact that he had been carrying the Major on his back with a load of equipment all night, Dwyer's thigh muscles were beginning to burn. At the point where the path now turned left back on itself where half a German lay, he stopped for a rest and lit a cigarette. He was now *definitely* sure he heard American voices shouting instructions to each other.

They were American voices, weren't they?
Definately.
You sure?
Absolutely positive!

He was about to shout over the bushes that obscured his view when he thought better of it. He was after all wearing a German helmet and jacket. He threw his cigarette to the floor and walked back up the path. He noticed that the rat had now gone.

Be grateful of small mercies, he thought and then somewhat unbelievably started to feel hungry again.

Amazing what you get used to.

On turning the last corner back towards the overhang, he glanced over to his right and stopped dead in his tracks. It took every ounce of willpower and self-control not to start jumping up and down and shouting at the top his voice to attract attention. He could definitely now see American soldiers scaling the bluff about fifty yards from his position. They were now further away than when he had heard their voices and appeared to be zigzagging up a path to the top of the bluff, albeit very slowly. He could not make out for sure how many there were as they went in and out of his sightline but his spirits soared through the roof.

Dwyer now sprinted back to the Major to tell him the good news. This however had not gone unnoticed by one of the men operating a machine-gun in the trenches above.

When Dwyer reached the area under the overhang, his heart flew up into his mouth. Carter was slumped against the back wall resting on his rucksack. His immediate thought was that he had been discovered and killed. He knelt down beside him and quickly inspected his torso and head for any injuries. On not noticing any, he gently shook his shoulder.

Carter immediately opened his eyes and on seeing Dwyer, he smiled.

'For fucks sake,' said Dwyer. 'I thought you were dead.'

Carter's smile broadened.

'Just had another tiny shot of morphine, I will be back with you in a minute,' Carter said and closed his eyes again.

A smile now appeared on Dwyer's face and he sat down next to him. He took yet another cigarette from his pocket, lit it and got busy getting lost in his thoughts.

There he was running around the French countryside killing the enemy, him being a civilian until just under a week ago, and there is this Major of the 101st Airborne spending half of his time out of his head on drugs.

Must be a nice way to fight a war.

Although he had never touched drugs in his life; if you did not count alcohol, the thought of a large quantity of it right at this very minute – alcohol that is, would definitely go down well.

Dwyer finished his cigarette and waited for the Major to come out of cloud cuckoo land.

9

Ten minutes and two further cigarettes later, Dwyer picked up the binoculars and looked down the bluff to his left. He searched in vain for the Americans he had seen on the bluff earlier. Anxious to see what progress they had made.

Where are they?

He looked at his watch and it was 08h10 hours. He had only left Greenham Common in the Dakota just over ten hours ago but it felt like a week. He was then hit by an overwhelming sense of tiredness and the urge to join Carter in his closing his eyes was irresistible.

He became fully alert, however, when he noticed a German soldier pointing his rifle at him and shouting, *'Warum sind Sie hier versteckt unter Feiglinge?'* He had just jumped down from the path above.

It was same the German that had noticed Dwyer sprinting up the bluff.

Dwyer had no idea what he had just asked, but he sounded mighty pissed off about something. He smiled, shrugged his shoulders and casually picked up his rifle. He made out that he was about to wake up Carter and then in one slick movement, aimed the rifle at the German and pulled the trigger.

For an instant Dwyer thought he had missed, as the German just stood still with a look on his face so surprised that it almost made Dwyer laugh. He had a flashback to the look on Gavin Evans' face in the police station in Portsmouth when Evans realised that he was leaving with Carter.

In slow motion, the German crumpled to the ground.

At the sound of the rifle shot, Carter suddenly became alert, picked up his rifle and started aiming at imaginary targets.

This was now too much to bear for Dwyer and this time he did burst out laughing. Carter stopped his deadly assault on thin air and looked at Dwyer quizzically, which had the effect of Dwyer laughing even harder. Whilst in the middle of his belly laugh he managed to point to the dead German, whose foot was still twitching, to indicate to Carter that their immediate danger had been taken care of.

With the effect of the morphine now abruptly worn off, Carter just nodded and rubbed his eyes.

'How are you feeling?' Dwyer said still smiling.

'Better thanks. Although I don't feel up to dancing the tango just yet.'

Dwyer snorted a laugh and shook his head at the same time.

'What did you find down there?' Carter asked and nodded towards the path and lit a cigarette.

Jesus you are a tight bastard. You could have offered me one.

Focus.

Dwyer made an exaggerated point of lighting one of his own before responding.

'I will get to the path in a minute. The good news is that I saw some Americans scaling the bluff off to our left about ten minutes ago.' He pointed west along the bluff. 'Looks like we may have some friendly company pretty soon. Perhaps we should invite them into our little home here and have some lunch.'

Carter closed his eyes and took in a deep breath.

He eventually opened them with broad grin appearing, 'That is very good news. How many of them were there?'

'It's hard to say. The kept going in out of my line of sight . . . maybe about thirty. I'm not sure.'

'Well thirty is better than none . . . and is probably only the tip of the iceberg. If they can make it, so can others.'

Dwyer nodded and took a drag on his cigarette.

'The other news is that the path leads to a bunker system. When I got there, there were three machine-gun nests firing down onto the beach . . . but not anymore.' He handed back Carter his ammo pouch with only one grenade left inside with his big foolish boyish grin.

'Give that man a Cigar,' said Carter and slapped him on the back.

Dwyer continued. 'The tunnel stretches both ways along the bluff. It must connect to others as I was joined by six others after taking out the machine-gunners.'

'Six? What happened to them?'

'I shot them,' said Dwyer with more calmness than he felt

inwardly.

'My, my. You have been busy,' said Carter smiling and then whistled.

'One of them shouted something at me before I shot him. Do you know any German?'

'Only the basics. Why? What did he say?'

'Something like, 'Polski'.

Carter burst out into a belly laugh of his own that made him grab towards to ankle to keep it from moving.

Dwyer started to smile not sure of what the big joke was but let Carter have his moment and waited patiently for an explanation.

'He was probably telling you not to shoot because he was Polish.'

Eh?

'*Polish!* What the fuck are the Polish doing here? I thought they would have been on our side considering the Germans invaded them.'

Carter shook his head. 'From what I know, many of the Poles have been conscripted and shoved on the front lines to do the Germans dirty work. The word is their hearts are not really in it though.'

'You could have fooled me,' said Dwyer nodding his head towards the beach. 'Looks like they are well up for the fight.'

Carter shook his head. 'No way they are all Poles here. They must be intermingled with a large helping of Germans to make sure they don't surrender too quickly. My guess is that they would have downed tools as soon as the bombs started to drop otherwise.'

As he finished his statement, Dwyer noticed Carter's eyes suddenly go wide.

'*Grenade!*'

On seeing the demise of his friend, whilst looking over the top of the trench above Dwyer's and Carter's hiding place, a further German had left the trench, crept down the path and tried to listen to Dwyer explaining his exploits. On hearing the odd word in English over the noise of battle, he reached down to where the edge of the overhang began and tossed a stick grenade backwards in their direction.

Dwyer looked to his right, and on seeing the grenade, which was very different in shape to the ones he had just used, he picked it up and threw it down the bluff. It exploded in mid-air.

'It looks like we have been discovered,' Cater said.

It promptly kicked-off.

10

At approximately 08h00 hours at Easy Red sector on Omaha Beach, a platoon of Americans that had survived the horrors of the beach landing had breached the sea wall. They placed two bangalore torpedoes together, and by shoving them under the barbed wire, they blew a gap in it.

On advancing through swampland, which was heavily mined, they engaged in small arms fire with the enemy and proceeded to start clearing the bunker systems. On seeing their exploits from the beach below, it gave many of the men still hung-up, the extra courage and inspiration they need to continue to advance. Up to that point, it had been pure living hell.

These were the Americans that Dwyer had seen earlier when returning from the bunker. His thoughts at present however were no longer on them.

Almost instantaneously as the stick grenade had exploded over the bluff, two machine-guns opened up on Dwyer's and Carters position. Not that they had any chance of hitting them hidden under the overhang, but they sure as hell made sure they could no longer go outside and check to see if it was raining.

Dwyer, who was seated, pulled his knees upwards towards his chest and repeated *'Fuck me,'* at least twenty times to himself. Carter did likewise ignoring his broken ankle for the moment only without shouting the obscenity.

The bullets were all kicking up turf on the path about fifteen feet in front of them.

The firing then stopped abruptly as it had started.

Dwyer picked up his rifle and got up onto one knee. He then shifted his position to the right slightly to slot anyone that dared to jump down onto the path. It also gave him a better chance of noticing any grenades that were thrown in from above. All of a sudden, the four-foot space under the overhang, that had been their home for the last two hours, seemed to constrict to four inches such was the vulnerability he now felt.

Carter lay flat on the ground and manoeuvred himself so that his rifle was pointing to Dwyer's right. They both waited for what they thought was the inevitable attack.

Nothing happened.

Dwyer was about to look back towards Carter when he noticed a hand appear holding a further stick grenade right above his head. He reached up and pulled it out. He then threw it down the bluff. It exploded in the brush setting of a further mine for a double whammy explosion. He then jumped out from underneath the overhang, pulled the German soldier over the drop and shot him between the eyes as he landed on his back. He then ducked down and pushed the body down the slope with his foot just left of the path. After the body had rolled down about six-feet, yet another mine exploded. Fortunately, for Dwyer and Carter, such was the angle of the slope the body parts were blown away from them although both were covered in the mist of blood that was created.

Dwyer wiped the blood from his face almost nonchalantly as if it was only sweat, and then resumed his firing position.

'That should make them think twice about trying to throw grenades in again,' Dwyer shouted over his shoulder to Carter.

A quick burst of machine-gun disturbed the path below them again. This time Dwyer did not flinch.

'Fire at the ground all you want, you stupid bastards, I aint coming out again,' Dwyer shouted at the Germans above. 'At least while you are wasting you ammo on the path you are not shooting at the beach.' He then added for good measure, 'Dick heads.'

All of the machine-gun positions above them then opened up again, but none this time, were aimed in their direction. On noticing that the earth on path was not being disturbed, Dwyer quickly reached for his binoculars beside him and looked out to the beach.

He groaned.

Why didn't I keep my mouth shut?

Carter struggled into kneeling position and joined him.

11

Further landing craft had arrived at the waterline and the troops were desperately trying to unload. The tide had come in over the last few hours and many of the obstacles that were clearly visible before were now half covered by the sea.

It was now 08h45 hours.

Dwyer continued groaning. It seemed to him that his earlier efforts in the bunker system had not made the slightest difference. The firepower that the Germans were throwing down on the advancing American troops was still ferocious.

He watched some of the landing craft back away after dropping off their troops to an almost certain death to go and collect yet more for the same hideous ordeal.

With a grimace on his face, he watched yet another craft go up in flames as the ramp opened. The men that were still inside were thrashing around as the flames consumed their bodies as if they were all trying to warn off a million swarming bees. He also could not see any further tanks that had made it onto the beach. Both of the ones that he had noticed earlier were now both out of action with smoke drifting upwards from them into the sky.

He then focused on one soldier that he could see crawling towards the shingle bank that appeared to be wounded as he was dragging his right leg incredibly slowly.

C'mon mate you can make it. Only a little bit further!

Just as he thought he was going to reach to some kind of cover behind the shingle bank, and go out of his sight, a mortar round hit him. One second he was there, the next he exploded into a red mist which seemed to Dwyer to be suspended for an unnatural length of time in the air as if the last remnants of his earthly form was desperately trying to hold on to every last second of life.

These men have families, friends, memories – then gone.

'You Goddamn bastards!' he screamed at the top of his voice, hurting his throat in the process.

His hands started to shake again and it took every ounce of his strength to keep the binoculars on a level plane.

He then turned his attention to a group of three troops that were rolling a dead body in front of them as they also lay flat on the beach and crawled along behind it. Every so often, they would stop and start firing on one of the German positions, then continue rolling the body towards the shingle bank. He eventually lost sight of them and assumed they had to be at the bank. He kept focusing on the spot that they had stopped at. They all then suddenly appeared again and started running and firing at the same time. Not one of them had been hit as they went out of sight and he made a further assumption that they had all made it to the sea wall. He punched the air in delight and then immediately regretted it as he hit the overhang above scraping his knuckles.

This is some kind of fucked up spectator sport.

What? This is no time for jokes – shut up you sick bastard!

I'm sorry – you're right. Just trying to keep you sane – keep things in perspective.

And what perspective would that be?

Silence.

Smoke still filled the channel as the ships were now intensified their assault, hammering away at positions inland and at certain strong points to the west of his position. The aerial bombing of the beach had thankfully stopped on the beach as far as Dwyer was concerned, but he could still hear the larger bombs and feel the aftershocks as they exploded further inland.

He briefly wandered how Garcia was getting on and if he had come round yet. He hoped so. The thought of him cowering in the barn brought a brief smile to his face.

Dwyer then turned his binoculars further westward down the beach and saw a warship in the distant unbelievably close to the beach in front of the screen of smoke. It was cruising along the coastline blasting away at enemy positions. Some other ships seemed to be following its example behind it although not as close in.

He now returned his focus to the Channel immediately in front of their position. There was still no sign of a significant amount of landing craft making their way to this sector of the beach.

He checked the beach again and followed the progress of another poor soul crawling along towards the shingle bank trying to make himself as small as possible. He thought for a horrible moment that the soldier had been killed, as he remained motionless for what seemed minutes. It was only in fact ten seconds. To Dwyer's relief, he then started crawling again with two others now immediately behind him. It seemed to Dwyer that he had been waiting for his buddies to catch him up. The lead soldier then looked up towards the sea wall and his head exploded. He had been shot by machine-gun fire.

Goddamn it!
Why are you putting yourself through this?
Look away. For Christ's Sake. Look away!

All the time, the machine-gun positions directly above them blazed away.

This was enough of observing the beach for Dwyer – his voice of reason had made a valid point. He decided to listen to it. He slumped down into a sitting position and turned towards Carter, realising that he had remained silent for some time now and had not been putting himself through the same overly curious hell as he had.

12

Carter was sat against the concrete wall smoking a cigarette and appeared to be aiming his gun at Dwyer with his left hand. His eyes were clouded and vacant.

Dwyer briefly felt his skin prickle again. All of a sudden, it was like looking into the eyes of his nephew when they had met in Portsmouth. *The cloud blocked out the sun – It's like looking into the eyes of a man with no soul.*

On eventually noticing that Dwyer was now looking at him – which at first with what seemed like a look of fear and dread in his facial expression – he started to shake his head slowly and said, 'I'm sorry, I just can't bear to watch anymore. What the hell has gone wrong?'

I have no idea why I did for so long.

It told you so.

Shut it!

Dwyer noticed that tears were welling up in Carter's eyes and that he appeared to be clenching his jaw in an effort to try to stop the floodgates from opening.

'Don't try and hold it in Ed, I had a good cry earlier without you noticing,' Dwyer said. 'Just let it go.'

With that, Carter instantly let his guard down and started to sob uncontrollably. Dwyer looked away to give him what privacy he could and lit two cigarettes and handed one to Carter.

'Here you go,' Dwyer said. 'You are always bumming mine of me you miserly bastard.'

Dwyer's attempt at humour did the trick as Carter now stopped mid-sob and snorted out a laugh instead. Not only did a laugh come out but also a huge amount of snot from both nostrils, which he quickly wiped away. Unbelievably, considering the circumstances, both men began to laugh together.

On joining Carter, sitting with his back against the concrete wall with his rifle pointing outwards to the bluff, Dwyer said, 'Well thanks for inviting me. It's been great.'

Instead of getting the laugh he was expecting and maybe another two snot balls, Carter said in all seriousness, 'You know, Davey, if we ever get out of this unholy mess you will have to come over to the States and visit me in North Carolina.'

'Only if you buy your own cigarettes,' was his reply.

Carter ignored this further attempt at humour and said, 'If I don't make it, I just want you to thank you now for everything. Getting you into this was total madness on my part. Total and utter complete selfish madness.' He ended his speech ruefully looking at the lit end of his cigarette.

'Still a story for another time?'

Carter appeared to Dwyer to be in conversation with his own voice of reason and just as he thought he was going to start talking, he nodded slowly instead.

I can't imagine what it could be.

Surely it can't be that bad?

He obviously thinks it is – or finds it difficult to talk about.

Obviously.

Dwyer turned away and picked up his binoculars again. He returned to his kneeling position and scanned beyond the waterline. The smoke that was blowing away to the east had slightly cleared. He could just make out what seemed to be huge number of landing craft off in the distance immediately in front of their position and even further craft off to his left. He studied their movements but they did not seem to be getting any closer. Only circling – or at least that what it appeared to him from this distance away.

Don't blame you.

I would be quite happy circling all day rather than trying to come ashore.

Fuck that for a game of soldiers.

This is no game – it is a real as it gets.

Really?

He sat back down again before speaking to Carter, 'Looks like there is a build up of landing craft out in front of us at the moment. When they get here I am going to try and do something about those bastards above us.'

Carter just nodded again. The clouds had returned.

'I wonder how the troops are getting on that I saw climbing the bluff,' Dwyer said.

'I wonder,' said Carter without enthusiasm.

The helmets of two German troops then appeared in the path below that both Carter and Dwyer both noticed at the same time. They appeared to have stopped and they could now see one of them pointing towards the top of the bluff to their left and behind them.

As if a gale force wind had blown the clouds away as quickly as they formed, the sun returned to Carter's now steely and alert gaze.

'They must have come from the bunker below. What do you think they are pointing at?' Dwyer whispered.

'Maybe they have spotted our boys up there,' Carter said.

The Germans both took two further paces up the path, which was the last they would ever make. Dwyer and Carter shot one each.

13

The machine-gun fire that had only been sporadic in the last few minutes from the trenches above now seemed to have stopped completely.

They could both now just about hear some panicked shouting coming from up above.

'I reckon that must be our boys arriving,' said Dwyer.

'Something is definitely going on,' Cater said. 'Fancy taking a peep?'

No.

Dwyer nodded instead and went to walk straight out from under the overhang to investigate.

Carter pulled him back and nodded to his jacket. 'You can't go out there with that jacket and helmet on. The Germans already know that we are the enemy and if our boys are up top, they will shoot at you.'

Good point.

Dwyer took off the helmet and jacket and replaced the helmet with his own that had been attached to his rucksack.

Without saying another word, he left their hiding place and crouched down so that only his head appeared over the four feet drop. He could not see anything but the fact nobody fired at him was definitely a bonus.

He then heard a rattle of rifle fire away in the distance. He stood up to his full height and could see two of the Germans were trying to turn around one of the machine-gun nests to point behind them instead of towards the beach.

Dwyer slung his rifle over his shoulder, pressed his hands flat on the bank above him and swiftly vaulted up the four feet drop. He then walked in between the bushes and slowly looked round the corner of them, first to his left and then to his right.

He had failed to notice it earlier, but the trench on his left as he looked inland seemed completely empty. He stepped out from behind the bushes and took a grenade from his ammo pouch. He pulled the pin and threw it into the trench right under where two German soldiers were scrabbling with the machine-gun nest. He ran and jumped back down the four feet drop and scared Carter half to death.

The grenade exploded.

'Looks like we are in business, I have not seen any of our lot yet but they were trying to turn a machine-gun nest round to fire to our left, or right if you look inland. That explosion you just heard was a grenade making sure they couldn't. Something is definitely going on. I'm going back up.'

'Take these with you,' Carter said and handed him three more grenades.

Dwyer put them into the ammo pouch that Carter had given him earlier and then checked his own to make sure that it was full as possible with magazines.

He then left the area from under the overhang again.

14

Dwyer vaulted the four-foot climb again and ran through the gap in the trenches. He then peered round the edge of the bush on his right into the trench below. He noticed that the grenade he had thrown in earlier had done the job and the two Germans who were trying to reposition the machine-gun were both dead. One of them had both his legs blown away from the knees down.

He grimaced and looked away closing both his eyes tight.
This is nothing personal.
Tell that to those poor bastards.
Focus.
At least there are not any rats.
Focus.

The majority of Germans he could now see were now not firing towards the beach. They were instead alternating between only briefly looking at the beach and away to their left – a definite element of panic was apparent.

What Dwyer was not aware of was that the Americans he had seen earlier had started to engage the enemy fifty yards in front of him, as he looked westwards, and had started to clear the trench gradually coming towards him.

Word had been passed along the trench by one big game of Chinese Whispers that their defensive lines had been breached.

On closer inspection, Dwyer could see that that trench below was similar in dimensions to the bunker complex he had entered earlier. Both sides of the walls were made of concrete and it zigzagged away in front of him leading to a pillbox, which was a square building also made of reinforced concrete with gaps near the top allowing the Germans to fire out of. He could clearly see two muzzles protruding out, firing. These though were continuously strafing the beach with their murderous, relentless firepower.

Whatever it is you are going to do, do it now.

He turned around to ensure that the trench behind was still empty. On satisfying himself that it was, he took four large strides to the manned trench and jumped down into it. He slowly stepped over the pieces of the machine-gun that he had destroyed earlier and then fired into the nearest German who was about ten feet in front of him. The German briefly turned towards him with a complete of utter shock on his face, holding the wound in his neck and as if slow motion, collapsed sideways into his companion.

His companion now turned towards Dwyer. On seeing this giant of man aiming his rifle at him, he immediately dropped his gun and threw his arms in the air. 'Don't shoot, Polish,' he shouted.

Dwyer, again, shot him anyway in the chest, which sent him sprawling backwards, which again attracted the attention of the next German or 'Pole' along the trench. Being on his own, he was in no position to start taking prisoners, and *after all*, he thought, *God knows how many Americans these bastards had killed firing down onto the beaches.*

This 'Polish' excuse is wearing a bit thin.

It's nothing personal . . . keep going . . . Focus.

They can't have it both ways. Shooting at us one minute. Thinking being Polish is an excuse not to shoot them the next.

FOCUS!

To Dwyer's amazement, the remaining four soldiers on noticing him simultaneously all ran away from him up the trench. They rounded the first of the slight bends in the trench out of sight. Remarkably, he now found he was stood in the trench all by himself. While briefly contemplating his next course of action, his mind was made up for him.

Jesus Christ!

A bullet flew over his shoulder that had been fired from behind him.

He quickly dropped to his knees and turned round. He saw three of the enemy running towards him through the eight-yard tunnel connecting the other trench who he had not noticed crouching down when he checked it seconds earlier. Their rifles were worryingly pointing towards him. The soldier in the lead was screaming something unintelligible.

Is he speaking Polish or German?

Who gives a shit – Not sure it matters at the moment!

Fair one.

Dwyer opened fire and for once, his aim was high and wide.

The German – or Pole – ducked and tackled Dwyer round the waist, which sent him sprawling backwards onto the floor of the trench. He had managed to keep hold of his rifle in his right hand. He aimed over the German now lying on top of him and fired off six shots at the two following. Both fell to the ground with wounds to the stomach and legs.

He then dropped the rifle, put his fingers in the inside of the mouth of man on top of him and pulled with all his considerable strength.

The German started to squeal like a pig and his eyes started to bulge.

Once Dwyer had pulled his face sufficiently away from his own, he pushed his body weight off him to the right and brought his left knee up to his combatant's groin. Not that it would have seemed to be possible, but the Germans eyes then grew even wider and his mouthed dropped open expelling almost all the foul smelling air from his lungs.

Ignoring the odour, Dwyer then jumped to his feet and kicked him in the stomach and once in the face, which put the German out of his considerable misery by being knocked unconscious.

'How do you like those onions?' He shouted down at him. Then gave him a good kicking.

Panting for breath, he looked back over his shoulder to ensure that the two soldiers that he wounded earlier were not crawling around looking for their rifles. As they both appeared to be motionless, he checked back underneath the tunnel to ensure there were no further soldiers advancing towards him. On not seeing any, he slowly walked to the bend where the previous Germans had run round.

Aren't you going to finish them off?
No. Only if I have to in future.
Why?
Because their dead eyes look up at me when I close mine.

Dwyer thought better of it than sticking his head round the corner so instead, he took off his helmet and slowly moved it round.

Jesus. The height you moved that round there will make them think they are fighting a dwarf!

Well, they will get a fucking shock then, won't they? When I walk round the corner.

His inner conversation ended abruptly when his helmet immediately received a barrage of bullets, one of which grazed it and sent it flying out of his hands. He quickly bent down to pick it up and noticed the scratch mark along its surface.

After placing it back on his head, he took a grenade from his ammo pouch, removed the pin, counted to three and then threw it round the corner. He then took two steps backwards and stood with his front flat up against the concrete wall. The grenade exploded.

THUMP!

He waited for a few more seconds before kneeling down and looking round the corner to see the damage it had caused. As the smoke and dust started too gradually clear, he could see two mutilated bodies about five yards in front of him and a further two that appeared to be crawling away towards a further bend in the trench, this time going slightly back inland to the left.

Dwyer quickly stood up, rounded the bend, and fired into the backs of the two injured on the trench floor. No further soldiers were visible. He then carried on and reached the next bend.

Only if you have to, eh?

Shut up. They weren't unconscious. And in any case, they were lying on their front and I couldn't see their eyes.

Rather than take off his helmet this time, he just aimed his rifle round the corner and fired off rounds until the magazine was empty. He then inserted a new clip into his rifle and peered round the corner. There were two further dead Germans and one more injured. Dwyer walked towards the not yet deceased and fired into him to make sure he joined them.

You could see his eyes.

Shut it. He was reaching for a pistol in his belt.

At this point Dwyer's hands started to shake. As soon as he fired into his latest victim, he had noticed that he could not have been more than eighteen years old.

This just gets better and better.

He rested his back against the concrete wall and fumbled for a pack of cigarettes in his pocket. When he eventually managed to light it, he took three huge drags and filled his lungs.

Oh my God! Did you see how young he was?
Silence.
What a waste! I said did you see how young he was?
Silence.

With the smoke fix now kicking in and making him feeling more relaxed, he quite understood why the majority of American troops smoked. No matter the insignificance of the act it itself, it now seemed to give him something to look forward to. Not to mention the fact that it definitely seemed to calm his nerves.

Dwyer had also now been awake for twenty-nine hours. Together with the considerable stress on his mind and body, he was starting to feel both mentally and physically exhausted.

He briefly closed his eyes.
You have to keep focused.
WAKE UP!

15

Dwyer obeyed himself. His eyes snapped open and he quickly threw his cigarette to the ground on hearing running footsteps from away to his left – the direction in which he had just come. He bent down on one knee into his favourite firing position and waited for the Germans to arrive. As the first one rounded the slightly angled corner of the trench, Dwyer opened up.

He cut him down with three bullets to the chest. The second and thirds momentum sent them stumbling over the former, which carried them straight into Dwyer's line of fire. They both collapsed onto the floor now creating a human obstacle in the concrete corridor. A further foolhardy German tried to jump over the pile of bodies. He was shot through the throat whilst in mid-air. He also collapsed to the ground, face down.

With his finger still poised on the trigger of his rifle, Dwyer held his breath and waited for more of the enemy. Instead of anyone trying to the run the gauntlet and round the corner, a stick grenade landed at his knee.

Shit.

He quickly picked up and threw it back to where it came from. His throw was too strong and it landed on the bluff to the right of where he was aiming. It had the desired effect however, as the German who had previously thrown it, came stumbling forward into his line of sight holding both his ears. They were bleeding profusely through his fingers.

Dwyer shot him in the head.

He gradually got to his feet, walked towards the angle in the trench and then quickly sneaked at glance round the corner. On not noticing any further soldiers, he immediately then took a further longer look.

All was clear.

He immediately turned round and started to jog along the trench, avoiding the bodies on the floor towards what new deadly adventures maybe waiting round the next corner.

As he reached it, he stooped and looked up towards the pillbox that was now only five yards in front of him. The machine-gun positions were still blazing away at the beach. He lifted his head over the top of the trench and realised what an excellent firing position it was.

The beach could be seen in every direction.

It was also obvious to him that the world and his wife – and by going on one of the enemy he had just killed, some of their kids as well – were now nearing the waterline in landing crafts.

Thousands of reinforcements were on the way.

Dwyer gritted his teeth. If he only managed to perform one more act in his life, he was absolutely determined to take out the soldiers in the pillbox. He could not calculate the number of lives it would likely save but even if was only one it would be worth it.

As he turned back towards the angle in the trench and prepared to take on anyone in his way, he wondered once more where the Americans were.

Surely, he would run into them sometime soon.

Surely.

Where the hell are they?

Keep going.

I know – Focus.

Little did he know that they were clearing the bunkers and trenches just five yards the other side of the pillbox. One of the machine-gun positions within the pillbox was now firing on them slowing their progress along the trenches.

16

Dwyer looked down inspecting himself and made sure that all his equipment was securely attached to his belt. He then prepared himself for yet another onslaught.

This time however he did not have to brave looking round the corner. Two Germans came running round it towards him. He did not have time to raise his rifle to aim and fire so he held it with both hands and slammed the first to arrive against the wall opposite by extending his arms. He then moved forward and brought his knee up into the groin of a further terrified teenager who let a terrified howl of pain and anguish.

An arm grabbed him from behind round the chest.

Bollocks.

He threw himself backwards with all his force and slammed the soldier that had hold of him into the tunnel wall on the opposite side. He then bent his knees pressing backwards at the same time and then quickly stood up pushing his head back. The effect was that his helmet crashed into the Germans jaw and knocked him out cold. Without thinking, he aimed his rifle and shot the young German writhing around the floor holding his groin in the back of the neck and then turned and fired two shots into the already unconscious victim in the chest.

Once again, Dwyer now checked that all was secure on his belt and without looking this time, marched round the angle in the trench with his rifle butt firmly placed in his shoulder, aiming forwards.

As he turned the corner, one further German was descending three steps from what seemed to him to be the entrance to the pillbox. One shot in the chest took care of him. After two stumbled steps, the German twisted slightly as he fell and landed on his side – his helmet came off and clattered towards Dwyer's feet along the concrete floor.

After carefully stepping over it, he now crept towards the entrance of the pillbox and looked through. The steps led to a small corridor about ten feet long. This in turn to some led to further steps leading down into a trench on the other side, which almost immediately turned left. In the middle of the corridor was an opening that led to the platform where the Germans were firing from.

The noise now was deafening. The urge to cover his ears with his hands was overwhelming.

He walked towards the opening, took out a grenade, removed the pin, counted to three and threw it in. He then slammed his back against the concrete wall of the trench to take cover.

After the explosion, the firing stopped immediately. This explosion however, shook the ground he stood on as all the ammunition inside exploded simultaneously. Flames and billows of smoke came out of the entrance, which made Dwyer start to cough, and his eyes began to water. He waited to see if anyone had survived and try to make an escape and run for the hills.

He doubted it.

After fifteen seconds had passed and he had wiped the tears from his eyes, Dwyer held his breath and ventured into the pillbox with his rifle aimed out in front.

There were four dead bodies and two machine-guns that had been destroyed beyond repair.

He slowly lowered his rifle, closed his eyes, and then suddenly raised his rifle into the air with both hands and let an enormous cheer.

'*Up your arse Hitler, how do you like that you dick?*'

This was then followed by a long and guttural scream. All the tension, fear and anxiety being expelled with one large frenzied bellow.

After its conclusion, he stood staring at the floor with his head slumped to his chest hyperventilating. The act of the victory cry had seemingly sapped every ounce of strength from his weary body.

He eventually raised his head and made an effort to regulate his breathing. He then walked towards one of the firing slits and looked down on the beach. More and more troops were now landing and were still taking heavy casualties when leaving the landing craft.

No more will be killed from here though, Dwyer thought to himself.

He took one last look round the pillbox, walked out into the corridor and looked to his right.

To his relief, he saw nobody.

He put his back to the wall and slid down it. He reached for his packet of cigarettes and realised he only had one left. He lit it anyway and smoked it with a contented smile on his face with his eyes closed.

17

Wow, did that really happen?
You are back then?
Same as earlier. You were busy. I didn't want to disturb.
I was speaking to you earlier. You didn't reply.
You were busy.
Did you see how young some of those Germans were?
Or Poles.
Whatever, did you see how young they were?

Theirs is not to reason why,
Theirs but not to do and die:
Into the Valley of Death.

What?
It's a poem.
Your quoting poetry, at a time like this?
Many poems are spawned out of misery and heartache . . . war.
I hated poetry at school.
You remembered this one.
I can't remember any poems, what are you talking about?
You must have.
Why?
I'm you.
You're me?
And you're me.
Did you see how young some of those Germans were?
. . . Silence.

18

Dwyer felt his right shoulder being prodded.
Whoever you are, go away, I'm in the middle of a serious conversation here.
Two more prods.
I said go away. I'm talking. Don't interrupt. I'm quoting poetry.
Prod.
Bugger off.
Dwyer opened his eyes and looked straight into the muzzle of rifle. Everything else behind it was a complete blur.
Oh, crap!
An American voice then shouted, *'Identify yourself.'*
The blur began to focus.
Was that an American accent?
It was.
Are you sure?
Positive.
'Corporal Dwyer, 101st Airborne,' Dwyer eventually replied now looking into the eyes of the owner of the weapon. To identify himself in such a manner, was one of the lessons Brooks had taught him while at Greenham Common.
Brooks . . . That rat gnawing at that German!
Dwyer shook his head violently to try to dislodge the image that was now forming in his mind.
The American took a step back.
'101st Airborne? The American troop repeated. 'What the fuck are you doing here?' He added with a mystified expression on his face.
'It's a long story,' said Dwyer smiling up at him. 'Am I pleased to see you. We have been here all night.'
'Are you alright man . . . it's just . . . it's just that you were talking to yourself when we came across you.'
'Talking to myself?'
'Yeah. Something about . . . I'm you . . . and you are me . . . or

something like that.'

'It is the only way you get a decent conversation . . . talking to yourself,' Dwyer said forcing a smile.

I told you to keep our conversations to ourselves – it's the first sign of madness.

What's the second?

Answering back!

'Your accents funny man, are you English?'

Dwyer just nodded.

'How the fuck can an Englishman be enlisted in the 101st Airborne?'

'That's an even longer story,' said Dwyer and then stood up. He was a full foot taller than his newfound friend was.

The American eyes grew wide at his size and then said, 'You are the one that took this pillbox out . . . right?'

Dwyer nodded and said, 'Yep, you got any smokes?'

The American obliged and said, 'My pleasure man, these mother fuckers in here have been laying down fire on us for about ten minutes. Two of our guys bought it . . . Thanks man.'

With that, they were joined by another six troops in the corridor and several more stood outside. All that could see Dwyer looked at him in awe.

Dwyer lit the cigarette and then said, 'I came through the tunnels from the opposite side to you,' nodding his head towards the direction. 'It should be pretty clear of the enemy.'

'Are you on your own?'

'No. I am with my Major who has broken his ankle. He his hiding under an overhang in the bluff about thirty yards away.'

'OK then, lead the way, I'm Lieutenant Richard Taylor, 16th infantry 1st Division, by the way.'

They shook hands.

19

Dwyer walked back through trench was that was littered with bodies on his way back to Carter's position. Although the journey back seemed quicker, every care was still taken when rounding the angles in the trench.

Dwyer was thankful that there were no further contacts with the enemy. . . even if he did now have company and there was now relative safety in numbers . . . he had had a gutful.

Halfway back, Taylor whistled through his teeth and then said, 'Wow . . . Are all this lot your handiwork?'

Dwyer just nodded and carried on leading the way. The two injured Germans that Dwyer had not *finished off* earlier were now dead also.

'This one is only unconscious,' said Dwyer nodding towards the German that he had fought with on the ground and left alive earlier.

He walked passed him.

A quick burst of rifle fire then changed that particular situation.

Dwyer closed his eyes briefly and shuddered before continuing along the bunker.

Maybe I should have kept quiet.

'This is it,' Dwyer said and climbed out of the trench when reaching the point he had jumped in earlier.

Taylor followed him out while the others continued under the tunnel to investigate further.

Dwyer then shouted, 'It's me Major. Don't shoot,' and without waiting for a response, jumped down the four feet drop. Again, Taylor followed.

Carter was smiling back up them both, 'Good to see you back Davey.' He then looked to his right and added,' I see you have company.'

'This is Lieutenant Richard Taylor. He has about thirty guys with him.'

'Delighted to see you, Lieutenant,' said Carter. 'What are you orders?'

'To clear the enemy line of trenches and bunkers and then move inland towards Coleville, sir. It seems your man here has done part of the job for us; on his own!'

Carter looked towards Dwyer and nodded approvingly.

'If you don't mind me asking, sir, why are you wearing a German jacket and helmet?' Taylor said.

'Courtesy of Corporal Dwyer here.'

Carter lit a cigarette.

'We were dropped about two miles away from here due to our plane getting hit last night. We had several contacts with the enemy on our way here, all of which he took care of and relieved some of their clothing for us. We thought it the best way to avoid capture.'

Dwyer, who had no desire to relive the night's experiences again, now interrupted the conversation.

'There is another bunker complex down the path there. I took out about six of them earlier but I did not check much further than the first few corridors. . . You may want to take your boys down and take a look.'

Taylor briefly glanced down the bluff and then slowly shook his head.

'No doubt that will be taken care of soon enough,' said Taylor and nodded to the hundreds of landing craft that were descending upon the beach below. 'Our orders are now to advance on Coleville. I suggest you stay here until the sea wall is fully breached. You can then take the Major here down to the beach to be evacuated. The landing craft are already taking the injured back to the ships. They have been all morning.'

Taylor ended is his statement with a slow mournful shake of the head and stared at the ground.

Without another word said, Taylor climbed up the drop and returned to the rest of his men.

'Heh,' shouted Dwyer after him. 'You are just going to leave without checking that bunker down there?'

Taylor acted as if he had not heard him. He and the rest of his men started walking towards the tree line.

'For fucks sake,' said Dwyer with exasperation and looked towards Carter in disbelief.

Carter just shook his head. 'Don't you think they've been through enough for one day?' He then nodded towards the direction of the beach.

Dwyer now felt instantly ashamed that he had now challenged Taylor, and with a grimace, nodded his agreement. His shoulders slumped.

He then bent down and moved in next to the major. He then took a packet of cigarettes from his rucksack, went to light one and then immediately thought better of it. He then said, 'How are you feeling?'

Carter did not respond. He was lost in his own thoughts.

'Good,' said Dwyer. 'I need to sleep. Wake me up if anything exciting happens.'

He then curled up into a ball, rested his head on his rucksack and feel asleep within seconds.

It was 10h15 hours.

20

This is 'Dream Centre Command,' we have incoming . . . I repeat . . . we have incoming . . . all hands on deck.

. . . When you look into the abyss . . .

This place stinks, Moose. Why did we get this shit detail? God, the smell. Why could they possibly want us to check this damn sewer?

Just keep going. The quicker we do it. The quicker we can get out of here.

The smell though. It makes me want to throw up.

I know. It smells like my jacket. Just keep going Brooksie . . . just keep going.

Silence.

Brooksie? . . . Brooksie? . . . Where are you?

It is dark in here, man.

Where are you?

I hope they are no rats down here . . . There is nothing I hate more than rats . . .

Where are you?

Oh God! They're everywhere . . . They're biting me Moose . . . Helppp meee!

Brooksie?

What goes around come, a voice said from behind him.

What are you doing here? I already killed you once.

My spirit will never die. It is in others around you. All around you – What goes around comes around.

Where is Brooks? What have you done with Brooks?

He is at peace with the rats . . . Down in the sewer.

Why don't you stop hiding in the darkness and come out and face me?

As you said, you already killed me once – What goes around comes around – Some of these rats are as big as dogs – Wow, mighty big – see ya.

Oblivion . . .

THUMP. THUMP. THUMP.
Open this door.
THUMP. THUMP. THUMP.
Who's there? What do you want? Why don't you just leave me alone?
Sally. It's me. Davey.
What do you want?
Sally open the door, it's me . . . Davey . . . Please open the door.
DAAVVEEYYY! Nooooo! . . . There's rats in here . . . Helppp meee!

. . . the abyss also looks into you.

And then finally.

Welcome oblivion again.

21

Garcia was now an emotional wreck. The aerial bombardment that had lasted for just over an hour had paralysed him with fear. Now at least, it appeared to him to be directed more in land than right down on top of his head. On three separate occasions he thought that the barn was going to collapse around him such was the ferocity in which the explosions nearby had rattled the wooden panels.

The smell was also becoming unbearable. He had previously thought about opening one of his field rations, but believed that the smell of burning flesh and the dead bodies that shared his hideout with him would cause him to throw it back up again as soon as he ate it.

Hunger however did get the better of him, so he forced himself to eat one of the breakfasts.

Much to his relief, he kept it down.

He then looked longingly at the soluble coffee after he had finished eating but there was nothing around to heat up the water. Not that it mattered; he had drunk all the water in his canteen anyway.

He was still sat in amongst the dead German bodies, up against the rear of the barn with his rifle still pointing at the door.

The fuel in the kerosene lamp had run out about half an hour earlier but daylight now filtered through the cracks in the wood panels. It gave the impression of a hundred tiny searchlights spreading out into the interior.

Garcia's thoughts were now consumed with retribution on Dwyer and Carter. He was rocking very gently back and forwards and singing to himself very quietly, 'I am going to get you. I am going to get you,' over and over again.

He was drooling.

As if someone had slapped him round the face, he suddenly snapped out of his deranged state of mind. He slowly stood up, wiped his chin and started to rub the top of his legs and backside. By sitting in the same position for over four hours, he had the worst case of pins and needles in his life.

'God my ass is numb,' he complained aloud.

Once his rub down was finished, he stretched out his arms and yawned as if he just got out of bed and slowly walked to one of the streams of light that were entering the barn. He raised his left wrist up towards the light and checked the time.

10h15 hours.

He then walked to the side door of the barn and considered opening it.

'Nope,' he said shaking his head. 'I aint going out there yet.'

Instead, he tried to look through one of the larger splits in the woodwork to try to see down the lane. On proving unsuccessful, he then opened the side door slowly, and even more slowly moved his head outside.

He noticed a bomb crater about twenty yards to his right that had hit right in the middle of the lane and further one on the bend to his left. He went back inside and closed the door congratulating himself on the decision not to use the motorbike earlier.

'That was good thinking, Tony. Very good thinking.'

He then stuffed his hands in his pockets and looked at the ground thoughtfully.

Surely the troops would have managed to get off the beaches by now . . . what is the damn hold up?

Although he still had no idea of his exact position, he believed that he must be pretty close to one of the landing beaches due to the amount of bombing that had taken place earlier. In addition, the sound of the raging battle could be clearly heard about two miles north.

Almost immediately, as the thought crossed his mind, he thought he heard what he believed to be a series of small arms fire. He started to pace up and down the barn trying to think what his best course of action would be. At one point, he kicked the foot of one of the dead German shoulders and told him to shut up because he was ruining his concentration.

He put his rucksack on, then he it took it off again. Then he put it back on, and then off again.

'What am I going to do?' He screamed at the top of his voice and then looked round the barn suspiciously to see if anyone had heard him.

If you could wake the dead by making a lot of noise, all the deceased in the barn would have stood up in unison.

He eventually pulled one of the chairs towards him, moved it to the side of the table and sat down. With his head in his hands, he started to cry like a baby. Barely audible through his sobs, he kept repeating, 'I am going to wait for someone to come and save me.'

22

Carter looked down on Dwyer while he slept. The effects of the morphine were making him drowsy at best and the thought of closing his eyes and escaping this horror for a few hours was very appealing.

This however was totally out of the question and would be unforgiveable as far as the Major was concerned.

The thought of compromising them both by not being on guard while the other slept made him shudder, the other in this particular case being the formidable Dwyer, now sleeping like a baby next to him. He was actually welcoming the pain that was now returning to his ankle as it was helping him keep awake.

His shifted his position slightly, reached for his rucksack and retrieved a 'dinner' K Ration. He chewed slowly through the canned cheese product, which to him tasted disgusting, the biscuits and the candy bar. He then placed the piece of gum in his mouth to try to get rid of the taste of the cheese.

It didn't work.

Next, he lined the four cigarettes that were inside the box on his lap and systematically chained smoke them. Rather than feeling energised by his meal, it had made him feel even more tired than before. He started to blink very slowly and his head lulled slightly forward.

Carter snapped his head back. He raised his left leg and brought it crashing down onto the ground, broken ankle first. This did the trick as he clenched his jaw trying not to scream.

Although the noise of battle below on the beach below was still horrendous, it had become marginally quieter since Dwyer had taken out the machine-gun positions above them.

His thoughts now returned to the sleeping giant next to him. He would never have requested Dwyer to investigate the bunker system below and the trenches above if he did not have every confidence that he could handle himself. The fact he had returned after taking it upon himself to clear out a stretch of tunnels and take out a pillbox was no surprise to him whatsoever.

His only concern was that he had undoubtedly changed this man's personality for the rest of his life. He was clearly starting to show visible signs of extreme stress, remorse and anxiety.

Nobody could experience what they had over the last eleven hours and not be affected by it.

Since landing in Normandy, Dwyer had had to turn into a cold-blooded ruthless killer, which Carter believed to be just as well, considering the shit they had found themselves confronted with. However, Carter could still see that behind all this he still had a good heart. He just hoped that he would not lose that part of his character for good.

Carter now opened the small packet of granulated sugar in his mouth and let it settle on his tongue for a while before swallowing. He hoped that it would give him some extra energy. He then did the same with soluble coffee from the two breakfasts that they had had earlier. Once finished, he returned to chain-smoking again.

After finishing six cigarettes that he lit by using the still lit end from the one he had just finished, he reached for his binoculars to check on the progress below. Just as he painfully got into a kneeling position, he noticed two Germans ascending the path below looking towards the tunnel systems.

Carter reached for his rifle and ducked down slightly. As their full torsos came into view, he shot them both in the chest. They both tumbled down the path and into the bushes where the path veered to the left. This time there was not the added explosion of a mine being set off.

He looked towards Dwyer. He continued to sleep blissfully unaware of the latest enemy contact. Not for the first time Dwyer was considered to be one hell of a heavy sleeper - albeit that his eyelids were manically twitching indicating that he was dreaming – *sweet dreams I hope* – Carter thought wistfully.

Carter now continued to concentrate on the path below. For a brief moment he thought that the bunker system below them might have been overrun by the American troops and that the Germans were now retreating. As there were no further Germans to be at shoot at in the next five minutes, it turned out to be a false hope.

He eventually then did pluck up the courage to pick up his binoculars and start to survey the scene below on the beach once again.

It was now 11h00 hours and hundreds of landing craft were with either coming towards the beach or leaving after dropping of their troops.

Unbeknown to him, between 10h00 hours and 10h30 hours, the 1st Battalion, 18th Regiment of the 1st Division, and the 115th Regiment of the 29th Division hand almost landed on top of each other, albeit that many of the landing craft were either late or completely out of position.

Despite the number of reinforcements, and the now many vehicles including tanks, bulldozers and jeeps, not much progress appeared to be being made in breaching the German defences. The troops that Dwyer had run into earlier were the only ones that he knew about that had made it to the high ground.

He looked towards the waterline and noticed that the tide had come in. The beach obstacles and some of the landing craft that had been destroyed earlier were now completely submerged. This appeared to be making it an absolute nightmare for many of the craft to land, as they were either in the middle of an enormous traffic jam. They were now cruising along the shoreline looking for the safest possible place to land. Some were being hit by mines attached to now submerged Belgian Gates and Hedgehogs. In addition, many of the tanks that had sunk in the first wave were not improving the situation by causing further obstructions.

The Naval bombardment had also picked up again in the last twenty minutes.

Carter assumed that word had made its way back to the fleet commanders that they were taking heavy casualties on the beaches and they were doing all they could to assist the infantry. He allowed himself briefly to wish that the invasion on this particular part of the coast should be abandoned. The loss of life up to this point had been horrendous. Still his fellow Americans came forward.

Away to his left, a German position received over 60 rounds within minutes, which ended in an enormous explosion. Carter thought at least that that particular battery would now be out of action and every little helped.

Still, Dwyer slept on.

Carter now passed the time by picking out specific landing craft that were headed towards the beach. The first of which made it to the beach and all its passengers dived to the ground as soon as they hit the beach as soon as the ramp lowered. He only noticed one casualty taken as they all went out of sight behind the shingle bank.

The next two he followed were not so fortunate. Half the troops on the first were shot by machine-gun fire as soon as the ramp opened sending the other half diving over the side into the water. The other was hit by a mine before reaching the beach. The men were sent flying up into the air in all directions.

He quickly averted his gaze.

It all been too much for Carter earlier watching the slaughter of his countryman. He now had the weird sensation that he was not watching from the bluff directly above the beach experiencing every bullet and mortar round fired. Instead, it felt to him that the events were unfolding in front of him on a monstrous movie screen.

Such had been the longevity and the intensity of the incredible noise that accompanied the now six hour-long battle, since the aerial bombardment had started, he had now almost completely blocked it out from his senses.

Any one of the shells exploding against the coastline, or the mortar rounds exploding on the beach and on the landing crafts would have ordinarily made him jump out of his skin. They all now seemed to blend into each other, and to Carter, had become the norm.

He found himself wondering if he would ever experience silence and tranquility ever again.

23

There were five ravines or 'draws' that led from the high ground to Omaha beach. The nearest to Dwyer's and Carters position were two dirt roads that led up to St-Laurent-sur-Mer and Coleville-Sur-Mer.

Carter was now scanning the beach as far as he could see from the west on his left, back towards his position just north of Coleville. When he reached the point about one hundred yards from his immediate front, he noticed a line of tanks that had begun to move out in formation and they were angling towards the bluff.

He followed their progress as far possible until they went out of sight to the east and all of which, at least to this point, remained unharmed.

His spirits rose as he thought maybe that the sea wall had been breached and the tanks could now start rolling inland firing on the German positions.

He went to wake Dwyer and tell him the good news, but on seeing that he was still dead to the world, he thought better of it. Any thoughts of his own tiredness had now disappeared. Despite the carnage he had witnessed earlier, he found himself feeling suddenly exhilarated.

With his newfound enthusiasm, he returned his attention back to the beach below looking for any more signs of significant progress made.

Over the next hour, he looked from the sea, to the beach, to his west and then repeated the process repeatedly. Although the machine-gun fire and mortar rounds were still extensive, the build up of men and machinery on the beaches had increased dramatically.

He started to gain further hope that it would only be a matter of time before the wall was breached in a number of different places and they could start engaging and clearing the enemy from the high ground.

This however was supposed to have been accomplished within the first hour of the troops landing. It was not lost on Carter that as the bombing and the naval bombardment had been largely ineffective, they were now relying on the infantry to belatedly fulfil the landings objectives as a result of their incredible courage and dedication.

As he now scanned away to his right, he noticed a large number of metal cans piled up high, which he assumed contained fuel. It was hit by a mortar round which sent an enormous fireball into the sky and engulfed four troops that were kneeling down next to it. Again, Carter averted his gaze away from the now burning bodies on the beach.

His spirits took a turn for the worst.

He now looked down immediately below him, and to his amazement, he saw two bulldozers driving towards him pushing an ever-increasing bank of sand in front of them. After briefly going out of sight as they reached the sea wall, he then saw them reversing back. They then started forwards again creating a further bank of sand in front of them. He guessed that they were blocking a German firing position down at beach level.

The bulldozers attracted a dozen men behind each who were taking cover behind it. Once the second bank of sand had been pushed forward, they all came out firing running forwards in front of the bulldozers and then disappeared from his view. Not one of them had taken a hit.

His spirits rose again.

Fifty yards to the left of the bulldozers, a further fireball erupted. Carter quickly turned his binoculars onto the scene and realised that two tanks had just exploded after being hit by mortar rounds. He could see clearly that one of the occupants was frantically struggling to get out of the hatch through the flames. His struggle was in vain, as he then appeared to be finished off by machine-gun fire, which left him slumped half in, and half out of the hatch. In case there was any doubt of his fate, a further explosion blew the tank in half as the ammunition exploded inside it. A handful of troops were killed by the flying debris.

His emotional rollercoaster now dipped again.

Carter then looked towards the waterline and noticed two further tanks that appeared to him to be swimming ashore firing on the same position away to his left that had taken a considerable bombardment earlier from the Navy.

He then felt a tap on his right shoulder and turned to see that Dwyer had woken up and was rubbing the sleep from his eyes.

'How are we doing?' He shouted as continued to rub away.

Carter handed him the binoculars to see for himself and then checked his watch.

It was now 12h30 hours. Dwyer had slept for a little over two hours.

24
10th July 1943
Autryville, North Carolina, USA
03h50 hours

Only muffled cries could be heard as the woman's face continued to be dragged from side to side across the carpet.

Such was the force that 'Mr Star Gazer' was using, it was now causing carpet burns to form on her forehead, nose and cheeks.

He then forcibly yanked her head back so hard that he almost pulled the hair from her scalp and moved her face to just six inches from his own.

'I have you had enough you dirty bitch – have you learned your lesson?'

Before she could make any kind of response, he thrust her face back down to the carpet and started rubbing again furiously.

He looked up to his three companions for approval . . . It was immediately given by three smiling faces.

Eventually, he stopped.

'I said have you learned your lesson?' He said through gritted teeth and yanked her head back up violently towards his own.

With hatred now blazing in her eyes, she spat in his face.

All other members of the group quickly looked towards each other all wearing open-mouthed surprised expressions.

Without any attempt to wipe the saliva away dripping from his nose, he said calmly, 'Well that is just disgusting . . . and not to mention very, very dirty.'

He then turned his attention to each of the group members, slowly turning his head and looking at each one in turn. All of their mouths remained open.

'Let's just see how really dirty she is, shall we?'

He looked to the member of the group to his right who was now enjoying himself immensely. He was showing his obvious excitement by moving from one foot to the other and rubbing his hands.

'Maybe I will let you loose on her after we are done,' 'Mr Star Gazer' said.

Frantic nodding of the head now accompanied the jigging about. He resembled a wind-up toy monkey that enthusiastically bangs his cymbals together.

'Mr Star Gazer' pulled the woman upright to her feet and then effortlessly threw her on the bed.

'Time to get down and dirty . . . WHOOP!'

The woman scrambled to the end of bed cowering against the headboard with her eyes shut tight.

Why did he do what I asked him too for once? She thought over and over again in her mind.

It would have been better if the gun HAD been loaded. Then this would already be all over . . . Welcome oblivion.

25

Dwyer felt awful. The short sleep he had just had made him feel worse than he did before. He felt sullen and irritable. He was also conscious of the fact that he had some kind of nightmare.

What WAS it about?

Don't ask.

But –

I said, don't ask.

As he scanned the binoculars from left to right on the beach below, everything appeared to him to be happening in slow motion and he now had a thumping headache.

His mood was not improved after witnessing yet another soldier on the beach disintegrating into a hundred different pieces after being hit by a mortar round.

He reached down to his canteen and poured half of the remaining contents of water over his head, only just remembering to take off his helmet before he did so.

After rubbing his hands on his face, which now gave him the appearance of some kind of hideous bog monster with greyish green skin, he turned to Carter.

'Seems to be loads of reinforcements now, have you heard any other Americans up top here yet?'

Cater shook his head.

'How long have I been asleep?'

'Just over two hours.'

Dwyer checked his watch. It seemed like more than eight to him; such was the deepness of sleep that he had fallen into immediately.

What was that damn dream about? Something about –

Forget about it. Don't ask.

He looked towards the rucksack with the rations in. 'I'm starving again. Do you want anything to else to eat?'

Carter shook his head. 'I ate while you were asleep.'

Dwyer then took out a 'K Ration' packet with 'dinner' printed on it and opened the can of cheese product. He spooned about a third of its contents and shoved into his mouth.

Oh crap. This tastes worse than the vomit.
It's better than nothing.
You reckon . . . it's like sucking dirty socks.

He immediately grimaced and started to chew very slowly. 'Jesus Christ, this tastes like crap,' he said aloud this time. His voice of reason nodding its head in agreement inwardly.

'Yeah well, I had to eat mine with you smelling like shit so stop complaining and just eat it,' Carter said with his trademark blank expression that how now returned to him.

Dwyer raised both of his eyebrows as he looked towards Carter to see if there was any type of joke implied, but on seeing no sign of humour in his facial expression, he finished of the can in just three other spoonfuls and quickly swallowed. He then took a gulp of water and swilled it round his mouth to try to get rid of the taste.

He then spat it out.

As he was about to reach for the candy bar, he noticed Carter go rigid and point his rifle forward down the bluff's path. He immediately reached for his own rifle and followed his gaze.

At first, he noticed four German soldiers all scrabbling up the path towards them. The first two had however fallen over and were blocking the paths of the others. They were joined about at least six others who were all now had to stand still and wait for the front two to get up.

Dwyer immediately knelt down into firing position and opened up. Again, his aim was off and he shot over their heads. Carter was busy struggling to get up and at present, was not providing any assistance.

Little help here . . . use a little help now . . . TODAY!

The Germans that were all still standing instantly crouched down and started to return fire. The bullets thumped into the top of the overhang sending soil and small stones down on top of Dwyer and Carter. Carter made the mistake of looking up. He was temporarily blinded as some soil landed in his eyes.

Dwyer did not flinch.

He lowered his aim and fired. Due to the incline, he only now had three heads looking up at him to aim at. After hitting two of them right between the eyes, the third went rapidly out of sight. He remained motionless in his firing position with his left foot flat on the ground together with his right knee.

One of the Germans then took it upon himself to try to charge them and stood to climb up the bluff. He was instantly cut down by Dwyer. Carter in the meantime had removed the soil and grit from his eyes and had was now kneeling on both knees for the moment ignoring the increasing pain in his ankle.

Nice of you to pop in – even if you are late.
Focus.

Carter took the last remaining grenade from Dwyer's ammo pouch and threw it slightly to the left of where the path veered to the left where he guessed the remaining Germans to be positioned. Due to the amount of adrenaline flowing within him, his throw was far too strong. It sailed over the Germans heads and into the bushes that lined the path, they were standing on. It landed further down the bluff. However, it did kill a further advancing German who had just left the bunker system. He was being followed by a further dozen.

The last thing what Carter was expecting now was for to Dwyer leave their defensive position and start to leap down the bluff. Especially as they had the advantage of the high ground. To his astonishment, this is exactly what he did.

Idiot!

Dwyer reached the corner of the path and planted his right foot firmly down to avoid following through into the bushes. He then immediately swivelled to his left and started firing indiscriminately down the path.

Two of the remaining Germans were both hit in the chest and were killed instantly, the third, that had dropped his rifle, shot his arms up in the air to surrender.

Dwyer hesitated, and then slowly started walking towards him. All the time aiming his rifle at the Germans head.

What? No don't shoot, don't shoot, I'm Polish, this time?
No. This one is definitely a real live German.

Whether it was the size of the man that was now walking down the path towards him, or that the fact he looked like he was wearing a

Halloween mask due to the amount dirt and blood that was smeared all over his face, the *'real live German'* panicked. His eyes gave him away by frantically searching the ground for the nearest weapon.

Dwyer shot him in the head. He landed in the bloody entrails of the mine victim earlier with a squelch that made Dwyer look away with a disgusted look.

He now cautiously walked down to the hairpin in the path where he had first seen the American soldiers scaling the bluff. He stopped and checked his magazine.

It was still half-full.

On rounding the corner, he almost bumped into the twelve Germans that had just left the bunker when the grenade that Carter had thrown had exploded. All of them were stood completely still but all had their rifles raised.

The fact that the path now increased in its gradient at this point worked towards Dwyer's advantage. He turned sideways and aimed a karate style kick into the chest of the German immediately in front of him.

The scene that followed was deliciously comical to Dwyer as the recipient of the kick flew backwards down the path and systematically knocked over two stood immediately behind him, which, in turn, had the same effect of the remaining nine. Once all bodies had reached the bottom of the gradient, he almost yelled out *'Strike.'*

There was now a mad scramble at the bottom of the gradient as all tried to stand at once resembling the aftermath of a collapsed rugby scrum.

Not many made it upright.

Dwyer carefully moved down the gradient as before, moving his left foot down and then joining with it with his right firing into the bundle of bodies at the bottom. Such was the melee amongst the Germans desperately now trying to cover behind each other, he even had time to casually replace a further clip and resume firing.

By the time he was stood over them, only two Germans were still alive. Two well-aimed shots to the head took care of that.

Excellent. You picked up the spares – double points next ball.

After one final check that none of them would be getting back up and bothering him again, he walked to the last bend before the path levelled out before the bunker and look towards it. He made like a statue, holding his breath, with his rifle raised at the ready for a full thirty seconds. Satisfied that there did not seem to be any further Germans attempting to come out and join the fray, he slowly ascended the path back to Carter.

26

On reaching Carter, he could not understand while he was looking so pissed off. After all, he had just taken care of just under twenty of the enemy, and without any help from him.

Jesus Christ. No pleasing some people.

'What's your problem?' Dwyer said when he got within five feet.

'You are the problem,' Carter said in a calm tone.

'I sorted it, didn't I? Why are you so pissed off?'

Carter looked away and sighed. He then returned his gaze to Dwyer and said, 'If you want to survive the day, do not ever do that again,' in a firm tone.

Eh?

Dwyer's mouth dropped open.

Carter continued before he could make any kind of audible response. 'When you are firing down from the high ground, you never give up your position. What you just did was reckless and totally unnecessary, not to mention completely insane. That's one of the first things you are taught at basic training.'

Basic training? Basic Training? You call two days of firing at rocks and jumping out of the back of a truck, basic training? Not to mention hurting my balls again.

Well f –

'Well fuck me,' Dwyer shouted aloud now sharing his thought process. 'Brooks must have forgotten to tell me that in my extensive two day training course. What the fuck was he thinking?'

A staring contest then ensued, with neither willing to back down and look away first.

Dwyer ended the stare down by shouting, 'What do you expect? I'm just a . . . I'm just a . . . I'm just a Citizen Soldier!'

After a brief silence between them, they both exploded into fits of laugher simultaneously.

When regaining composure, Dwyer said, 'Time for a ciggie,' and took a further packet out of one of the rucksacks and offered one to

Carter.

While enjoying their smoke, both with their backs to the wall under the overhang, Dwyer suddenly burst out laughing again.

Carter looked towards him to see what the new joke was.

Dwyer shook his head and said, 'I wished you had seen that. The path is pretty steep down there and I literally walked into twelve of them why they were walking up. I kicked the first one in the chest which sent him back into the others.'

Dwyer then paused, as he could not now talk for laughing and coughing. Carter still was not seeing the funny side of it.

He eventually added, 'They all fell over down the slope and it looked like the Key Stone Cops when they all tried to get up again.'

Carter looked at him quizzically and then said, 'Twelve of them? Where are they?' As he turned his attention back down towards the path.

'Dead,' Dwyer said simply.

'All of them? None of them just injured?'

'Nope, all of them are dead.'

'That's a shame. We could have done with one alive to try to interrogate him about their other positions,' Carter said matter of factly as if they were discussing the weather.

Didn't think of that, did you?

No.

Too busy throwing strikes and picking up spares.

You were there. Why didn't you say something?

Silence.

Don't tell me. I was busy. Didn't want to disturb?

Silence.

'I'll bear that in mind next time,' Dwyer said shaking his head and lit another cigarette.

27

Dwyer picked up the binoculars and checked the beach once again. It had become more and more crowded but was still taking a lot of fire. He could still see the effect the machine-gun positions and mortars were having. He focused on one troop who appeared to directing traffic. It reminded him of the local coppers in the roads in Portsmouth, although this bloke seemed to be doing a better job of it.

He scanned away to his left and noticed two columns of tanks moving out.

'What do you think of that?' Dwyer said and pointed towards the area of the beach to Carter.

He slowly got up to a kneeling position and looked.

'I saw something similar earlier although there were fewer then. It definitely seems to me that we have breached their defensives somewhere along the line and are advancing inland,' Carter said.

'Well I wish they would hurry up and advance up here. I am getting sick to death being stuck in here,' said Dwyer resembling a petulant child.

'Imagine how I feel,' Carter said without looking away from the beach.

'What do you mean?'

'You still stink like shit.'

Dwyer sniffed his jacket and thought, *'Fair one.'*

28

Dwyer and Carter both noticed the movement down the path together. As Dwyer was about to raise his rifle, Carter moved his right arm across his chest to prevent him from doing so. On further inspection, Dwyer realised why.

'101st Airborne here, identify yourself,' Carter shouted.

'115th of the 29th Division,' came the reply.

'The path is clear. Come on up, lads,' said Carter.

With that what seemed to Dwyer and Carter an endless line, the Infantry walked up the path towards them. Dwyer felt like running down and hugging each one of them individually, so pleased he was to see them.

Captain David Wells looked down on both of them with a look of utter confusion on his face and then turned to his men to tell them to carry on up over the overhang to the top of the bluff above.

'Aren't you a bit lost?' Wells said when he looked back towards Dwyer and Carter.

'You could say that. I am Major Edward Carter and this is Corporal Davey Dwyer.'

'Captain David Wells, sir,' was his response and then bent down and shook Carter's hand.

Dwyer moved from underneath the overhang and stood up.

'What happened to you?' Wells asked.

What hasn't happened, Dwyer thought.

Carter then proceeded to provide a very quick summary of the day's events since parachuting in and praised Dwyer every step of the way throughout his commentary. Wells kept looking towards Dwyer every time he was mentioned, who stood staring at the ground almost embarrassed by the praise being heaped upon him.

When Carter had finally finished, Wells whistled and said, 'That is quite a story.'

'It's nothing compared to what you just had to go through,' Dwyer said and nodded towards the beach.

Wells did not venture a comment and refrained from looking

back.

'What are your orders, Captain?' Carter said.

Wells just shook his head. 'Our orders, Major, are now shot to shit. We were supposed to land about a mile from here. It seems nobody is in the right place. I fully expected the beach to be almost clear by the time we got here.'

Carter just nodded and waited for Wells to continue.

'It's an absolute mess down there. The dead or dying are all over the place not to mention the body parts spread around everywhere. Most of my men have puked at least twice since landing. It's a Goddamn nightmare.'

'How did you manage to get off the beach?' Dwyer said.

'We were some of the lucky ones I guess. We circled around in the Channel for God knows how long until we finally got the go ahead to land. When we did reach the beach there were landing craft all around and in front of us so we had to move east. When we finally did find a spot to land, the coxswain was shot.'

Wells then paused and said, 'You two got any smokes? Mine got soaked coming in.'

Dwyer took his out from his pocket and gave him the whole packet.

After lighting one up and taking a deep drag, he blew the smoke up into the sky with a satisfied look on his face.

'As I was saying,' he continued. 'The coxswain got shot and nobody knew really how to work the damn thing. Once we finally did manage to get it moving, the ramp got stuck. The craft either side of us were hit by mines and both blew up. In the end, we all just jumped over the side and swam in.'

Wells paused for another lungful of smoke.

'Once we hit the beach, we actually managed to get to the sea wall without too many dramas. We must have landed at one of the only spots, which they did not have covered. As I said, we were lucky.'

'I take it you have cleared the bunker system below,' said Carter.

Wells nodded. 'We got through the barbed wire using bangalore torpedoes and then walked through a mine field. One of our guys bought it there.'

Wells paused again and looked visibly upset whilst staring at the ground. He cleared this throat and continued. 'As we flanked to our left one of the boys looked back and saw what he thought was an entrance. It was hidden behind some bushes. Sure enough, it led straight into a maze of trenches and bunkers. When we started throwing grenades in, most of them ran.'

'That would explain why they all came charging up here then,' Carter said looking at Dwyer.

Dwyer nodded.

'Yeah we wondering about that,' Wells said. 'We found some dead inside just before the exit to this path and saw a whole lot more outside all the way up.'

'That was me,' Dwyer said with his stupid schoolboy grin on his face.

'All on your own?' Wells said.

Dwyer now realised that he probably look somewhat smug. He wiped the grin of his face and just nodded.

Wells whistled again and said, 'Sure could do with you coming along with us. You seem to be able to care of yourself.'

He turned to Carter and said, 'How about it Major? Any chance of taking him with us?'

Before Carter could reply Dwyer said, 'I have got a couple of things to take care of first. I will find you later.'

Wells was somewhat surprised that the Major had allowed this huge Corporal to speak for him but something else was bothering him about Dwyer.

He looked at him quizzically and said, 'Are you English?'

Dwyer nodded and said, 'It's a long story.'

'I bet it is,' said Wells. He took one last drag on his cigarette and then threw to the ground and extinguished with his boot. 'Well, good luck to you both. We are now going to head towards St Laurent and try to meet up with the rest of our guys. You never know, somebody there might know what the fuck is supposed to happen next, hopefully see you later, Dwyer.'

Wells then climbed up over the overhang and joined the rest of his men that had been admiring Dwyer's earlier efforts in the trench above.

Dwyer followed him up and noticed other American troops off to his left that had also scaled the bluff that were now headed inland. He thought that was the best way to take the Major down to the beach for evacuation. He did not like the idea of walking down the path and through the bunker system, which according to Wells, led out into a minefield.

He jumped back down the four feet drop and said, 'Ready to get out of here?'

Carter said, 'You said you had two things to take care of to Captain Wells. Assuming that one of them is escorting me to the beach – at least I hope it is. What is the other one?'

Dwyer looked Carter in the eye and said, 'There is no way that I am going to leave Danny's body in that field. I am going back to get him.'

'I see,' Carter said. 'And when did you decide that you were going to do that?'

Dwyer then felt the colour drain out from both of cheeks . . . *the dream . . . the rats!*

'Are you okay? You look like you just saw a ghost,' Carter said.

'As soon as we left him there,' Dwyer said trying to ignore the ghost comment . . . *the voice in my dream . . .*

Carter took out his pack of cigarettes and said, 'Sit with me and have a cigarette first. I am going to think of ways in the next five minutes to talk you out of it.'

As Dwyer took a cigarette out of Carter's packet he said, 'It's about time I had one of yours you tight bastard,' and smiled.

Carter did not.

29

Carter finally broke the silence between them. It was however not heartfelt. It was always the American way never to leave their dead behind.

'You cannot go running the countryside on your own in order to bring back one dead body. The chances of you making it back alive are almost nil.'

On not receiving a response from Dwyer, he continued.

'I am sorry, Davey, I simply cannot allow it. Brooks' body will be no doubt be discovered soon enough. You are just going to have to let it go. That is an order.'

Dwyer stubbed out his cigarette. He picked up the German jacket, moved out from underneath the overhang and tied it round his waist.

On realising that Dwyer had absolutely no intention of listening to him, Carter said, 'I am on my way back to England today, and if I have my way, you will be joining me.'

Dwyer just stood and stared at Carter without responding.

'If you should get killed now on a suicide mission, what would I tell your girlfriend back home? That I let you go off your own to look for one person that was already *dead?*'

This seemed to Carter to have an effect on Dwyer, as he now turned round to look at the beach below. Carter wondered if eyes were searching across the Channel back towards his homeland.

Focus.

Focus on Sally.

Dwyer then turned back to Carter and said, 'Brooks had a girlfriend too you know. Would you tell her that you allowed his body to rot in some field and made no attempt to bring him back?'

'I have already said that his body will be discovered later at some point,' Carter said angrily.

'At some point, maybe,' said Dwyer. 'Don't you think these boys have a bit more on their minds at the moment than looking for dead Americans that they don't even know are there in the first place?'

'What difference does it make when he is discovered? It's not going to bring him back to life, is it?' Carter was now unable to conceal his exasperation.

Dwyer took a deep breath and looked back towards the path. After reliving the horror of witnessing the torso of the German being consumed in his mind, he returned his gaze towards Carter.

'Okay. Let me tell you something,' said Dwyer. 'You know the first German you shot earlier that set off the mine when he fell down the bluff?'

Carter nodded.

'Well, what is left of his body is laying down there on the path had company. When I walked past it earlier, there was a rat the size of a small dog having his breakfast, lunch and dinner all at the same time.'

Rats the size of dogs. Mighty big . . . The dream.

Dwyer stopped to see the effect this was having on the Major and to try to eradicate the horrendous now vivid memory of his dream from his mind.

Carter looked away from Dwyer's stare. He looked horrified towards the ground.

'There is no way I can live with myself thinking the same thing is happening to Danny,' Dwyer said, 'I would wake up screaming every night having nightmares about it.'

You already have had one.

Thanks. I was there. I know.

So was I, remember? That was some scary shit.

Carter looked back up towards to Dwyer, and such was the intensity of his stare, Dwyer felt like he was looking through him searching for his soul.

Eventually, Carter slowly nodded his head and said, 'Okay then, go and get him. I will wait here for you.'

Dwyer immediately turned to his left as if to leave until Carter shouted at him to wait.

What now?

'Take the last of the fragmentation grenades before you go and make sure you fill your other ammo pouch with clips.'

Fair one.

Dwyer stopped in his tracks and went towards the rucksack with the ammo in.

'And have something else to eat before you go. You are going to need the energy.'

'Yes mum, anything else before I go?' Dwyer said now smiling and turning back towards Carter.

'There is as a matter of fact. When I eventually go down to the beach I would very much like it if is you that takes me there . . . Make sure you come back.'

Dwyer smiled. 'You're not getting all sentimental on me, are you?'

Carter looked away and said, 'Just make sure you come back.'

PART FIVE

Reunion

gathering, get-together, meeting.

I

'If an injury has to be done to a man it should
be so severe that his vengeance need not be feared.'

- Niccolo Machiavelli

After Dwyer had finished his K Ration, which he had carefully checked to ensure that it did not contain the cheese product, he stood to get ready to go. He took one last look at the beach below and noticed that troops continued to land on the beach. The mortar and machine-gun had now seemed to ease and there was an ever increasing amount of vehicles coming ashore. It now appeared to him that many of the mortar rounds now only appeared to be fired from German positions inland.

He turned back towards Carter and said, 'How long do you think it will take me to get back here?'

'Good question,' Carter said. 'I have just been trying to work that out.'

He took the map out of his inside pocket and briefly studied it, scratching his chin as he did so. Scratching of the chin then turned to scratching of the head.

'I would say that the barn is about two miles from here, at most. If you go back exactly the same route.' Carter then paused and shook his head.

'What is it, what's wrong?' Dwyer said impatiently.

'You are sure you want to go through with this?' It was Carter's last throw of the dice to try to persuade him otherwise. He then shook his head again realising what a feeble attempt it was.

'Yes, what is it?'

'Well, let's put it this way. Our German friends will be a tad more alert than they were earlier. Walking down the dirt track between the hedgerows will be not possible now. The only problem is, after studying this map I cannot see a different route.' He lied.

'Maybe it will be,' Dwyer said and pointed to the German jacket round his waist, he then added, 'Do you know what 'I am German' is in German?'

'*Ich bin Deutcsher,*' Carter said. 'And add '*nicht schieBen*' on. It means do not shoot.'

'*Ich bin Deutcsher, nicht schieBen*' Dwyer then repeated to himself a dozen times in a truly horrible attempt at a German accent.

Carter grimaced.

Satisfied that he had now committed the phrase to memory, he checked his watch.

'It is 14h10 hours now. If I am not back by 17h00, try to go down to the beach without me.'

Carter did not respond. Instead, he looked away to his left trying to hide his feelings of despair.

Unsuccessfully.

Dwyer could not help but notice that Carter appeared to be struggling emotionally and said, 'I tell you what. I *will* bet you your house this time that I make it back before then.'

Carter broke into a smile. He then turned back towards Dwyer and said, 'No bet.'

2

The gentle rocking back and forth had ceased.

Garcia had clearly heard the sound of running of feet outside the barn. It then had come to an abrupt halt, right outside the double door entrance in the small driveway.

He slowly stood up from the chair and slowly walked towards the side of the barn. On placing his right ear to one of the doors, he listened while holding his breath. He could clearly hear one voice shouting panicked stricken instructions in German.

As he listened further for any kind of response to try to ascertain how many others there were, he looked down at his rifle and checked that his safety was off. He then ensured that his knife and pistol were securely attached to his belt.

Once satisfied that all was in order, he took two paces back from the doors and pointed his rifle towards the slight gap in the middle of them. He waited to see if the Germans would open them and venture inside. An unwelcome surprise was now ready if they did.

The voice stopped.

Garcia slowly walked towards the doors and squinted through a thin vertical crack in the left door. He could barely make out at least four figures.

He then started to smile.

They now appeared to be walking towards the end of the driveway. Two of them appeared to be carrying something. The excited instructions continued. The voice slowly trailed off into the distance. They were leaving.

'See you later, sweethearts,' he whispered. This was then followed by a quiet cackle of laugher.

Now fully confident that they were not coming back, he walked towards the right door and gently pushed it open. On glancing left and not seeing anyone, he slowly stuck his head round the side of the door and peered to his right. The lane was empty.

He breathed a sigh of relief, cackled again and then took a tentative step outside. After one further check to his left, he started to giggle insanely, only this time, much louder.

With his back against the barn, he slowly edged his way along to the gate at the rear, continually looking back to his right to ensure there were no further Germans approaching from the lane.

He was starting to enjoy himself.

Every time he realised he was still alone, the giggling intensified.

On reaching the gate at the end of the barn, he quickly glanced round the corner into the field behind. He briefly noticed the Germans walking along the edge of a hedgerow. On closer inspection, he realised that two of them were carrying a machine-gun that was still attached to its tripod.

As if he was out for a ramble in the countryside, he gently opened the gate towards him, which slightly creaked due to the rust, and started to follow.

'Need some oil on that baby,' he mumbled to himself glared down at it. 'You could have given me away.'

The gate was soon forgotten. A smile now started to appear on his face as he very quietly started to whisper, 'A hunting we shall we go,' as he started to make his pursuit.

The Germans suddenly stopped and appeared to him to be looking through the hedgerow. Garcia stopped behind them. From his angle, he had no idea what now held their attention.

Instead of remaining stationary, he casually walked along with his rifle pointing at them closing the distance . . . 'I'll get you rabbit,' he said to himself and then chuckled. He then started to whistle a tuneless tune.

When he had closed the gap to about ten yards, the German nearest to him turned to his left and spotted him.

Immediately recognising Garcia as the enemy, he let out a startled yelp, which immediatley got the attention of his three companions. They all looked towards the smiling American approaching them. Two of them had been positioning the machine-gun to point through a slit in the hedgerow and had placed their rifles on the ground. The other two were so surprised by the sight of the grinning American they did not raise theirs in time.

'How's it going boys?' Garcia said in cheery voice and then

without any hesitation, he opened up on them.

The German nearest to Garcia was killed instantly as a bullet passed through his throat. His hand immediately shot up to it as he collapsed to the ground with a gurgling noise escaping from his mouth. Two of the others were hit in the chest. Both were still alive but collapsed moaning on the ground. The fourth had dived down into the mud and was frantically trying to aim his weapon at Garcia.

Without seemingly being the least bit concerned, Garcia casually strolled up to the uninjured German and stamped down on his rifle, which pinned it to his chest.

'Now what do you think you are going to do with that?' Garcia said. His smile then broadened as he shot the German right between the eyes.

Hysterical laughter followed as looked down on the now very dead German and said, 'Look at you now, you look like a Cyclops. Oh yeah, one dead cyclops rabbit.' He then added, 'No time to skin you though, rabbit.'

What was it that James to say at times like this, he thought. *He would have loved this. Oh yeah, he would have absolutely loved it.*

Still grinning inanely, he took his foot of the Germans chest and turned his attention now to the two injured Germans that both continued to moan on the ground. One was making a very slow attempt on trying to crawl towards his rifle, which was two yards away from him.

'And where do you think you are going? Not leaving already, are we? The party is just getting started.' Garcia said and then sprayed three bullets into the Germans back. After studying him for a few seconds, ensuring that his escape attempt had come to an abrupt halt, Garcia looked towards the remaining injured German and walked towards him.

As he reached him, the German looked up and said in English while gasping for breath, 'I surrender. Please, I surrender.'

Garcia smiled down at him and said, 'I bet you do,' and then stamped down on the Germans throat. 'I bet you do,' he repeated and then shot him in the forehead. Insane giggling erupted once again. 'Your one dead cyclops rabbit too.'

The giggling then suddenly stopped.

The earth to his right then suddenly started to erupt into the air. Two Germans manning a machine-gun nest placed on the other side of the field had eventually, after hearing Garcia's first shot, had turned their tripod round and had now started firing towards him.

Garcia immediately hit the deck and dived for cover, using the last of his victim's body as shelter. He pushed it so that it was lying on its side. Immediately, bullets started to slam into the back of the dead Germans body. There was a brief pause and then a flurry of bullets hit the same target.

'What the fuck are you shooting at me for?' Garcia shouted. 'I was only having some fun.' He then went off on one and started to recite the words to a nursery rhyme.

> *Ring-a-Ring o'Rosies*
> *A Pocket full of Posies*
> *"A-tishoo! A-tishoo!*
> *We all fall down.*

This was greeted by another burst of machine-gun fire just above Garcia's head, which this time, thumped into the mud bank behind him.

'What's a matter with you, don't you like my rendition. This is getting personal now boys,' Garcia shouted as he slowly brought his rifle up to his side. He then took the quickest of glances over the body and could see that the Germans firing on him were about seventy yards away, slightly to his left.

He quickly moved his rifle up and while resting on top of the shoulder of the corpse, he fired two shots. The first of which hit one of the legs of the tripod holding the machine-gun. The other hit the German that was firing the machine-gun in the knee.

Garcia could hear the scream of agony clearly and looked up to see one of the Germans writhing around on the ground.

'Hurt, did it?' He shouted.

He then slowly positioned himself into a kneeling position and fired off three more shots. The German, who was now frantically trying to take over the firing position, was hit twice in the stomach.

He joined his partner on the ground, squirming and gasping for breath.

Garcia aimed again, more deliberately this time. He fired two further shots. Both shots were bulls-eyes. Each of the Germans was now put out of their suffering by receiving fatal injuries to the chest.

Garcia slowly stood up.

'Now that's what I call good shooting,' he shouted whilst pumping his rifle up and down over his head with both hands.

On eventually turning his attention back to the two Germans across the field, and seeing that they were now completely still, Garcia carried out a complete three hundred and sixty degree surveillance of his surroundings.

Unbeknown to him, Carter had carried the same exercise earlier and he now also realised that such was the height of the hedges, he could not see anything else apart from the tops of some trees in the distance.

Two planes then flew by at low level about a mile away to his right, which he recognised as American. 'Go get em boys,' he shouted up to the sky and then added, 'You fly-boy faggots. That aint no way to fight a war. Get your asses down here and fight like a man.'

After one final cursory glance around, he continued following the hedgerow walking away from the barn and then noticed a huge German that was now slumped against a machine-gun. At first, Garcia thought he had fallen asleep guarding an exit to the field.

He stopped, and then inexplicably, began to recite a further demented chant.

Hush a bye baby, on the tree top,
When the wind blows the cradle will rock;
When the bow breaks, the cradle will fall,
And down will come baby, cradle and all.

Garcia crept towards him with his rifle pointing directly at his head. On reaching him, he kicked one of his feet. 'Wakey, wakey,' he said.

The German did not respond.

On closer inspection, he noticed that the Germans head was severely bruised and partially indented towards the right side and back.

Garcia's thoughts immediately turned to Dwyer.

'I bet he put a hell of fight though. Look at the size of this mother, mighty big as James would say . . . and damn ugly . . . damn ugly!' He said aloud to himself. After giving the corpse one final prod with his rifle, he said, 'See you later. Probably in hell.'

Garcia then casually strolled out into the dirt lane and looked both ways along it. As soon as he glanced to his right, he saw American troops slowly advancing towards him. They were all in crouched firing positions. The troop on point raised his rifle at Garcia.

Unfazed, Garcia just casually raised his thumb into the air smiling at the same time.

The point man lowered his rifle, stood up and returned the gesture.

This was the last action of his life.

A machine-gun opened up on him from the field opposite on the dirt other side of the lane. Such was the ferocity of the burst; it almost decapitated the young American.

All the remaining troops following him dived for cover.

Garcia did not. He casually walked towards the slit in the hedgerow, where smoke was now coming out of, and tossed a grenade gently over the top. The explosion killed the two Germans behind the hedgerow instantly and destroyed the machine-gun beyond repair.

'All clear,' Garcia shouted, who had not even bothered to dive for cover from the exploding grenades.

The other twenty-five Americans now all returned to their feet and then cautiously walked towards Garcia who was standing in the middle of the lane as bold as brass.

When the leader of the Group reached within five feet of Garcia, he stopped and said, 'Captain Wells, 115th of the 29th.'

'Private Garcia, 101st Airborne.'

'Oh yeah?' Wells said. 'We ran into two of your buddies back at the beach, a Major Carter and a Corporal Dwyer. Were you on the same plane as them?'

Garcia's face darkened. He then slowly nodded and then said,

'Thank God they made it, Dwyer is like a brother to me.'

'Is that a fact? You don't sound like you are English to me.'

'It's a long story,' Garcia said.

Wells snorted a laugh and said, 'Yeah, that's what he said. From what the Major told me, sounds like your buddy is a hero already. Apparently he took out a whole stretch of trenches on his own.'

Garcia smiled and said, 'That sure sounds like him. He sure can handle himself. How far is it to the beach from here?'

'Just under two miles I'd say. Why? Are you thinking about trying to join up with them?'

'That would be just great if I could. I mean, if you would permit me, sir.'

'Sure,' Wells said.

Garcia smiled. 'Can you tell me the way and where their position is?'

Wells took out a map and briefly showed Garcia the route they had just taken from the beach. While folding it up once finished, he said, 'We are going to advance on St Laurent and then probably dig in for the night. Your buddy Dwyer said he would try to join us later.'

'Okay, thanks Captain. If it's alright with you I am going to try and find him and help him get back here.'

Wells nodded his agreement. 'Okay then, but watch out for German snipers.' He then added, 'Thanks for your help here by the way. Hope to see you later, if you find him. Remember, we are heading for St Laurent.'

'Will he be bringing the Major with him? Garcia said.

Wells shook his head. 'No. Seems the Major has broken his ankle when he landed last night. Dwyer had to carry him on his back all night. He is going to take him down to the beach later and get him evacuated.'

Garcia became anxious. 'Will Dwyer be going back with him?'

'Maybe, who knows? Although, he did say something about doing something else first.

'What was that?' Garcia said quickly. He then glanced down the lane over Wells' shoulder, assuming that Dwyer might well be coming back to finish him off. If not completely, then at least ensure that he was arrested.

Wells shook his head. 'He didn't say. Anyway, good luck. Hope you find him.'

'Thanks Captain,' he said. 'I am sure I will. It would be good to see the Major as well before he goes. He is a good man.'

Wells went to walk away when Garcia stopped him. He said, 'This field is clear. I took out all of the machine-gun crews earlier. That one was a bit a problem though, he said with a wicked grin on his face.'

Wells looked towards the dead German slumped against the machine-gun at the entrance to the field, and then said, 'Jesus, he's huge, and ugly too.'

'Aint he though? Just about the ugliest mother, I ever did see. All in a day's work though,' Garcia said still grinning. 'See you later, Captain.'

Wells watched Garcia walk away down the lane passing his men, high fiving some of them as he went. He knew he was telling lies about the dead enormous German. Carter had included that part earlier in his commentary on their night's events. If he had any idea just how big a liar and insane Garcia was he would have stopped him there and then and put a bullet in his head as if he were a rabid dog. Instead, he turned and led his men cautiously down the lane towards St Laurent-sur-Mer.

3

Dwyer jumped up over the overhang and walked between the two trenches. He double-checked them both to ensure that they had not now been reinforced with further German troops.

His mind was put immediately at rest as he now saw a steady stream of American troops away to his left that had scaled the bluff. As he started to walk towards the tree line, an American who was leading a group of men, walked towards him with his rifle raised. It was pointed directly at him.

Oh, crap.

Dwyer raised both his hands in the air. 'Easy mate, I am on your side.'

'That's some souvenir,' the American said lowering the rifle and nodding down to the German jacket tied around Dwyer's waist.

Dwyer nodded. 'I am going to need it where I am headed. Don't fancy coming with me, do you? I could do with the help.'

Dwyer's request was ignored. The soldier's interest in Dwyer had completely disappeared. He walked past him along the top of the bluff.

'I take that as a no then,' Dwyer said, noticing that his eyes seemed to be completely vacant. He then shuddered at the thought of what he had gone through and witnessed while advancing onto the beach.

After the last of the line of troops had passed him, Dwyer put his hand to his head and realised that he had not put on his helmet before leaving the bluff. A smile appeared on his face as he wondered how the previously attentive Major could possibly allow him to leave without it. He quickly thought about returning but then dismissed the idea.

His voice of reason spoke up.

That's a mistake.

I'll be okay.

If you say so, but I am telling you now. That's a mistake.

After consciously ensuring that he did not look back down at the beach, as he had had enough for one day, a lifetime in fact, he walked into the woods.

In the daylight, all now seemed very different. It was nowhere near as dense as Dwyer thought it to be in the darkness. The Major's voice then entered his head.

'Be careful of the mines.'

He became rooted to the spot.

His own voice then entered his inner conversation.

Get on with it.

What about the mines?

You can't stand around here all day. Get your thumb out of your arse and get moving.

He took notice and eventually started to put one foot in front of the other. However, at first, he did so with extreme caution as he made his way through the woods, following a path roughly in the direction they had come from during the early hours of the morning.

Be careful of the mines. The Major's voice had returned.

Such was his concentration of looking at every tree to ensure there were no Germans taking cover behind them; he nearly jumped out of his skin when an American shouted from about ten feet behind him to remind of that fact again.

'Fuck the bloody mines,' he grumbled to himself. 'You nearly killed me by giving me a bloody heartache attack! Why the fuck does he think I am walking so slowly for? . . . Moron!'

Dwyer realised he was going in the right direction when he came across the German he had killed with his knife earlier while he was carrying out his ablutions. It seemed to him that every fly in France was now hovering over the corpse and he then started to think about rats again.

He shuddered and reached inside his pocket for his cigarettes. After lighting one and having two large tugs on it, he continued. He kept reminding himself to blink every now and then as his eyes were literally out on stalks searching every blade of grass, bush and tree in front of him.

On reaching a clearing, which was about ten yards square, he came to an abrupt stop. He had definitely heard a branch snap away to his left. As he slightly crouched down to peer into the trees and bushes, a shot was fired. The bullet missed his head by about an inch. He felt the warmth and rush of air as it passed over him.

Shit, that was close.

He dived head first onto the ground, even finding time to swear aloud when he realised that his face was now in a pile of animal droppings, not as much as the cows earlier, but incredibly smelly all the same.

What is with you and ability to roll in every piece of shit you find in northern France?

Goddam it.

Now really is the time to focus.

After wiping his face frantically, he slowly raised his head and tried to figure out the exact direction from which it had come from, albeit he did not have a clue.

He started to crawl towards a two-foot tree stump when a further shot rang out from immediately in front of him. The bullet passed over his left shoulder and he started now to regret the fact that he not gone back for his helmet.

I could say I told you so.

I like it better in times like this when you don't want to disturb.

Silence.

I said –

A further shot sent splinters flying all around him.

Dwyer thought he was hearing things when a childlike cackle could now be heard from his front-left. He also believed he had heard a voice saying something about rabbits. He strained his ears to ensure that he was not imagining it.

Some idiot can't be shooting at rabbits, can they?

Not unless you have suddenly grown two big ears and a tail.

He shook his head instantly dismissing the thought and then wiped the remnants of crap of his face. He then crawled the few feet further required to reach the base of the stump.

As soon as he reached it, the top erupted into a hundred splinters as four shots thudded into the top, just above his head. One of the largest of the splinters was now embedded in his forehead. He quickly reached for it and pulled it out which caused a gush of blood to flow out straight into his right eye. As he was trying to wipe it away, he noticed out the corner of his left eye a figure crashing through the bushes towards him.

So much for shooting at rabbits.

He frantically tried to roll over onto his back and tried to move his rifle into a position where he could fire it at the same time.

He was too late.

Just as he managed to get onto his back, a boot came crashing down on his chest. As he looked up, he found himself staring straight into the muzzle of an M-1 rifle.

4

'Hello again, shit head,' Garcia said to him with his insane grin all over his face. 'Did you miss me?'

'Desperately,' said Dwyer.

'Where is that son of a bitch Major?' Garcia hissed.

'Probably half way across the Channel by now,' Dwyer said.

'Is that so, Davey my old mate?' Garcia said with a truly pathetic imitation of a London Cockney accent.

'That's so,' Dwyer said.

'Well then. It seems to me that you are not being very honest with me now, don't it?'

'Nope, I took him down to the beach to be evacuated,' thinking, *how the hell could he possibly know that.*

'Well, what you doing here then? Why didn't you go with him?'

'I was going to get Brooks' body and bring it back.'

Garcia bellowed an insane laugh and said, 'Well aint that real nice of you. What a little sweetheart you are. What about Hickey and Henderson? Are you going to bring their bodies back too?'

Dwyer just stared up at him. Considering his current predicament, he was actually feeling incredibly calm.

'Well here's the thing. I just ran into a Captain Wells who you met earlier.'

Dwyer tried not to show his sudden disappointment. He knew now where this was headed.

'He tells me that you were going to take the Major down to the beach and then do one other thing. Now I know what that other thing is. There aint no way you had time to get down to the beach and get over here, is there now?'

He has a point.

Dwyer just continued to stare up at Garcia.

'I took the major – '

Garcia stamped down harder on his chest to cut him off midsentence. 'And if I'm right, which I know I am, that tells me that I was right earlier also. You are not being completely honest with me,' Garcia said with his insane grin growing wider.

Dwyer just shook his head.

'Don't matter anyhow. The Captain told me where you roughly were. I will find him right after I have taken care of you.'

'And how are you going to do that?' Dwyer said desperately trying to buy time and think how he was going to get out of this.

More insane laughter erupted. 'You are one big dumb son of a bitch. I aint the one with a gun in my face now, am I?'

Another good point.

Yeah, you can't fault his logic. Even if he is a sandwich short of a picnic.

Only one sandwich? This one is missing the whole hamper.

Dwyer now started to laugh, or pretend to at least, and said, 'You have a good point I suppose. What are you going to do, just shoot me in the head? Wouldn't you rather have a good old fist fight and see who wins?'

As if they were playing a game of 'Laugh Tennis' it was now Garcia's turn. Unfortunately, for Dwyer, he never took his eyes off him.

'Yeah sure, you would like that wouldn't you?'

Yes. Very much.

'Do you take me for some kind of moron or something?'

Again, yes.

'I know you are a big tough guy,' and emphasised his point by pressing harder down on Dwyer's chest.

'Don't flatter yourself Garcia. You give morons a bad name. From what I have seen of you, you are just a coward piece of shit,' Dwyer said calmly.

Excellent. Antagonise him, why don't you?

This instantly wiped the smile of Garcia's face. 'Okay tough guy. I am getting bored now. Get on your knees and beg for your life.'

'Go fuck yourself.' Dwyer said.

Garcia then rammed his foot even harder into Dwyer's chest and shouted, 'I said get on your knees and beg,' and then took three steps back away from him still pointing his rifle at Dwyer's head.

Dwyer slowly eventually got to his knees never breaking eye

contact with Garcia as he did so. He then made a conscious effort to make his eyes go wide and looked over Garcia's left shoulder. He obliged. He looked round behind him.

Moron.

Dwyer then sprang to his feet and grabbed the end of Garcia's rifle. He pulled it towards him and head butted Garcia on the bridge of his nose as he turned his head back towards him. Garcia crumpled to the ground.

After kicking him in the stomach, Dwyer then threw the rifle about ten yards away into the bushes and then casually moved his own behind the tree stump.

He then returned to Garcia and stood over him who was only semi-conscious on the floor.

'I cannot believe you fell for that you stupid bastard. That's the oldest trick in the book. My little sister stopped falling for the 'there is someone behind you routine' when she was about four years old,' said Dwyer.

He then grabbed Garcia by the scruff of the neck and pulled him too his feet. He slapped him twice round the face, which had the effect of Garcia's eyes regaining focus and looking into his own. Blood was pouring from Garcia's broken nose and mouth.

'What we are going to do now is play a game of 'May the best man win.' My rifle is over there by that tree stump. Whoever gets to it first gets to shoot the other. That's fair . . . isn't it?'

Garcia did not respond. He just stared at Dwyer with petrified bulging eyes.

'I will even give you a head start,' said Dwyer and let go of him.

Garcia stumbled sideways and looked towards the rifle that Dwyer had placed behind the tree stump. As he made his first step towards it, Dwyer stamped on the back of his right knee which sent him falling to the ground.

'Too slow I am afraid,' Dwyer said matter of factly as he stood over him smiling.

He was beginning to enjoy himself.

Garcia then eventually got to his knees and started crawling towards the rifle. Dwyer let him get within about two yards and then kicked him in the side of the stomach, which sent Garcia flying sideways, and onto his back. He lay there gasping for breath making no further attempt to move.

As Dwyer moved closer and stood over him, Garcia looked up and said through blooded and missing teeth, 'I met your sister when we were in Portsmouth. She is the easiest lay I have ever had . . . Not very good though . . . But real easy.'

The smile was wiped from Dwyer's face. Garcia realised from the look on his face that he had now sealed his own fate. He whimpered . . . like a little girl.

'Is that a fact?' said Dwyer. 'I should have realised that you would go round shagging dead people . . . No woman alive in their right mind would want to go near you. Not without being drugged or being banged on the head first.'

He then bent over, grabbed hold of Garcia's jacket with his left hand and pulled him to his feet.

Further whimpers escaped Garcia.

When standing, Dwyer hit him in the jaw with his right that sent him back crashing to the ground again. His head just missing the tree stump.

That's a relief. I want him conscious for what is coming next.
Indeed, this is fun.
Really. You sure?
Really.

Dwyer casually walked up behind him and placed one foot either side of his back. He bent down, picked up Garcia's head and pulled back with both hands under his chin. Just when he thought he was actually going to pull his head off his shoulders, he said, 'What goes around comes around . . . *You sick fuck!*'

Garcia screamed . . . 'Nooooo.'

He then twisted Garcia's neck violently to his left, which killed him instantly by snapping his neck like a twig.

As if 200 lbs had just been lifted of his shoulders, Dwyer felt as if that he had exorcised at least one of his inner demons that had been plaguing him since landing in France.

'One less enemy within,' he said aloud to himself.

After taking two deep breaths, he wearily let go of Garcia's head, stood up, walked towards the tree stump and sat down. He lit a cigarette and looked all around him. Just as he turned to his left, a further bullet flew over his head.

Goddamit... what now?

A German soldier had been hiding in the bushes watching on in amazement as the two Americans had fought each other. When Dwyer ended the contest, he left his hiding place to shoot the winner.

Fortunately, for Dwyer, he was a horrible shot and missed him by a good three feet.

Dwyer almost casually picked up his rifle and shot the German in the chest in one swift movement. On seeing him crumple to the ground, he said to himself, 'When it rains, it certainly fucking pours.'

You did well again, Davey. Very, very well.
Thanks.
Now go and get Brooks.
Yep, just have to take care of one thing before I go.
Good plan.
Thanks.

Dwyer finished his cigarette, stood and then picked up Garcia's body. With ease, he threw it over his shoulder. He then looked around for the thickest bushes he could find, casually walked towards them and then threw his body into them.

Once he was satisfied that it could not easily be spotted, he said to Garcia's dead body, 'Hopefully the rats will get you before anyone finds you. You don't deserve a proper burial.'

As he picked up his rifle, he said to himself, 'That Major owes me one hell of an explanation when I get back. This story for another time shit stops right now.'

He then proceeded to march off through the woods towards Brooks' body.

5
10th July 1943
Autryville, North Carolina, USA
03h55 hours

Two of the group quickly moved to opposite sides of the bed holding both of the woman's arms, while a third ripped off her nightdress. They then proceeded to rip two long shreds and tie them round her mouth.

All her previous spirit and fight had now left her and she lay on the bed without attempting any resistance. She simply stared at the ceiling. No further tears were rolling down her cheeks. She had accepted her fate.

'Mr Star Gazer' stood and the end of the bed and slowly took of his trousers and underwear. He took the belt from his trousers and wrapped around his fist with the brass buckle prominent at the front.

He waved it towards the woman. 'Now, you don't want me to use this on your old haggard old face now, do you?'

She made no response.

'You just lay back and enjoy it . . . WHOOP.'

The woman's eyes now went wide and then abruptly closed.

'The four of us are just going to have a bit of exercise, then after that, who knows,' he said as he now climbed up onto the bed. He entered her without hesitation.

His three companions all watched on with glee.

With her eyes now wide open, she stared at the ceiling trying to divorce herself from her immediate horrific reality. *I never noticed that stain on the ceiling before* she found herself thinking. *I really must paint over that when I get the chance.*

The whole group then took their turn.

There were only so many stains on the ceiling and cobwebs in the corners to look at. She could not divert her attention away from the horror forever.

She begged to God to end it . . . Just end it . . . NOW . . . HAVE SOME FUCKING MERCY, PLEASE!

God was not listening. She silently cursed him.

'Over to you now,' 'Mr Star Gazer' said after the fourth member of the group was spent and looked towards the cymbal banging monkey. 'Do your thing.'

He did not need asking twice. A knife with a six-inch blade was immediately taken out of his inside jacket pocket.

He smiled down at her with the most hideous bedside manner imaginable. 'Now then,' he said. 'This is really going to hurt,' and lowered the knife to her abdomen.

Two hands were clamped over her mouth to prevent the inevitable screaming.

Twenty minutes later, the entire group left the house through the front door and walked out casually into the night.

The woman lay on the bed upstairs with her now lifeless eyes still staring at the ceiling. If her face had not been slashed in twenty different places, it would have been noticeable from her expression that she was actually relieved . . . Total and utter complete blissful oblivion had descended upon her.

'Wow. It's gone past four o'clock,' the Star Gazer said. 'Time sure goes fast when you are having fun, eh fellahs? . . . WHOOP,' he added when he sat down inside the jeep. He then started singing . . .

> Hickory Dickory Dock,
> 'Why scamper?' asked the clock.
> 'You scare me so
> I have to go!'
> Hickory Dickory Dock.
> **WHOOP-WHOOP**

6

Dwyer had reached the edge of the wood. He had only just remembered in time to stop himself from striding purposely across the thirty yards of open ground between the tree line and the gate, which lead into the first of the two lanes that he was going to have to negotiate.

He took consolation from the fact that it was now light and he was not carrying the Major on his back. It would no doubt make the task easier to study the ground for possible evidence of the ground being disturbed.

Be careful of the mines.

He stood still for a full two minutes suspiciously looking forward and downwards and then turned round back into the woods. After collecting a bundle of fallen branches from the trees, he returned to the spot where he had left the wood originally. He then took his first tentative step and closed his eyes.

Dwyer's somewhat blasé attitude towards the mines had now changed after seeing the remnants of the German soldier on the path leading to the bunker system.

He bent down and placed a branch where his right foot now was and then stood up and brought his left forward to the same spot. He then looked towards his intended target of the gate.

He cursed.

If anything, it looked further away to him.

His vision now seemed to him to have a tunnel effect, which made the gate the only object in his focus, all his peripheral vision had seemingly disappeared.

Focus.

I am . . . Just shut the hell up, will you?

Focus on Sally.

The second step was then taken with the branch placing process being repeated. He then bent down again and picked it back up. After counting the amount branches, he had found in the wood, he now realised he only had ten pieces left. He quickly calculated that he would have to place one after every third step.

Oh, crap. This is bollocks.

Silence.

I said this is bollocks.

Silence.

By the time he placed the last branch on the ground, twenty minutes had elapsed from the time he first left the tree line. He checked his watch.

It was 14h55 hours.

It had taken him forty-five minutes to cover only a sixth of the total distance. At this rate, it would take him four-and-a-half hours to return to the major.

Not so good.

No. Get you arse in gear.

Ignoring his last instruction to himself, Dwyer quickly consoled himself further by thinking that the journey back would be quicker due to not having to deal with Garcia. In addition, he could now quickly walk across the open land between the gate and the start of the wood by following the branches. He took the last three steps to the gate without further hesitation and opened it.

For Gods sake! Is there no end to this bollocks?

He then had to stop again immediately. There were three German soldiers were running towards him from his right.

They were oblivious to him.

He knelt down into his now favourite firing position and fired off six rounds. The lead German was killed instantly while the two following fell to the ground severely wounded after both being hit in the chest.

Dwyer stood up and glanced to both his right and left to see if they had further company. To his relief, it soon became apparent to him that they were on their own. At this point, he did not intend to finish off the two injured on this occasion. However, one of them made the mistake to start screaming so loudly for help, his actions only had the effect of ending his life along with his friends who had remained silent. Dwyer walked towards them and ended the noise with two well-aimed shots to the head.

Was that really necessary?

Yes.
Really?
Shut it.

He now tried to block out the general background noise of the battle on the beaches still raging behind him to the north of his position, and the aerial bombardment that continued inland to his south. He was desperately trying to concentrate on his immediate vicinity.

As he looked skywards, he saw three planes flying at low level strafing targets below. He briefly followed their progress as they eventually ascended with one carrying out a victory roll. He assumed they had been successful in destroying whatever it was they had been aiming at.

He punched the air in delight.

Dwyer now turned his attention away to his right. He could make out the sound of small arms and machine-gun fire. This time he assumed that the Americans that were now advancing inland were having contacts with the Germans in and amongst the hedgerows. As the fighting taking place seemed to be some distant away, he ran to his left towards the junction of the lane.

On turning the corner, he stopped and looked round. As with the woods, it seemed very different in the daylight. It went off into the distant in almost perfect straight line slightly angling to his right. It was was flanked by the hedgerows on both sides. These now appeared to be higher to Dwyer, as the tops of them did not now blend in with the earlier darkness.

He considered for a moment that the end of this dirt lane would lead onto the lane where the barn was situated. He quickly dismissed the idea, as although he believed it would, he thought it best to stay to the exact same route they had followed earlier. He did not have time to get lost no matter how unlikely he considered that would be.

Remembering the Germans that had challenged them before, when Carter had been literally spurring him on how a jockey would his horse when approaching the finish line of a race; he then crouched down and started to proceed cautiously down the lane. He briefly smiled to himself of the previous thought he had of *Straight Deal* ending up in a sandwich.

All appeared to be quiet.

So much so, it actually started to worry him as opposed to giving him comfort.

Stay focussed.

Sweat was continually pouring down his face into his eyes as he studied every inch of the hedgerows looking for openings where the Germans could fire at him from. Every time he had to pause and wipe it away with the sleeve of his jacket. Every time, this was an unwelcome reminder of the amount of the amount of crap and blood that was now completely dried on it.

After taking a few paces forward, he looked to his right and could clearly see a small opening in the hedgerow. After staring at it for a full thirty seconds, he kept to the hedge on his right taking tiny steps, concentrating on not making the slightest of sounds.

He started to sweat even more profusely when his right foot stood on a branch and split in half. He held his breath, swore silently to himself and then eventually, continued.

On reaching the gap in the hedge, he stole the quickest of glances through the slit. Not for the first time in his life, he was thankful of his size. A smaller man would not have been able to reach it and see through.

To his complete relief, he noticed that the two Germans that had been guarding the post appeared to be dead in the field. The machine-gun lay in pieces around them. He confirmed this to himself by taking a longer more considered look.

Yep. Will not be getting any trouble from them anytime soon.

He then crouched down at looked both ways down the lane. He was still on his own.

The thought now occurred to him that the advancing American troops might have been down here earlier. His mind wandered back to his meeting with Captain Wells and assumed it had been him and his men.

It must have been them.

Maybe.

After a brief period of further consideration, he stood up to his full height to put on the German jacket that was tied around his waist.

Once he had put one of his arms through the jacket, he stopped and paused. He then removed it again, threw it on the ground and started to jog as his newfound confidence made him think that who else would have taken them out?

Dwyer now reached the entrance to the field where he had fought with his worthy opponent. To his amazement, the German was still slumped against the machine-gun where he had placed him earlier.

This time, he had company.

A large black bird, which Dwyer thought to be a crow, was perched on top of the dead Germans head and was helping itself to some lunch by pecking at the corpses eyes.

His mouth dropped open in horror and he immediately raised his rifle and fired at the offending scavenger. This had the effect of sending up a hundred feathers up into the air and then slowly spiralling back down to the ground.

Dwyer instantly thought of Danny's body and now started to sprint.

The rats . . . Don't forget the rats!

He sprinted faster.

His pace only slowed when he noticed a further four dead German bodies in front of him and eventually Dwyer thought it wise to stop completely and make one further check of his surroundings.

Away to his left, he noted a further German machine-gun position with two bodies laying face down in the mud. They too were attracting a number of the local bird population. This time however, they were cautiously walking around the bodies bobbing their heads as they went, trying to muster up the courage to approach their proposed snack.

The four bodies in front of him appeared to be, for the moment at least, not to be on any of the wildlife's menu.

Dwyer took one further look round the entire field and then nodded his head as it to confirm to himself that this area had been cleared by the Americans.

The fact that Garcia had told him that he had run into Captain Wells and his men entered his mind. He suspected it must have been them; that had cleared the field. Wells had said that he was on his way to St Laurent and Dwyer remembered the road sign earlier when the Major thought it a good idea to get rid of the bike.

Starting to sprint again, Dwyer did not notice the four Germans that had entered the field at the northeast corner behind him.

Now within twenty yards of the gate, Dwyer had to take a slight detour to his left to avoid a bomb crater in the field. As he did so, he glanced to his right to check on the barn. It appeared to him to have completely remained intact. This made him slow to walking pace, as he feared their maybe now further of the enemy hiding in it.

He quickly realised that Wells may have led his men straight down the lane as opposed to entering the field after taking out its previous German occupants.

Having now reached the gate, he slowly opened it towards him, which again creaked and slowly looked round the corner into the driveway. He then became even more alert when he saw that one of the doors was open slightly obscuring his view of the lane.

Unbeknown to him, he now followed Garcia's example of slowly moving along the exterior of the barn with his back against it. On reaching the opening, he quickly bent down and moved into the doorway with his rifle at the ready.

Now frantically moving his eyes from left to right, he realised that it was empty of any live bodies at least, and that the motorbike was still inside. His spirits rose when he noticed that the keys were still in the ignition.

Now backing out of the barn, he walked down the driveway and turned right instead of left towards Brooks' body, after noticing the crater in the lane if front of him. He walked to the edge and looked to see how deep it was.

'Shit,' he said to himself, ending all thoughts of checking to see if the lane that led to the woods did end at a junction with the lane he was now standing in.

There was no way he could get the bike past this twelve feet hole that covered the entire width of the lane. *I am definitely going to have to carry Brooks' body back*, he thought.

He checked his watch.

It was 15h20 hours.

'Plenty of time,' he said to himself as he now abandoned all caution and turned round and sprinted back past the barn towards the slight bend in the lane. His progress was halted as he nearly went sprawling head first into a newly formed additional crater.

After skirting round the edge, he jogged the final distance to the point of the wall where they had found Carter. He looked down on the surface of the lane and could still clearly see the pool of now dried blood that had been created by Hickey when he had cut Brooks' throat.

Dwyer looked towards the wall and paused. He was now reluctant to see what was on the other side. He closed his eyes and said to himself quietly, 'Please let him be okay,' and then without further hesitation, he placed both hands on the top of the wall and vaulted over.

7

Carter was staring off into space trying to calculate Dwyer's progress on retrieving Brooks' body. What he had not taken into consideration was his meeting with Garcia and the amount of care Dwyer had taken in crossing the open ground between the edge of the wood and the gate that led to the first lane.

He glanced at his watch to check the time and estimated that if all had gone relatively smoothly, he should be at least half way back.

After lighting a cigarette, he went over the journey again in his head and then nodded agreement to himself that his calculations were correct.

He could hear more and more Americans above his position under the overhang now. On one occasion, a soldier had jumped down to investigate where the path led. He looked scared half to death when he turned round to notice Carter pointing his rifle at him.

As a result, his Captain then joined him and Carter once again gave detail of his activities throughout the night. After being informed by the Captain that they were also heading for St Laurent, Carter asked him to keep an eye out for Dwyer, as he would be returning from that rough direction.

The Captain and his company left after Carter had refused his offer of help. He was adamant that he wanted to wait for Dwyer's return before heading down to the beach to be evacuated.

Carter now turned his thoughts to how he could ensure that Dwyer joined him on his premature journey back across the Channel.

At one point, he started to smile about the thought of shooting Dwyer in the foot. He quickly dismissed it however as he did not want to be on the receiving end of his wrath. He hoped that he would be the most senior officer in the immediate vicinity of the beach and just 'pull rank' on his subordinates.

With that, he picked up his binoculars and checked the progress below him. Mortar rounds and sniper fire still rained down on the troops below. He took some consolation in the fact that it now appeared to be less intense.

He grimaced at the thought that there was still one big last adventure to be had. The thought of the carnage that now awaited them on the beach below.

He now sat back down, rested his back against the wall and looked towards his rucksack. After a brief moment of contemplation, he decided against a further small shot of morphine. He wanted to be completely alert when Dwyer returned.

Instead, he lit yet another cigarette and resumed his thoughts on Dwyer's progress.

Surely, he must be nearly back any time soon.

8

Dwyer landed on the other side of the wall between the bodies of Hickey and Brooks. He immediately looked down to his right and noticed that Hickey had appeared to remain a scavenger free zone.

He then slowly turned his head towards Brooks, hoping that the same applied to him.

It did.

Oh my God! . . . Thank you.

He still aint listening to you.

Really? Oh well, thank you anyway.

He bent down and rested his knees on the ground with his eyes closed when he noticed that all was okay, apart from the flies.

No rats . . . or birds.

Praise the Lord.

You're not fooling anyone about this suddenly finding religion thing.

Thank fuck then!

Another 200 lbs of weight now seemed to fly off his shoulders. Inner demon number two had been exorcised.

He could not imagine being able to close his eyes ever again if Brooks had become lunch to a hungry rodent. He hoped and half-believed that that particular dream would never haunt him again.

After a futile attempt to bat away the flies with his hands, he studied Brooks' face more closely.

It had turned completely white and his eyes stared upwards towards the sky. Dwyer made an unsuccessful attempt to close his eyelids that just refused to move downwards.

After checking his jacket pocket to ensure he still had Brooks' letter and picture of his girlfriend inside, he said, 'C'mon then mate, let's get you home.'

He pulled Brooks' body towards him that had now started to stiffen due to rigamourtis setting in and positioned him over his left shoulder. He gently pulled his legs back towards him so that they were flat against the left half of his chest and waist and then stood up.

Dwyer now realised the full meaning of the expression 'dead weight' as Brooks was considerably heavier that he could have possibly imagined. He then lifted his left leg over the top of the wall and gently lowered it the last few inches to the lane below. Now straddling the wall, he very slowly brought his right leg over concentrating on not losing his balance.

Once accomplished, he adjusted his rifle that was slung over his right shoulder so it was pointing forwards and then started walking back towards the barn, already starting to work up a sweat.

As he reached the slight bend in the lane, he was confronted with the four German shoulders that had entered the field earlier, all pointing their rifles toward him. He stopped dead in his tracks and quietly said to himself, 'Fuck it!'

9

'*Setzen Sie den Korper und Ihre Waffe und legen Sie Ihre Hande auf,*' one of the Germans shouted.

You what?

Dwyer just stared at him and remained motionless. This phrase was not the one Carter had previously taught him.

'Put down the body and your gun and put your hands up,' he repeated in English, this time a lot louder and with a lot more urgency.

Yeah right!
Maybe you should do what he said.
Not going to happen.

Dwyer slowly angled his body so that his left side was now facing the Germans and gradually bent his knees as if to lower Brooks to the ground. In the same movement, he angled his rifle round his waist, placed his right index finger on the trigger and fired off two shots.

One German was shot in the leg while another was hit in the stomach.

Both went down.

The other two returned fire.

Dwyer lumbered forward and dived into the crater in the middle of the lane with Brooks' body falling away to his right, oblivious to the bullets that were ricocheting off the lane around his legs. He then reached for one of the grenades in his ammo pouch, pulled the pin and threw it over the top.

On hearing the explosion, he slowly peered over the top of the crater. The two injured Germans were now dead lying next to each other face down in the lane. He looked from left to right to see where the fourth was.

He was nowhere to be seen.
Where the hell did he go?
Probably in the barns driveway.
You reckon?
Probably.

Crawling upwards on his elbows and knees, Dwyer left the cover of the crater and moved to the right side of the lane. He then stood and slowly inched his way to the entrance of the barns driveway. When within three feet of it, the remaining German raced round the corner from behind the hedge. He was screaming his head off and was pointing his rifle straight at Dwyer's chest.

Dwyer instantly grabbed the muzzle of the rifle and pulled it towards him. Instead of the desired effect of pulling the German closer to him, he was left with the rifle in his left hand.

The German had let go.

Dwyer threw the rifle to the floor and lunged forward. He grabbed the German with his right hand and then twisted him towards him in a headlock. He then shouted into the Germans left ear, 'You can either live or die, it's up to you.'

'I live, I live,' the German shouted instantly in a panicked stricken voice.

'Good decision,' Dwyer said. 'Now you can make yourself useful.'

He kept his hand on the scruff of the now terrified Germans jacket and pulled his head up within inches of his own face.

'You can help me carry my buddy back to the beach,' he said through gritted teeth.

'I help, I help,' the German agreed trying to nod furiously. Dwyer's grip was preventing him from doing so.

'Good lad. Now, I am going to let you go. If you even look at me in a way I don't like when I do, I am going to ram my hand down your throat and rip your fucking heart out. Do you understand?'

'Yes, yes, I understand, I help.'

Dwyer released the German who slowly turned and looked up into Dwyer's face. 'I help,' he said again, in a concerted effort in trying to appease him.

'Take off your jacket and helmet and throw them away. I don't want any Americans shooting at us.'

The German did as instructed now revealing a naked torso.

'What is your name?' Dwyer said.

'My name is Friedrich.'

'Okay then, Freddie, you go and pick up his arms and I will carry his legs. You can walk in front.'

'Friedrich then started to walk towards the crater and picked up Brooks arms. He looked up at Dwyer who had been following and said, 'Okay, I carry his arms. We go to the beach now.'

'One other thing, Freddie,' Dwyer said. 'Do not even think about dropping him and then try to run away. You have more chance of out running me than getting a whale up you arse.'

The combination of whale and arse in the same sentence obviously confused the German who just nodded and said again, 'I help.'

Dwyer and his newfound helper carried Brooks the same route round the back of the barn and through the field. On leaving the entrance, a further bird was helping himself to the carcass of the dead German leaning against the machine-gun.

Dwyer looked away and Friedrich dropped Brooks' arms and started to vomit. Dwyer allowed him a few minutes to recover before insisting they continue.

Fair one. I did that when I first saw the rat.

Yep. Doesn't make him a bad person – how come you are okay about it now?

Amazing what you get used to.

By the time they had reached the gate leading to the open ground in front of the woods, they had passed a platoon of Americans coming towards them along the lane.

Friedrich panicked. He dropped Brooks' legs and shot his arms up into the air. 'Don't shoot, don't shoot,' he said in a panicked voice. 'I help, I help.'

Oh, bollocks.

Dwyer was left holding Brooks' body by himself under the armpits. '101st Airborne,' he quickly shouted. He then gently lowered Brooks' body to the ground. 'I am taking my friends body back to the beach. This bloke here is my prisoner. He is helping me.'

'Is that so?' One of the Americans said.

Dwyer did not like his tone. He walked towards him and stopped when only a foot away. He loomed over him and said. 'Yes. That's so. I also have to help my Major down to the beach to be evacuated. He broke his ankle when landing last night.'

'Bit lost, aren't you?' The American said. 'And where are you from? Your accent sounds funny.'

Here we go again.

Dwyer rolled his eyes. He gave him a brief account of their exploits and informed him that next five hundred yards were clear of the enemy.

Friedrich remained silent staring at the ground.

Eventually, both wished each other good luck and they went their separate ways.

On reaching the gate, Dwyer said, 'Okay Freddie, you see those branches placed in a line leading to the woods?'

Friedrich nodded.

'Make sure you follow them. We don't want to step on any of your mines now, do we?'

After his eyes had grown wide with terror, he nodded and eventually started to follow the line . . . very carefully.

On reaching the wood Dwyer said, 'Okay, that's far enough. You can put him down here.'

Friedrich placed Brook's arms on the ground and looked up towards Dwyer with the hint of a smile on his face and said, 'I helped.'

'Yes you did, Freddie, and thank you. I am now going to turn my back and count to ten. Make sure you out of my sight when I turn round. I will take him back from here.'

Friedrich looked at Dwyer with a disbelieving look on his face. When Dwyer shouted, '*ONE*,' he ran for it when he realised that he was not joking.

That was very decent of you.

I have had enough of killing to last a thousand lifetimes.

On hearing him starting to run, Dwyer smiled to himself and bent down to pick up Brooks. He was then thrown to the ground after being hit by the shock wave on an explosion. He quickly picked himself up, dusted himself down and looked behind him.

Why are you bothering to do that? You are already covered from head to toe in God knows what.

Friedrich, in his eagerness to escape, had not followed the line of branches on the ground that Dwyer had placed earlier and had stepped on a mine. He was now dead on the ground with only one leg.

Jesus Christ. There WERE mines in that field!
Really. You reckon?

Dwyer looked back towards the lifeless mutilated body of Friedrich, slowly shook shaking his head, and said, 'You stupid, stupid bastard,' and then returned his attention back to Brooks.

Before picking him up, he checked his watch.

It was 16h20 hours.

PART SIX

Evacuate

abandon, leave, relinquish, vacate, withdraw from.

1

Carter looked up as somebody jumped down from the overhang to his right. He was greeted with the smiling face of Dwyer.

'Fifteen minutes to spare,' Dwyer said trying to look as nonchalant as possible.

He did a piss poor job of it. His elation was obvious.

'What the hell took you so long?' Carter said trying hard not to smile.

Dwyer was about to go off on one when he realised that Carter was joking. A smile had started to develop, slowly across his face.

Dwyer began to laugh.

He then sat down next to Carter, took out his cigarettes and lit one. A contented smile appeared on his face as he inhaled deeply into his lungs.

'I take it you have been successful and brought Brooks back with you?' Carter said.

Dwyer nodded slowly and as he took a further long drag and then said, 'I left him up top.' He then looked round to Carter and added, 'I had a bit of excitement on the way though.'

'Really? What shape was Brooks' body in?' Carter asked referring to Dwyer's concerns about rats. He left the specifics unsaid, just in case.

'He's absolutely fine.'

Carter raised an eyebrow and waited for Dwyer to continue regarding the excitement he had on the way.

'What?' Dwyer said, enjoying the moment.

'You mentioned some excitement.'

Dwyer nodded.

'The first thing is you should know is that I had help. I ran into a few Germans by the barn. I took three of them out with a grenade, the fourth, after a bit of persuasion, helped me carry him as far as the woods.'

'Where is he now?' Carter said.

'I let him go. Two seconds after I that, he blew himself up by stepping on a mine. In that part of open ground between the gate and the wood.'

Carter up until now had been listening intently with a serious look on his face. He now burst into hysterical laughter. After eventually controlling himself he said, 'I'm sorry. I am not sure why I am laughing. That just sums the day up, I suppose.'

'Aint that the truth,' said Dwyer. 'There is one other thing though.'

'And what might that be?' Carter said still smiling.

'I ran into Garcia.'

The smile was instantly wiped from Carter's face. 'What happened?' He said now staring at Dwyer anxiously.

'Well let's just say that he is now hidden amongst a load of bushes and is now hopefully rat food. He won't be bothering you again, that's for sure.'

Carter stared off into the distance, seemingly focusing on nothing in particular. Dwyer studied him intently, looking for some kind of reaction. He looked away when none was noticeable.

'Why did you kill him?' Carter said eventually.

'Because the bastard shot at me, stuck his gun in my face and then made me beg for my life. That's why.'

Carter looked away from Dwyer. He then started to nod his head and said, 'Sounds fair I suppose.'

After returning his gaze back towards Dwyer, who was staring at him intently again, both men erupted into fits of the giggles simultaneously. It was a welcome macabre relief.

After the merriment had subsided, Dwyer said, 'Okay Eddie, let's have it.'

'Have what?' Carter said, fully realising as to what Dwyer was referring to.

'What is the reason for me being here? Why did you need me to protect you from those three bastards?'

Carter looked upwards towards the sky and then back at Dwyer. 'Let's have another cigarette, shall we?' He said.

2

Dwyer lit both cigarettes and handed one to Carter. He then looked at him with an expectant look on his face.

Carter took one long drag, slowly blew out the smoke and then started to tell his sorry tale.

'Corporal James Carter was abandoned as a baby. As my brother and his wife could not have children, they adopted him and brought him up as if he was their own. There was nothing they wouldn't do for him.'

Dwyer's brow furrowed. 'Not your nephew? You said at the station in Ports – '

'Do you want to hear this or what?'

Fair one.

Dwyer looked to the floor with the look of a scolded schoolboy and nodded his head.

Carter looked away briefly to stifle a grin when noticing Dwyer's demeanour.

He then continued.

'By the time he was about five years old, it was obvious that something was seriously wrong with the boy. He used to spend most of his time in the backyard pulling the wings of butterflies and burning ants through a magnifying glass.'

'Sounds like some of my old school mates,' said Dwyer.

Carter carried on without any indication that he had heard him.

'When he was in his mid-teens, his father knew that his three best friends were as screwed up as he was. They were inseparable and on countless occasions my brother had to bail them out of the local police station, mainly for public disorder offences.'

'Garcia, Henderson and Hickey,' said Dwyer.

Carter nodded and continued. 'As they grew older, not one of them managed to hold down a job and they seemingly spent every waking hour in the local bars. God knows where they got the money from, not to mention the fact they started drinking when they were still under the legal age.

After much pleading from my brother, I eventually agreed to try to get James into the 101st. We agreed that the army discipline might do him some good. If he and his friends had any ounce of moral fibre they would have volunteered anyway.'

Carter then paused and looked towards Dwyer. On noticing he was hanging on his every word, he continued.

'After James had found out from his father that I had been successful, he paid me a visit on his own and point blank refused unless his buddies could join him. Somewhat stupidly in hindsight, I agreed to this and managed to get it organised.'

Carter paused and took a further large drag on his cigarette. Again, he looked at Dwyer's reaction, who nodded at him to continue.

'Last year my brother and his wife died,' he said. He then paused and looked upwards to sky.

'How did they die?' Dwyer said eventually to prompt Carter to continue. It appeared to him that he was now clearly struggling to finish the tale.

'That adopted piece of shit nephew of mine killed them with his buddies. That's how.'

Dwyer's jaw dropped open. He looked at Carter disbelieving and then eventually said, 'Why the hell weren't they arrested then? How the hell were they allowed in the army?'

Carter shook his head. 'There was never any evidence, everyone suspected it was them, even the police, but they could never prove it.'

He stubbed his cigarette out angrily on the ground and then immediately lit another one.

A grimace appeared on his face on face as the painful unwanted memories returned.

'I was called to the scene when their bodies were discovered. They never even bothered to close the front door when they left. Eventually, a neighbour went to investigate when they noticed the door had been open all day.

By the time I got there, my brother was still laying on the floor in the hallway, with a pool of blood round his head. His wife was upstairs in the bedroom.'

Carter now stopped and closed his eyes and tried to compose himself in readiness of what he was about to say next. Like Dwyer, he had his own personal demons, which he too had now partially exorcised thanks to Dwyer's handiwork.

'We found her naked on top of the bed. We found out later that she had been raped, repeatedly, but that was by no means the worst part.'

He paused again. Dwyer now grimaced trying to imagine what is was that could be possibly worse than being gang-raped.

He did not have to wait long.

'I suspect it was Garcia, as he always carried a knife. He had carved her body up so badly, that you could barely recognise her.'

Carter then became silent.

'How did you know it was them?' Dwyer said eventually.

'It was three things that convinced me. I walked into the kitchen after discovering my brother and noticed a red tin on the side by the sink along with some other tins of food. I knew that was where my brother kept a stash of cash. He used to save for a fishing trip with his friends. They used to go every year. It was empty. Only his wife and probably James would also have known about it.'

A further cigarette was lit.

'The second was that afterwards, Garcia did not appear to have his knife anymore. He was always playing with the damn thing, or cleaning his fingernails with it for God's sake. He obviously ditched it somewhere after cutting her up.' Carter then paused again.

Dwyer nodded and said, 'What was the third reason?'

'Whilst I was still in the kitchen, James arrived. To be fair, he made a fine effort of acting distraught and horrified. He started to vow his revenge on whomever it was that did it. He then noticed me looking at the red tin. I could tell instantly by the look on his face that he knew I thought it was him and his crew that had killed them.

Since that day, the four of them have been watching me like hawks. As soon as they got a chance to take me out as well, it was obvious to me that they would go for it. Once we came over to England I knew once we invaded, a stray bullet would probably end my fate.'

Carter looked Dwyer in the eyes and with an earnest and sincere expression on his face.

'What I could not allow to happen, was for me to be preoccupied whilst leading my men once in battle. After hearing from the two MPs that witnessed your fight with them all in Portsmouth, I quickly developed a plan in my mind to get you on my side. They were very impressed with your efforts.'

Carter then looked wistfully at the lit end of his cigarette. He then took a long drag and blew four perfectly formed smoked rings.

'And how did you do that?' Dwyer said, following the progress of the four circles of smoke until they dissipated.

'First of all, I told all the details to my superior officer Colonel Harrison.'

'When?'

'The night you were unconscious in the cells when I met him at Southwick Park. He is a good man and he approved my plan straight away.'

Dwyer nodded.

'He was already aware of the fact that I believed James and his friends had committed the murder before we left for England. I had requested that they remained at base back in the States as I was convinced they were going to come after me next.'

'Why didn't he agree to it?' Dwyer said. 'It seems the sensible thing to have done.'

'Let's just say that he had more on his mind with the planned invasion. He also did not want to take any chance of it getting out into the open and ruining the men's morale.'

Carter then paused again and then added, 'What he did do, was that he assigned two under-cover MP's to watch their movements continually. Whether they were suspicious about being watched I don't know, but they managed to keep themselves out of trouble until we came to England.'

Dwyer puffed out his cheeks and expelled a long breath of air. 'From what I have seen, morale would have been improved if they stayed behind. Nobody had a good word to say about them when were back at Greenham Common. Sergeant Nelson told me that everyone suspected them of thefts and beating up a Private on base. That's why you sent them to Portsmouth. To improve morale to get rid of them for a day at least.'

Carter nodded and then limply shrugged his shoulders.

'For what it is worth, I think your Colonel must be some kind of idiot letting them come over here. What the fuck was he thinking?'

'Maybe,' said Carter and then added, 'His judgement has always been pretty sound though. Anyway, hindsight is a wonderful thing. As I said, there was never any real proof. What could he do?

Once I informed him of James' death and informed him about you, he compromised by allowing me to take you in with me, to watch my back as it were. It believed that was preferable than choosing one of our own men. Again, for morale purposes.'

Carter then smiled at Dwyer and continued.

'Second, I told all the details to Detective Williams. It was then that I suggested to him to give you an alternative to prison. That was the hard part. He is a man of great honour and the thought of interfering in the correct justice process played heavily on his mind. He has taken a great risk by possibly harming his reputation and career. That would be inevitable, if word of this ever got out. However, other circumstances came to light and I then realised why he went for it.'

Dwyer was looking at the ground thoughtfully. He shoulders then sagged and he said in a tired voice, 'Well, your problem is sorted now. Do I get to go back to England with you?'

Carter nodded, 'If I get my way you will be.'

'That's not a yes. Who is likely to get in your way?'

'Hopefully nobody, but we can cross that bridge if we come to it. Shall we go?'

'Just one more thing,' Dwyer said. 'You said other circumstances came to light which is why you realised Williams went for it. What were they?'

'That my friend is definitely a story for another time.'

Dwyer looked away and began to laugh again. 'You son of a bitch,' he said and began to stand up.

'You son of a bitch, *sir*,' Carter said.

Oh yeah, etiquette.

3

Dwyer packed all the loose equipment back into the two rucksacks and remembered this time, to put his helmet on. He then bent down to help Carter up and then lifted him up over the overhang and onto the path above.

Four rifles immediately pointed in their direction and then lowered again. Four Americans soldiers had been looking at Brooks' dead body that Carter was now sat next to.

'You might want to shout a warning next time you appear out of nowhere,' one of the troops said. 'You nearly got your heads blown off . . . Dumb sons of bitches.'

'Very true, private,' Carter said. 'Can the four of you come over here please?'

The soldier immediately regretted his comment about their mothers after now noticing the Majors rank.

Dwyer climbed up over the overhang and then joined Carter after taking one last look back to make sure he had not forgotten anything.

'Jesus Christ,' a different one of the four said. 'Look at the size of this mother.'

'Yes he is large, isn't he?' Carter said smiling. 'However, even he will not be able to carry me and Private Brooks here down to the beach. Can I have two volunteers please?'

All four troops took one pace backwards in unison.

One of them said, 'We have just spent two hours of hell getting of that beach. If you think that we are going to go back down there, you can forget it. Our orders are now to go inland and engage the enemy. And that is exactly what we are going to do . . . Major.'

Okay. Enough of this crap.

Dwyer walked towards him and said calmly, 'You can shove your orders up your arse mate. If two of you don't offer to help to carry him to the beach, I will throw all four of you back down there from here.'

Carter turned away and suppressed a grin.

The two troops nearest immediately bent down and picked up Brooks. 'Lead the way,' one of them said.

Carter then climbed onto Dwyer's back carrying the rucksacks and they walked to their left to start their descent.

4

Although it now appeared that German defences, had in the most part, been cleared from their immediate area, it was not exactly a stroll in the countryside to negotiate the bluff down towards the beach.

It was now 17h30 hours but still mortar fire was exploding on the Americans still landing on the beach below from positions further inland and German sniper fire was still prevalent directed by yet undetected observation posts from the bluff.

It appeared to the two infantry troops of the 115th Regiment of the 29th Division that were carrying brooks, that Dwyer appeared to be oblivious of it. They had noticed the eagles head on the sleeve of their jackets identifying them as 101st Airborne and wondered how long they had been here. However, they were not about to start questioning the giant Corporal – with the funny accent – who strode along with a Major on his back with the ease as if he was carrying a small child.

The fact he was covered in what appeared to be dried blood from head to toe, none of it appearing to be his, and not to mention his size, ensured they kept their own council. They certainly did not dare to comment on the fact that he absolutely stank to high heaven.

After about three hundred yards of walking along the top of the bluff, they came to a dirt road. It was filled with tanks, jeeps and men slowing going upwards.

Dwyer turned to check the progress of the two infantry and noticed they were struggling.

'Time for a cigarette break,' Dwyer said and carefully lowered Carter to the ground.

The two troops were only too eager to agree and literally dropped Brooks' body to the floor.

THUD.

Dwyer jumped to his feet and shouted angrily, 'Be a bit more fucking careful with him, will you?'

'What difference does it make? He's already dead, aint he?' One of them replied and then immediately wished he remained silent or just offered up an apology instead.

He was now staring at the ground after noticing the look on Dwyer's face following his blasé comment.

Dwyer now walked towards him, bent down so he was right in his face, and said through gritted teeth, 'I said be more fucking careful with him, okay?'

The soldier looked away and looked towards Carter for support. Carter was too glaring at him, so he now just looked to the ground once more and mumbled, 'Sorry.'

'You will be if you do that again,' Dwyer said, and then stood upright and walked back to Carter.

'Stupid moron,' he said as he sat down next to him.

They have been through the ringer too Davey.
I don't care.
It's nothing personal.
If they treat Brooks' body like that again, it soon will be.
Silence.

He took out a cigarette from his pocket and lit it. He looked towards to the endless stream of vehicles and men going up the dirt lane in the bluff. He then noticed a red-faced soldier glaring down at him as he travelled in a jeep towards him.

Oh for Christ sake, what now?

Dwyer returned the angry stare until the jeep stopped right in front of him.

What the hell is he looking at?

'What are you doing sitting there smoking, soldier, as if you're on a goddamn Sunday picnic? Get up off your ass and get up this hill.' The tone of his voice was full of contempt.

Up your arse . . . you red faced arsehole.

Before Carter could intervene, Dwyer said instead, 'I am taking the Major here, down to the beach so he can be evacuated. He has had his ankle broken. We are just having a rest if that's okay with you?' The tone in his voice suggested that the red-faced officer should not dare to argue.

I seem to remember something about etiquette.
Bollocks to him.

The officer looked toward Carter said, 'Is that right?'

Carter nodded.

The officer then gave Dwyer one final angry glare and then signalled to the driver to carry on.

It was returned.

The red-faced officer was then immediately driven away from them up the bluff, now paying no further attention to them.

'Who the hell does he think he is?' Dwyer said.

'A Colonel,' Carter replied.

Dwyer just nodded and then put out his cigarette out on the ground.

'Does that outrank you?'

Carter nodded.

'Fucking arsehole,' Dwyer said.

Carter nodded again.

'C'mon then, let's get going,' Dwyer said and stood up.

He looked towards the two infantry to do the same. They did without protest and picked up Brooks' body immediately.

5

At first, the dirt lane twisted gently downhill away to the right and then more steeply when it turned back to the left. This now afforded a view of the beach. Up until now, their view had been obscured by tall bushes on each side.

All of a sudden, Dwyer now felt terribly vulnerable. Not that the bushes would have saved them from a haphazard mortar round or burst of machine-gun fire, but being now out in the open felt far more unsafe just the same.

Dwyer put his head down and focused on the point where the sand began, now only twenty yards in front of him. He puffed out his cheeks and quickened his step.

The two infantry troops struggled to keep up behind him.

Without any hesitation, Dwyer turned left as soon as he hit the beach and marched towards the cover of the sea wall. On reaching it, he kept going for a further fifty yards. He then gently bent down and positioned Carter so he could lean against the wall between the other injured and the already dead.

For the entire fifty-yard walk along the sea wall, he had kept his focus on the ground immediately below him, determined not to look around and see the carnage at close quarters that he had witnessed from the bluff above. He continued to look down at Carters feet as the two infantry troops, carefully this time, placed Brooks' body next to Carter and then walked back towards the dirt lane to once again, ascend the bluff. They did so without saying a word.

6

Dwyer then mustered the courage to lift his head and took in the scene around him. Witnessing the slaughter from the top of the bluff was one thing, now he was slap-bang right in the middle of it.

Oh my God!

There were countless dead and injured up against the sea wall as far up the beach as he could see. The injured were suffering from a wide range of horrific injuries.

To his right and towards the Channel, were all kinds of vehicles either moving towards the lane they had just walked down, or were motionless and on fire after being hit by mortar rounds. Men were still running towards him from the landing craft that were still approaching the beach. Others were running back towards the Channel with the injured on stretchers. Body parts could still be seen strewn around everywhere. There was nowhere Dwyer could look to avert his gaze from them.

Maybe you should just close your eyes.

Dwyer waited for two stretcher-bearers to arrive back to the sea wall. He walked towards them as they were about to pick up a further soldier that had lost his right hand.

'Whenever you are ready, lads. The major here has a broken ankle.'

They both looked over at him with disdain on their faces. One of them then said, 'He is going to have to wait his turn. There are far worse cases here than a broken ankle to deal with.'

The look on Dwyer's face made him quickly reconsider.

'If you carry him to just short of the waterline, we will take him from there,' he added.

Dwyer turned towards Carter and saw that he was now in a serious debate with another soldier who was kneeling down next to him, continually shaking his head. He was about to interrupt and pick him up and then hesitated.

That doesn't look like that is going well.

No.

What do you think they are arguing about?
At I guess, I would say about me leaving with him.
Oh, bollocks.
Indeed.

Dwyer stood making circles in the sand with his right boot. He then immediately stopped after uncovering a single finger with a ring still on it.

The foul tasting cheese he had eaten earlier violently reappeared. He grimaced at the fact that it actually tasted worse on the way out. He would have not believed it possible.

He shut his eyes and tensed every muscle in his body in an attempt not to heave again. His earlier session of reaching had made his stomach ache.

When convinced he had everything under control and there was not going to be any more Mount Vesuvius scale eruptions from his stomach, he walked towards the clearly irate officer; that he guessed was Carter's senior.

'Mr Irate' had now stood up and Dwyer clearly heard him say, 'Not a chance, Major, he stays here. We need everyman we can get.'

Carter tried in vain to argue his case again. He was cut short.

'I am not arguing with you any further, he stays . . . and that's final. I don't care what he's done.'

Carter had provided the Colonel with the highlights of their night and day activities and demanded that Dwyer should be able to accompany him. He would later regret not informing the Colonel of how Dwyer had been recruited in the first place which may possibly made a difference.

Again, Carter tried to plead a case for Dwyer. Again, it was dismissed out of hand.

This time, Dwyer did interrupt. He walked towards them both and said to Carter, 'C'mon, I will take you as far as the water.'

'But – '

'It doesn't matter,' Dwyer said. 'There aint no point in arguing. He has made up his mind.'

The soldier turned to Dwyer and said, 'I'm sorry, son, if I let you go uninjured, everyone else is going to want to leave. I could end with some kind of damn mutiny on my hands.'

Dwyer nodded. 'I understand.'

You do?

He bent down so that Carter could climb on his back.

Carter did so reluctantly throwing a filthy look at the Colonel, as he did so.

It was ignored.

As they walked towards the water, a mortar round exploded away to their right. It sent sand flying up into the air and all over them both. Dwyer just carried on as if nothing had happened. Carter frantically wiped it away from his eyes.

When they had reached two yards from the water, Dwyer stood upright waiting for the stretcher-bearers to return from the converted tank landing craft that were being used as makeshift hospital ships.

He glanced behind him and to his right. The officer that was preventing him from leaving was not taking his eyes of him. The urge to give a one-fingered salute was overwhelming. It was only the fact that he was still carrying Carter prevented him from doing so.

Dwyer's thoughts were then interrupted by Carter.

'I will sort it out when I get back to England.'

Dwyer made no comment as he was far from convinced that that would be possible.

Carter continued. 'Don't worry I will get you out of here soon enough. The Colonel there is having none of it at the moment.'

Dwyer nodded and said, 'Make sure you get a message back to my Sally when you get to Portsmouth. Tell her I love her and I am okay. Constable Evans at the police station knows where she lives.'

'Will do, don't worry about that,' Carter said. 'I have left both the rucksacks at the sea wall, make sure you go and get them. They have all the cigarettes in.'

Dwyer had noticed the break in Carter's voice.

'How long do you think it will take for you to sort something out?' Dwyer said.

'I'm sorry, I can't answer that honestly, I have no idea.'

Thought so.

Carter was still struggling to control his emotions. 'I will work on nothing else when I get back to England . . . Nothing else until

I get you home.'

'Just in case you have any problems, please can you at least make sure you get a photograph of Sally for me and somehow try to send it to me. . . although I don't suppose the mail service is going to be that regular at the moment.'

'I will do whatever I can that is possible,' Carter said with a now stoic expression.

The stretcher-bearers returned.

Dwyer lent back gently so that Carter could ease himself onto the stretcher. The bearers went to move off immediately towards the waiting landing craft.

'Wait a minute,' Dwyer bellowed.

They both froze and looked back towards him.

Dwyer walked towards Carter, took out Brooks' letter and photograph of his girlfriend from his pocket, and said, 'Make sure that gets posted will you?'

Carter took the envelope and picture and nodded. He then said, 'Thank you, Davey, it has been an honour a privilege to meet and serve with you,' wiping the tears from his eyes.

Dwyer stared at Carter and said, 'The privilege is mine,' and then added, *sir.*'

He then stood bolt upright and gave Carter an exaggerated salute.

It was his first.

The stretcher-bearers moved off towards the landing craft and loaded Carter in. The whole time Dwyer remained saluting until it pulled away and started to make its way back across the Channel.

He then became aware of a presence standing next to him.

'Very touching, son, now let's get the hell off this beach. The Major told me you are a good man and I can't afford to lose anymore,' said the Colonel from behind him.

Dwyer completely ignored him and walked towards the water.

It was 18h30 hours.

'Where the hell do you think you are going?' the Colonel shouted.

'I am going to wash the crap of my clothes. I stink.' Dwyer said without looking back.

One more word out of him and I will knock his fucking head of his shoulders.

You have my blessing.

Really?

Really.

'I would not do that if I was you, son,' the Colonel shouted after him.

Dwyer looked down towards the waterline.

The sea had turned red.

Epilogue

Between the hours of 18h30 and 21h30, Dwyer sat with his back against the sea wall staring at the English Channel. Although the beach was the still the hive of activity, if asked the next day what had taken place during those hours, he would never been able to remember. He stared at the Channel – smoked – stared at the Channel - and smoked some more.

Even the intermittent explosions that were still erupting from all areas of the beach still did little to snap him out of his trance like state staring across the water.

Due to the fact that the beach now resembled one huge traffic jam, the mortar rounds that were still being fired from positions inland could hardly miss a target.

The colonel, once satisfied that he was not going to try to swim home to his freedom, and had observed him just slumped against the sea wall, lost interest in him and let him be. From what Carter had informed him earlier of his exploits, he felt he had deserved to at least sit and rest.

Dwyer eventually became aware of two soldiers digging a large hole in the sand five yards to his right, who when finished, lay down in it and looked to be trying to get to sleep.

Dwyer got to his feet, walked over and took one of the shovels without asking or even acknowledging the incumbents of the hole. He then started to dig one of his own.

Neither ventured a comment towards him.

He then looked once more towards the Channel and noticed that the last of the daylight appeared to be disappearing just beyond the horizon.

He then started digging again, oblivious to his immediate surroundings.

When he considered that his own 'fox-hole' was sufficiently deep enough, he placed the two rucksacks at one end of it, took out a packet of cigarettes from his jacket pocket and laid down with his head on the rucksack, looking up at the stars above.

He wondered if Sally was looking at the very same ones that he was - right at this very minute. He lit a cigarette and then practised blowing smoke rings. Two cigarettes later, he had mastered it.

His thoughts then turned to the Major. He wondered if he had made it back to England yet – *no probably not - how long ago did he leave?*

Seems like days.

He then tried to go over the day's events in his mind since landing in Normandy. He soon gave up, however, as some of the vivid images that appeared were just too painful to remember.

To think, I tried to volunteer for this crap.
Who could possibly know it could be like this?

Now trying to console himself about his current predicament, he thought how different it may of been if they had landed where they were supposed to.

Maybe they would have engaged the enemy in an all out fight and been shot. Maybe in the confusion Garcia, Henderson or Hickey could have had the chance to kill him and the Major with a couple of 'stray' bullets . . . Maybe . . . Maybe this had all happened for a reason. Maybe the events of the worst twenty-four hours of his life had somehow perversely saved his life. Sally was always saying that things are meant to be and everything happens for a reason.

Maybe she is right . . . Maybe . . .

Why then, did all these brave men, American, German, and not forgetting the Poles of course, have to die attacking and defending this, until now, insignificant piece of beach? . . . Why?

Did that all happen for a reason?

If it did, he would never understand the reasoning behind it as long as he lived.

What lies beyond the beach? More maiming and killing? Undoubtedly, for the foreseeable future.

His thoughts now turned to Private Baker and he now believed that he spent most of waking hours wasting his time.

If there was a God; how could he have let what he had witnessed today take place? How? To serve what purpose? To end the rule of tyranny brought about Hitler and his hench men. Why then would he have created Hitler in the first place? What was that saying about the chicken and the egg?

If there is a God and a Devil then the Devil is winning the war at the moment. He believed that his recent prays to God would not be repeated any time soon. He would just have to look out for himself.

They certainly didn't do Baker any good, as he was now convinced that he had not made it out of their plane before it crashed.

And what about Danny Brooks? What could possibly convince his girlfriend that being killed by one of his own side, *murdered* by one of his own side, had happened for a reason? Dwyer wondered if she would ever be told how he really died. He doubted it. Wouldn't look very good on the recruitment posters.

JOIN THE ARMY

Health Warning:
You may get your throat cut by one of your own regiment!
Beware of insane murdering bastards at all times.
WATCH YOUR BACK.

After one further cigarette, he closed his eyes and tried to get off to sleep, desperately hoping that he would not have a reoccurrence of the nightmares that haunted him earlier in the day.

That was one hell of a day.
It was. Master of the understatement.
You did well, very, very well.
Thanks. I could not have got through it without you.
My pleasure. Likewise . . . I am you . . . You are me.
My only concern is that I am going to have to do it all again tomorrow.
You'll be fine.
Really? I'm just a . . . I'm just a . . . I'm just a Citizen Soldier.
Just remember to keep –
Focused?
That's right. Keep focused.
Focus on Sally.
That's right. Focus on Sally.
Do you think the Major will get me out of here?

He said he would do nothing else until he did — I'm sure he will. He's a man of honour. A good man.
He is. One of the best. I am lucky to have met him.
You need to sleep now. You really need to sleep.
I do. I'm so tired.
Goodnight Davey.
Goodnight . . .

The End

Lightning Source UK Ltd.
Milton Keynes UK
19 September 2010
160089UK00001B/120/P